Maybe Once,
Maybe Twice

ALSO BY ALISON ROSE GREENBERG

Bad Luck Bridesmaid

Maybe Once,
Maybe Twice

A Novel

ALISON ROSE GREENBERG

ST. MARTIN'S GRIFFIN
NEW YORK

To Mom and Dad

I'm incredibly lucky to have you both as my rocks. Thank you for
always believing in me, and please don't read the sex scenes.

First published in the United States by St. Martin's Griffin, an imprint of
St. Martin's Publishing Group

MAYBE ONCE, MAYBE TWICE. Copyright © 2023 by Alison Rose Greenberg.
All rights reserved. Printed in the United States of America. For information,
address St. Martin's Publishing Group, 120 Broadway, New York, NY 10271.

www.stmartins.com

Library of Congress Cataloging-in-Publication Data

Names: Greenberg, Alison Rose, author.
Title: Maybe once, maybe twice : a novel / Alison Rose Greenberg.
Description: First edition. | New York : St. Martin's Griffin, 2023. |
Identifiers: LCCN 2023016946 | ISBN 9781250791627 (trade paperback) |
    ISBN 9781250791634 (ebook)
Subjects: LCSH: Self-realization in women—Fiction. | LCGFT: Romance
    fiction. | Novels.
Classification: LCC PS3607.R4468 M39 2023 | DDC 813/.6—dc23/eng/20230414
LC record available at https://lccn.loc.gov/2023016946

Our books may be purchased in bulk for promotional, educational, or busi-
ness use. Please contact your local bookseller or the Macmillan Corporate and
Premium Sales Department at 1-800-221-7945, extension 5442, or by email at
MacmillanSpecialMarkets@macmillan.com.

First Edition: 2023

10 9 8 7 6 5 4 3 2 1

Lightning strikes
Maybe once, maybe twice

                              -STEVIE NICKS

Prologue

——

THIRTY

I SHIFTED ON MY BARSTOOL, faraway eyes watching my best friend, Summer, float past the neon exit, her four-inch heels barely touching the ground, a mauve silk duster moving behind her model frame. She grazed the earth's surface like a polished, gorgeous superhero on a casual mission to make heads turn.

It wasn't until I etched my fingers into the bar counter with a full-body exhale that I realized I had been holding my breath all night. Thankfully, there was only one friend left to con tonight in this grungy Nolita dive bar. Garrett Scholl and I were the last two patrons, sitting side by side on creaky stools as the bartender restocked cheap vodka. Historically, Monday nights had been *our* thing, but today I was forced to share it with other people. This is what happens when you turn thirty: your friends want to celebrate you. *Selfish assholes.*

Garrett swiveled on his barstool, one eye on my distant expression, the other on the dart pinched in his large fingers.

"What's my prize if I get the bull's-eye?"

I glanced at the dartboard, which hung yards away on the other side of the bar. While I lost to Garrett every time we played darts, making this bull's-eye was the equivalent of a kicker making a sixty-yard field goal. It was never going to happen.

Which is why I said, "You get . . . a truth."

Garrett grinned at me, his square jaw, ocean-blue eyes, and clean-shaven face slicing me open. I sucked in my cheeks, resting my chin on the palm of my hand so that drool wouldn't escape. He squinted at the dartboard, flexing his wrist back and forth.

"A truth, huh? I thought I had all of Maggie May's truths."

My heart blistered with the painful reminder: he did *not*. Tonight, I had gone the extra mile to pretend like I wanted to celebrate my existence. I effusively hugged one friend after another with a big smile until my cheeks matched my insides, until I hurt everywhere. Spending all night thinking about your age when your future has just been stolen from you will do that to a woman.

Garrett steadied his eyes on the dartboard, and with extreme precision, he let it fly. The dart moved across the bar like it was tied to a string, landing dead center: bull's-eye.

"Goddamnit," I said, shaking my head.

He spun back around to me with one fist frozen in the air, savoring every ounce of victory as his mouth found a coy smile, one that erased the ache in my chest. Garrett's entire personality was a crisp ray of sunshine, wrapped around the heart of a music nerd, wrapped in the body of a Greek god. He lit up a dark night the way no one else could, with a smile that gave hope to my shattered heart.

His fingers performed a drumroll on the bar's counter.

"Truth time, Maggie May."

With my deep inhale, the smell of stale beer and cleaning solution ran through my lungs like a warm hug. I had spent the first part of my twenties playing music in tiny bars like this one, and even some nights working behind the counter.

"C'mon, tell me something good," he said.

I chewed on my bottom lip—a nervous childhood habit. Growing up, according to the monsters in my fourth-grade class, my lips were "too aggressive" for my petite face, so naturally, they started calling me "fish face." I didn't stop resenting my pillowy lips until I was fourteen—until my face was reflected in the amber eyes of my first love, Asher Reyes— until he grazed my bottom lip with his thumb and whispered, "How is everything about you this perfect?"

There were a couple truths to spill out of these flawless lips of mine. One was truly horrible. The other was horrible only if Garrett didn't feel the same way. The maybe horrible truth: I was in love with Garrett

Scholl. I loved him in a way that kept me up at night. I loved him the way Johnny Cash loved June.

I exhaled and laid my head on the warmth of his broad shoulder, a place I felt both safe and uncertain. I let myself sit there for a while, just two unrealized soulmates closing down a dive bar the way soulmates do.

"You okay?" he asked brightly, because Garrett would only question pain if it was through an optimistic tone.

It was a question no one had asked all night. Not even Summer. My best friend usually sniffed out bullshit from a mile away, but tonight she was distracted. In Summer's defense, she was in the middle of a fight with her wife, Valeria, who had "rescued" a goldendoodle from a pet store window without first asking Summer. It was occupying all of Summer's emotional bandwidth, which, like the internet in the nineties, was limited. It struck me as odd that Garrett was even asking me about my feelings. Nine times out of ten, he sidestepped any hint of morose with a sparkly distraction. He could always tell when I wasn't myself, but he knew how to make the corners of my mouth dance with a dirty joke or a guilty-pleasure nineties song.

"Hey . . ." I felt Garrett's shoulder shifting under me as he swiveled his body on the barstool, now facing my lifeless profile. His eyes narrowed on me, and I weakly attempted my hundredth smile of the night.

"I'm fine."

"If I've learned one thing from all my past girlfriends, it's that no female has said she was fine and meant it."

His one-sided smirk sent me to another planet, allowing me to feel the masculine version of fine: *totes fine!*

"I'm fine," I said again, with my forehead tilted toward his gorgeous face.

"No, you're not." He pointed upward to the ceiling. "The song's almost over, and I haven't heard one '*What's going on?*'"

My ears shifted, hearing Linda Perry's low register croon through the speakers. I had never, in the history of ever, kept my mouth closed during 4 Non Blondes' "What's Up?" and Garrett knew it. He knew it because he knew how my heart beat out of my chest for anything I loved, making it impossible for me to cage my emotions—which is why it felt like I swallowed a sunrise whenever his eyes met mine.

"Maggie?"

He put a hand on my shoulder and craned his neck so I'd meet his scrunched-up face. Our eyes locked, and my heart beat faster. Taxi headlights beamed in through the glass window, lighting up his blue eyes in an unfair way. His face tightened on my lack of response.

I swallowed hard as the horrible truth battled its way toward the surface. He was the one person in my life who would make something treacherous feel less devastating. *I should tell him.* I opened my mouth, but the thought of reliving it strangled my throat.

Garrett's eyes widened as he clasped his hand around my numb fingers.

"Maggie, you're shaking."

I studied his hand on mine, my heart pounding in my eardrums, my throat dry and tight. All at once, the only way to breathe was to crack open my mouth.

"Tonight . . . tonight when I blew out the candles, my birthday wish was for us to end up together."

The maybe horrible truth fell out of me, and I couldn't put it back in. Garrett studied me like he was dropped inside a play without knowing any of the lines. My lips stayed parted in the air—stunned by their own handiwork. There was a familiar blazing adrenaline coursing through my body, the kind of bravery I only felt when I sang under a spotlight. Which is why I kept going, even as all rationale screamed, *STOP SAYING WORDS, MAGGIE.*

"If we're not married in five years, promise me you'll show up at my door and marry me," I heard myself say.

"You . . . you want me to marry you?" he asked slowly, as if he needed to say the sentence aloud to understand it.

I shook my head. "Scratch that."

"You don't want me to marry you?"

"I do. But *I'll* show up at your door—you're horrible with timing."

Garrett opened his mouth, but no words followed. His brows pressed together for a long moment as my breathing became more rapid. I couldn't feel my fingers, and there was a ringing in my ears.

Did I just spring a marriage pact onto Garrett Scholl?

I knew I was in a bad place, but I didn't know I was in a reckless one. I bent my neck forward with my hand around my throat, fighting the wave of humiliation rising from my stomach. I turned toward the bar, focusing hard on the freshly washed glasses, as if they were a time machine. Garrett reached his hand down to my seat, twisting my barstool toward him and bringing us face-to-face. My heart thumped as his eyes scanned every line on my face. And then, Garrett stretched forward, the heat of his mouth against mine.

"Why do we have to wait until we're thirty-five?" he whispered against my lips.

1

THIRTY-~~FUCKING~~-FIVE

THE ONLY PROMISE IS THAT nothing is promised to us. Someone should have told me that at seventeen. I should have known better by thirty. Much, much better at thirty-five. A childhood therapist once told my mom I was "filled with promise." I had been promising for over three decades—like a drug that could work, but lacked federal funding.

While I was filled with promise, I was not so much filled with eggs, according to my gynecologist's tight smile. He loomed beside my paper-gowned body like the grim reaper, while his scythe—a rubbery ultrasound probe—searched for signs of life inside my dying planet. He pulled the wand out of me, sighing in my direction with a slight head shake. I recognized this look. Like my former math teachers, this doctor expected more from me. He snapped the gloves off his hands, flicking the latex into the trash can as if he were the LeBron James of vaginas.

"I don't want you to take this personally. Most women lose ninety percent of their eggs by thirty."

I went to scream, *"How am I NOT supposed to take MY personal body personally?"* but instead, air huffed between my slack jaw, which I had forgotten to pick up off the not-so-cute floor of infertility. It was a thrilling way to ring in the elder age of thirty-fucking-five.

I studied the receding hairline atop my gyno's round face. He appeared to be in his late forties, and my eyes slipped down to his hand, where there wasn't a wedding ring in sight. I wondered if he was like me: childless and single. I wondered if it scared him.

Of course it didn't.

Men under fifty stroll through dark parking garages the same way they approach their birthdays: without a second thought. They don't lose sleep over their place in the world—not until they find themselves inside a midlife crisis. Women don't have midlife crises, because we've spent our lives constantly in crisis. If only I had done a better job of leaning into the societal role that a woman should play. Every birthday should have been a gentle reminder that I was losing a war against time—that my branch on the family tree might hang aimlessly in the air. Instead, the End of Days had crept up on me like an asteroid in a Michael Bay movie. I had wandered the halls of my future with the false confidence of a mediocre white man, and I would pay for it like a woman.

I had made this appointment with the vain hope that I would be declared "a fertility marvel." My doctor would pat me on the back with a wowed smile and reassure me that I had plenty of years left to strum through life without permanent repercussions.

Maggie Vine was not a medical marvel. Biology was holding me at gunpoint. I was walking the tightrope of regret. "Kids, one day" had become "kids, now or never."

"If you have a partner, you should start trying," he said. There was an inflection of hope for the hopeless in my doctor's voice as he spun on a little stool below me, poring over my medical chart on his iPad.

If I have a partner . . .

My love life shared the potential of my uterine lining: outlook *not* good. One might best describe it as a fuckboy warfare hellscape. The word "relationship" was always in finger-quotes. My "relationships" were a lot like my music career: constantly on the verge of becoming something until they became nothing. Optimism spiraled me toward the joys of lovesickness and watched me lose myself in some angular jawline's undertow.

"We should talk about your options," he said, taking my silence for what it was.

"What do those bad boys run these days?" I asked, flipping through the IVF pamphlet.

"Well, I think you should try IUI first, which could be about five hundred to four thousand dollars, depending on the meds, bloodwork, and insemination—"

"Those are two *very* different numbers."

"And then you'd have the price of a sperm donor on top of that," he continued, handing me two more pamphlets. "If IUI doesn't work, we'd shift to IVF, which is much more invasive and costly, but generally more successful. Now, yours would be considered a geriatric pregnancy, so I don't want you to get too excited when you see these fifty percent success-rate numbers."

"I'm sorry, did you just say 'geriatric'?"

Apparently, it was time for my ovaries to take a starring role in one of those arthritis commercials. She would find a silver fox and run in slow motion down the beach, toward a bright light. Maybe they handed out AARP memberships to retiring reproductive organs. If my fertility was going to wave a white flag, at the very least, I deserved a discount at Red Lobster.

"There's always freezing your eggs, but freezing eggs this old . . . I don't know. If you were smarter, you would have done it sooner."

"Smarter" shot through me like a bullet. I wasn't exactly stupid, but I was overly hopeful. Which was possibly a very stupid way to approach life. Wide-eyed, I studied the silent nurse in the corner who awkwardly played with her hands, trying not to meet my eyes. I looked back at the doctor, just as he flicked a smile my way. It made me want to end his life.

There was nothing I hated more than proving a shitty man right. He was about to find out that I was much less smarter than he didn't give me credit for. I had wasted my adulthood by choosing to play a game of risk, and it was not rewarding.

I shivered in front of the mirror at the Upper East Side exam room, dissecting my reflection—unfortunately under fluorescent lighting. Here I sat on my thirty-fifth birthday: cold ultrasound lube dripping onto my pale thighs; lime-green eyes open far too wide; long, wavy hair framing a heart-shaped freckled face; last night's mascara creating an unintentional kind-of-hot smoky-eye. Here I sat: a woman out of options.

I was staring down the edge of my dream, completely unaware that two other doors were about to swing open.

2

THIRTY-FIVE

"It's just . . . I didn't think I'd have to adult this quickly," said a thirty-five-year-old fully grown woman to her best friend.

I had just divulged my lack of fertility options to Summer Groves, who responded to my pain by allowing me to open up an egregiously expensive bottle of pinot. A purple haze poured in through the arched windows of Summer's Tribeca kitchen as the red wine burned down my throat. Summer lived in a generous three-bedroom condo, which was soon to be featured in *Architectural Digest*. It was the kind of place that made your mouth hang open when you walked in: bright, playful colors set against honed dark marble, one-upped by unobstructed views of the Hudson River. It was the kind of place you lived in if you were crushing adulthood.

"Hi there, Billie girl," I cooed.

Summer's goldendoodle, Billie, panted up at me with her apricot tail wagging. I scrunched my face down to Billie's wet nose. Summer flinched, uncomfortable around the ease at which I let an animal's warm tongue bathe my cheeks. Summer never grew up around affection, and it showed. She got high cheekbones and full lips from her model-actor father and icy veins from her emotionally stunted mother. She casually breezed into rooms and sent jaws to the floor. Summer was a knockout without trying—an intimidating combination that I would have died for. Unless you were one of the very few people inside her bubble, everything about Summer was terrifyingly untouchable—the kind of woman who you worried was judging you, whose silent approval you would go to the ends of the earth to retrieve. If not for my world turning on a dime when I was seventeen, Summer would have just become a distant memory—*that bitchy college roommate whose name I can't remember.* But my father had to go and die. I joined the Dead Parent's Club, a club Summer was already a member of, and my grief brought her walls down. Thankfully, I got to know the hilarious, ballsy, honest woman cloaked in sharp teeth.

"Your mommy loves you," I said into Billie's well-groomed face, with an eye on Summer, equal parts reassuring the dog and the dog's indifferent owner. "Can't you and Valeria just have a cute pair of twins, and then hand one over to me? *And* be financially responsible for said child?" I asked Summer, batting my eyelashes and pouting my lips toward her.

Most recently, Summer's wife, Valeria, had dropped hint after hint about starting their journey toward motherhood. I didn't press the issue, because with Summer, it was never a good idea to ask questions before there were answers—unless you enjoyed eyes that cut like knives slicing your soul in half. Unlike myself, Summer had both the financial security to create a child of her own, along with the emotional and physical support of a partner. The common road—climbing a career ladder and getting hitched—had shiny benefits.

I spun aimlessly on the barstool, feeling Summer's pointed eyes on me across her oversized marble island—which was the size of my entire kitchen. I stopped spinning, meeting Summer's glare as she took in my dull gray T-shirt and black ripped jeans.

"Maggie, you have to at least *look* like you care. It's your thirty-fifth birthday, not your funeral."

"Feels a little like my funeral."

"Well, if we're going to bury you tonight, wear something that shows off your tits."

"It would take a surgeon to show off my boobs. But . . . there is that blue Reformation dress that almost makes me look like I have curves?"

This was not a subtle hint. I had subwayed it over to Summer's apartment for pre-birthday drinks, but also, for her to dress me. Summer owned an excess of beautiful clothes. Even though I stood four inches shorter than her, we wore the same dress size. She was my very own Rent the Runway.

The corners of her lips danced into a grin, softening her usually deadpanned expression.

"You little mooch," Summer said, shaking her bleach-blond long-bob at me. She swirled the stem of her wineglass and her eyes darkened as she walked out of the kitchen toward the closet. "Just wait until you see what Valeria did now."

I giddily followed Summer down the herringbone-floored hallway, coming up with possible shoe/dress combinations in my head. Yes, we also wore the same shoe size.

I pulled my neck back as we entered the walk-in closet. The room had been transformed into a worrying dedication to ROY G BIV. The closet was sparse, but it was *specific*. I cautiously opened a drawer. *Dear God.* Rainbow color-coding had even come for her thongs.

"What happened to all of your clothes?" I asked, surveying the half-empty hanging space.

"Netflix happened," Summer said through gritted teeth. She huffed, tugging a flowy blue dress off the hanger and tossing it my way.

Three months ago, Valeria had sold a direct-to-consumer frozen smoothie company for seven million dollars. As a result, Valeria went on a work sabbatical before diving into her next venture. During the last few months, Summer had discovered a new piece of information about her wife: Valeria should never go without a job. Valeria was a glorified work-aholic who thrived under pressure. Without the thrill of the grind, Valeria was the kind of person who decided to retile a ten-thousand-dollar "boring" fireplace, by hand. Valeria had started making her own cheese a few weeks prior, and it appeared that this week, she had discovered the freedom of giving away every article of clothing that did not spark joy, *while* organizing her socks by color.

"She watched two Netflix home improvement shows, and now I'm living inside my own personal hell. Has *my* life improved? *No.* I should sue Netflix for emotional damage."

Summer was a powerhouse publicist—CEO and co-founder of a thriving fashion PR company. She was a shark, and she enjoyed the casual threat of a lawsuit more than most people.

I tugged her dress over my half-naked body, pulling the ruffled off-the-shoulder neckline past my clavicle. It worked with my white Converses, but I could do better.

"Are you gonna need this back?" I asked, twirling the fabric in my hand. I knew what the answer was before the question even left my lips.

Summer smirked. "Happy birthday, you little shit."

I grinned, scanning the pristine row of rainbow-colored heels. "Don't worry about Valeria. She'll find another company to take over," I said.

"That, or she can find another person to go down on her."

Summer and Valeria met about seven years ago. Historically, Summer lusted after love but turned her back the moment lust faded. With Valeria, Summer had to try harder than she was used to, a rarity for her—a fight that she stayed in, one that allowed her to see that underneath Valeria's painfully gorgeous and painfully shy armor, there was extreme warmth and loyalty for those she loved. And she adored Summer. I could see it reflected in Valeria's eyes when she looked at her wife, and vice versa. I had yet to personally bask in the rays of Valeria's affection. She often looked at me wide-eyed, body tense, like my curse-filled stories and songs would tear their paintings off the wall. But I didn't need Valeria's approval to know that she and Summer had what I was looking for: they had It All. Together, these beautifully polished women would have an offspring or two and continue to live out a slice of the American Dream. The dirty truth: I was jealous of their road traveled by.

I recognized it was careless to purposefully bring life into the world while I was still getting knocked out by the universe. But the difference between aching for a child that didn't yet exist and aching for a child that would never exist is the difference between hope and agony. Maggie Vine always chose hope.

"What if the moment just passes me by?" I sighed, as hope's fragile light flickered inside my chest.

Summer looked over at me as I studied my reflection in the mirror. My faraway eyes came back down to earth, catching her worried expression. Summer was accustomed to watching me leave the present—she knew when my mind was wandering. It was simply my brain's fault: I gravitated toward building irrelevant scenarios in my head. Unfortunately, today's scenario was all too relevant.

Summer cleared her throat as she clasped a thick gold bracelet around her wrist, letting me know it was Less-Devastating Topic Time.

"So, is Garrett coming tonight?" she asked.

I froze. Her words found my chest: a fist tightening around my delicate heart.

"I doubt he's coming," I muttered.

Summer had sent the invites out five weeks ago—a casual birthday comingling thanks to a free Dave Matthews Band concert in Central Park. Shamefully, Garrett Scholl's was a courtesy invite—one I was certain he would turn down, but one I knew I had to have Summer send. Let me be clear: it was a courtesy invite for *me,* not for Garrett. Leaving Garrett off the guest list would have been an acknowledgment that we had fully died. I wasn't ready to bury one of the most important friendships of my life, even if the coffin was already sitting in the earth, waiting for the ground crew.

"You told me you guys had a good chat—I figured everything was cool now. Back to being besties."

"The conversation was good, it's just . . ." I shrugged. "He's been kind of distant since then."

Distant was generous. *Dead silent* was more accurate. Summer stepped closer to me with her steely Olivia Benson expression.

"What aren't you telling me, Maggie?"

"Nothing."

I grabbed a pair of black matte Louboutins from the shelf behind Summer, deflecting with high fashion. Summer rolled her eyes.

"I told you, men like to compartmentalize. He's got you in a box."

"I *opened* the box," I said forcefully.

Summer's eyes widened.

"You opened the box?"

I nodded.

"You're in love with him again, aren't you?" she said.

"Again" implied I had stopped loving him. I had spent the last year adamant about the fact that I wasn't in love with Garrett, shutting the conversation down so that Summer would stop convincing me to pour my heart out to him already.

I had, unfortunately, not stopped loving Garrett Scholl since the night I heard his voice.

3

TWENTY-THREE

THE SKIES DECIDED TO OPEN up *after* Summer and I concluded that we were too close to our next destination to slip into a cab. We had just finished drinks with a small group of friends who all had big workweeks ahead and couldn't rage on a Monday night. Summer also had a huge week ahead, but she refused to let me go home before midnight on my *goddamn twenty-third birthday*. I had a big week as well: playing two different night gigs, singing at a wedding ceremony, cold-calling bookers around the city, and trespassing. My lunch hour was spent hovering around the doorsteps of recording studios, until I curved my body in behind a delivery messenger. I'd slide my demo onto their packages and duck away—just hoping my voice would land in a producer's hand. My second demo was five songs long, homemade inside my mom's sound-proof closet. Maybe twenty-three would be the year someone listened to one of the songs.

Summer and I sprinted through three rainy blocks on the Lower East Side and arrived at Arlene's Grocery, a former bodega turned iconic dive bar, soaked from our heads to our heels. My white ribbed dress was see-through, and underneath I wore a black bra, so all in all, I looked ready to rock.

It was live music karaoke night at Arlene's Grocery, and our first stop was the amber-lit packed bar. Summer ordered us two cheap beers, and suddenly, dopamine hit the back of my brain. The chords thumped against my heart—E minor, C, G, D over F sharp—the grungy electric guitar tugged my body away from the bar, edging my bare wet shoulder past the crowd of hipsters and toward the purple-lit stage like a moth to a flame.

My guitar teacher introduced me to The Cranberries' "Zombie" when I was ten. It was the melody behind my ears when I was told that my brain was wired differently. "I like the way this song sounds—dark blue and mustard," I said as my guitar teacher played it for me on his boom box. Up until that point, I thought everyone heard music this way, but my guitar teacher looked at me wide-eyed, before explaining that I had a special neurological gift: synesthesia. I could see music in color, and I could taste specific words—some were bitter against my gums, and some danced on my tongue like a packet of sugar.

I peered over the heads to see who was responsible for this time machine, for the taste of salt and vinegar on my tongue and midnight blue behind my eyes. Strangely, the buzz of nostalgia shifted—now strangled inside my throat—as I locked eyes with the voice. He was wearing a vintage R.E.M. T-shirt and was built like a machine gun, with biceps that flexed as he gripped two white-knuckled fists around the microphone shaft with such intensity that I was certain the cord was an extension of his lips. I, Maggie Vine, was so, so, so fucked.

"You're so fucked," Summer whispered in my ear.

I aimlessly seized the cold beer from Summer's hand, with my eyes glued to the singer. What good were eyes if I didn't use them to take in every inch of this guy?

This singer—whoever he was—sent my body into a tailspin. He swept his thick, wavy blond hair to one side of his angular jawline, revealing a face so handsome it belonged inside the pages of a magazine—a face teenage Maggie would have torn out of *YM* and taped over her bed. It wasn't just his beauty that leveled me, it was the way his entire body stirred with the song: music *meant something* to him, which meant everything *to me*. He moved in slow motion as sweat poured down his neck and onto his tightening veins, his raspy voice turning Dolores O'Riordan's mezzo-soprano voice into something both violent and gorgeous. The live backup band was at his mercy—their eyes just as wide as mine.

"So, so, so fucked," I said, open-mouthed.

He finished the song to a chorus of applause and effortlessly jumped off the stage with a one-sided grin. I watched him wrap one arm around his friend, a cheering young woman. I didn't know which was worse: the thought of him belonging to someone else, or the thought that he could belong to me. He laughed into a drink, going on with his normal life as if he hadn't just brought a complete stranger to her emotional knees. Instantly, I knew that loving this man could only destroy me.

"You're next," Summer interrupted.

She flicked her eyes up to the ceiling and sipped her beer with a straw, refusing to let cheap ale ruin her perfect magenta lips.

"What? I can't follow him. Are you serious?"

"I called ahead and they slotted you in, birthday girl," Summer said as she bumped her shoulder against mine. "And don't be ridiculous. *No one* can follow *you*."

Under normal circumstances, sure. I was the best act you'd see at any karaoke bar, unless Lady Gaga strolled on in. The measuring stick for wowing drunk dive bar patrons in New York City wasn't set too high. That was then. Before this guy.

"Maggie Vine, get on up here," the MC said into the mic.

I panicked, eyes darting toward Summer.

"Which song did you choose?" I asked.

Arlene's Grocery had a list of nearly two hundred songs: *classic rock* songs. I was an indie folk singer. I did not wear AC/DC well. Summer smiled innocently at the ceiling.

"Fuck me," I whispered into my beer.

Performing on a stage was an adrenaline rush that I chased, night after night. I longed for the feeling of a hot spotlight on my lashes. I didn't want to follow this guy, but I could feel my ego thumping as I made my way onstage. I couldn't resist a live mic.

I darted my eyes down toward the mystery singer. My chest twisted, alarmed to find his playful grin on me. His gaze tightened every muscle in my body. It was not safe to make eye contact with someone this offensively gorgeous. I quickly looked away before his smile could turn me into a puddle.

The MC flipped the songbook pages, displaying the lyrics to "Maggie May" in front of me. I could make Rod Stewart work with my folksy voice. But performing a song that shared my first name was wildly masturbatory.

"I hate you, Summer Groves," I said into the mic, glaring down at my best friend sandwiched in the crowd. She raised her beer up to me with a sly smile.

The opening guitar riff plucked through the air as I gripped the mic's shaft. It was still warm from the mystery singer's touch and damp from his sweat. That alone was a high like no other. I let my dark red lips grace the windscreen, and then I shredded Rod Stewart to pieces. I knew my voice was different. It was soft and dreamy, yet there was always an unsettling yearning behind my tone, as if I was trying to reach the other side of a void—and I *was*. Gold stars didn't fall naturally across my chest. My undiscovered talent was drowned out in dingy dive bars, night after night, as cackling groups of people turned their backs to the stage. I supplemented my lack of income as both a solo-act wedding singer and a glorified cater waiter—trying *not* to spill trays of amuse-bouches inside every exclusive event from Manhattan to Montauk. You could hear it in my voice—the distance between my real life and my dream. And boy, did I want him to hear it.

I let the last verse melt away, and I blinked back the violet spotlight with a wide smile. I could hear Summer yelling too loudly, a high-pitched shriek among civilized cheers. And then I made the mistake of glancing down, because without even knowing him, I cared too greatly about how he saw me. My throat tightened upon his hardened eyes. He was staring at me like he wanted to take me home and keep me up all night.

"You stole my soul, and that's a pain I could do without."

I should have listened to Rod's words. I should have just hopped off the stage and made my way back to Summer. Instead, the song came to a close, and I jumped offstage, landing right in front of his body. The post-show adrenaline had made me braver than I had any right to be.

His eyes were the color of the fucking ocean. *Of course they were.*

"Hi." I smiled at him, breathlessly.

"Well, hey there."

I extended my hand.

"Maggie."

"Maggie May." He grinned, taking my hand in his. "Garrett."

His grip was strong. I made sure mine was stronger.

"I think I've seen you play before at the Parkside Lounge," he said.

I nodded. "I'm there a few times a month."

"First Tuesday of every month—our band kind of sucks, but our drummer knows the booking agent," he said, indicating that he also dabbled in this unprofessional life.

He smiled, admiring my eyes and my lips and my shoulders.

"Well, that's good to know," I said.

I smiled coolly and inhaled sharply, as if breathing him in for one more second would be akin to sitting with tear gas for too long. I knew what would have happened if I had stayed. I wasn't yet ready to be ruined by this man, so I walked away without looking back.

4

THIRTY-FIVE

SUMMER STARED ME DOWN, AS my eyes locked on the chandelier above me in her closet. Garrett and I had been inseparable since our early twenties, and the dissolution of our complicated relationship was a fault I'd tried to remedy six weeks ago. I thought our conversation had gone well. I assumed we'd be back to being Garrett and Maggie—or maybe something more—after we hugged goodbye in the coffee shop, his chiseled jawline brushing my cheek; his musky vanilla scent filling my lungs with a chaos of lust and regret. We went our separate ways with smiles—mine was genuine, his turned to agony.

A week after we'd sat side by side, I texted him a simple hey—a casual, unassuming, can't hurt a fly, lowercase "hey." Three dots immediately followed. My heart fluttered, and then, the dots disappeared. I had spent the last several weeks masochistically going back over our text chain, staring hopelessly at his non-response. After a successful night gig, I'd plop on my bed with tequila and coffee swirling inside me, grab my phone, prepare to text him every thought in my brain, but I was only brave enough to graze the keyboard. The woman who fearlessly sang her heart out in front of one hundred strangers couldn't even text a dude.

Hey! Did you get MY "hey"?

Did I say too much?

Every unsent text became a new ache in my chest—until the collective weight punched me down to a devastating reality: I poured my heart out to the man who used to light my soul on fire, I told him a horrible truth, and it made him go away.

I let my teary eyes float back to Summer, who shook her head at me.

"Can you two get it over with already?" Summer said, rolling her eyes.

"There's nothing to get over. We were never *under*."

I turned away from Summer so that she couldn't see my ears and cheeks reddening.

Why do I have to wear my emotions all over my skin?

"Just go make babies with him. No time like the present."

"Summer, he has a girlfriend." He did. And she was perfect. Her hair fell across her shoulders like a Garnier Fructis commercial. "You know . . . I have a better idea. Why don't I roam the bars, bring a guy home, and let him come inside me? Cheaper than embryo shopping and IVF rounds."

"Playing Russian roulette with herpes sounds like a cool plan, Maggie."

"I *do* enjoy being STI free. . . ." I mused. "Ugh, I should have just stayed with the Vine Group. I had health insurance, steady pay . . . if I hadn't jumped ship, I would be able to afford like half an embryo, probably."

Summer grabbed my chin, forcing my eyes onto her.

"You were fucking miserable, Maggie. I'm not letting you work for your mom ever again. Plus, you just booked your largest gig in five years. You should be looking forward, not playing a game of What-if."

Summer Groves was a realist, yet somehow my biggest cheerleader, which made her belief that I could succeed the most important belief in my life—second to me believing in myself. A part of me wished she'd give up on me already, so I could have another reason to give up on myself.

"Back to Garrett. It's not the worst idea I've had. And I shaved my head in solidarity with Britney in 2007, so that's saying something. He's financially stable, you totally love him, your babies would be gorgeous, and he'd support you while you got your career back on track."

"*Summer.* It's never going to happen."

I hated the sound of saying it out loud. The words tasted bitter against my gums—like a Creed song.

"Never say never," Summer said.

"Never."

I poured the wine down my throat, willing away the tingling in my chest. It was a flutter I had bargained with for the last decade: the possibility that Garrett Scholl was maybe, kind of, just a little bit, *absolutely* my soulmate.

5

TWENTY-THREE

IT TOOK ME ONLY ONE first Tuesday of the month to gather the courage to run into Garrett at the Parkside Lounge. Except, I didn't work up the courage to do it honestly. I called the booking manager and begged him for his free 11 p.m. slot. I knew Garrett's band, The Finance Guys, went on at nine. I was pissed that he hadn't come to see me play first. Society had taught me that men should try harder than women in the world of romance. But as Summer suggested, "You probably scared the shit out of him when he met you. Men are sad, fragile creatures."

She wasn't wrong. That night, I walked into the back room at the Parkside Lounge, the Lower East Side's oldest dive bar. It was dimly lit, but I could hear his unmistakably husky voice the second the front doors swung open.

I stepped farther into the room, seeing the crowd of females stare up at Garrett as if he could read their fortunes. As his cover of Paramore roared on, he found my face in the crowd. There was an instant catch in his throat as his eyes met mine, and my ego did a somersault. I could throw this confident man off his game, and that meant everything to me.

I went onstage right after him, with no room for pleasantries. Garrett hung around to hear my entire set, but when my eyes brushed against his, something had changed. He didn't gape at me like he wanted to fuck me; he looked at me like he appreciated my beauty, but was fucking someone else.

Fuck me.

After my set, I walked around the stage and he motioned for me to join him at a high top.

"I loved that last song," he said as I scooted into my chair.

"Thanks."

"You wrote it?"

I nodded. "I wrote all of them."

He smiled even bigger. "Who was it about?"

"My mom."

Garrett tilted his head, as if surprised by my answer. "'Did he steal the sparks from your sky/When he waved goodbye'—I didn't expect that to be about your mom. Is it also about your dad?"

He was trying to understand a verse of my song, which made me feel like he was trying to understand all of me. My insides were throwing a goddamn parade.

"Yeah. My mom had me when she was twenty-one, and my parents divorced right after. And she's been kind of . . . a rigid bitch ever since."

His eyes widened. I shrugged, unfazed. I wondered if my candor scared him. Most men were amused by my vulnerability, but only for a night. Garrett grinned and stretched his body closer to mine.

"Has your mom ever heard that song aloud?"

I cackled, shaking my head. I had written that song before I left for NYU, after a huge fight with my mother. My dad, William, had been her one wild card—the rebellious class clown who she met in college. I was the unexpected result. She gave birth to me right after her college graduation. After I was born, my mom traded in the joker, held on tight to the queen, and returned to a lifetime of serious, well-calculated goals—never taking a gamble again. My mom was so focused on "what's next?" that she refused to embrace the electrifying romance of "right fucking now." I was all about right now.

"We were oil and vinegar living under the same roof for seventeen years—and it was mostly a special kind of hell."

"So, she's not the kind of mom you sing your stories to."

"I'd rather die than unleash that song in front of my mother. Actually, I'm certain she'd kill me if she heard it."

"My dad doesn't even know I do this," he said with raised brows—as if he were proud to have something rebellious of his own. "Oh!"—he snapped his finger—"your bridge! That key change, from A minor to F sharp . . ." He placed his hand on his chest and leaned back. "Knocked me out."

I fought a smile, afraid that my cheeks would show what was happening under my skin.

"What age did you start reading music?" I asked.

"First piano lesson at four. Then I picked up an electric guitar at nine, and I was done for. It was like breathing."

His smile was so big I wasn't sure the table could contain it.

I shifted in my seat, fixed on the way his bright blue eyes scanned my face.

"You never came to watch me play," I said.

His eyes stayed locked on mine as he sucked in air.

"Well, Maggie May . . . I really wanted to. But to be honest . . ." His eyes flickered away from mine, and he stirred a little straw into his whisky with a gentle smile. "To be honest, I started dating someone a handful of weeks ago, and I thought it wasn't a good idea to fall in love with you. And when you sing, it's hard to not fall in love with you. So, that's why I didn't come see you play."

He looked up at me with a shy smile, the tips of his ears reddened by the admission.

"Oh."

The word fell off my tongue like it was acknowledging the death of a loved one. I stared at him for a moment, and then bit down on the inside of my cheeks.

"Well, I should go," I said.

"Let me buy you a drink first."

He put his hand gently on my wrist. His skin on my skin felt worse than I had imagined it could feel.

"I think it's best that I don't fall in love with you, either," I said.

I turned and walked away from him, and it felt like my heart was breaking with each step. I recognized I had no right to ache for someone whose middle name I didn't know. I had no clue where he was born, if he went to college. I knew next to nothing about Garrett, and losing someone I never had was about to make me hold my body in the fetal position on the hardwood of my shitty apartment.

Two weeks later, I elbowed through the crowd in New York's hottest Monday night spot: the Trader Joe's in Union Square. I shivered past the frozen foods cooler, untying the flannel around my waist and throwing it on over my T-shirt dress.

I had come here for one thing: the frozen chicken chile verde burritos, so naturally, I found myself smack-dab in the center of the beer aisle—studying creature comforts that I could not afford. I was more of a wine drinker, but New York state law refused to allow a grocery store to sell wine or liquor—so the Two-Buck Chuck was next door at a separate entrance: the Trader Joe's Wine Shop. And I was too impatient to brave two lines.

I weighed the can of Boatswain Chocolate Stout in my hand, which seemed more like a gamble than a thought-out beverage. It would either be the greatest invention in the world, or leave me scraping my tongue with a napkin. I knew I couldn't afford it, but the mere knowledge that it existed was not enough: I had to taste chocolate beer on my tongue. Summers in New York City did the most damage to my lack of savings. It was almost impossible to book kids' birthday parties with school out—so there went my Saturday morning income, singing "Kiss the Girl" in my cutest Sebastian voice at four-year-olds' princess parties. My cater waiter gigs moved to the Hamptons for the season, where they preferred to hire local. So, for the past two months, I had taken on a temporary job of bartending at a grungy bar in SoHo. Not one famous singer was discovered there, nor would they be, because there was no stage. I was bartending three times a week and playing music at different coffee shops and dive bars the rest of the time. Monday was my night off from both. I had a hard time coping with nights off. The sun plummeted against tall buildings, reminding me how far away I was from my dream . . . how my light felt like it might be dimming. Hence: the need for chocolate beer.

"I can't let you buy that," said a low, husky voice. It was a voice I could recognize anywhere.

My heart raced as I turned to find Garrett smirking at me, swinging a brown bag full of whatever he had just purchased next door at Trader Joe's Wine Shop. My eyes widened upon his outfit. He looked like he was moonlighting as another man. Instead of his rock and roll vibe, he was giving "Very Fuckable Brooks Brothers"—a crisp white collared shirt tucked into belted dark blue khakis. I glanced down at the shopping basket in his other hand, seeing lean chicken breasts, spinach, bananas, and protein powder. I surmised that the guy I knew very little about was a nine-to-fiver, and likely the proud owner of zero body fat.

I cradled my chocolate beer lovingly to my chest, letting my eyes dare to graze his.

"Weird beer has gotten me through some rough times," I said.

"But who's there to hold you after a chocolate beer hangover?"

Was he slyly asking if I had boyfriend, or was he trying to tell me what I already knew: there was a price to pay for consuming sweet alcoholic beverages.

"Oh, so you're saying that your"—I squinted down at the pinot noir in his brown bag—"twenty-seven-dollar-wine hangover is better than *my* hangover?"

He opened his mouth with a comeback, but then he quickly pursed his lips together.

"Come on, don't be shy. Let's hear it," I said as I crossed my arms.

A devilish grin hit his lips. "Nothing about me is shy."

That smile—coupled with the warmth of his Adonis body inches from mine—made me consider taking off my flannel and laying my body on top of the frozen treat aisle. I watched his chest rise and fall, and each inhale played a game of tug-of-war with the buttons, which I wished would pop and give me the view of a lifetime.

"I caught myself about to use the word 'congener' in a sentence and decided I had too much life left to live before I turned into my father, so I kept my mouth shut," he said, twisting a shiny silver watch on his wrist.

I clocked that he grew up rich, and he was trying to keep his upbringing from showing. But no matter how hard we try, our childhoods, one way or another, find a way to scratch the surface.

We floated to the neighboring aisle, and I grinned as he grabbed a box of the Smashing S'mores.

"What?" he asked, studying my wide eyes.

"I'm relieved that your body knows the taste of chocolate."

"Oh!"

All at once, his face lit up. He pointed to the ceiling as if God had suddenly decided to bless us all in this TJ's . . . with Fall Out Boy. "Sugar, We're Goin Down" blasted from the speakers, and Garrett's broad shoulders moved with the beat of the drums as he spun on his wingtip shoes, his body dancing backward toward the nuts section, his fingers playing the correct guitar chords, a killer smile fixed on me.

"Oh, so you're one of *those* . . ." I mused.

"I'm not one of any, Maggie May."

I went to open my mouth, but he stopped me. "Don't you dare say it."

"Say what? That you're emo?"

"I told you not to say it."

"I would *never,* because clearly you're pop punk."

He stopped dancing for a quick moment, as if I'd warmed his entire universe. He smiled big. "You see right through me."

And somehow, in the absolute best way possible, I did. He put his large, calloused fingers over a bottle of olive oil, using it as a microphone.

"But you're just a line in a song," he belted, with vocals so rich and loud that every human in the packed aisle darted eyes at him. I watched as the pointed glares softened into adoration the moment strangers saw his gorgeous face.

He smiled and kept dancing, confidence bleeding through his skin. I had never cared for this song before. And now, I was doomed to go home, stare at the ceiling fan, and listen to it on repeat. Fall Out Boy lyrics would flutter inside my heart until I died, probably.

He continued shimmying toward the vegetable section. Garrett already had spinach in his basket, and it occurred to me it was possible he was re-shopping just to spend more time with me. Or maybe he just couldn't *not* dance to Fall Out Boy. Either way, I had only come here for a frozen burrito, and I was *absolutely* window-shopping just to keep him in my orbit.

Garrett stopped and stared at me as if he was trying to unwrap my skull and see what was inside. I felt my cheeks grow hot, until he finally spoke. "Indie folk, indie pop," he declared.

I took a proud curtsey.

"That's me. Lover of the *Who Hurt You?* genre of music."

"Who hurt you first?"

I didn't even have to consider the answer.

"Tracy Chapman."

He put his hand on his chest and closed his eyes, stumbling backward, implying that Tracy Chapman did things to his heart.

All I could do was nod as a memory snapped against my heart like a rubber band. I was suddenly nine years old, sitting cross-legged on a shag carpet, a silly grin across my face, wide eyes looking up at my dad as he danced away from his record player. He pulled the coffee table to the corner of the room, shimmied down to me in his dingy Queens apartment, tugged me up from the floor, and twirled me in his arms.

"Break it down for me," I yelled over "Fast Car."

My dad never blindly loved a song. He knew the entire backstory to all his favorites. It was habit—he was a music theory professor. He taught me to appreciate intention behind the lyrics, and he shaped my brain to fall in love with words before melody.

"Mags, this song is about a woman who drops out of school because her dad's an alcoholic, her life gets worse from there, and eventually the hope she placed in her lover's arms turns to rust," he yelled back to me. As a kid, I loved that my dad treated me like I was smart enough to understand concepts that I was not yet smart enough to understand.

The memory of my dad bubbled inside me until my chin quivered, and I came back down to earth—begging my stupid lack of a poker face to hide the fact that I was one move away from weeping openly in the vegetable aisle of a Trader Joe's in front of a man I wanted to see naked.

I glanced away so he couldn't see my eyes glassing over, and we approached the checkout line, now just a few people deep. Garrett tilted his blue eyes at me, tall frame looming over my warring expression. Instead of asking what was wrong, he *fucking smiled*—a goddamn Cheshire cat smile. Was he aware he could heal people with a grin? Because the pang of grief melted away as I lost myself in his sparkling whites.

He pointed to his chest, announcing, "Blink-182."

I exhaled a laugh. "Blink-182 hurt you first? *Yikes.* You're officially no longer allowed to make fun of my chocolate beer."

"Excuse me? 'Dammit' is a national treasure."

"You cried to '*I guess this is growing up*'?"

"I don't cry. The song just . . . spoke to my soul."

He didn't cry, but he had a music-nerd heart. Was he repressed, or did he have emotional restraint? Because I had a music-nerd heart, and I cried all the time. I was once reduced to the fetal position over a holiday minivan commercial. I could always find something that would bring me to my knees. And here he was, announcing "I don't cry" as if it were a shrug.

He grinned at the checkout lady.

"One check."

"Two checks," I said gently.

I smiled at Garrett, my heart-shaped face saying, *I appreciate the gesture, but not necessary.* He raised his hands in the air, backing down.

I was uncomfortable with the idea of being indebted to anyone, except Summer—and it took me *years* to ask to borrow her white T-shirt. My mother had a spot-on way of making me feel guilty for being born. Every tiny thing I accomplished or failed to accomplish either shined a light on her achievements in spite of me, or her lack of achievements because of me. At my college graduation, my mom tucked my hair behind my ears and adjusted the cap on my head, musing, "I never got to walk at my college graduation. If only you hadn't decided to come four weeks early." My existence was one giant favor owed. And this is why I paid for four-dollar beer instead of letting a nice guy do a nice thing for me.

Nice Guy and I pushed our bodies outside onto Fourteenth Street, the balmy August night hitting my cheeks as I turned to meet him. Garrett had just finished redistributing his purchases among his four bags—probably so he could perform evenly weighted bicep curls with his groceries on his walk home. The orange sunset cast a glow on his wicked smile, a smile that was impossible not to match.

"I'm that way," Garrett said, nodding behind me.

"I'm that way," I said, pointing behind him.

He stepped forward, his blue eyes just inches from my face. My heart fluttered as he took my free hand in his and set the handle of a brown paper bag onto my open palm. He closed my fingers around it.

"Good night, Maggie May."

Before I had the chance to find words, he curved past my body and disappeared into the packed street. I slowly peered down at the bag. Inside was the nice bottle of red wine and the box of s'mores. A stunning swirling sensation fluttered to every inch of my skin—neon glitter exploding in my chest. This wasn't the discomfort of being indebted to someone—not even close.

You know the moment you realize the person across from you could be the person who fills the blanks inside your soul? I'd felt this once before—but at fourteen I didn't understand how rare it was.

For the first time in nearly a decade, I was drunk on the possibility of someone else.

I glanced down at the time on my phone: 7:15. I would come back to Trader Joe's next Monday at 7 p.m. I would wait for him by the eclectic beer. I could only hope he would do the same.

And he did.

6

THIRTY-FIVE

IT WAS MY THIRTY-FIFTH BIRTHDAY, and I had just been told that I was as fertile as someone approaching menopause. I tried to remember how to pretend that I wasn't dying inside, which was hard for the woman who wore her heart on her sleeve.

I couldn't escape the incoming demise of my unrealized dreams, but I could get drunk and high. I was crushing both of those things, swaying against the summer heat on the Great Lawn in Central Park, surrounded by fifty-five thousand strangers as the Dave Matthews Band jammed on-stage. Concerts in the Park had been my favorite thing. They were free, they made the park come to life with a melody, and they were absent of New Yorkers who were too good for summers in the city. The loyal lot of us got to party inside my favorite park in the world, while lamenting about how we almost suffocated underground waiting for the C train. Beginning Memorial Day weekend, affluent New Yorkers fled the city's humidity, camping out in the Hamptons for the summer like absolute assholes. I wanted *very much* to be an asshole. It was *hashtag goals*. Summer was a rich asshole who owned a home in East Hampton, but she had stayed behind to embrace the heat and celebrate me amid a sea of Dave Matthews Band bros, like a true best friend and masochist.

I stood on an oversized towel, swaying drunkenly with a charcuterie board, Summer and Valeria below me. Summer's eyes were the size of saucers as she scanned the crowd, experiencing a specific kind of culture shock: her first Dave Matthews Band concert.

"I've never been more of a lesbian than I am right now," Summer announced to Valeria. Valeria held her tighter, as if physically shielding her lover from a sea of straight white men in cargo shorts.

"Let's donate to feminist causes when we get home," Valeria said.

I smirked at the grown men in the crowd. Dave had reduced them to mere teenagers: dudes fumbling over lyrics that housed the emotions of their easy-breezy nineties childhoods. They were booze-soaked and high, clutching their koozies, reliving the memories of their first few Dave concerts. None of these guys had attended just one DMB concert. Seven, *minimum*. This Dave Matthews concert was an attempt for forty-year-old men to recapture the magic of their long-lost youth.

I let my cheeks find the violet sky, and I closed my eyes, promising the music gods that I would go home and cry to some Phoebe Bridgers to offset my secret bro-ey heart. I couldn't fake it, or fight it: I was a product of nineties music.

I looked down, seeing Summer's body wrapped around Valeria's. No one had held me like that in public since I was seventeen. Men had held me, with passion and lust on their fingertips, but not in a way where I could exhale into their chests—not in a way that felt permanent. The lawn was lit up by the neon spotlights on the band stage, and the glow of the city's skyline surrounded the stretch of freshly cut grass as the bass and saxophone plucked through the air. The dusty purple clouds gave way to the dark night as I swayed to my favorite Dave song. I'd had a lot of sex to this song. A lot of sex with my first boyfriend, Asher Reyes, to this entire album, which is why I defended *Before These Crowded Streets* with an ache. It was like I was defending my fragile teenage heart. Young love had a qualifier for a reason: it was made to get smaller in the rearview. But our love felt too big to fade— and the strange ache inside me was a reminder that it had done just that. I breathed in the epic yearning inside the lyrics.

"God, I want you so badly."

I was right there with Dave—I wanted It All, so badly: the American dream, the road less traveled, the blue skies, the fireworks. Summer was *not* swayed, as evidenced by her pursed red lips.

"C'mon, you can't *not* like this song."

"Stop trying to make me fall in love with Dave Matthews!" she yelled, rather viciously.

I raised my hands to the sky, backing off. Suddenly, I tilted my head, seeing Valeria own an expression I had never seen from her: a wistful smile. I followed her eyes across the lawn, toward a woman swaying with a BabyBjörn strapped to her body—her infant asleep against her chest. Valeria smiled at Summer, nodding to the infant. Summer smiled back, but as Valeria brought her focus back to the child, Summer swallowed hard, the smile fading into a straight line.

My eyes widened in alarm, just as Summer looked my way. I had caught a glimpse of something I wasn't supposed to see, as evidenced by how quickly Summer stitched on a pointed grin. She grabbed her phone, using the screen as an emotional shield to hide behind.

I turned away to study the crowd, and my body froze.

There he was. Standing on the other side of the fence, curiously, his eyes were dead set on mine. My expression brightened, as I realized Garrett looked like a version of his old after-hours self. Tight white V-neck that his biceps wore too well. Thick, untamed blond hair. Garrett hadn't looked this ways in years. Usually, he was loosening the tie strangling his neck, with his hair combed neatly out of his eyes. He'd stepped down as lead singer of the band a handful of years ago and traded in his sweaty rock and roll nights for midnight finance deals and IPOs. But here he was, looking ready to grip a mic and unleash his soul onstage. His eyes were drawing me in, but with a hardness that I did not recognize.

Below our chins, there were groups of people drinking out of red plastic cups, cackling, chatting, singing off-key. We stared at each other like two empty bookends standing above the crowd—no one and nothing else needed to exist between our bodies.

The chords of "Crash Into Me" plucked though the air as tall bodies filled in the gap between Garrett and me. The park was thick with nostalgic romance. Maybe that's what pulled my bare shoulders through the crowd and outside the lawn's fence so effortlessly. Maybe that's what landed me right in front of his strong body.

We stood inches from each other. We'd been here a couple times before. And this time didn't feel any different—like if our lips didn't touch, the world might end.

My chest pounded as the verse moved into the chorus. *"I'm bare-boned and crazy for you."* Garrett's eyes searched around my face, and I waited for his usual grin to cut through my intensity. My heart beat faster with the realization that there wasn't a joke in sight.

"Happy birthday," he said.

Garrett managed a quick smile, but his expression hardened into something else. His eyes washed over me like a tidal wave engulfing the shore, rendering me powerless. But I wasn't. I was a grown woman. Suddenly, I felt my age: all of thirty-five. I felt every painful moment under my skin: from my dream getting callously torn from me, to time refusing to be on my side, to watching the men I love slip away. I felt what it was like to come *so close*, and I didn't want to feel it anymore.

Happy birthday felt like a dare.

A yellow spotlight warmed the entire park, and I took a step forward. "Kiss me," I said.

7

TWENTY-FOUR

I SAT ON THE TOILET seat in the dingy bathroom of Arlene's Grocery as Summer applied bronzer to my pale cheek.

"So, I finally get to meet Grocery Garrett."

"You were there when I met Garrett," I reminded her, through my sucked-in cheeks.

"Doesn't matter. He didn't get to meet *me*."

Summer was bitter. For a year, she'd listened to me wax poetic about a gorgeous guy who existed only on Mondays inside a Trader Joe's. "If you don't ask him to your birthday, I'm going to march to TJ's and do it myself," Summer had threatened two weeks prior. It was the nudge I needed to ask Garrett to see me outside of the frozen food aisle—to ask him to come to my birthday party at our original meeting place, Arlene's Grocery. He said "I'll be there" faster than I'd ever seen a word fly out of his mouth.

"I can't believe it's taken you this long to invite him out," Summer said. She applied magenta matte lipstick to my mouth and handed me a piece of toilet paper to blot.

Summer knew exactly why it took me a year to suggest that Garrett and I see each other outside a grocery store: I was terrified to mess with something so flawless. I was a perfectionist when it came to things I loved, and I didn't want to shatter our glittery snow globe—a foul-mouthed Hallmark movie inside a Trader Joe's.

There was the household goods section, where he insisted that Duran

Duran's "Lay Lady Lay" was better than Dylan's. I laughed straight into his earnest blue eyes, and like a *lady*, I told him to "fuck right off." He shook his head at me with a grin—it was an expression that looked a lot like love, and then his eyes darted away from mine.

The dairy aisle, where we rapid-fire listed nineties one-hit wonders. Where he tried to convince me that Blues Traveler was "so much more than a one-hit wonder," and before I could give him my trademark Maggie Vine smirk, his hand brushed my cheek, one earbud went into my ear, and right there in front of the 2 percent milk, I fell in love with "Hook" because it was the song playing when Garrett Scholl's hand lingered on my face for a moment too long as his eyes stared at mine, unflinching.

The pots of mismatched wildflowers, where I forced one of my favorite unrequited love songs, Fiona Apple's "Paper Bag," onto him, hoping he would catch the non-subtle hint: *Not being with you keeps me up at night.* Truthfully, "Silver Springs" stood tallest on my podium of musical heart-ache, but Garrett wasn't Lindsey Buckingham—we were in our early years, he hadn't broken my heart, *yet*. Part of what kept me up at night was knowing Garrett had the potential to turn me into That Girl sitting on the subway, the one rage-sobbing *"was I just a fool?"* to complete strangers. He had the potential to break my heart and fill the cracks with fury. He had the potential to make me go Full Stevie Nicks—to turn me into a woman hell-bent on haunting his existence with my voice. So I went with the more optimistic approach, the second-most brutal song in the back of my mind, "Paper Bag." I watched Garrett's jaw clench as Fiona Apple's *"hunger hurts and I want him so bad"* met his rock and roll eardrums. We were inches apart, the headphone cord dangling between our chins, and the line buzzed on my gums like a drunk cigarette. He stood motionless after the song ended, slowly handed me back my earbud, and, eyes locked on mine, without a hint of his usual smile, said, "I've been there." I wanted to ask, *"Are you there, right now, with ME?"* I longed to step forward and close the gap between us with a simple, *"We don't have to be there,"* against his lips. But all that followed was a head nod, because I wasn't sure I could recover if I received confirmation that he didn't feel the same way.

The mixed nuts section, where, holding a package of salted pistachios, Garrett opened up about his late grandfather, a man who would leave tiny pistachio shells strewn throughout his Connecticut Tudor home. His grandfather was hard on his father, so his father was hard on Garrett. I watched Garrett's jaw clench with emotion as he finished telling stories of emotionless men who shared his last name. He painted on a smile, burying his hurt inside, but I saw it just the same: there was pain inside the man who radiated sunshine.

The vitamins section, where I broke down after a typical fight with my mother—an argument spurred by my refusal to take the real estate license exam and follow in the footsteps of the thirty-year plan she had set out for me. He stepped forward, wrapped his huge arms around me, leaned down, and held me tightly. I loved how my head fit under his chin. "I envy that you're brave enough to put your dreams first. I'm not," he whispered. He pulled back and smirked at me, using his hand as a ruler as he measured the top of my head, coming just to his neckline. "*Seriously,* how short *are* you?" I elbowed him, laughing as I wiped away tears.

Garrett wasn't fearless enough to put his dreams first, but I didn't blame him. We were both only children, and we concluded that our parents should have made more options for success instead of setting their legacies on top of our shoulders. My mother was waiting on the moment I would come to my senses and follow in her real estate broker heels. Meanwhile, Garrett was acing the role of the golden child, a child who by definition doesn't deviate from the path laid ahead. He was going to follow in his father's venture capitalist shoes, even if he spent a couple nights a month moonlighting as the lead singer of a band. The Finance Guys, true to their name, was a bunch of finance guys in their midtwenties who refused to give up their nights to a job they would soon have to give up their nights to. Music was what he wanted to do for the rest of his life, but he was smart enough to know that music *wasn't* what he would do for the rest of his life. In some ways, I envied Garrett, but I also felt a sense of pretentious bitterness. What gave him the right to take up space on a stage if he wasn't prepared to wake up on it? He could afford nice wine and healthy food, and he got to enjoy the spotlight once in a blue moon. But gun to my head, I would rather bleed for every penny and go to sleep in a shitty apartment with a smile on my face than the alternative. Garrett's glory days were about to be behind him. I got the sense mine were approaching.

Over the last year, steam had started picking up. I was playing at different venues in the city five nights a week. I sold a handful of demos after each show. It was a high like no other when people put cold hard cash into my sweaty palms just so they could hear me sing again. A few months ago, I crushed an open mic night in Murray Hill, and the director watching offered me a Wednesday residency. I was starting to recognize the faces in the crowd, and I realized the same people were coming back to drink cheap beer in an old dark bar just so they could hear me sing, *again*. My Stevie Nicks cover on YouTube did a crawl from 12 to 5,245 views. I had *fans*. But it was inside a chilly, bustling TJ's on a Monday night with no spotlight on me, where I felt the most seen.

I was aware that Garrett had a girlfriend. He probably looked at her the same way he looked at me in front of the checkout counter, and the possibility of witnessing his affection for another woman made me want to meet an untimely death. Equally appalling: Garrett believed I was the most authentic person he'd ever met, and if he stepped into my world, he would see Maggie Vine faking it with someone else—which was exactly what I had been doing for the last two months.

His name was Craig. He was an estate lawyer who I met at a child's birthday party. Summer said there was no bigger red flag than a forty-year-old man giving his number to Sleeping Beauty at his niece's birthday party, but that's what happened. I threw his number away, because nothing about a man who wore his company logo stitched onto his puffy vest which he then wore *over* a button-down shirt screamed, *"I will find your clit!"* When I didn't call Craig, he got my number from his sister and called *me*. He was wildly charming on the phone—charming enough for me to forget the fact that he purposefully popped his shirt's collar. Craig was the type of guy you want to introduce to your mom. He adored his family—half of the pictures in his phone were of his niece, Noa. He made more money than he knew what to do with, so he donated to the Frick, the Met, MOMA . . . yes, he cared about art. He traveled from Tribeca to the worst bar on the Lower East Side just to watch me sing on a rainy Tuesday night. He had a soft speaking voice, cute dimples, and a sparkly smile. I enjoyed his company, and there was absolutely no good reason to stop seeing someone this perfect in person and on paper. He was blue skies. But unfortunately for Craig, every Monday night when I stepped into Trader Joe's, I was reminded that fireworks existed.

I exhaled as I looked at my newly bronzed, newly twenty-four-year-old face in the mirror. "Mr. Brightside" boomed through the walls, where outside this bathroom, blue skies and fireworks would light up the night, bursting my bubble.

Summer opened the door, grabbed my hand, and tugged me out of the bathroom. We shoved our way past the shoulder-to-shoulder crowd, toward the stage room's bar. I slowed my steps, my insides growing hot as I spotted Garrett by the bar. He leaned one broad shoulder against the brick wall with a beer in his hand, watching the drunk singer onstage butcher the Killers. Garrett went to Trader Joe's straight from work, so the only casual I was used to seeing Garrett wear was business. Rock and Roll Garrett did *everything* for me—forest-green Henley, fitted dark jeans, damp tousled hair.

My heart pounded faster as I approached his body. He turned in my direction and momentarily froze, clenching his jaw, swallowing hard, and blinking me back. I glanced down at my floral off-the-shoulder dress, realizing that Garrett hadn't seen me this dressed up . . . *ever*. He inhaled, then melted into a smile, wrapping his arm around my bare shoulder and bringing me in close for a hug. He was freshly showered, and spicy musk and vanilla swirled around me, a scent I had only gotten a hint of, because he rarely held me this close inside a grocery store.

"Happy birthday."

"Thank you."

"Are you going to introduce me, or what?" Summer interrupted.

We broke out of the hug, turning toward Summer, who stared at us as if we were a complicated painting. His arm was still loose around me, his fingers grazing my waist.

I'd give anything to stand just like this—his skin pressed against mine— until the sun comes up.

"Summer, Garrett. Garrett, Summer."

Summer nodded at him, tipping her wine to his beer. "Grocery Garrett."

"Oh, is that what she calls me?" he asked, giving me the side-eye.

My cheeks grew hot. Now he had confirmation that I talked about him outside our bubble—that he also mattered to me on Tuesday through Sunday.

"What do you call her?" Summer asked, playing the role of the protective parent.

"Maggie May."

"I think that one's my fault," Summer noted.

I hid my mouth behind my empty drink, my cheeks burning.

"Can I get you another?" he asked me, nodding to my beer.

"It's my birthday, so I'll allow it."

I'd allowed him to buy me *a lot* of things over the last year. He did so slyly, never outright asking, but rather, he would place random food, candy, or drinks inside my shopping bag as we left Trader Joe's. I would sprint the long three blocks back to my tiny apartment, race up the four flights of stairs, giddy to discover what mystery lay inside—what little piece of Garrett I could bring into my real world. And here we were, in the real world.

"Let me guess. You're drinking some fruity, made in your mama's backyard, weird drink disguised as beer?"

"It's blueberry beer, and it's delicious."

Garrett shook his head at me and turned to Summer. "Can I get you something? Maybe something less offensive?"

Summer's eyes were pointed across the bar, at the bartender with a tattoo sleeve and long red hair.

"No thanks. I'm good," Summer said, not breaking eye contact with the bartender.

We watched Summer float around to the other side of the bar, where the redheaded bartender shot toward her like a magnet, taking her drink order.

"It happens wherever she goes," I noted as Summer leaned her head back in a cackle, charming the bartender. "I wonder what it's like to be that beautiful."

Garrett leaned in closer to me.

"Tell me. What's it like?" he asked, his eyes dead-set on mine.

I gripped one hand onto the counter to keep from falling over, as his hardened stare unscrewed every joint in my body.

"What do you want?" I heard a voice ask.

Him. I want him.

I couldn't look away. Garrett tugged his eyes off mine and turned to the impatient bartender, ordering our drinks. Meanwhile, my mind went into a free fall. Had Garrett just implied that I was beautiful? Had he just looked at me, here in public, like he wanted to take me somewhere private?

My phone pinged, bringing me back to earth. I pulled my phone out of my crossbody, seeing a text message from Craig.

Stuck in traffic, almost there xx

I swallowed the guilty lust in my throat, glancing to the ceiling. I had forgotten about Craig. Garrett did that: made me forget about the world outside his smile. In public, Garrett and I had other people who looked at us the way Garrett had just looked at me. I didn't definitively "have" Craig, but we spent a couple nights a week together, and he had asked me if I was sleeping with other people last week, and seemed pleased when I said no, and even happier when he asked if we could keep it that way, and I said "of course." Even worse, Garrett was in a year-long serious relationship with a speech pathologist. Maybe he needed a reminder, so we could cool down before Craig walked in on us tearing each other's clothes off in the middle of the bar.

Garrett handed me my beer, and I broke eye contact quickly, looking down at the drink in my fidgeting fingers, wondering how to seamlessly bring up Other People. Masochistically, I wanted to know everything about Quinn Parker. Garrett rarely brought her up, but when he did, he called her affectionately by her last name, which made me hate her blameless existence even more. The less I knew, the less I could hold on to and tear apart in my head. The more I knew, the more it hurt my heart.

"So, I thought . . . I thought you might bring Quinn tonight. I really want to meet her," I said in a high-pitched voice that made my statement wildly unconvincing to absolutely anyone with ears.

Garrett shot me a one-sided grin, which called "bullshit" louder than he could have said it.

"Quinn and I broke up."

Oh.

He pursed his lips together in a blank expression. He wasn't even referring to her as Parker anymore. She was just Quinn. Dead-to-him Quinn. My heart beat faster as I stared wide-eyed up at Garrett, the way you'd look at someone who had gone from a fantasy to a possibility.

"I'm sorry."

I was not sorry.

"Are you okay?" I asked.

"I'm fine. Honestly. It was a long time coming. It's kind of . . ." He trailed off, and I watched his strong jaw twitch.

The guy who had the perfect response for everything was suddenly having a hard time finding the right words. Garrett seemed to effortlessly turn a phrase, with a bright smile to go along with it. Here, he was missing both: the words and the smile. He looked down at his beer bottle, unpeeling the sticker with his fingers, until his eyes settled back on me.

"It's actually what I wanted to talk to you about," he said.

"You wanted to talk to me about your breakup?"

"No. I wanted to talk to you about *why* I broke up with—"

"Garrett Scholl, to the stage," an MC said over the loudspeaker.

Garrett drew a deep breath of air and set down his beer.

"Hold that thought," he said.

He turned and hustled toward the stage as Summer sidled up to me. I glanced at her flushed face.

"What's her name?" I asked.

"Azi."

Summer tilted her head, watching Garrett climb onto the stage.

"This guy really does it for you?"

"*Summer.*"

"He's just . . ." Summer shrugged her shoulders dismissively.

"He's objectively *very* attractive."

"Not my type."

"Well, yeah, he has a penis."

"Speaking of, he wants to use it to fuck you."

"Ew. Can you say that nicer?"

She crouched down to my eye level, speaking slowly the way you would to a toddler. "Maggie, do you see that guy onstage? He wants to make sweet, sweet love to you."

I smiled like an idiot at the thought, doe eyes watching Garrett unfold the songbook, staring longingly at him as he ran a hand through his thick blond hair.

I wonder what those fingers would feel like running up my thigh?

I swallowed the thought, realizing that I shouldn't be openly drooling over a man.

"No. He doesn't. And I don't . . . I like Craig," I said, reminding myself.

I took a sip of my blueberry beer, hoping the sweetness would wash away the taste of Craig's name—wet cardboard on my tongue.

Garrett shut the songbook and locked eyes with me. His hardened expression melted into a slow smile, one that softened his jaw for longer than it should. I could see Summer shaking her head at me out of the corner of my eye.

"Apologies to Craig," Summer said.

Garrett lowered the mic stand with a devilish grin on me.

"Yeah . . ." I nodded, with my lips parted in the hazy air.

"Let's make some noise for Miss Maggie May over there. Today's her birthday," Garrett said into the mic.

The room cheered. I rolled my eyes at him and playfully waved to the crowd around me.

Garrett covered the mic with his hand.

"Come sing with me," he yelled down to me.

I wasn't the kind of person who enjoyed harmonizing with others. Most voices stomped all over mine, or tried to compete. And his voice was huge. I shook my head. He let his lips settle into a playful pout, one that tore apart every defiant bone in my body.

"Goddamnit," I said.

I handed my beer to Summer and made my way through the packed crowd toward the ramp leading up to the stage, with the violet stage light shining behind Garrett. His smile reeled me in until his lips were inches from mine—only the mic between us. My favorite place. My favorite person.

I covered the mic with my hand and leaned toward him.

"You *know* I don't sing with other people."

Garrett sidled up closer to my body, his hard torso dangerously pressed against my pounding chest. He looked me straight in the eyes.

"Well, now you do."

Garrett playfully danced one eyebrow upward. I could feel my heart thumping in my throat, as the swell of an electric guitar filled up the room. I gripped the mic in my fist, and adrenaline shot through my body.

"Everlong" was over four minutes in length. Our eyes didn't find the crowd—not once—in those four minutes. We had both watched each other sing in every corner of Trader Joe's for a year, and somehow our voices had never actually met, but they knew each other.

Garrett and I were trapped inside our own universe, irises locked, desperate voices gliding against each other with urgent wanting. It didn't help that my senses were cross wired. Singing with Garrett was a cotton candy fever dream, and "Everlong" exploded behind my eyes like a purple and orange sunset. It left the taste of buttermilk frosting on my tongue. I didn't want the sensation to end.

"And I wonder . . . If anything could ever be this good again."

Good fucking question, Dave Grohl.

I was a solo act. I felt most confident and at ease when it was just myself and a guitar. But singing inches away from Garrett felt like I had injected an illegal substance into my veins. My voice had found its other half, without even trying.

I didn't know how I was supposed to go back.

I didn't think I wanted to.

After the song ended, Garrett jumped offstage and lifted his arms up to help me do the same—steadying my waist until my feet found the floor. I moved to back my body off his, but he held me tight. The feeling of his strong grip against my bones—one hand above my hip, the other hand in mine—was a scenario I had only closed my eyes on. My eyes were open, and his touch on my skin was very real. Garrett scanned my face with hungry eyes, and I felt the warmth of his mouth growing hotter and hotter against my lips. I felt his body thumping against mine—cotton shirt pressing on my strapless dress. Out of the corner of my eye, I saw my maybe-boyfriend, Fucking Craig, parting through the crowd.

Fucking Craig.

"I . . . I can't," I said, the heat of the words echoing against Garrett's lips.

I wanted nothing more than to kiss him. But not when it would hurt someone else. I didn't want us to begin that way.

Garrett nodded and painted on an uncomfortable smile.

"Okay. I—I guess I misread . . . sorry."

I shook my head, wanting to tell him he had nothing to be sorry for, that he didn't misread a thing. But I was frozen in the moment, unable to speak.

"I have an early morning, I should go." He leaned toward my cheek, brushing his lips against it. "Happy birthday," he whispered into my ear.

He turned away from me, parting the crowd and edging his body out the door.

IT TOOK ME EXACTLY FORTY minutes to find the right vowels to piece together kind sentences—sentences I used to break up with Craig. I decided to spare him the knowledge that I was in love with someone else, and instead went to the holy grail of breakup scapegoats: it's not you, it's me. Craig responded by showing me that he was not, in fact, perfect in person.

"This is what happens when you fuck an aimless twenty-three-year-old," he said, shaking his head at me. I fought the urge to correct him with *"I'm actually twenty-four."* He kept going. I was a "self-sabotager" who would "never be successful or happy." Normally, these possible half-truths would swirl around in my chest and tug me down to the hardwood of my apartment until I was sure they were facts, until they turned into a brutal breakup song about why Maggie Vine was forever doomed. But Craig's cruel turns of phrase didn't break the surface. All I could think about while he was calling me out on my own bullshit was finishing what Garrett had started.

An hour later, I approached Garrett's Gramercy duplex, my insides buzzing with nerves. A few months ago when we played New York geography, I realized he lived a few blocks away from our Trader Joe's. Technically the one-bedroom pre-war co-op I was staring at belonged to his parents—they kept it only as an investment property. Garrett sheepishly assured me he paid them rent.

I stood in front of the burnt-orange brick façade and ornate wooden door, finding his last name on the call box. I pressed my chipped red nails on the buzzer, twirling my necklace in my fingers as I impatiently waited.

"Um . . . it's one a.m.," a breathless female voice finally answered.

I reddened, squinting at the call box, realizing I'd pressed the wrong button.

"Parker, who is it?" sounded Garrett's voice.

I had not pressed the wrong button.

The fluttering that had consumed my body on the subway ride to Garrett's apartment darkened to nausea. I somehow remembered how to use my limbs, and I backed away from the call box. Hot tears fell as I held my bare shoulders with eyes drawn down to my heels, walking through Stuyvesant Square alone. I should have just let him kiss me in the crowded room, the outside world be damned, but I overthought everything. He should have sat with rejection for more than a couple hours, but Garrett hated pain, and Quinn was a fast Band-Aid.

We sucked at timing.

We could fit like the fairy tale
But you're growing out of Us before we can try Us on
Don't walk someone else's line
Take me back to the "Once Upon a" time
Before this magic wand hits you like a hired gun
'Cause I can see us dancing through the years
When someone else's dream outruns its run
Come to me undone

8

THIRTY-FIVE

"Kiss me," I said again, the words trembling with my heart in my throat.

Garrett and I had been here twice before—an inch of thick air between our lips.

He stared at me, his chest rising and falling through his thin cotton shirt, his blue eyes steady, for what felt like a lifetime. The box was open. He swooped forward with his hand on the back of my neck and tugged me desperately onto his open mouth.

His fingers running down my throat. My hand clenched in his thick hair. A complicated love song come to life. My willowy frame tangled up with his strong build. Twelve years of bad timing seemed to melt away over and under our tongues. It was tender and full of yearning. His fingerprints on my damp skin lit tiny fireworks on delicate places he'd only explored once before. All at once, I could feel wind where there had been fire—he was no longer touching me.

Garrett stepped back as quickly as he'd stepped forward. I couldn't catch my breath, but by the looks of it, he was searching for more than air. Garrett's gaze was fixed on his feet, with one hand pressed onto his reddened neck, as if trying to get confirmation that he was the owner of the body that just kissed me like it was the end of the world.

I went white, with my eyes widening under the visual of sunshine battling a storm. Garrett inhaled sharply, blinking back tears—tears which didn't dare fall. But I'd never seen water gather at his eyelids, not in the twelve years I'd known him. Garrett's insides were coming undone, even though his armor refused to split open.

"Garrett?"

Brows pressed together, I moved forward with my arm stretched out toward his cheek, but he gently grabbed my hand before it could find his jawline.

"I'm . . . I'm engaged," he cracked, barely able to get the betrayal out.

The words wrapped around my brain, and I tugged my hand sharply out of his grip. His eyes darted away from mine, shame all over his face.

"I wanted to tell you when we had coffee, but you—you said what you said, and . . ." He trailed off, eyes frozen on the ground.

Shock opened my jaw and strangled my throat, until a current of anger pushed the words out of my mouth.

"Why did you kiss me?"

My heart pounded faster under the realization that I had just gotten something I desperately wanted, but under horrible circumstances. Garrett slowly met my damp eyes. I was aghast, my palms open toward him.

"Today, I kept looking at my door, Maggie. I kept staring at my door *waiting* for you to show up." He kicked the dirt below him, as if the emotion punching his ocean eyes was the dirt's fault. "I always thought that we'd"—he looked up to meet my eyes, so that the line would further delight and destroy me—"I always thought we'd end up together. I thought the cards would fall the right way. You didn't show today, of course you didn't. And it should have been an exhale. I'm with someone else. But staring at that door, it consumed me . . . until it felt like . . . like I couldn't breathe. Like I was inhaling smoke or something. I left my apartment to get some air . . . I started walking . . . I walked the entire city to stop thinking about you, and I ended up at the very place I knew you'd be."

His hands were limp at his sides, as if none of his thoughts or actions were his fault. As if I'd put a pistol against the back of his head, marched him here, tugged him onto my lips, and forced him to inflict emotional torture upon me. I hugged my shoulders, watching him stare helplessly at me through a puddle of hot liquid behind my lashes.

All at once, inhaling the wind was painful—shock turned to fury, insides tightening and boiling. I stepped in to his face, brows pointed together, anger showing. He froze, stunned by a version of Maggie Vine that he hadn't yet seen. Few got to meet her.

"Are you bringing up my thirtieth birthday? Bringing up that promise?" I asked, my voice loud and mad. "We were sitting across from each other six weeks ago, and you failed to mention you were engaged. I poured my heart out to you, you hugged me—you fucking hugged me, and you left. And then, you iced me out. You couldn't even text me back. And you're bringing up a stupid promise we made five years ago?"

"It was more than that and you know it."

"You put a ring on someone's finger! If it meant more to you, if you wanted to start a life with me today, you wouldn't be starting one with someone else," I said, forcefully.

"Goddamnit Maggie, I thought you were turning me down on your thirtieth birthday," he said, exasperated. His voice got quieter. "After that night, I thought that for you, the idea of me was always going to be better than the real thing. And then you told me—" He stopped for a moment, words stuck in his throat. "When I proposed to Cecily, I'd . . . I didn't think I was a possibility for you. I'd put it out of my head. What am I supposed to do now, knowing that *we* should be together? You waited until after I'd put a ring on my girlfriend's finger to tell me that for the last however many years, you were in love with me. And you knew I was in love with you."

I couldn't speak, tears were everywhere.

"I would have walked away from anyone for you. *Anytime. Anyone*," he said, inches from my face, tears still holding tight in his eyes.

I let my lips part, knowing that the result might throw dirt on our coffin.

"And now?" I cracked, my voice quivering.

He swallowed hard and looked to the darkening sky before his eyes came back down to mine. His lips searched for words, even though it was clear he already had them. He just wasn't sure how to make the delivery.

"I'm getting married." He said it like an exhale that hurt.

I felt my chest caving in, my breathing turning rapid.

"That was always your answer, wasn't it? She was your endgame when your feet led you to this park, when you saw me standing here, and you kissed me anyway."

I was fully aware of what we had just done. The kiss would live inside me forever, filling me up and then bleeding me dry. From this day forward, "Crash Into Me" would land like tiny paper cuts all over my skin. Silent tears rolled down my chin as I stepped back from him.

Hope is The Unknown wrapped in a safety net. It's wading through rough waters, clinging to the possibility that a big wave might push your shivering, tired body onto the balmy, sun-kissed shoreline, and ignoring the fact that a big wave might sneak up and drown you. When sparkly hope gives way to a cruel reality, when you can nearly taste the shoreline but you're caught in the undertow, it's heartbreak.

I felt my chest split in two. The possibility of Garrett was one of the things that I had allowed to pull me further away from reaching the shore, from finding the right man to start a family with. I believed no one else measured up to him, so I didn't give myself a fair shot to test the hypothesis. There was a part of me that believed he'd show up on my thirty-fifth birthday and put it all on the line. He'd kiss me, and that kiss would be the beginning of the rest of our lives, just like I had promised. Instead, it was confirmation that Garrett and I fit perfectly, but we would never be. I was thirty-five, and the road less traveled was officially a dead end.

9

TWENTY-SEVEN

I SUCKED THE FRESH BLUE ink off my index finger, rereading the outro. It was beautiful, but thanks to the swaying tour bus, I was certain I wouldn't be able to decipher my jittery handwriting come tomorrow.

> *Twisting tides breaking your fisherman's bend*
> *I like it when I'm afraid of how it ends*

I grinned, steadied the open notebook on my bare thigh, and reinked the lyrics as the minor key danced in my brain. The tour bus's bunk alley had become my favorite place to write. It was a warm cocoon: velvet blackout curtain around my twin-size bed, the lingering smell of frequent palo santo cleansings, and miles of blurry fields and crisp stars out my window. The road swayed my body like a hammock—ideal for focusing and sleeping, not so much for eligible penmanship.

I glanced up from the rewritten words, seeing my phone brighten under my notebook's leather binding. My heart stayed neutral as I read Garrett's name atop the lock screen.

When are you getting back here already? It's peak NYC. Sheep Meadow awaits!

I clicked on his text's accompanying photo: a picture of barely clothed New Yorkers sprawling all over Sheep Meadow's green lawn—enjoying the first warm day of the year. I spotted Summer in the corner of the photo, flipping the camera off. While I was on tour, Summer had invited Garrett to come to one of her client's fashion shows, and apparently, they shut down the after-party together, getting happy-drunk and sharing a cab ride home. And then they started going for coffee. And now my two best friends were sitting in Central Park annoying the hell out of each other in a loving way. I smiled big, comforted by the idea of them becoming friends. I took in the photo, reminded of the first time I saw Garrett running through that patch of grass.

I didn't see Garrett for three weeks after my twenty-fourth birthday. I couldn't drag my body through the front door of a TJ's on our Monday nights, as the humiliation and unspoken awkwardness from our almost-kiss *and* the fact that he'd gotten back with his girlfriend within the hour played like a horror movie in my mind. I was furious with both myself and him, but I recognized he didn't do anything wrong. He thought I was turning him down, and so he turned to the next best thing. Three weeks after that mess, he texted me a picture of a bunch of his friends with Solo cups on blankets, sunbathing in Sheep Meadow. Come hang, we'll be here all day! his text read. He was the bigger person—the person willing to blow past the awkwardness for our friendship. Mortification left my body, I grabbed a light jean jacket, and ran out the door. I walked over to the red plaid blanket from the photo, searching for Garrett, when I got a tap on my shoulder. "You must be Maggie!" said this blond, bubbly, wide-eyed angel. It was Quinn, his on-again girlfriend. With her four words, my heart thudded against my rib cage: I was officially in the Friend Zone. I wasn't a threat to his girlfriend—I was someone Garrett told his girlfriend about. I had two choices: embrace my role as the next best thing, or walk away. As my heart sank, I saw Garrett running yards ahead, shirtless, jumping in the air to catch a Frisbee like a golden retriever. He turned around and locked eyes with me, grinning from ear to ear as he swooped the sweaty hair out of his face. My body lit up at his smile, and I decided a life without Garrett would ache more than a life spent wanting more from him. Since that moment, I'd met three women who hugged me just as tightly as Quinn, squealing a "You must be Maggie!" in my direction. With each introduction, the pain lessened.

I grinned at the photo of Sheep Meadow, and I curled my body up to the bus's window, snapping a picture outside of the sun setting on West Virginia farmland.

I'll be back next week! Keep Central Park warm for me, I wrote, attaching the picture.

I was officially in remission from Garrett Scholl, and my entire body was better for it. Wanting something you can't have is an all-consuming ache, and if you're not careful, it can darken your insides. It had been a couple years since my last pine—since I closed my eyes and fantasized about standing next to him in a courthouse or pushing out his blue-eyed babies. I was also incredibly busy, which helped with rumination. Nothing is worse for heartache than idle time.

I was opening for the Violet Bride—a beloved indie band with a small but loyal following. I had made friends with a booking manager in New York City, Josh Wheeler, who knew to call me whenever opening acts backed out anywhere around the tri-state area. It meant playing at midsize venues and selling my demo with the bigger band's merch—which was incredible exposure and much less horrible pay than I was used to. So, when the Violet Bride's opening band announced they were breaking up—one month before they were set to leave on their North American tour—Josh sent my YouTube channel their way. I brought my guitar to their lead singer's apartment at two in the morning, belted six songs for the three-person band, and they responded by telling me to clear my schedule from February to April.

"Can I bug you?" I heard a voice ask.

I sat up in the bunk and pulled back the curtain, smiling as Drew Reddy slyly lifted his eyebrow. I patted the empty space next to my crossed legs, and he hopped up, pulling the curtain closed and putting his scruff on my neck.

I met Drew the first night of the tour at the historic Aladdin Theater in Portland. My set started out the way most unknown opening acts do—noisy chatter and laughter competed with my voice. But by my last song, I noticed a hush had fallen across the room. The sold-out crowd of 620 people was transfixed, staring up at me in silence so I could be loud. I floated offstage to a chorus of deafening cheers, my skin on fire and my insides vibrating from the rush of captivating my largest audience.

Seconds later, Drew found me backstage at my sexiest—my sweaty forehead pressed against a giant box fan, the neckline of my off-the-shoulder dress tugged below my bra. Just a girl, standing in front a fan, asking it to cool her post-show adrenaline boob sweat.

"You were something out there," said a faded Southern accent.

I quickly pulled my dress's neckline above my chest and turned to find myself staring directly into a wide 85mm lens. The shutter clicked, and the photographer glanced up from his camera, his playful expression widening my eyes. He looked like the kind of guy who built log cabins with his bare hands—a beanie, flannel, and blue jeans.

"Drew," he said, outstretching his hand to mine. "I'm joining you guys for the rest of the tour." He pointed to his chest. "The photographer."

"Maggie Vine. The opening act," I announced.

"Yeah, no shit."

I grinned, cheeks reddening.

"What?" he asked, amused.

"It's just . . . I'm not used to someone knowing who I am before we've been introduced."

"Get used to it, Vine."

The sound of my last name on his lips made my face burn even hotter.

Later that night on the tour bus, after I beat him in a game of Bullshit and gloated shamelessly with a victory dance, he stared into my eyes for five seconds and announced, "You're trouble."

I knew better. I knew that when a man calls a woman trouble, *he* is in fact trouble. But Drew was right, and so was I: we were both trouble. I wanted so badly to feel something real, and Drew lived life like it was one big game of Dare. If we had an extra day in a small town, he would find us a cliff to dive off, a lake to get naked in, a country club to sneak into so we could go on golf cart joyrides. Every night, in the time between sets, Drew and I would find a closet backstage, he'd press me up against a wall, tug up my skirt, I'd rip the leather belt off his jeans, and we'd have the fastest, wildest sex of my life. I had a hard time coming down from performing, and I discovered that Drew's hands on my body was the best way to expel the remaining adrenaline.

Drew was a talented up-and-coming music photographer who would go back to LA and find another indie band to tour with when ours ended, and I would go back to New York and start playing bigger venues and work on getting actual representation. I would miss him instantly. I knew I would. I would be left with my willowy body curling over my dad's old Gibson Hummingbird, ugly cries echoing against the hardwood of my pre-war studio, wine-stained lips birthing earth-shattering breakup lyrics. We had a week left on tour, and I was dreading the inevitable. I was subletting my studio in the city, I was doing what I loved without having to worry about paying rent or feeding myself, or fighting to get my next gig—my adult life felt taken care of for the first time. And I liked embracing my wild side. New York City didn't give me a chance to feel this kind of freedom. You can't live on the edge when an entire city is watching. You can't sneak out of your studio apartment and run naked into cold moonlit lakes without a second thought. Drew made me feel like a teenager again—like the Maggie Vine who snuck out of her camp cabin to find wanderlust with her first love, Asher Reyes. Drew made me forget about the constraints of adulthood.

I lay naked in Drew's arms, my nails tracing one of his many tattoos on his biceps, my soul at peace. He grazed his fingers up and down the side of my breast, eyes pensive.

"We should keep seeing each other. After this," he announced to the ceiling.

I slowly sat up, shifting so I was on top of him—so his eyes met mine. I searched his face, shocked to find his expression dead serious. This was a man who scoffed at people who wanted to put down roots, and here he was, discussing *our* future.

"You want to keep seeing each other?"

"I do," he said, expression unwavering. "What do you think about me coming to spend some time in New York?"

My mouth hung open in a smile. I pinned his wrists back, scrunching my face up to his. "Those AC units drippin' onto your mouth when you aren't lookin', all those people in a hurry to go nowhere," I said in my best Southern accent, mocking his pretentiousness. "I thought you hated New York."

His dark green eyes scanned my face.

"I do. But I love you."

Heat enveloped my chest, as a sparkly sensation floated through my body. My hands went limp around his wrists.

"You . . . you love me?" I found myself grinning stupidly under the words. They were lavender and honey. *Love.*

He sat up and grabbed the back of my neck, pulling me into a kiss and rolling me over. Drew's mouth found my ear as I arched my hip upward, feeling my protruding phone on my back. I set the phone on the windowsill, and out of the corner of my eye, I saw a text from Garrett light up the screen. His words, miss you, made my heart beat even faster.

10

THIRTY-FIVE

THIS WASN'T THE FOLLOW-UP MOMENT I had pictured after I kissed Garrett Scholl on my thirty-fifth birthday. It had played very differently in my mind over the last five years, like a glorious rom-com montage. I figured our courtship, most of it existing in the All Is Lost moment of act three, would send us straight to Happily Ever After once our lips met, once one of us kept that promise. *Not so much.* I was not "I-wanted-it-to-be-you" Meg Ryan. I was crying-hysterically-in-her-bed Meg Ryan. More specifically, crying-on-the-subway Maggie Vine. Here I was, failing to hold back tears on the C train, weeping to "Silver Springs" because Garrett Scholl wasn't mine.

"Was I just a fool?"

I unstuck my sweaty, bare thighs from the bucket seat, avoiding sympathetic eyes as they floated in my direction. I ducked my head behind the heat of my phone as an elderly woman, likely in her mideighties, wobbled toward me.

She stopped, clutching the bar next to me, looming over my seat. "I've been there, honey," she said, giving my shoulder a firm squeeze.

Have you? Did you make a promise with your best guy friend to marry each other when you turned thirty-five, only to kiss him on your thirty-fifth birthday, just to learn that he was engaged to another woman? HAVE YOU BEEN HERE, SHIRLEY!?

"He's not worth your tears. Or she. Or them. My grandchild is a them. Isn't that wonderful?"

I bit the fire on my tongue and blubbered, "Yeah. Thanks."

Progressive grandmas are national treasures, so I decided to protect her against my personal devastation at all costs. If only I owned a car, then I could sob from one destination to another in peace, without all of New York Fucking City as an audience.

One 10 Minute "All Too Well" later, I stormed up my Union Square apartment walk-up, narrow wooden stairs creaking, and with each step, devastation gave way to a punch of anger. By the time I made it up the four flights and edged my shoulder past the door of my studio, I was *give-me-back-my-scarf* enraged. I flicked on the AC window unit and pushed my songwriter journal from the bed to the floor, plopped face-first down on my floral quilt—puffy red eyes smothered amid the smell of Garrett's cologne in my hair—which only made me cry harder.

I heard a buzzing on the floor, and I stretched my upper body off the bed to grab my phone. *Fuck.* It was Summer. I had forgotten that there were a handful of humans still sitting on the Great Lawn because of my birth.

"Hi—" I barely got the word out before she cut me off.

"Did you seriously just ghost me on your birthday and leave me to fend for myself with Dave Matthews bros?"

It sounded like she was driving in a car, and no longer in a sea of cargo shorts.

"Sorry . . . I was too high to be a human," I lied.

I couldn't stomach reliving the earth-shattering news that I once again knew what Garrett's body felt like pressed against mine; what his hands felt like in the back of my hair; what his tongue felt like inside my mouth. The answer was, unfortunately: still hot as fuck. I would tell Summer about it later, after I had a chance to let it ruin me, just like our first kiss had. The engagement, however, was eating my soul alive. I bit into my chipped nail, nervously wrestling with the words.

"Did you, umm . . . did you know Garrett's engaged?" I asked.

There was silence on the other end of the line.

"He's *what*?"

"Yeah."

"No way. I mean I guess I've been a shitty friend, I haven't seen them that much lately."

"Like, not in the last six weeks?"

"Well, I saw them at that gallery opening last month. I didn't notice a ring on her finger—obviously I would have told you if I did."

"I know," I said, my voice small, as I picked the gel polish off my thumb.

"Remember, I told you watching them together that night was like watching wet paper dry. They were so bored with each other. I was certain he was going to break up with her, honestly."

"Well, he did the opposite."

"Well . . . shit." Summer's voice turned unusually delicate. "Do I need to come over there? Are you okay?"

"I'm totally fine. Doesn't affect my life," said the *totally* unaffected woman wiping hot, angry tears off her cheeks.

"Maggie, I'm coming over right now—"

"No. Summer, I can't go there, not yet. I need—I need to sit with it," I said, tears enveloping my vocal cords.

"Okay, I'm here if you need me," she said. "Oh, shit. I forgot to show you something earlier tonight—I saw it yesterday. Hold on . . . Okay, check your texts."

I put Summer on speaker and clicked on a linked *Deadline* article.

"Isn't that the book you made me read freshman year?" Summer asked.

My face went blank. I couldn't even answer her.

There he was.

Olive skin that hadn't seen a clogged pore in two decades, copper eyes that tugged at the world's heartstrings, trademark chiseled jawline that threatened to break into a million-dollar smile. There. He. Was. It wasn't the photo of the first guy I ever loved that sent my body into a tailspin—I had grown accustomed to seeing his image everywhere. It was the headline. I hovered over my phone; eyes unblinking on the article: "Asher Reyes Set to Adapt *On the Other Side*."

The headline punched like closed fists on my heart. I hadn't spoken to Asher since I was seventeen years old, yet my first thought was: How could he not have told me? How could Asher Reyes not have called me with this information?

All at once, I was flooded with a memory that had been tucked away—lost amid eighteen years of navigating a sea of men that never held me the way Asher Reyes did. Years of awkward first dates, forgettable one-night stands, intense short-lived relationships, and unrequited pining. Long before my complicated relationship with love, Asher Reyes made me a promise. Yes, we were only teenagers, but the way he and I said things to each other . . . Asher Reyes and Maggie Vine made blood oaths look casual.

He *promised*. But instead of finding me before midnight on my thirty-fifth birthday, he was dangling the glittery parts of my adolescence in front of my face.

"Maggie? You still there?" asked Summer on the other end of the line.

"Yeah, give me a second."

I silently reread the last line of the article: "'We've got our lead, and the next step before production is to go out to a few different producers and songwriters for music—which is obviously one of the most important parts of this beautiful story,' says Reyes."

Obviously. I sat up farther and scooted to the tower of books chaotically stacked next to my bed. I bypassed the IVF pamphlet taunting me on my nightstand—a reminder of the baby I couldn't afford and the time I didn't have left to try. My fingers found the weathered copy of a book, *On the Other Side*. I hesitated, then delicately opened it, wet eyes blinking back the inscription in messy black-ink cursive, "To My Maggie, Love Daddio." My father bought this book at an indie bookstore in Boston—a recommendation from the bookseller whose favorite aunt had written the novel. He gave it to me for my eleventh birthday solely because the main character was a singer. But she became more than that for me. She became fictional proof that you can do what you love and be loved.

I leafed through the dog-eared and underlined pages—the glitter gel pen notes written in the margins. The only person who this story was "obvious" to was me . . . and maybe six other people. I loved it that way.

When I was a kid, *The New Yorker* did a write-up about my mom's favorite neighborhood hole-in-the-wall restaurant. Overnight, our quiet dinner spot became overcrowded. The food tasted the same, but the atmosphere was different. Fury swirled inside me at the thought of Asher doing this to my favorite book. I was an artsy gatekeeper: the things I loved that the masses didn't yet have their fingers on felt like they were made for me. It was a false sense of ownership, a defense mechanism—like sticking your nose in the air and telling people you sobbed to "All Too Well" in 2012, or you saw *Hamilton* off-Broadway.

The pain inside me morphed into a raw energy. It was as if I could glean a hint of sunlight under a closed door. And like a moth who kept coming back for more fire and pain, I asked Summer for a favor.

"Can you get me to Asher Reyes?"

If Asher Reyes wasn't going to find me, I would go find him.

11

FOURTEEN

I WAS AN ADULT TRAPPED in a kid's body, and everything was the end of the world. I was intense and serious about one thing: music. There was no point in frivolous pursuits—such as the pursuit of friends or an active social life. My peers were lawless creatures who wanted to scratch every hormonal itch. I was a scholarship kid who navigated the oak halls of my Upper West Side prep school with my lungs sucked in and headphones around my ears. I could only exhale once I was behind the closed doors of my tiny childhood bedroom—guitar slung around my freckled neck, eyes shut inside my own little fantasyland. I had no real friends, unless I counted my English teacher, Mrs. Churchill, or my guitar teacher, Mr. Cunningham. They were the ones I spent my lunch periods with, where I ate vending machine candy and word-vomited to adults who recognized that I did not belong to the age group I was forced to walk with. I was misunderstood, and I didn't want to overextend myself so that people I couldn't care less about might understand me.

Not helping the end of my freshman year was the fact that my father had decided to offset his lack of in-person parenting by shelling out cash for me to go to sleepaway camp. Instead of spending the summer in Boston with him, he was sending me to an art-based sleepaway camp in the middle-of-nowhere Connecticut, where I could be among other weirdos. My father had moved from Queens to Boston when I was nine, so I spent summers with him to make up for the other three seasons. Unlike my mother and I, my dad and I got along like two peas in a pod. He taught me

tricks on the guitar, let me jam in the living room until 1 a.m., took me
to concerts, and made me cackle. I adored everything about him, *when I
was with him*. When I wasn't, I felt like there was a hole in my heart where
a parent should be. He was always just an arm's length away, but never
in my company long enough for me to grip on to him with both hands.
When he put me on the bus to camp, I was instantly homesick for the
time we wouldn't get together, and my chest ached with the possibility
that he didn't feel the same way.

I stepped off the bus into Buck's Rock Camp with tears in my throat,
but all at once, they disappeared. My wide eyes found lanky kids with
guitars slung around their backs, with colorful paint under their nails,
and cameras in their hands. Every part of me lit up—this was belonging.
Instead of putting on headphones and walking with my head down, my
body felt like it was outstretched: opened wide to the world. This was how
Maggie Vine was meant to live.

My counselor said it was an unusual heat wave, but it was only the
second day of camp, so I had almost nothing to compare it to. All I knew
was that the June air was so stifling that the tiniest breeze did more harm
than good, pooling winds of fresh-cut grass and wildflowers from the
surrounding Connecticut fields into the back of my throat until my eyes
stung. The heat soaked the front of my red floral dress and effortlessly
upended my efforts at taming my untamable hair—beachy curls framing
my face. I sat on the stage of the open-air arena, looking out at a grassy
field surrounded by a purple lupine meadow. My bony legs swung back
and forth as I aimlessly plucked my guitar. There was one song I hadn't
been able to stop singing, and goddamnit, it wasn't mine. Train's "Drops
of Jupiter" had taken over my universe and frozen me in a state of writer's
block. I was unable to come up with anything better. I was jealous of every
yearning verse and the sweeping melody. I longed to write a love song
like it—one that tasted like dark chocolate. And then I found out it wasn't
actually a love song, which made me envy the words even more. Before
leaving for camp that summer, I listened to an interview on the radio
with Train's lead singer, Pat Monahan. "Drops of Jupiter" was about his
mother, who had died of cancer. He imagined her returning from all the

joys of heaven, only to reveal that we shouldn't take the little things on earth for granted. I was desperate to find someone else in my atmosphere to make this premonition come true. I wanted nothing more than to have feelings so strong that even the *idea* of heaven would feel "overrated." I was tired of thinking of soulmates as a hypothetical.

Yeah. At fourteen, I was *a lot*.

I edged at a jumbled-up verse inside a song I couldn't untangle, and I pivoted to hum "Drops of Jupiter" instead. Suddenly, I heard a soft voice speaking in the distance—the kind of voice that floated through the air like a beautiful feather. I frowned up from my guitar, eager to stare away any human who would dare invade my writing-procrastination zone. My expression softened, eyes widening.

Oh.

I sat still, but my body was in a free fall, losing control as it soaked in a stranger. This guy stood tall in a white T-shirt with a plaid flannel shirt tied around his waist. He was lanky, like he hadn't had a chance to grow into his new growth spurt. There were headphones over his ears, and his eyes were glued to a crumpled sheet of paper in his hands. I could see an iPod poking out of his black skinny jeans. He was every emo fantasy come to life—instantly the most gorgeous guy I'd ever seen. Severe jaw-line, olive skin, puka shell necklace, thick black hair, and cheekbones that he—a male—had no right to be gifted with.

This mystery guy had no idea he was walking into my space, nor that I was committing his entire being to memory, just in case I needed to close my eyes and relive him until my dying day. He walked right past me, and I made a point to breathe him in with the breeze. Sunblock and a hint of musky citrus, most likely Abercrombie and Fitch's Woods.

"*Sit by my side, and let the world slip. We shall never be younger,*" he muttered under his breath.

I knew this one. It was Shakespeare. He spun on the toes of his All Stars with an air of confidence that I envied, walking right past me again, repeating the line.

"*Sit by my side, and let the world slip. We shall never be younger.*" He said the last line emphatically, with so much conviction that the hair on my arms stood up. And then, his copper eyes locked on to mine.

I sat frozen in his stare, with my entire body slanted to the side and my guitar limp in my hands. His eyes softened as they searched mine, twisting my insides up into knots. There was a vulnerability in the way he looked at me—like his default was to lead with compassion. Finally, he took the headphones off his ears and sucked in his reddening cheeks.

"I didn't see you there."

The way words danced on his tongue . . . I wanted to dance there, too. He crossed his arms and raised his cheekbones into a warm grin, melting the knot inside me and sending a wave of heat toward every inch of my body.

"Well, I guess it's only fair that you show me yours," he said, nodding to my guitar.

He wanted me to sing for him. *Oh, fuck NO.* I felt my cheeks burn, and I tried to open my jaw, but it was suddenly wired shut.

Open your goddamn mouth, Maggie. Use it to form a sentence.

"I—I don't sing for other people," I said, trying hard not to trip over every vowel.

"What's the point of that?" His eyebrow danced upward in amusement, waiting for my answer.

It was a good question, one I had wrestled with for years. Music was my lifeline, but music was mine alone. My voice was not for sharing. I was best behind a closed door where I could live in the fantasy of being talented without someone telling me that I was maybe, just super average. The possibility of disappointment—of being told that I didn't have the talent to do the only thing in the world that I wanted to—was stifling. "I hope I'm good" was safer than "tell me if I'm bad." "I hope my dad shows up to my guitar recital" was safer than "you know he'll never show, Maggie." Hope's reality had mostly let me down, but the sliver of possibilities pushed me through all the same. Head in the clouds, false safety net at my feet.

I took in the beautiful boy standing in front of me, waiting for me to sing. I hugged my guitar closer to my body. Maybe he couldn't see through me if I had an armful of carved mahogany covering my heaving chest.

"It's okay for people to have things that are just for them," I said, barely believing my words.

He chewed at the inside of his cheek, clearly in disagreement, but wanting to be gentle about it.

"I think art should be shared," he said.

He sat down cross-legged on the field below the stage and peered up at me, twisting long pieces of grass between his fingers, for what felt like minutes. This was the first time a beautiful guy looked at me like he wanted to *know* me—like he wanted to see all sides of me. I felt the air thicken, and I swear, the second hand on my watch moved slower.

All at once, I heard the sound of my own guitar. I felt calluses strumming C, G, F, F. Then I heard my own voice. As if for the first time.

"Now that she's back in the atmosphere, with drops of Jupiter in her hair."

Train's song echoed against the arched wooden arena surrounding me. His mouth parted, just slightly, as his amber eyes widened against my tone. My voice was lighting up someone else's face. It was a high like no other.

I planned to stop singing after the chorus's end, but a stupid grin broke across his face, and I could do nothing but keep going, until the entire song was finished.

This was love at first sight.

The final note left my lips, and I realized he was holding my gaze—his eyes staring deeply into mine, unblinking. Heat curled down my spine, and suddenly I was back in my own body—dress damp and tight against my fluttering chest, as if stage fright had simply been a fever that needed to break.

He opened his mouth slightly, but he couldn't find the right words. Something about the way he searched for them made me think that when this guy found the words, they meant something.

"I could listen to you sing every day until I die."

It was better than *"I love you."*

He sat down next to me on the edge of the stage and outstretched his hand.

"Asher."

I opened my mouth, which was suddenly dry. "Maggie," I said, without actually saying it. Because I couldn't speak.

He gave me my limp hand back, his attention shifting to the worn paperback book on my guitar case. He picked up the book, handling it with care, as if it were a relic in a museum.

"On the Other Side," he said, reading the title. His hand brushed over

the illustration on the cover: an oil painting of a young woman gazing up at the lonely moon.

"It's—it's my favorite book," I found myself saying.

"Can I borrow it?" he asked.

I was dumbstruck. What did this gorgeous guy want with my book?

"Don't you want to know what it's about first?" I asked.

"It's your favorite book. What more do I need to know?"

We had only known each other for the length of a song, but somehow, Asher wanted to understand the things that made me come alive.

Train was right: heaven was overrated.

12

THIRTY-FIVE

THE BEST WAY TO FOLLOW an existential crisis is to sing "Hallelujah" during a dead oil baron's memorial service, on an eighty-foot sailboat schooner off Sag Harbor. I belted Leonard Cohen's gospel as a wealthy man's black-tie-clad family scattered his ashes into the sea and, thanks to the high winds, into my mouth. "Hallelujah" was, without a doubt, my most requested song. It was one of my favorites, but I didn't have the heart to tell the grieving widowers and beaming brides that they were asking me to sing a very Jewish song about being undone by sex.

"She tied you to a kitchen chair."

"Morty was a devoted husband to his wife, Sue Anne. . . ."

"Remember when I moved in you."

"There's nothing Morty loved more than spending time fishing with his grandsons, Morty the Third and Mason."

After doing Leonard Cohen proud, I gave the family space to mourn, retreating to the other side of the boat as the service continued. I drew in a deep breath of the sea air, when a tiny, sticky hand wrapped around mine. I looked down, seeing a little girl, no more than three, grinning up at me.

"You're like a princess," she announced.

I crouched down to her big cheeks and fixed the undone bow around one of her pigtails.

"So are you."

She smiled up at me with all her teeth.

"I wish I could sing like you and Ariel. Did you know all the best princesses sing?"

I touched her little button nose. "Did you know that if you can talk, you can sing?"

"Not like you."

"Do you want to try and sing with me?"

"I'm scared of singing to strangers. I only sing to my Elsa microphone."

"Well, I used to be afraid of singing aloud to strangers, too."

She opened her jaw, her blue eyes widening against the wind in disbelief.

"It's true. Do you know what helped me sing in front of people?"

"Your mommy promised you a chocolate?"

"No. But I do love chocolate. What helped me is I would search for the friendliest face in the audience. Because when you're new to singing in front of other people, there's always one person you love in the audience."

"So, I'll make my mommy bring my Ariel Barbie next time I sing. I love her."

"It's nice that you love your mom."

"I love my Ariel Barbie the most."

"*Oh.*"

"Whose mommy are you?" she asked.

I fought to keep the smile on my windblown cheeks.

"I'm actually no one's mommy."

"Why?" she asked, patting my wanded curls.

Several years ago, I started seeing a therapist. She told me that the father wound I thought I'd skirted had in fact punctured deep below the surface. It was why as a teenager I was afraid to sing to a crowd, because I had a special kind of anxiety when it came to rejection. She also let me know that I was using the trauma of my childhood to put off my feelings about having children of my own. It was ironic, but in doing the emotionally exhausting work, I realized what I wanted for myself. I realized I wanted children, and

I had just been told that they were nearly impossible to get. If only I'd stayed in the shadow of my childhood, convincing myself that the fear of being a neglectful parent meant I shouldn't become one—convincing myself that the genes my father gave me could break some little kid's heart one day. If only I'd stayed frozen in my past, then I wouldn't be aching the way I was right now, staring at this tiny little girl who wasn't even mine. I wanted to be able to say I was someone's mommy. I wanted to give a child the emotional support I rarely got from my mother and the time of day I rarely got from my father. I could one day do both, but I didn't have many days left to try.

"One day," I whispered to the little girl, with hope strangled inside a sea of tears in my throat.

I patted her on the head, and she grinned and ran back to the other side of the boat, into her mother's arms.

Maybe it was because there were the ashes of a successful dead old man inside me, or the fact that a little girl had just made my ovaries weep, but the service only reaffirmed that I needed to create a legacy. I pulled my shoulder blades back and untucked my phone from my purse, dialing Summer.

"Hey. Did you find anything on Asher?" I asked.

"Top of the morning to you, too. You used to be so much more timid about asking for favors, you know."

"What can I say? Your lack of personal affection has rubbed off on me."

"*You wish.* I was just about to call you," she said. "I did some digging, and my colleague is best friends with Reyes's PR person. Asher's here, in New York City. Did you know that?"

Summer was a PR shark who had a Rolodex that boasted one degree of separation from absolutely anyone. I was not surprised in the least that it only took her two days to find Asher. But the knowledge that he was roaming the same streets as myself made my insides flip.

"Honestly, I had no idea we were in the same city."

And it was the truth. Sure, Asher Reyes was *People* magazine's Sexiest Man Alive, but he was wildly hush-hush about his private life. He performed the studio-mandated PR circus for one Oscar darling after another, and then he found remote islands to hide out on. He ignored personal questions in interviews, said very little about his family, and never commented on his relationship status. He was an enigma, and I liked keeping him that way. I stopped googling his name in my early twenties as a form of self-preservation. There was a lingering pang after our breakup, and for the first few years that followed, a giant "What-if?" consumed my mind: *What if Asher Reyes was The One, but I met him too soon?* I'd be lying if I said the thought didn't also visit me into my thirties. But we no longer knew each other, and keeping up with a celebrity ex-boyfriend who didn't keep up with me made me feel small.

"So, he's going to be at the DGA event tonight."

"The *what* event?"

"Director's Guild. He's speaking on some panel, and then there's a cocktail hour after. It's only for members, but because I'm the most amazing human ever, you're on the list."

A dizzying wave took over my body, and I gripped onto the boat's railing to keep from tipping over. I would be seeing Asher, *tonight.* It had been eighteen years . . .

"You know, it's a rite of passage to backslide around a big birthday," said Summer. "The confirmation that time has passed and your ovaries are withering away is a perfect excuse to finally find and fuck your super-famous summer camp boyfriend. Frankly, I'm surprised it's taken you this long."

"I don't want to have sex with him, Summer."

"Sure, sure, sure," she said. I could picture her in her spotless West Midtown office, rolling her eyes at me.

"I *don't.*"

I didn't. Having sex with Asher Reyes was the furthest thing from my mind. I wanted something more from him.

13

FIFTEEN

ALL I WANTED IN THE world was to have sex with Asher Reyes that summer. I wasn't trying to rush us, but I had the entire sophomore year to think about what my long-distance boyfriend might look like naked, and what his naked body might feel like pressed against mine.

My insides were screaming with the thought as the large bus entered the gates of Buck's Rock Camp grounds. I was sandwiched in a bus-full of loud New York City kids, while Asher's flight in from San Diego had already landed. Knowing he was waiting at the bottom of the hill for me made my heart race faster.

The past school year, I spent nearly every night with the phone cord wrapped around my fingers, whispering so my mom couldn't hear, discussing everything and nothing with Asher until my eyelids grew heavy and my cheek hit the pillow. And now, I'd get to do it in person. I could still taste our first kiss on my lips. Lilacs and salt and fireworks and Mountain Dew—explosions in the sky over the lake. I could taste our last—full of salty tears, blubbering voices making promises we actually kept. We'd made our long-distance relationship work since we left camp, even with him in San Diego and me in New York City.

We had spent every free moment of last summer together. We snuck out of our respective cabins after our counselors were asleep, our lips colliding under the moonlit gazebo. We pulled each other farther toward the outskirts of campgrounds and talked for hours under the stars. He'd read me poetry, I'd sing him a fresh love song. We were in love, intoxicatingly and blindly. And now, after three seasons apart, we'd get to do something about it.

I ran off the bus like a bullet, straight toward his wide grin, my large backpack banging against my spine, my body in a free fall until my arms were wrapped tightly around solid ground—his neck. He smelled the same: like sunblock and musky citrus. But he was taller now, and his shoulders were broader, allowing him to lift me above the ground with ease. I clenched my eyes shut and exhaled—the way I exhaled when I walked into my bedroom after a long day. I was home. He was home.

Asher set me down and put his hands on either side of my face, tucking the windblown hair behind my ears. There were giddy tears in my eyes. And my heart soared, seeing the tears in his. Asher was a lot like me: casual about nothing. He saw the world as intensely as I did, and he made me want to dig deeper—to see the underbelly of *everything*. He was gorgeous, moody, creative, and he was standing right in front of me in screaming color.

14

THIRTY-FIVE

THE STAGE FRIGHT OF MY early adolescence had returned and decided to attack every cell inside my body. Thanks to the subway breaking down on the way to the Director's Guild, my nerves had an extra hour to multiply, so by the time I arrived outside the Midtown brick-and-glass complex, I could hear my heart pounding in my ears. I had missed the panel, and was ushered to the small reception, where I kept my eyes on the floor and chewed on my bottom lip as I darted toward the open bar, refusing to make eye contact with anyone. Finally, tequila and lime swirled hot in my chest, slowing my heart rate to a normal pace.

Asher Reyes and I were in the same room, and I would need more than a stiff drink to quiet my insides: I would need a tranquilizer dart. My eyes dared to scan the crowd of professionals wearing their best creative casual, as my trembling hand clenched around the cold glass. I flicked my attention to my phone, pretending to read an important email, so as to not look entirely out of place. In many ways, I wasn't. I was surrounded by creatives who loved the sound of their own voices—there wasn't a quiet talker in this room, which is what happens when you gather impassioned people under one roof. Normally, I would join in on these conversations and match their intensity word for word. But these weren't normal circumstances.

I was in the middle of pretending to read a riveting email from Lyft when a low, soft voice broke through the crowd. The hair on my arms stood up and my heart galloped like a racehorse.

The first night I met Asher, I sat alone on my top bunk. Lit only by a small book light, I scribbled "I fell into stars" into my songwriter journal with my entire mind racing and unblocked. I wasn't expecting Asher Reyes to do this to my adult body. But eighteen years later, and all I can say is . . . I fell into stars.

15

THIRTY-FIVE

IT SEEMED IMPOSSIBLE—ASHER WAS PHYSICALLY standing only yards away from me. My entire body felt like it was floating outside itself, gazing at him in surround sound. I could hardly move; all I could do was take him in. Across the room, Asher was surrounded by half a dozen seemingly influential people. A famous Broadway actress and a blockbuster director among them. They stood tall, not reduced to a puddle by his celebrity, but they leaned in to his body when he spoke—they recognized how important he was. Asher used his hands to paint a picture—to tell a story of something only he could make come alive. His eyes brushed mine for half of a second. His attention went back to the actress he was impressing, but then his jaw stayed slack, wide open midsentence. His eyes widened and floated back toward me, and I smiled as he pulled his neck forward, blinking me back. The bodies around him turned in my direction, prying eyes trying to see the reason Asher Reyes had lost focus. He tilted his head slightly toward the lapel of his leather jacket in disbelief.

Before I could catch my breath, I realized he was walking toward me. The chandeliers above existed just to follow the angular slopes of his body, until all at once, he stopped giving the crystals a reason to shine. Asher Reyes was standing right in front of my face.

I soaked in the freckles swimming in his yellow-brown irises, the two-day stubble on his jaw. He had grown into a man that no picture could do justice. A *man*. A *gorgeous* man. Asher's lips parted, but just silent air floated between us. His wide-eyed expression curled into a soft, stunned, one-sided grin, he took one more step forward, and I let the arms of the first man I ever loved fold around my body in a tenderly unfamiliar way. We had never hugged, *ever,* where it hadn't meant something more. Our hearts had never beat against each other in a platonic nature. But here we were, pretending. I pulled back, letting my cheek brush his stubbly neck, inhaling the scent of wildflowers after a rainstorm, the smell of a rebellious cowboy who took refuge in a Connecticut lilac field. His hands lingered on the open back of my dress. My throat went dry amid the sur-reality of his skin on my skin. I wondered if he still remembered the ways we used to touch each other.

"What—how . . . what are you doing here?" he asked, with a stupefied grin splashed on his face.

His hand left my body, and I cracked open my jaw. It was hard to re-member how vowels and consonants worked together to form sentences with his eyes peeling the protective layer off my skin.

"I . . . I saw the *Deadline* article."

"Oh . . . ?"

I wanted guilt to be plastered all over his movie-star face, but there wasn't a hint of *"my bad for stealing that thing you loved without telling you"* in sight. Instead, he fought a smile, and a part of me was thankful to replace stars in my chest with a punch of anger.

"You got the rights to my favorite book," I said, trying to remain cool while seething.

"I did . . ." he replied.

He was now full-on grinning, giving my spite permission to thunder to the surface. I crossed my arms over my chest.

"If you think I'm going to let anyone else write the music for *On the Other Side* without a fight, you're out of your mind."

His eyes widened, surprised by the undercurrent of anger in my voice. He turned sheepish. "I—I had no idea you'd want to work on it."

"A heads-up would have been nice. You wouldn't know *On the Other Side* existed if it weren't for me. Reading the article . . . it felt like you took something that belonged to me and threw it to the wolves. It felt careless."

His jaw clenched, letting the pain behind his eyes shine through.

"Careless," he repeated.

An ache in my chest replaced the fire. I had just told the guy who historically cared too much that he was careless. I opened my mouth to try and soften my previous words, but he spoke first.

"I've had the book rights for a decade. I've been renewing them every eighteen months. Do you think it's a coincidence it was announced before midnight on your birthday?" he asked.

The air left my lungs. The article about my favorite book was published before midnight on my thirty-fifth birthday. The very day we were supposed to find each other.

"Before midnight . . . You remembered . . . ?" was all I could manage to say.

"Of course I did," he stated, as if any other option was impossible.

Of course he did.

"Where's my ring?" I asked, jokingly.

He twisted a cocktail napkin in his fingers, his cheeks reddening.

"I'll get right on it," he said.

Asher exhaled a little smile as his eyes brushed mine, and I felt my insides hum.

"You could have just . . . DMed me."

He shook his head, playfully offended by the suggestion.

"There's nothing romantic about that," he scoffed, letting a half-grin splinter his jawline.

The twinkle in his eye was a light switch, turning on the galaxy inside my chest. I paused to stare at him—to really look at Asher Reyes. He was offensively stunning.

"It's really unfair to the rest of the world that you look like this," I found myself saying.

His eyes refused to leave mine, indicating he didn't hear my words—indicating he might be thinking the same damn thing about me.

Fuck. FUCK.

"Hi," he said softly.

"Hi," I exhaled, trying not to melt under his gaze. I stood up taller, as if to remind myself that I wasn't fourteen again—that I didn't come here to drown in All The Feels.

Asher exhaled a chuckle, breaking into the same thoughtful smile I had fallen for two decades prior. There was still a thread of sadness stitched around his expressions of happiness—adulthood hadn't changed that. It comforted me and broke me all the same. His smile faded as he pursed his lips together.

"I'm sorry you're upset. That was never my intention. I always loved the story, and it *really* meant something to me—" He closed his mouth, as if he was worried he might say too much. "We actually had a big name attached to do the music and lyrics, but she had to drop out for personal reasons. So, we're on the hunt."

"Yeah. I read that in the article."

"I have a co-producer on the project, and he's *not* easily charmed. What I'm trying to say is: the buck doesn't stop here. I don't make these decisions alone. I can't just give you a gig."

"And I wouldn't want you to *just give* me anything."

"I know you wouldn't," he said with a smile, remembering.

I took a step forward, eyes level on him. "No one else can do this better than I will. I know that book inside and out. The only thing I'm asking for is a shot to prove it to you and your producer."

"Full transparency: we're going out to another songwriter exclusively next week. So if you want to be considered, you'd need to get me a song in two days."

I didn't flinch. "No problem."

Dolly Parton wrote "I Will Always Love You" and "Jolene" in the same day. I could get my ex-boyfriend a song based on my favorite book in two—easy.

He brought his phone out from his back pocket. "Same email?" he asked.

I nodded, fighting a smile. It never occurred to me that Asher still had the same email address. Instead, in true Maggie fashion, I took it to the extreme and showed up at an event I wasn't invited to, to confront him. To be fair, his Maggie Vine Bat-Signal was a movie announcement.

"Reply to me with your home address, and I'll have someone messenger you the script tonight." He tucked his phone into his back pocket. "You'll see the placeholders in the script for the songs—I'd work on the breakup number in the first act. It's the biggest emotional block."

"Sounds good."

"I'll send you times that work for Amos, my co-pro. Plan on coming to me to perform the song. . . . If memory serves, you're pretty convincing in person," he said with a warm smile.

There was a familiar spark enveloping my chest, spreading to my fingertips and toes. Hope was dancing inside me, gloriously letting me forget what rock bottom felt like. Asher must have noticed optimism breaking through my cheeks, because he shifted uncomfortably. He was unaware that the glowy optimism that fueled my youth had met its match five years prior.

"Listen, I wish I could, but I can't make you any promises," he warned.

I kept the smile on my face. "I didn't come here for promises."

He grinned to the floor, hesitated, then locked his brown eyes onto mine.

"I was kind of hoping you did," he said.

It was jarring, the way my heart threatened to grow, right in front of him. The way his finger brushing over the faint scar on his chin made me want to hold him. The way I longed to erase our last kiss from my memory by taking one step forward. It was dangerous, the way his eyes searched my face, as if in slow motion. I was a woman drunk on hope and something more.

Neither of us moved, we just drew each other in, as if recommitting each other to memory.

"Caroline wants a word," said a voice behind Asher.

Asher blinked me back, turning toward a short man in a suit.

"I'll be there in a second," Asher said, his voice unusually low.

I had to get out of there. I had to pour a bucket of ice water on my body.

"It's fine. I've already taken up enough of your time. I'll see you in two days," I said, putting my hand on his arm. I took a step away, and he caught my hand before it left his body. He squeezed his fingers around mine, and then let me go.

I shot him a polite smile and beelined for the exit with my cheeks flushed and my heart pounding. There was a giant wall mirror by the doors, and inside the reflection I could see Asher's eyes on me, watching me leave. It was the reflection of his pure, boyish grin as he looked down at his shoes that nearly made my knees buckle to the floor.

I made it to the elevator banks and lay my back flat on the cool brick wall. Sweat ran down the back of my neck as my chest pounded against my ribs. A part of me had come undone. A part of me had come back to life. Maybe it was the best part of me. She was worthy. His smile mattered the most.

Fuck me. I was fifteen again.

—∼—

16

FIFTEEN

I CLUTCHED THE THIN SILVER chain around my neck, rubbing the metal guitar pick charm between my fingers—a present from my dad. It was beautiful, and it had arrived a few months ago in the mail instead of in person. He was now a music theory professor at a Boston community college, and it was even more difficult for him to get into the city with this full-time job. Even though I should have gotten used to him not showing up, it stung every time. And that feeling—the anxiety of my dad's rejection—it was currently invading my body. Unfortunately, this had nothing to do with my father. This circumstance was new. But my mouth was dry, my stomach churning, my throat constricting all the same.

I ran my hand along the neck of my guitar, sweat dripping down my temples, eyes blinking back the direct sun and the fuzzy faces in the crowd. The small stone amphitheater stood in the middle of an open field adjacent to the animal farm, and it was used primarily for drama camp to run their lines or try out new material. This mini-Colosseum and sun magnet was now being used for Asher Reyes's girlfriend to overcome her stage fright. A dozen theater kids were scattered on the concrete steps above me, waiting for me to disappoint them.

We were three weeks into the summer, and the goal of taking the next step in my relationship with Asher had been replaced with the goal of telling my stage fright to kindly fuck off, forever. I had signed up for Talent Night with the intention of ripping off the Band-Aid. Performing at Talent Night meant that I would play in front of my largest audience—the entire camp—roughly three hundred people. I had asked Asher if he would help me overcome stage fright, since he was born to be onstage. Like everything thrown at Asher, he took my request seriously. Some (me) might say, *too seriously.*

He jumped down from the stone steps and walked over to me, his kind eyes trying to offer reprieve in a sea of nerves.

"This is your fault," I said through gritted teeth. I clenched my trembling hand around my guitar. "I can't believe you audience-bombed me."

"You're mad I didn't tell you they'd be here?" he said, searching my face for the usual smile that his closeness brought out of me.

Being with Asher was my safe space, and he had yanked the safety net out from under my feet with his own two hands, without warning, which felt like a special kind of betrayal. He had asked a dozen theater kids to show up here so that I could have my first crowd to sing to.

Anger swirled in my chest as I saw him fight a grin. Truthfully, he'd been breathing down my neck all day. I knew I only had a day left to overcome stage fright before Talent Night, but he had barely let me think about anything else since this morning. I needed an exhale, and he was refusing to give me one. And not only that, but some part of him was enjoying pushing me outside of my comfort zone. Maybe that's because it was my usual role. I was the first one to kiss him, the first one to suggest we sneak out of our cabins at night—I was the only one who gave him permission to embrace his wildness. To have fire in his belly instead of being so careful. And here he was, lighting a fire under me.

"What's so funny?" I asked, taking in his grin. I tugged at my throat, which felt as dry as the hot concrete under my feet.

"Would you have come if I told you I had gathered an audience for you?"

I stared at him with steely eyes, confirming whatever point he was trying to make. Asher set a hand on my chin and raised it to his.

"Look at me," he demanded.

His eyes swallowed the sun, and I watched him breathe in and out, deeply. I echoed his breathing, still mad at him, but also less mad because when he looked at me this way—unflinching—I wanted to fall onto his lips.

Last summer was spent working with different camp directors to polish

my songwriting skills and vocal techniques. I learned the fundamentals—
from developing my vocal sounds, to understanding different rhyming
patterns. I was relaxed when singing and playing guitar in front of a paid
professional—because I knew they wouldn't tear me to shreds. Singing
in front of my peers was a different story. I was at a sleepaway liberal
arts camp—every camper here thought they were The Next Big Thing. It
didn't help that my mother believed singing and songwriting was a cute
hobby that I'd one day outgrow. What if I was just mediocre, and singing
in front of everyone proved her right?

"I'm not ready."

"You know the song backward and forward. Mags, you have nothing
to be scared of when you're this great."

He placed both his hands on my shoulders and tilted them back.

"Your confidence goes the way of your spine."

I let my shoulders fall back into their protective place. "Did Mr. Greenway teach you that?" I asked, rolling my eyes.

Mr. Greenway was his high school drama teacher—a man who I gathered was more important to Asher than Asher's parents. Asher talked
about him more than his mom or dad, which was odd, because when
Asher described his parents, it was always with such warmth. One would
think he'd have more stories to share about his family, but it was always,
Mr. Greenway THIS. And *Mr. Greenway THAT*.

"Wanna know my secret?"

"If you say, 'picture everyone in their underwear,' I'm going to physically harm you."

"Find one person in the audience who loves you no matter what. No
matter if you're great or good or just okay." He pointed to himself. "Sing
to the person that feels like home. Everyone else will disappear."

"You must think very highly of yourself."

He tilted back on his heels. "'*Your eyes look like the stars I couldn't see
out my childhood window*' was quite the ego boost," Asher said, quoting
my lyrics.

"That might be the last nice thing I write about you," I hissed.

"Somehow, I doubt that."

Asher grinned and backed away from me, his eyes still on mine. He
took a seat toward the right side of the terraced steps, purposefully next

to a lanky kid named Peter, whose fingers were twisted around a worn yo-yo string. My insides softened as I watched Peter smile up at Asher. Asher became a theater god the second he opened his mouth onstage last year. He had that *thing* you can't teach—and while theater was competitive, he was so great that everyone wanted to learn from him, rather than wallow in the fact that they couldn't measure up. Asher first noticed Peter last summer—he was the kind of kid who walked around camp like he had an invisible friend. After Peter bombed an audition for *My Fair Lady* and cried onstage, Asher ran after him and asked Peter if he wanted to be his understudy. Asher used his quick camp celebrity not to boost his own profile, but to fill in the lonely space of a kid without a friend.

Watching Asher trade smiles with Peter, my angry insides gave way to gratefulness. My eyes locked on the guy I loved—the kind of guy who went to the ends of the earth to make sure others would thrive—the guy who was bringing me out of my comfort zone just so I would succeed. I inhaled deeply from my diaphragm, opened my quivering lips, and let my first love song, "Invisible Skies," find new sets of ears. It was the song I had started writing the very first night I met Asher. Adrenaline beat through my chest as the folksy, soft love song echoed against the stone wall behind me.

I had never seen Asher smile this wide. I felt the warmth of the sun on my cheekbones as my eyes moved from Asher onto the other faces that were glued to me. I watched as the booming bridge made each jaw in the crowd go slack. The last note left my lips, followed by the longest second of my life: dead silence. All at once, they rose from the stone steps and effusively clapped and whistled. I pursed my lips together, trying to keep from screaming. This adrenaline was new. It was big. It had pulled my spine upright so I could touch the sun. My voice made strangers come alive. I wouldn't ever let another person convince me that I was meant to do anything else but this. I wouldn't let another stage intimidate me.

Asher mouthed, "Told you," in my direction with a proud smile stuck on his face.

The theater crowd jumped off the steps and onto the field quickly, shooting me effusive compliments as they passed. Wide-eyed, I watched them disappear down the grassy hill. My heart was pounding in my eardrums, my entire body shaking as I set my guitar down into its hard case.

The second gong sounded, and the remaining bodies flew past us into the dining hall. Asher propped open the door with his foot, waiting for me to walk through it. I hesitated, and he nodded, as if to tell me to move. Suddenly, an arm clasped into mine, tugging me inside. I looked up, seeing my bunkmate, Gracie, with a huge smile on her pointed face.

"Wait till you hear what Conner Lee did in glassblowing," she sang. Gracie scrunched up her nose. "Why do they do this to us? Sloppy joes are an assault on our digestive systems."

She tugged me toward the buffet line, where a hot wave of mixed meat made my stomach turn even more. I looked back, seeing Asher's lanky frame lingering in the doorway. He glanced around the dining hall quickly, and then curved his body outside, disappearing behind the closing door. I felt it for the first time: a pang of romantic heartache. A puzzling uneasiness settled inside my gut.

Ten minutes later, I sat squished toward the edge of a long wooden table, anxiously force-feeding myself crinkle fries. I had just divulged Asher's bizarre behavior to my bunkmates, and I was waiting for them to tell me something hopeful, *anything* to make the growing knot in my chest disappear.

Gracie stuck a bobby pin in her wild magenta hair and leaned back with a booming laugh. "He wants to have sex with you tonight," she said, biting her pierced lip for juicy effect. No one loved the idea of a good story more than Gracie. She was here working on her playwriting—and we were all subject to her wild theories. I shook my head and rolled my eyes.

"No he doesn't. He—" My throat closed up with the memory of my hand tugging at the elastic of Asher's shorts, just moments ago. His fingers under my shirt. His body hard against me.

"Oooh my God. Does he?" I searched around the table for confirmation, scanning all the shit-eating grins. My eyes stopped when they got to our cabin sexpert, Pria, who had lost her virginity two weeks before camp. "Pria?"

Pria set her chin on her hand and leaned forward. There was oil paint on her cheek and under her nails. "A *hundred* percent," she said. "You better shave your vag tonight. I can help you prep if you want. Want me to give you an artsy vag? I can do a heart or something, depending on what canvas I'm working with."

I hesitated, picturing Pria using my pubic hair as her latest art project. "I'm good, thanks," I said.

But I was *not good*. The fries inside my stomach were bubbling to the surface. I showed up to camp Prepared with a capital *P*. I had spent all nine months fantasizing about Doing It with Asher. I had a journal full of weird sex tips I'd torn out of *Cosmopolitan*. I had a runway and I was ready for landing! So why was there suddenly a wave of terror spreading across my limbs? I set my arms across my chest and inhaled deeply, trying to push my shoulders back, but it didn't help. While I had confidently found my voice, a new kind of stage fright had hopped aboard.

FIFTEEN

I GRABBED MY FLASHLIGHT AND quietly edged myself down off the top bunk. Most nights, I tiptoed out of our cabin like a spy, and then sprinted past the rows of cherry-red bunks, through the fields to get to the dock at the lake, giddy to run into Asher's arms. But as I made my way toward the lake, my feet moved slower, each step making my heart pound faster against my rib cage and louder in my ear.

I took in the full moon hanging over the small lake, with miles of dense trees behind the water's edge. Fireflies danced overhead, and it was the perfect night to seal the deal with the perfect guy under a sky full of stars, except for the fact that I felt like I might be dying.

My throat was closing up with panic. I set my hand under my shirt, pressing my fingers onto my belly button and drawing in a deep inhale. I exhaled slowly through my mouth—a "sing with your diaphragm" exercise that my vocal coach had taught me. I'm not sure what kind of result I expected from a basic singing drill, but as thick muggy air swirled in my lungs, I wasn't ready to sing or get naked.

Asher's silhouette on the dock's edge turned to life as I stepped closer to his body. He came into crisp view—kicking a hacky sack on his ankle, while muttering his monologue to himself.

"Hey," I cracked, as my flip-flops slapped the dock.

He turned, catching the hacky sack in midair. His shoulders dropped at my presence, a relieved grin splashed on his face.

"You made it," he said.

I painted on a smile and walked toward him, clenching my fists to try and get my fingers to stop shaking as he wrapped his arms around me. His body was cool against my sweltering skin, and the feeling of his ribs rising and falling against mine only made my heart pound faster. I inhaled the scent of wildflowers and musky citrus on his damp hair, arching back and twisting my curls up into a bun, curiously avoiding eye contact with the one person whose eyes felt like home.

"Circus camp?" he said, raising his brows suggestively and taking my hand in his.

The circus camp was the ideal makeout spot, once you got past the terror of oversized clown paintings on the wall. Soft gymnastic floor mats were stretched over two-thirds of the room. It was the most likely place I would lose my virginity, and I came to camp this summer prepared to do just that. So why wasn't I tugging his body there? Why was I dropping his hand? Why was I inching away from his outstretched palms? Why was I stepping out of my sandals? Why were my toes curled around the edge of this dock? I felt a rush of blood to my head—heat blinding my vision with white spots as my throat closed. I had none of the answers. All that I knew: the only way to breathe was to jump.

The cool lake water hit my body like a fever breaking—splintering against my summer skin. I came up for air, cutting past the surface with a desperate inhale—taking in the familiar scent of a muddy rainstorm.

Asher stood on the dock, looming over me with his head bent in confusion.

"What are you doing?" he asked.

Solid question.

"Swimming?"

"It's pitch black down there."

"It's a man-made lake. It's not like there are monsters in here."

He stared at me, waiting for a better answer. "You just . . . jumped in," he said in disbelief.

"What can I say? I'm an enigma."

I wasn't. I was an open book begging to be read. Asher was the mysterious one. But I guess tonight he was unaware that I had jumped into dark waters because it felt like a less-scary alternative than getting naked in front of him.

He tugged his shirt off and sat at the edge of the dock, lowering his perfect abs into the water on the side ladder. He was always so cautious, testing the waters before he dove in. I rolled my eyes as his torso delicately met the lake. He waded toward me, and on instinct, I splashed my hand against the moonlit water—as if acting like a toddler could delay becoming a woman.

He blinked the water back from his thick lashes, glaring at me with liquid dripping down his striking jawline.

"Come here," he demanded, tugging the hem of my T-shirt, bringing me against his body.

His fingers went into my drenched curls, pulling my face toward his. Our lips were cold, our tongues were white hot, and I lost myself in his kiss, until I felt his mouth leave mine. The heat of his breath was now on my neck, his hand grazing up my torso.

"Wait," I said.

I sucked on my lower lip and pulled back from him, leaving his mouth parted in front of me.

"I'm—I'm not ready."

My mouth hung open as I felt every joint in my body exhale with the truth: I wasn't ready to have sex. The air around me shifted, straightening my spine to the moon. I was not ready for something I thought I wanted, and I felt no shame. This was not stage fright.

"Not ready for what?" Asher asked, interrupting my virginity epiphany.

"I'm not ready for sex," I stated, obviously.

He squished his eyebrows together, replaying my words.

"O-okay." He tilted his head. "Did you . . . did you feel like I was pressuring you?"

"No, I didn't feel like you were pressuring me."

"Mags, I'm a little lost here."

He scanned my wide eyes, the realization that we were on two very different pages bathing my body in a different kind of heat, the kind of embarrassment that not even the cool lake around my skin could take care of.

"You didn't want to have sex with me tonight," I slowly realized, aloud.

He tilted his head, pursing his lips together.

"I wasn't planning on it. I don't want to rush us. I mean, we haven't even talked about sex."

He put his hand on my chin, staring at my wide eyes. *Of course* he didn't want to rush us. Asher Reyes was a bleeding romantic. The same way he held a stone in his hand—looking at it from every angle—was the same way he held my face in his palm.

"Then what's wrong?" I asked. "Why have you been weird all day? I thought it was because you were nervous about—you know." He squinted at me with a slight head shake, as if to tell me he didn't follow. "You haven't left my side all day. You spent ten minutes walking to lunch admiring the woodwork on the gazebo—I had to practically tug you into the mess hall before the final gong," I continued. "You wanted me to skip dinner, you. . . ." I trailed off, seeing his jaw tighten.

Asher's gaze moved to fix on the moon's reflection in the water. The sound of the lake pattering on the dock behind us somehow grew louder in the seconds that followed, and I felt his hold on me loosen. He swam a couple yards toward the ladder on the dock and pulled himself out of the water.

I wanted to go after him, but I was frozen in confusion, treading water by myself, watching my boyfriend stand above me, motionless, eyes like gunmetal staring at the moon.

"Asher?"

His eyes floated toward me, filling to the brim with tears. All at once, his chest caved in, and he folded his body down onto the wooden slats, setting his head between his legs. Asher was an emotional guy, but I had only seen his tears fall twice: when he was performing onstage, and when we said goodbye to each other last summer. But this wasn't a soft cry, it was painful and loud, like a boy splintering in half. My heart broke out of my chest, and I tugged myself onto the dock, folding my wet arms around his shaking body and holding him tight. He gripped onto my hands with his body frozen in agony.

We stayed like this for ten minutes—neither of us moving, until he finally looked up at me—eyes puffy and red. There was anguish on every line of his face as he wiped his tears with the back of his hand. I shifted my body so I was sitting in front of him, my knees folded on his, his hand clenched inside mine.

"Today"—he inhaled sharply, trying to find his voice amid tears—"today is my brother's birthday."

My heart dropped. We had spent an entire year talking for hours upon hours, night after night, and Asher never mentioned he had a brother. He was the only person in my life, besides my mother, who knew I had an absent father. And here I sat, not even knowing he had a sibling. Instantly, I felt a sting of pain. Pain that whispered, *maybe Asher means more to you than you do to him.*

"I didn't know you have a brother," I whispered.

"Had," Asher corrected. He steadied his breathing, as if dreading the words that were about to leave his mouth. "My brother died. Four years ago. He . . ." The reality strangled Asher's throat, and he swallowed hard. "He killed himself." His tears fell effortlessly, wide brown eyes now on mine. "I hate this day. Last year was the first time that I didn't hate this day so much. Because I got to spend it with you. I didn't have to spend the hours listening to my parents talk about how old he should be. I didn't have to listen to them talk about the person he didn't get to become. I got to just be with you, and it made me happy. I should have told you last summer. I'm sorry."

I found my hand wiping away my own tears, crying at the mere thought of Asher losing someone. I set my fingers on his wet, quivering jaw, my thumb wiping away his flowing tears.

"You don't have anything to be sorry about. It's okay," I said softly against his cheek.

"I wanted to tell you, I just . . ." He clenched his hand over his chest. "When I talk about him, it hurts *everywhere*."

I nodded, as if I understood, but I didn't know this kind of pain. Asher was living with the kind of hurt that hope couldn't fix. My father's absence was different, and the ache shaped me. I was strikingly aware of the gap between what my father gave me and what a daughter deserved. So, I let hope fill in the middle. Hope was my drug of choice. It dulled a painful, fatherless reality. I twirled toward bright lights despite strong winds against my cheeks. There were no bright lights here.

"I understand," I said, pressing my cold lips against his forehead.

It wasn't exactly a lie, because while I didn't *understand*, I now fully understood Asher Reyes. I understood why he led with caution. I understood why he longed to slip into other roles. I understood why he made lonely kids feel wanted. I understood the reason for the pain behind his eyes. I understood why he looked at me like I mattered—and why he made sure to tell me, every day. The mysterious side of Asher was no longer a mystery to me, and I loved him even more. I ran my hands through his hair and kissed the tears off his cheeks.

"I don't want to be alone tonight," he whispered into the curve of my neck.

I didn't leave his side until the moon traded places with the sun.

18

THIRTY-FIVE

IT WAS WELL PAST MIDNIGHT, but I knew my eyelids wouldn't find reprieve until after the sun came up. My body was still floating through space after its encounter with Asher, and the hopeful adrenaline built upon itself with each page-turn of the script in my hands. I reached the end, and the scope of the adaptation of my favorite book left me wide-eyed, with my palm on my soaring chest. It would be the second feature he'd direct, but this was Asher's first screenwriting credit—a co-write, to be fair—but Asher had fully undersold what he'd done to it. He took a story that let me feel *seen* as a child and made it more grown-up, while keeping the thoughtful and tender parts intact. It was the same beloved character study that I fell in love with, but it didn't feel like a small indie—it felt cinematic, like it needed to exist on the big screen and be heard in surround sound. This wasn't my favorite little red sauce restaurant on the Lower East Side—I couldn't gatekeep something this epic, and as I grinned from ear to ear, I realized I didn't want to.

I set the script down and started poring through my songwriting note-book, dog-earing prewritten verses and lines that would work perfectly—ones that could bloom into full songs and help make the lead character's arc come alive. She was a singer-songwriter caught between two worlds, and only music could guide her way home. She was a lot like me—longing to make footprints on her planet, but unsure of which step to take to make her wishes come true.

I just needed one verse to start. One perfect verse to bring this breakup number toward the top of the story to life. I scanned a couple lines—but I stopped. I needed to understand how the lead actress sang first. If I couldn't do her justice, I wouldn't get the job.

I lifted my laptop up from the dusty wooden floor and pulled up You-Tube, searching for Raini Parish—an actress I had never heard of before, the young woman who would be taking the lead role.

I pressed play on a video of a delicate-looking twenty-one-year-old in a sundress. She was sitting on a messy kitchen counter, eyes closed, heart-shaped face casually nodding as she sang Olivia Rodrigo's "Drivers License." She sang it a capella. She approached the huge bridge like a casual shrug, and the result knocked me out. Raini seemed to hold all the world's angst behind her large brown eyes—a gift we both shared. I was in love with her instantly. A buzzy grin splashed on my lips—when suddenly, my face fell. I couldn't have read it right. I blinked back white spots of terror, confirming that I wasn't hallucinating.

The email notification bounced atop the right corner of my laptop like a casual middle finger, a warning to the hope sparking through my body that I would never get off this easy.

> To: Ms. Maggie Vine
> From: Mr. and Mrs. Robert Scholl
> Subject: Garrett and Cecily's Engagement Party

My heart folded onto itself as my shaking hand clicked on the Paper-less Post invite.

Why was I invited? What kind of masochist invites the other woman he loves to his engagement party?

The invite was an ode to muted florals—which reminded me of Ce-cily: classy, not too loud, in control, the kind of window dressing that made you sigh and say, "That's nice." Unlike Maggie Vine, who enjoyed chaotically mixing patterns and jumping up and down in quiet rooms. My eyes scanned the invite: dinner and dancing at Wölffer Estate Vine-yard in the Hamptons. In two weeks. TWO. FUCKING. WEEKS?!

Why was I clicking "accepts with pleasure"? What kind of masochist goes to the engagement party of the man she loves?

I did not accept with pleasure. I accepted with deep, melancholic longing. But I accepted all the same—and I had no philosophically sound reason why. I went to text my therapist for a long-overdue emergency appointment, but I was hit with the reminder that she was on maternity leave. I cursed, then silently forgave my hero for bringing a human into this world just as my life was blowing up—because her starting a family was not about me, even though, right now, her choice to push a baby out of her body felt super fucking personal to me! *Fuck you, Wendy!*

I ran through the scenarios in my head. The first hypothesis seemed like the most mature: I accepted this invitation for the same reason Garrett sent it—to move onward and upward, to acknowledge we could somehow get past this and be in each other's lives as friends. The second hypothesis: my name was on the original guest list, and Garrett felt like there might be some explaining to do if he scrapped me from it, especially since Cecily knew how close we once were. The third hypothesis was the devil on my shoulder: Garrett sent this invitation because when you choose wrong, you want your soulmate present so you can blow your life up like in the movies! The selfish monster inside my brain liked this unlikely scenario the most—which meant it was probably the reason I RSVP'd without thinking about the brutal consequences.

I backed away from my laptop like it was a land mine, swallowing angry tears that were bubbling to the surface. Why were Garrett and I doing this to each other? Hadn't we done enough? My chest caved in, and I curled into a ball on my bed, clutching my shoulders, letting mascara stain my pillow. All my relationships ended this way—with me in the fetal position. I had spent the last decade trying to prove to myself that I could love someone the way I loved Garrett Scholl. In doing so, I fell hard and fast, so by the time a "relationship" ended, I was already holding my knees. Secretly, my songwriting was at its best when I was at my worst— when I was learning how to stand again. Heartbreak fueled my art, and it was almost always worth it. *Almost.*

I angrily wiped the hot liquid off my cheeks, sucked in a furious breath, and sat upright. I was ready to pull the blade out of my chest and turn the ache into words that would cut like knives.

My favorite songwriting teacher at camp taught me that I should be able to boil down the premise of a song—the chorus—into one Big Idea. To do this, I had to know three things: what story I'm telling, from whose point of view I'm telling it, and the emotion it expresses. *On the Other Side* told Yael's story, as a teenager desperate to escape a rough childhood. The Big Idea was that sometimes we have to leave the best of us behind to leave the worst of us behind. Yael was a teenager with dreams to travel to another planet and leave her restrictive childhood in the dust—but in order to flee, she'd have to leave the love of her life back on earth. She'd leave with nothing but the hope of one day ending up with her soulmate. In this scene, she's imagining what her future will look like as she studies the galaxy from the roof of her childhood home. She dreams of herself all grown up, floating through the atmosphere in a place where all her dreams have come true—all but one. The emotion was complex: clinging to blind hope in a moment of loneliness. I wanted the song to look like golden rays exploding through charcoal.

I could feel the bleak finality of Garrett and Maggie swirling in my gut as I opened my songwriter notebook. My fingers knew exactly where to go. It was a line I had written when I was in my late twenties, after I introduced Garrett to a guy I was dating, Drew Reddy. For years, I tried fitting it in somewhere, but it never felt at home in any other song. It was a verse that I knew, without a doubt, would change my life. Here it was, in bright blue ink, calling me home.

Hope's always the last friend to leave

19

TWENTY-SEVEN

"How many shoes can one woman own?" Drew asked, wide-eyed. He shook his head, watching me step into a pair of white Vans.

"Never enough."

I angled my body toward the full-length mirror, squinting at my reflection. The bottom of the epically distressed jeans—meant for a non-vertically-challenged human—were bunched on my shoes. I stood on my tiptoes, confirming that the jeans I had borrowed from Summer (and had forgotten to return) were meant for Summer's long legs. I swapped the sneakers for heeled booties and studied all my angles in the mirror. *Better.*

Drew stood up off the bed and folded his strong arms around my body, pressing his lips to my ear and taking a playful nibble. We'd had the best couple days coming down from the tour, holed up in our cocoon with our bodies trying to remember what it was like to fall asleep in a room that wasn't swaying and our lack of inhibitions enjoying the spoils of my queen-sized bed. But it was time to leave our lovemaking nest, which meant it was time for me to introduce Drew to the two people who mattered most. I was giddy about the disastrous potential of having Drew and Summer under one roof. Drew could be a little chest-puffy when faced with a fellow alpha, and Summer wasn't shy about letting you know she was the smartest person in the room. I knew Summer would have no problem testing the limits of The Male Ego, and I knew Drew could more than take it. Tonight, the big question mark curling my insides was the equation of Drew plus Garrett . . . plus *me*. It wasn't the idea of Drew seeing me interact with Garrett that made me uneasy. Rather, it was the thought of Garrett seeing me with another man. I had never introduced Garrett to a guy I was dating. *Ever.* And I couldn't figure out why this specific scenario made me want to vomit on my suede booties. I wasn't in love with him anymore, I had met plenty of his girlfriends by now. We were friends. Friends meet the people you're having All The Sex with, so why was I about to take off my top and try on a fourth blouse to delay the inevitable?

I narrowed my eyes on my reflection in the mirror—twisting the bottom knot on the pink button-down shirt.

"I look like I'm about to host a playdate, don't I? It's a little too suburban mom chic."

Drew ran the tip of his finger up the side of my rib cage, grazing the small single-needle tattoo of the moon—a tattoo I got when I was seventeen. A tattoo that my mom lost her mind over.

"No one's mom looks like this," Drew whispered into my ear.

"That's sexist. And ageist. My mom looked like this, but even younger."

I stepped out of his hold and peeled the shirt off my body, tossing it onto the chaotic pile of clothes on the bed. Drew pulled me by the clasp of my bra and spun me around so I was facing him. He tilted his head at me.

"Woman, *what* is happening here?"

"*Oh.* This is me getting dressed," I explained. "It's always a production. Get used to it."

"You were never this way on tour."

"That's because Summer sent me on tour with only five dresses, which I rotated. There was no room for decision making."

He stared at me with a dropped-jaw smile.

"You're nervous."

"I don't *do* nervous," I said, elbowing his gut. He had never seen me nervous, because I was my best self on tour. I was Confident Maggie Vine—the way God had intended me to be. My chest was pattering now as I looked at the time on my phone, realizing we were going to be late.

Drew crossed his arms and scoffed at me. "You're afraid to introduce me to your crew, aren't you?"

"No."

Yes.

He tugged me toward him by the loop of my jeans and bent down to my ear. "Maggie Vine, I give good friend," he assured me, his faded Southern accent and the heat of his mouth against me sending sparks to my skin. *Goddamnit, why did he have to make everything sexy?* His lips went to my neck, and his fingers moved downward, unbuttoning my jeans.

"I just put those on."

"I have faith that you can do it again."

His cool thumb brushed past my hip bone, playfully tracing my underwear line. My breathing quickened as his hand slid lower.

"Summer will hate you, but don't take it personally," I said, swallowing hard as he pressed gently on my clit through the lace thong. I closed my eyes and steadied myself.

"I'll try not to take someone's personal distaste toward me personally."

I felt his touch leave my body and opened my eyes to find his hands on my waist, pushing me onto the bed. He tugged the booties off my feet and my jeans to the floor. He bit the inside of my thigh, then his finger hooked inside my underwear, and his tongue was inside me, his hand clenched on my ass, my fingers wrapped around his waxy hair, my body writhing, my chest pounding.

"We're . . . we're going to be . . . super late," I moaned, as my breathing quickened.

He glanced up from my legs, his lips wet, and his eyes hardened.

"I don't fucking care," he growled.

"Then put your tongue back where it belongs," I bit back.

"You're a real piece of work, Vine."

We were provocatively brash with each other when our clothes came off. This had never been my thing. I was a romantic when it came to sex—when it came to *everything*. I thought the fever dream was a man kissing my naked breast as I read him poetry by candlelight. But with Drew, his large hands on my wrists and his crass, "Shut your mouth so I can fuck you like it's the last time my cock will ever meet your pussy!" got me wet faster than *"Shall I compare thee to a summer's day?"*

I ADJUSTED THE BRA UNDER my V-neck as Drew and I walked into the Biergarten, a cute outdoor spot hidden under the Highline, with Ping-Pong tables and a couple different bars stretched through the space. I froze, amused to see Summer laughing hysterically at Garrett. They stood on opposite ends of a Ping-Pong table, as Garrett fished a ball out of the beer in his hand.

"You are *horrible* at this game," he told her, playfully throwing the wet ball at her face.

Summer ducked, letting the ball hit a hipster behind her. She stared ahead at Garrett, wide-eyed, not taking responsibility. I exhaled a chuckle, watching Garrett and Summer make silly faces at each other. Summer told me that they had "gone out a few times" while I was on tour—but I didn't know they were this comfortable around each other. Summer adopted the role of Smarter Older Sister to most people in her life, even those who were older than her, like Garrett. Garrett needed someone to lovingly give him a hard time, because he was a gorgeous, tall, privileged, white male. She didn't fall for any of his bullshit, and after he became less scared of her, he really appreciated her candor.

I watched as Garrett's girlfriend, a stunning tall creature with wavy blond hair, rubbed his shoulders. Apparently, they started dating after I left for tour, and all the information I received from Summer was that Blaire was "very hot and very temporary."

I felt Drew grip on to my hand, and I pulled him closer as we approached the table.

Summer threw her paddle down as her eyes met mine. "There she is!" she yelled.

Summer opened her arms, letting me hug her as tightly as I wanted, and reciprocating—which for Summer, in public, was not a small deal.

"You missed me," I said. "Look at this hug! Someone record this! See how her arms are gripping me tight? She fucking missed me!"

Summer pulled back and glared at me. "What can I say? My clothes and I have been very lonely without your needy presence."

Summer looked over my head, sizing Drew up with a nod. He smiled nicely at her.

"Summer, Drew."

"The photographer."

"The best friend."

"One of them." Summer grinned, nodding to Garrett, who was approaching behind me. I inhaled his familiar scent—musk and vanilla—a combination that I wished wouldn't make my heart beat a little faster. But oh boy, *it did*.

I swallowed hard and turned, meeting Garrett's beaming smile. He was Casual Garrett, a sight I loved to see. And he was tanner than usual, making his blue eyes appear even brighter, and his smile even more ridiculously perfect. He took me in his arms and lifted me up in a tight hug. It felt odd that Garrett was doing this in public, while the people we were having sex with watched directly below my head. Drew shifted in place with pursed lips, trying his best to act cool, despite being visibly uncool with another man's arms around my waist. Garrett set me down and beamed at me with a sly grin. He glanced over my shoulder, eyes scanning Drew.

"Hey, man," Garrett said, not coldly, but not warmly, either. Like it was a chore. He stuck his hand out and Drew shook it. "Garrett."

"Drew."

"I'm Blaire!" the super-hot woman said, squeezing her body between Garrett and myself. "You must be Maggie."

"That I am." I smiled into her doe eyes.

"Babe, I'm gonna go get us some pretzels. They look *so* good," Blaire cooed.

It didn't upset me that she owned *that* body and could enjoy carbs. It didn't. Because that would make me petty as fuck. And I wasn't. I was a feminist! Feminist with an asterisk, apparently.

Drew tightened with each body and beer that curved past his broad shoulders. "So many humans," he muttered. I glanced up to find Garrett's eyes on mine, with a look that said he'd heard it, too. I chewed the insides of my cheeks.

"Not a fan of New York?" Garrett asked Drew.

Summer's eyes widened toward me. She fought a grin, her gaze darting between Drew and Garrett, as if she were eager to grab a bag of popcorn and stay a while.

"Everyone here is always in a hurry to go nowhere," Drew said with a scowl.

Garrett nodded silently, but he made a point to put his eyes back on mine. I felt the tips of my ears redden. I was being judged for someone else's opinion. Which I guess is what happens when you choose to date Someone Else.

Drew tightened a grip around my waist. "Big fan of hers, however," he said, holding me close against his large body. "Drink?" Drew asked into my ear, with eyes that were not on me. I was certain they were on Garrett, but my chest was pounding too hard to turn and make the confirmation.

I nodded and smiled brightly, purposefully, as if to show Garrett I was happy.

"Yes, please."

Drew turned and tilted my chin up to him, kissing me hard. As he left, I let my eyes dance toward Garrett, who looked away instantly, picking up a Ping-Pong paddle as a worthy distraction.

Summer sidled up to me with a shit-eating grin.

"Don't say a thing," I warned between gritted teeth.

"I wish I had filmed that so I could replay it whenever I'm sad," she whispered.

"We playin' here, or what?" Garrett asked Summer, twirling the paddle in his hand, eyes refusing to meet mine.

"First, while she's gone, we need to talk about your girlfriend."

Garrett set his paddle down, his attention on Summer.

"I don't know how to tell you this, but your girlfriend likes pussy," Summer announced.

"Summer!" I said, recovering from choking on my own spit.

I arched my neck back farther, realizing Garrett was unfazed. He was grinning, actually.

"I think you could have tried a little harder to tell me that differently?" he suggested.

"I couldn't have. It's not in my nature. *But* I attempted a qualifier." Summer looked across the bar at Blaire, who was engaged in a conversation with Summer's new fling, Shira. I had received multiple effusive screenshots of Shira's dating profile while I was on tour, so I could pick her long blue hair out of any lineup. Blaire's lips were parted, her body hanging on Shira's every word. "Blaire was very fast to tell me she's an 'above-the-waist lesbian,' but give her time."

Garrett smirked. "Good to know."

"Great legs," Summer added, her eyes exploring Blaire's legs in a micro miniskirt. I was certain her vagina was going to pop out at any moment.

"Are you asking for my blessing to steal my girlfriend?"

"Gross. I don't do commitment. I don't want to steal her, I just want to have sex with her."

Garrett shrugged half-heartedly. "You know what? If she wants to do below-the-waist stuff with you, you both have my blessing."

Summer batted her big blue eyes up at Garrett. "I can't believe I ever thought you were just a dumb meathead."

"Keep the compliments coming."

Summer patted Garrett's head and floated across the bar toward Blaire. My eyes shifted from Summer to Blair to Garrett as I pressed my brows together.

"*Really?* You're cool with that?" I asked.

"I'll just find another girlfriend."

"*Garrett*. Women aren't expendable creatures. We have hearts and feelings, and we should be treated with a full spectrum of humanity."

"Blaire asked me in the middle of sex last night if I was into threesomes—we've only been dating two months, and she's already getting bored . . . not exactly an ending to lose sleep over."

I grabbed Garrett's beer from him and took a sip, hoping the light ale would wash away the bile rising to my throat thanks to the image of Blaire's naked body wrapped around Garrett. I knew this was the kind of information best friends shared—but it was playing like a horror film in my brain.

"Well . . . great relationship, Garrett."

"I don't have big feelings for her, Maggie. Not everyone has All The Feels All The Time."

His arms were limp at his side. I'd never seen him this cavalier.

"What's going on with you?"

Garrett shrugged, eyes refusing to meet mine. I punched his biceps, bringing his attention down to me.

"Stop doing that!" I said.

"Doing what?"

"Shrugging. Acting like life is just a sequence of events that happens to you."

"Isn't it, though?"

I narrowed my eyes on his face and grabbed him by the hand. Garrett's gait was slow as he let me drag him toward a hidden archway on the other side of the Ping-Pong tables, where no prying eyes could find us.

"Spill. Right now."

He looked away from me and rubbed the side of his neck for a moment, a vein pulsing with emotion under his skin. He paused, then his eyes came back toward mine.

"I had to give up playing in the band."

I uncrossed my arms, my eyes moving quickly around his sad face. The band was his lifeline. "You did?" I asked gently. "When?"

"Last month. And I'm just—" He pinched his forehead and slid his hand down his clean-shaven jaw. "Work is all-consuming. My dad's eyeing early retirement, so I'm on this fast track to become him." He looked down at his fingers for a long moment. "I thought I had more time. It feels like I'm entering a life sentence." I took Garrett's hand and stepped forward into his personal space, forcing his eyes to meet mine.

"It's going to be okay. I know this feels overwhelming right now, but I'll help you figure it out. You won't live in a world where you aren't getting to do what you love. Even if it means you have to join me onstage after finishing paperwork at midnight—I'll make sure you get on that stage."

He swallowed hard, before quickly painting on a smile and shaking his head. "This is stupid stuff. I know how lucky I am to have the opportunity and the job—"

"*Hey.*" I set my hand on Garrett's cheek, bringing his eyes onto mine and silencing him. "Stop it. You don't have to do that with me. You can be honest about your feelings."

He put his hand on mine and brought it off his cheek.

"I've tried that before, Maggie."

He shook his head, revealing a tiny, sardonic smile. I winced and tugged my hand out of his hold. This was the first smile I'd received from Garrett that thundered inside me like a storm.

"What are you talking about?"

"I don't want to do this right now."

"Do *what*?"

"Bring up shit while some guy you're sleeping with waits for you on the other side of the bar."

Garrett stared at me and shrugged, *again.*

My mouth fell open as thunder trembled to the surface. I pressed my hand over my pounding chest. Holy. Fuck. He had the nerve to be mad at me because I was happy with someone else.

"That's not fair. I've watched you with woman after woman. Do you think that's been easy for—" I stopped myself from going further. This was the closest I had ever come to telling Garrett how I felt about him, and I could feel the truth flying too close to the sun. My eyes darkened, shifting me back to a place that couldn't burn me—the storm. "You can't just play it cool the *one time* you meet a guy I like?"

Garrett didn't flinch. His eyes stayed locked on mine.

"He's not for you."

"That's not for you to decide," I said forcefully, an inch from his face.

Garrett studied my expression, tears in my eyes, and all at once, his shoulders dropped. He inhaled and shook his head slightly, as if appalled by how we got here.

"You're right. You're right, I'm sorry."

"You and I: we're friends. Best friends."

"I know," he said.

"So don't do this. Don't do this when it's convenient for you, and not for me. That's not fair."

We both knew what the *this* was. The *this* was one of us actually telling the other how we felt. The *this* was the elephant in the room of our friendship.

"You're right. And I'm sorry. I'm being an asshole. It's no excuse, I'm just having a rough couple months. I feel like I'm losing grip on—on the stuff I thought that would always be there. The music, and . . . " He trailed off, open palm in my direction. "It's stupid, I—" His voice cracked, and he glanced up to the ceiling, begging vulnerability to stay inside his throat. Garrett swallowed his emotions whole and turned back to me with a smile shining through. "I'm fine. Go have fun."

"Come here, you big idiot."

I wrapped my arms around Garrett's tall body. He didn't move for a long moment, which made me squeeze him tighter. Finally, I felt his body exhale inside my grip, and his arms folded around me, hugging me back.

"I'm happy that you're happy," he said, genuinely.

"I know you hate him."

"I don't hate him," he lied.

"He's not forever, Garrett."

"I know," he whispered into my ear, without skipping a beat.

I tilted my head up at Garrett, stunned and slightly horrified. I had just admitted to the outside world, and to *myself,* that I wasn't deeply in love with my boyfriend, and I never would be. And the kicker? Garrett already knew.

Garrett grinned, reading my wide eyes and folding a stray curl behind my ear. "I know, because I know you." His grip loosened around me. "Go have fun, Maggie May."

I gently stepped out of his hold. "Only if you come have fun with me."

"Well, of course. I'm the essence of your fun."

I elbowed him in the stomach as he laughed, and we walked back toward the bar's main room.

"A little TJ's action this Monday?" I asked.

"I was just thinking that I hadn't made fun of your beer choices in four months."

"Usual time?"

"Can we make it eight thirty? I don't get out of the office until—"

"Say no more. For you, I will miss *The Bachelor.*"

"What a sacrifice."

"I'm basically Mother Teresa."

He smiled at me—a big one—and we entered the main room where, in the corner of the bar, Blaire, Summer, and Shira shared a laugh. I watched them with a head tilt.

"Are you really going to have a threesome?"

"Come on." Garrett waved it off. "I'm not having a threesome. *Two* women? *Naked?* I'd come in like, five seconds."

I countered his head shake with a knowing smirk. "You would *totally* have a threesome if the offer presented itself."

A grin broke across his gorgeous face. "Totally," he admitted.

I rolled my eyes at him and kept walking. He was a few steps behind me when I froze in place and turned around.

"Hey, Garrett?"

"Yeah?"

"If it happens, I don't want to hear about it."

He sucked in a grin, staring at me for a long moment, as if comforted by my request.

Across the room, I watched as Drew cut through the crowd with my beer in hand, frowning as he navigated a sea of people who refused to count personal space as a virtue. Garrett turned to see where my attention had gone to.

Garrett's raised brow met mine—those ocean-blue eyes and half grin silently screaming what I already knew: I could do better. Better's shoulder playfully bumped against mine, and all at once, the backs of our hands were touching in a dark room. Neither of us moved. I tugged my eyes away from Garrett, staring ahead, chest pounding, arms limp at my sides. My throat went dry as I felt his fingers curl around mine. We weren't exactly holding hands, but we weren't *not* holding hands, and we stayed like that, *maybe* holding hands, until the very second Drew outstretched a beer toward me.

It was just the back of his hand. No one should put this much hope inside something so small. But I did. I couldn't unfeel him.

That night on the subway ride home, Garrett's skin buzzing against mine played like a film reel behind my eyes, with one verse echoing in my head. It was as sweet as the maple-flavored beer on the back of my tongue, and I shifted my body away from Drew so I could text it to myself.

Hope's always the last friend to leave

Garrett was back in my heart. Who was I kidding? He never left.

20

THIRTY-FIVE

THE FLOOR NUMBERS IN THE elevator climbed, and I held on to the guitar around my neck like it was a life raft, until *PH* lit up bright red. It wasn't just the possible life-changing moment that had my sweaty palms clenching for solid ground, it was the fact that the elevator was going to open, Asher Reyes would smile at me, and I'd forget how to breathe—which wasn't ideal when tasked with digging deep into my diaphragm to belt a folksy love ballad.

The elevator chimed, and I cleared my throat, reminding myself that I couldn't let Asher melt me, because I was here to be a force of nature: a hurricane that he and his producer wouldn't be able to look away from, not a puddle on the floor. I stepped into the airy industrial loft, with the smell of fresh roses and crisp lavender swirling in my lungs—thanks to the enormous vase of flowers on the marble kitchen island. All at once, Asher came into view, walking right by me, holding a steaming mug of tea as he crossed the living room.

"Hey," I said.

He jumped, startled, spilling half the mug of tea on the front of his white linen button-down shirt.

"Shit." I winced and ran to grab the hand towel hanging from the oven door.

I don't know what possessed me to press the towel onto his hard, pounding chest, without thinking about the consequences. But I did. I could feel his heart thumping beneath me, and my breathing slowed as

I dared my eyes upward. It was worse than I could have imagined. He was staring fixedly at me, and I watched him swallow hard, golden eyes locked on mine. I sucked in my reddening cheeks, slowly removing my trembling fingers from his body, handing him the towel and backing away.

"Sorry."

He stared at me, unblinking, holding the towel to his shirt.

"That's okay. It'll dry."

He set the towel on the counter with a grin and leaned against the honed marble. I held my guitar tighter, lifting my hand in the air. *Yeah.* I fucking waved, like a toddler greeting a stranger in the supermarket. He slowly lifted his hand up in a little wave, and then his hand went to his soaked chest as he steadied his eyes on me. The last time we saw each other, he did All The Things to my body, but I wasn't sure if it was as intense for him. There was no question now. I didn't even need to ask him why he looked like he was about to reach forward and tug me against his wet chest. It was the same reason I wanted to let him. Teenage Maggie Vine was standing in front of Teenage Asher Reyes. Had any time passed? Shouldn't rational people fill in the blanks of adulthood before picking up where they left off? Did the blanks even matter? The acknowledgment of how absolutely surreal and fucked-up it was that we were both able to do this to each other was a light switch to my soul. I felt my bony legs weakening. Asher Reyes was, as Train would say, back in my atmosphere.

I looked past his angular lines, trying to focus on anything else besides how magnetic he was. The living room was open to the kitchen, with the sun blaring through silk sheers—gorgeous cream beams against white brick. It was a blank canvas, unlike my apartment, which was a chaotic pile of messy patterns. I let my eyes float back to Asher, finding his attention fixed on the Gibson in my hand. He tilted his neck at me, surprised.

"That's your dad's guitar."

All I could do was nod. *How did he even remember—* No. NO. NOPE. I shook my head and straightened my spine. I would not sob onto his ripped torso, telling him that my dad died two weeks after we broke up. I wanted to. I was dying to see if he still held me the same way. I hugged my guitar tighter to my chest—a reminder that my career was in both our hands. I didn't come here to press play on a tape that had been paused for eighteen years. I came here for my career. If only he'd stop looking at me like he wanted to press play because I wanted to press play and dear God what would that film look like because I'd watch it every fucking day— *No. NO. NOPE.*

"You—" I left my mouth open, unsure how to finish the sentence I'd started. He took a step forward and stared at me harder, waiting. "You aren't allowed to talk until after I sing," I finished.

"Huh?" he said with a baffled laugh.

"That's a word," I said, my eyes darkening.

Asher fought a smile, miming stitching up his mouth and throwing away the key. He nodded to the door in the corner of the loft, which led outside to an expansive wraparound patio.

Thankfully, the outside breeze blew the lust out of my lungs as I folded my hair behind my ears, with wide eyes taking in Asher's private patio. No one should have this amount of square footage to himself in Manhattan. It was the kind of space that made you think the impossible was possible. It was the romantic's side of reality, and I loved it instantly. One side housed a gorgeous dining area with twinkle lights, while the other looked like a modern meditation garden atop faux grass—full of colorful poufs, candles, and low couches. Asher kept his mouth shut as he outstretched his palm, pointing to a lanky man standing by the patio's edge. Asher's co-producer turned toward us, tucking his phone into his jeans and adjusting his thick wire-frame glasses. He forced a flicker of a quick smile, as if being polite wasn't his default.

"Maggie," I said, outstretching my hand.

"Amos."

Amos shook my hand, then glanced at his watch. I nodded, completely fine with the personal disconnection. I wasn't here for pleasantries, either. Maggie Vine was here to blow him away.

I sat cross-legged atop an oversized Moroccan pouf, loosening the strings on my guitar until my ears were dancing. I eyed Amos and Asher sitting across from me on a maroon couch, with Asher's eyes refusing to leave my guitar. Amos flicked lint off his jeans, waiting for me to disappoint him—already bored. I sucked in a deep inhale from my diaphragm and took my eyes off the skeptical producer and set my attention on Asher.

A smile hit Asher's cheeks, shooting a spark of adrenaline through my bones and sending my song "Up North" out of my whole body. The song started out dark, with lyrics that tasted like metal: *A silver lining in a barren atmosphere.* Then it dipped into something savory and hopeful—a lemon bar on my tongue, blinding rays of sunshine: *Come bring your crown, I'll wear a gown.* I could relate to the main character, Yael. The wild spoke to her soul, and she couldn't help but be pulled into a scary, gorgeous, scorching, florescent orbit. As the song turned golden, I tore my eyes off Asher to focus on Amos. Amos chewed on the edge of a plastic coffee stirrer, and while I had a hunch that this guy didn't show his hand for a living, I sang louder and deeper, with eyes like gunmetal, until Amos's expression finally widened upon my key change at the haunting bridge.

Holding on to you is like wishing upon a star I can't see
But hope's always the last friend to leave
So come keep me warm up north
I know, it's a reverie
Fold your arm around my shoulder
We could be the real thing

I let the outro hang in the air until there was silence, and I realized Asher's entire body was leaning forward, his lips twitching with a smile. He was so much like me—horrendous at hiding a beating heart. Unlike Amos, who stood up and nodded at me. I shot up quickly and slung my guitar around my back. My ego rebuilt itself every time I sang in front of an audience, giving me the spine to openly smirk at Amos, a smirk that let him know that *I knew* he fucking loved me.

Finally, a fleeting grin betrayed Amos's face. "We'll be in touch," he said.

"Awesome," I said, ever so coolly.

Asher and I walked toward the door in silence, entering the living room. We crossed the room, eyes flickering up at each other, both of us chewing on big smiles. I hesitated, then pressed the elevator button, even though all of me wanted to take a seat on the sunken linen couch and never leave.

Asher stepped forward, amber eyes taking in mine.

"Can I talk now?" he said, grinning.

I lifted my chin and crossed my arms. "I'll allow it."

He stared at me like he was about to recite Shakespeare.

"Your name should be in lights."

I pressed my hand to my reddening cheek with a grin. Funny enough, I rarely suffered from imposter syndrome. When things went well, I knew I was exactly where I needed to be at the exact right time. But things hadn't gone well in a very long time, and his effusive tone wrapped my beaten ego in a gold-leaf bandage.

"Thank you," I finally said, daring to match his soft smile.

"Why haven't you made it?" His tone was casual, as if the answer should be just as simple.

I choked on a laugh.

"Why haven't I made it . . . ?"

My tongue searched the corners of my gums for the words. There was too much to say, and while he was the guy I historically said *everything* to, right now, silence was easier. So, I shook my head. Without tearing his eyes off me, Asher stepped forward, catching the now-closing elevator doors. I hadn't even heard them open. He pressed his back against the elevator door, keeping it ajar. His eyes followed mine, to the delicate tattoo of a crescent moon on the underside of his hard biceps.

"It's still my only one," he said quietly.

I set my finger on my rib cage. "Same."

He studied my fingers on my stomach, and his eyes stayed there for a moment longer than they should have, until coming back up to me.

His spine was holding the elevator door open for me, and I eyed the gap in the doorway, wondering how to physically sneak past him with my guitar without invading his personal space. There was likely a way to get in the elevator without my body pressed against his, but that would be criminal. I took two steps forward. His eyes were hardened on mine as I lifted my chin up to his face, as my arm swept against his torso. I hesitated for a moment, lost in the way his face seemed to be moving closer to mine, then I exhaled and stepped inside the elevator. I spun around and set my back against the elevator wall. He stood tall, sizzling eyes on me, and suddenly, he took a step forward, pressing one finger on the DOOR

OPEN button with his other hand right next to my face. His lips were just inches from mine.

"Maggie Vine, I could listen to you sing every day until I die," he whispered, real low.

Asher pressed his hand against the wall, pushing himself out of the elevator bank, with eyes that refused to leave mine as the doors shut between us.

It took me five whole minutes to remember how to use my legs.

21

THIRTY-FIVE

IF YOU'RE VULNERABLE ENOUGH TO put your heart on the line for an audience, nothing screams louder than the silence that follows. The moment before the applause. The moment before you get a yes or a no. The moment when someone studies your work—the art you bled for—and decides if spilling your guts was worth it. Most of us are born with an instinct to safeguard against failure and rejection—to put ourselves in positions to win. We don't run headfirst into situations that will likely break our hearts. Artists do the opposite, every day. We tear down our own walls to dig into the center of our glittery souls and fashion something that's uniquely ours—something that no one else can create. We present a slice of our humanity to the world, and nine times out of ten, the world tells us it isn't for them.

Asher Reyes historically had a way of filling the silence with noise—of making rejection seem impossible. He'd squashed the tiniest hint of doubt a week ago when I was leaving his loft, but now, in the silence that followed, rejection seemed inevitable. I hadn't heard from Asher in six whole days. Not one fucking word.

I paced in my apartment, hands on my phone, his email address beaming in front of me. There was a fine line between desperation and assertiveness, and since my career was in his hands, I was afraid to cross the line. I plopped down on my bed, my insides twisting with the probability: their answer was a no. Asher was likely trying to come up with the perfect way to let me down, because Asher was the kind of person who would take the long way home if it meant avoiding a pothole. So often we count vulnerability as a prize, but I wondered how many more scars I could take before I decided to stitch up my wounds for good and leave music safe inside the center of my soul, where it could never hurt me again. I had tried doing so four years prior, but that decision sucked the life out of me.

I huffed off the bed and tugged a short black strappy dress on over my body, then slipped on my black Converses. I inhaled deeply with my eyes clenched shut, opening them into the mirror of my apartment, shaking off the probable bad news. Now wasn't the time to play in the Worst-Case Scenario mud, not when I needed to sing to my largest audience in five years. Tonight, I was playing at the Bowery Electric. And while I'd done a lot of work over the last few years to get my body ready for this moment, my palms were sticky and sweaty just thinking about it.

The Bowery Electric was a historically important stage for indie artists and was a nominal step above the other venues I played. Like, three or four steps above. It was also a triggering place for me, the place where I was *sort of* discovered five years prior. Their main room held two hundred people standing, which would be my largest crowd in these last five years.

Five years ago, I was supposed to play the Bowery Electric, but I pulled out at the last second, drowning in a panic attack thirty minutes before stage time. The panic seemed to swirl in the back of my throat—the memory sitting atop my shoulders like a dumbbell. I inhaled deeply, clenching my fists, reminding myself that I had gotten to a place where I believed I could look into a large crowd and *not* search for his face.

I walked toward the window to grab my guitar, just as the sinking orange sun cast a shadow over my dad's old hard case. The case leaned against the wall, with faded stickers covering every inch of his Gibson's home. I ran my fingers over the curled edges of each sticker, as if I was memorizing the shape of someone's face while she took her final breath. I LOVE NEW YORK, Stevie Nicks, John Lennon's "Imagine" illustration, acid house smiley face, Boston Celtics, the *Village Voice*—each sticker was a reminder of his youth, his hopes, his *what-ifs*—a reminder that he never got those answers. I felt the weight of Making It settle atop my shoulders, while a staggering monster put down roots inside the walls of my chest, twisting all the way through me, past the soles of my bare feet, until I was frozen in place, anchored to the hardwood floor.

My father's unfinished dream was my burden. It was wrapped around my bones, standing on my shoulders, prickling my eyes. My dad never made it as a musician—not the way he wanted to. He had immense talent, but once he hit the age where he could starve to go all-in on his dream, he had another mouth to feed. My parents split up when I was one, he became a music teacher to help pay child support, he stopped playing night gigs with his band, and he refused to go all-in on anything, including his role as a father. Even to this day, a part of me felt like I held my dad back from becoming who he was supposed to be. I wanted so badly to make it for the both of us. I wanted to be the phoenix rising out of the ashes of his unrealized dreams. I was terrified of another possibility: What if I was just a little girl covered in her father's ashes?

My body jolted from its heavy roots, thanks to the vibration between my fingers. I looked down at my phone, seeing that Summer had texted me four times.

Meet you at the side of the stage.

Answer your phone!

Why aren't you standing in front of me right now?

Get your ass over here, or I'll come drag you out of your apartment by your hair.

I looked out the window, studying the musty afterglow. The dark violet night shined on my face, and I grabbed my father's guitar case, letting my legs pull my body out the door.

I CHECKED MY PHONE ONCE before I stepped onstage. I could hear the crowd grow louder behind the curtain, and a swirl of nerves and bravery fought inside my chest. I closed my eyes on the image of Asher's smile as he watched me sing six days ago.

Fuck it.

I brought my phone up to my face and furiously typed an email.

So, when are you going to tell me I got the gig?

I pressed send before my subconscious could catch up to my fingers. Before I had time to regret it, my name was on the loudspeaker, followed by scattered cheers behind the curtain.

Seconds later, I walked onto the stage with a sizable crowd below me. The blue spotlight hit different than I had imagined it would when I got the booking notification a month ago. It didn't feel like the start of something, it felt like a Hail Mary into the end zone. I grabbed the cold mic and my eyes found Summer, who was cheering too loudly.

I stared down at my guitar, letting the spotlight hit it, just right, the way it deserved. The first song would be about my father. After his funeral, I didn't know how to direct my anger and my unsaid words at a dead man. So I wrote him a song.

Wide eyes on a clock that stood still
Waiting for you in rooms you never did fill
Tiny hands folded like paper on my lap
When I dreamed about them outstretched around your neck

You made some other house your home
You crushed your little girl to the bone
If home is where the heart is
Then what was I to you

I felt hot tears on the surface of my eyes. These words were harder to sing aloud than they were to write. This song was like opening a page of my diary and sharing it with strangers.

I decided to slip into the next song faster, without a break, knowing that even reaching for a sip of the water bottle below my dangling feet would give me time to think about the loss stuck in my throat. So, I pivoted from *my daddy did me wrong* to *first love kicked my ass*. Clearly, the theme tonight was Pain.

I wrote "Under Different Skies" the night after Asher and I had that agonizing final phone call. I was sitting on my twin-size bed in my dorm room, choking back tears, thinking that life couldn't get any worse. I had no idea my father would die two weeks later. So the moral of that story is: little girl, it's so much easier to cry over a boy than it is a man.

I sang the chorus, taking a moment to scan the crowd, soaking in their beaming faces, letting their expressions bring a smile to my lips, even as I unleashed the saddest breakup song I'd ever written. My mouth opened to belt out the bridge, but all at once, there was fire in my chest, a ringing in my ears—my insides too hot and loud for any words to escape. My wide eyes were locked on Asher as he made his way from the back of the room toward the stage, his head down, his eyes covered by the brim of a baseball cap. Muscle memory kept my fingers dancing on the chords as my heart beat faster and faster, like a young child following a trail of bread crumbs out of the dark woods. He stopped below the stage and glued his eyes onto mine, the spotlight bathing us both.

22

THIRTY-FIVE

I COULDN'T CATCH MY BREATH, but somehow, I belted out five more indie folk songs. The crowd caught on during my last song—when one woman shrieked in the audience, catching Asher's eye. *People* magazine's Sexiest Man Alive was staring at me like I was the most important person in the world. There were, I swear, tears in his eyes as he watched me sing. Phones were pointed in both our directions, and a gaggle of college-aged women started to swarm him for selfies. I had never seen so many little flashlights, or had so many people care about what came out of my mouth. Asher didn't seem to love the attention, and he made it a point to keep his eyes on me—even as flashes blinded his face.

When my set ended, I tugged my wide eyes off Asher's, and I disappeared behind the stage curtain, hyperventilating backstage and texting Summer to get her ass there immediately. I laid my back against the brick wall with deep breaths, my chest pounding wildly.

Summer danced her body past the curtain and grabbed both my wrists.

"Okay, what in the actual fuck—"

"I don't know!" I said before she could finish. I shrugged, baffled, with wide eyes.

"Did you invite him?" she asked.

"No. How did he know I was here?"

"The internet, you dum-dum." Summer tilted back on her heels. "Oh boy," she said, with her signature wicked cackle.

"Stop doing that. Your big smile freaks me out."

"I can't believe you didn't tell me you guys had sex when you went to play him your song. You lying slut!" Summer swatted my shoulder.

"We didn't have sex! I didn't even touch him." I tilted my head. "Okay—maybe like, my arm *touched* his chest, and my hand, but that was . . . just like two touches."

Two super-fucking-sexy touches.

"So, you guys just look at each other like that, for no reason at all?"

I shrugged, even though it was nothing to shrug about. "It's how we are—*were*. How we *were*."

"You're going to go viral, you know that, right?"

"What do you mean?"

"You're a normie who just had eye-sex with Asher Reyes *in public*. He's a notoriously private A-lister, and if you don't think you're about to be the top story on *E! News,* think again."

"There was no eye-sex—" I stopped talking, shifting back to the meltdown at hand. "Summer, I think he's here to let me down in person." I held my chest, feeling my body crouch to the ground. "I can't go out there. I can't hear another no. I don't think I'm strong enough to keep doing this, to keep trying to make it—"

All at once, Summer grabbed my elbow and tugged me up, pulling me toward the stage curtain.

"Shut up and go say hi to that gorgeous man and let him slice your face open with his jaw," Summer demanded, as she pressed her palm onto my spine, shoving my body past the curtains.

I whipped my head back to her, mouthing, "Come with me," but she returned my plea for a best friend life raft with a smirk, letting the curtains close between us.

My heart thumped as I stepped offstage and into the main room. A few yards away, a group of young women had formed a circle around Asher, giggling like fangirls as he spoke to them. I watched Asher shift uncomfortably, but he held a warm smile toward the women, grinning past his unease to make each one feel valued. Asher Reyes could have become That Asshole, but he didn't—not even a little bit. He turned toward me, and I watched his body light up the moment we locked eyes. I lifted my hand up in a slow wave.

He squeezed past his fans, his eyes refusing to leave mine, until we stood inches apart. Asher glanced around, increasingly uncomfortable with the peering eyes on us. He leaned in and whispered in my ear.

"Can we get out of here?"

I'd go anywhere with you.

All I could do was nod. I felt his hand squeeze mine, and lightning shot through me as if I were seventeen again—a girl with an entire world of opportunity in front of her in screaming color. After a moment, I realized my hand was still in his, as the biggest movie star on the planet, my ex-boyfriend, was pulling me past a gaping crowd and into a shiny Escalade.

I sat in the seat next to him in the SUV as his driver sped away from the Bowery Electric, my mind tripping over itself. He grinned out his window—brown eyes watching the lights and the people pass us by, taking in the universe the way he always had. I used to drown in his eyeline, collapse in the way he saw the world. I felt my body melting into the leather seat as he looked at me.

"Now," he said.

I squished my brows together, confused.

"Now . . . *what*?"

Asher smiled, holding up his phone—the email that I had forgotten I sent him. "Now is when I'm going to tell you that you got the gig."

My eyes were wide and there was a ringing in my ears.

"I got the gig? Are you fucking with me?"

He grinned even wider. I blinked back white spots in front of my eyes, and I felt heat envelop my body. I was floating. My jaw was wide open.

"I can't believe you're serious right now."

"When have I *not* been serious?" Asher asked.

The answer was never.

"Amos loved you. He watched a few of your songs on YouTube after you left, and he was sold." Asher smiled to himself. "*I* never needed any convincing."

"Holy fuck."

"Sorry to drag you out of there. I didn't want to tell you in front of all those people. You're in Union Square, right?"

I nodded.

"I have a super-early shoot tomorrow for Rolex, so we're going to take you home first. Is that okay?"

I nodded again, still in shock.

"Can I take you out to dinner Wednesday night? We can talk shop, and . . . catch up?"

He waited for my reply, hopeful eyes on mine as his fingers fidgeted with the thin chain around his neck.

"Sounds good," I finally said, bringing a smile to his lips.

"And you're going to need an entertainment lawyer for your deal," he noted. "Do you want me to send you some names?"

I blinked at him, shock once again holding my tongue captive. His eyes scanned mine.

"Maggie . . . ?"

I let out a grin.

"What's so funny?" he asked.

"It's weird. Weird to hear you call me Maggie."

He leaned toward me, the city lights shining in his kind eyes. "Hey, *Mags*. I can't wait to see what you do with this music. You're going to blow us away."

I beamed back at him, because I believed it to be true.

Later that night, after I let his cheek brush mine for a moment too long, I hopped out of the Escalade with my guitar case in hand and a huge grin on my face. I had gone to my own funeral and I had been resurrected—which was complicated for a Jewish girl.

I floated into my studio apartment, ignored the mess of cascading dishes on the kitchen counter, plopped onto my bed, and smiled at the ceiling like an idiot. Before I could wrap my head around tangible success, my phone pinged with an email from Asher: the contact information for four different entertainment lawyers. He made sure to note that they were "the best of the best," but also explained that none of them repped him, so there would be "zero conflicts of interest."

With a clear road ahead of me, I googled the only female lawyer on Asher's list, seeing that she was listed as one of *Variety*'s top entertainment lawyers. With a widening smile, and with the paper cuts on my soul mending, I emailed her.

THIRTY-FIVE

I TUGGED MY ARMS INTO a pair of long blue gloves, sweating as I looked at the time on the broken microwave in my studio. Like the genius I was, I set my phone alarm for 8:30 p.m., which was of zero help to wake me up at 8:30 *a.m.* I was about thirty minutes away from officially running late for today's gig: singing "Do You Want to Build a Snowman?" at a three-year-old's birthday party inside New York's glamorous event space, the Rainbow Room. I stood on my bed, which was the best way to get a good look at myself in the full-length mirror, and I haphazardly tugged on Elsa's blond wig. The cape, the blue boots, the dress . . . I was a three-year-old's dream.

I skipped down the stairs and opened the front door of my building, when suddenly, camera flashes blinded my eyes. Aggressive, sweaty men with loud voices and large lenses crowded my personal space.

"Maggie, how long have you been with Asher Reyes?"

"How did you meet Asher?"

"Maggie, is he in your apartment right now? Did he spend the night?"

"MAGGIE—"

I grew up envisioning what my eventual fame would be like, running through all the usual fame rite-of-passage scenarios: hearing my song on the radio for the first time, holding my Grammy as I thanked my dead dad, selling out Madison Square Garden. When I imagined what my first time being chased by the paparazzi would look like, I was not wearing a flammable Party City Elsa costume.

I shoved my way past the line of photographers, thrusting my body into oncoming traffic. A taxicab screeched to a halt behind me, and I glanced back as the driver held a labored honk and aggressively flipped me off. I twirled around and sprinted to the other side of the street, my blue cape flapping against a crowd of people bustling toward me, my wig now facing backward—a blond braid swaying in front of my horrified face.

I could see it yards ahead: the Fourteenth Street subway entrance. Relief took over as my blue boots found the stairs, leading my shaking body belowground—just as a smarmy man with a camera lurched into my face. Because I wasn't born with the ability to just be a chill, suddenly famous person, I shrieked directly into the wide lens. The camera's flash washed over me, memorializing me at my absolute best: jaw opened midscream, wild eyes of terror, and an Elsa braid cascading down the wrong side of my skull. I stumbled down the stairs with a ringing in my ears, my name getting louder behind me.

My MetroCard was buried deep in my purse, and I didn't have time to fish it out. I took a running start and jumped over the turnstile, forever scarring a small child who pointed at me and screamed to her mother, "Elsa didn't pay, Mommy!"

The R train screeched down the tracks as I tore across the platform, spinning into the subway car just as the doors opened—like a hot mess action hero.

My trembling body folded against the cold bucket seat. I dangled my head in between my legs, catching my breath, and before I had time to wipe the sweat off my lopsided wig, I realized that my lap was vibrating, incessantly. With my gloved hands shaking, I twisted my braid right-side-around and dug for my phone.

I arched my shoulders back, alarmed as I studied my buzzing phone. I hadn't checked my cell all morning, not since I had overslept and given myself only fifteen minutes to emerge looking like a put-together princess. Missed calls and texts from every person I'd ever met were cascaded all over my lock screen, with links and question marks.

E! News: "Does Asher Reyes Have a New Leading Lady?"
Page Six: "Reyes Sets His Eyes on Unknown Singer"
Just Jared: "Get Yourself a Person Who Looks at You the Way Asher Reyes Looks at This Random Woman"

My chest pounded faster and faster until I got off the subway, hustling up to street level on Fiftieth Street, getting off one stop early, just to have access to better cell service. I pushed my way through a packed West Midtown as I buried my slack jaw in the heat of my phone.

I swiped through the surprisingly flattering, ethereal photos of myself onstage at the Bowery Electric, with Asher gazing up at me. In each photo, he looked at me the same way I looked at him, like there were thousands of unfinished love songs between us. My heart plummeted with the realization that these storybook images would soon be replaced with today's photos of Hot Mess Elsa. I moved to click on *The Cut*'s article, "Asher Reyes Goes for a Normie—There's Hope for Us All!" but a call from Summer flashed across my screen. I pulled the phone up to my ear.

"You are *everywhere*," Summer said.

I barely let her finish. "Every-fucking-where."

"Please tell me you had sex with him."

"*What?* I didn't have sex with him."

"Restraint? That's very unlike you."

"What are you talking about? I overthink everything."

"That's true, but you also like one-night stands."

"I can't have a one-night stand with a man I share a childhood tattoo with!"

"You have a point. Hey, have you checked your Insta?" Summer asked, her voice brimming with a disproportionate amount of excitement.

"What did you do?" I asked, warily.

Summer had a login to my Instagram, where she used her PR and marketing background to amplify my singing posts with the appropriate hashtags. I pulled up my Instagram with widening eyes, seeing that Summer had uploaded the video of me singing at the Bowery—singing the song I had written about Asher, *to* Asher.

"Check the views, babe."

I blinked back the view count under the video: 53,680 views. My hands started to shake as my eyes floated up to my follower count: I had 22,000 new followers. I had *fans*. Well, fans of gossip and Asher Reyes—but still.

"Where are you right now? We need to spin this the right way," Summer said.

"I'm a block away from Thirty Rock. I have to sing at a kid's birthday."

"Ew. Why?"

"I can't let an innocent three-year-old down. It's the swan song of my princess gigs, okay? Also, it might be a little late to spin this in the right direction."

"What did you do?" Summer asked, her tone shifting, rightly foreboding.

"You know the part in *Frozen* where Elsa accidentally sends her cute little town into eternal winter?"

"Yeah . . . ?"

"So, the good news is: I didn't do *that*."

"Crap—I have to roll into this nine a.m. Just come to me this afternoon—don't you dare go back to your place. I'll stop at your apartment after work and grab all your shit."

"You're the bestest friend there ever was."

"And hey: don't Story all the stupid memes you see today, got it?"

"The memes I find aren't stupid!"

"And stop screenshotting and sharing tweets on your Instagram. Tweets should stay on Twitter. Also, we need to start branding you, now— *Oh!* I almost forgot. I assume you're driving with me to Garrett's engagement party this weekend? Valeria is out of town," Summer said, before abruptly hanging up.

Summer was never one for goodbyes. It was a PR habit—one crisis folded into another at lightning speed, so she would word-vomit everything she needed to say before she hung up. She happily left conversations without pleasantries, and now, she'd left this conversation with a reminder that I had masochistically inked my name atop the "accepts with pleasure" line.

I pointed my chin up to the towering skyscraper above me, 30 Rockefeller Plaza, closing my eyes and inhaling the balmy air, the timeless city stench of hot sewer and early morning street meat.

Somehow, I hadn't thought about Garrett—not for one second since Asher walked into the Bowery Electric. I looked down at my phone, seeing a candid photo of Asher and me after the show—his body leaning toward mine, my eyes taking in every inch of his face—on *E! News*. I wondered if Garrett had woken up to these photos. I wondered if it bothered him the way it bothered me when I saw a picture of him on Cecily's

Instagram the night after Garrett kissed me. I felt sick admitting it, but I hoped the idea of me with another man twisted Garrett's insides.

I didn't know how I was going to exist in the same room as Garrett without crumpling. How was I going to pretend that I didn't know he liked biting my lower lip? I shook off the cruel reminder, choosing to heroically point the shoulders of my flapping blue cape up to the sky, like a princess with boy trouble who had to save herself.

I SPENT THE FOLLOWING TWO hours inside the Rainbow Room belting out Elsa's, Anna's, and Olaf's greatest hits while the Empire State Building glared at me through the windows. More money went into this party than *Frozen*'s actual premiere. There were chocolate milk ice luges for the toddlers, and beluga caviar served on blocks of ice for the adults. After my final encore—a wildly gorgeous indie-folk rendition of "Let It Go"—I cut through a pack of strollers on West Forty-Ninth Street in my Elsa costume, sans the wig, holding my breath as I dared to venture back online. I wasn't sure how to fully prepare myself to come Elsa-to-Elsa with the paparazzi photos from this morning—mainly, the one in front of the subway where I had casually shrieked into the camera. Just as I was about to type "Enews" into Safari's browser, a text from a 917 number came on-screen.

> You're about to get a call from an Unknown Number. It's me—Asher

He attached the very photo I had been dreading: Elsa Gone Bad—my nostrils flaring into the camera, wig swaying backward over my seething face. It was . . . not super flattering. If your friend tagged you in this picture, you would not only untag yourself, you would ask your friend to take the photo down completely. It was "also delete this pic from your Recently Deleted folder" kind of horrible.

My hands trembled, and then my phone rang. UNKNOWN NUMBER flashed on the screen.

"Hello," I said.

"Well, hello there."

I let my cheeks blanket in heat as I took in the photo.

"So my PR intercepts all things Asher Reyes, and I have to say, I really enjoyed getting that photo this morning," he said.

"I've looked better."

"I think it's . . . charming." I heard him exhale a little laugh. "Would you like that photo to go away forever?"

"Very much so."

"Good. 'Cause I agreed to have a window-facing drink with you tomorrow night at Marea, so that the piece-of-shit photographer can get one photo of us and destroy this one."

I put my hand on my chest, exhaling the mortification from my bones. "Really?"

"PR photo-ops aren't my thing, but . . . for you . . ."

"Seriously, thank you," I said.

"It's a date."

A date. My hands were shaking again. But I wasn't sure it was nerves. I think it was anticipation. Like, my fingers were itching to curl around the back of his neck.

"It's a date," I echoed.

A date. I had never seen a photo of Asher on a date. The closest I came to seeing him candidly in a relationship was a photo of Asher hand-in-hand with Penelope Lynn—his stunning co-star—leaving an *SNL* after-party two years ago. That was it. The rest of the photos were red carpet appearances with different starlets on his arm. He was willing to open himself up to a mountain of scrutiny, to go on a date with a nobody, just to save this nobody from a lifetime of embarrassment.

"I'll see you Wednesday. Also—I'm sorry, but I wouldn't go home if I were you," Asher warned. "The paparazzi are going to camp out at your place for a day or two—it's their style. Do you have a friend's place you can stay at?"

"I'm actually on the way there now."

"I'm sorry," he said.

"It's not your fault."

"It is. I didn't think it through—just showing up at your gig like that. I got the final word from Amos and the studio, and I was so excited for you that I . . . Mags, I don't do crowds like that. *Ever.* I'm sorry, honestly. I don't know what came over me."

"Yes, you do."

I didn't mean to say it aloud, but the words fell out of me fast. There was silence between us as I bent my legs and crouched to the ground in the middle of the sidewalk, silently mouthing "fuck me" with my eyes clenched closed. I heard him exhale.

"Yeah, I do," he agreed.

I opened my eyes to the blue sky, my chest beating even faster.

"Bye, Asher," I said quietly.

THIRTY-FIVE

I HAD A MANAGER. I, Maggie Vine, was officially being managed by a professional person. I, Maggie Vine, had a contract.

I grinned stupidly at the massive stacks of paper in front of me in the white-on-white room, with the city's skyline shining in through the floor-to-ceiling windows. The guaranteed money from this deal—the money I would get once I delivered all seven tracks—was enough to build a future. The money that would come once this movie was made was enough to keep that future a reality. I could create an embryo, I could become a geriatric singer-songwriter and then have a geriatric pregnancy. Life was officially full of options—the weird, young-geriatric, good kind. The joy inside me was so big that I wanted to scream, but I was pretending to be a professional, so instead I swallowed hard and stared ahead.

My brand-new manager, Shelly Pier, sat across from me at the huge oval conference table—just the two of us dwarfed by a room meant to house twenty people. Shelly looked like the spiritual granola type, with fringe bangs covering her purple glasses, chunky mixed-metal rings on her fingers, and a dizzying oversized patterned dress swallowing her figure. According to Asher's Grammy-winning musician friend, Shelly was everyone's fun-loving, mama bear manager, but if you tried to screw over one of her clients, she would become the scariest person in the room.

Shelly smiled brightly at me and reached across the table, pulling the paperwork toward her.

"All done," she said, tucking the papers under her arm and shooting up like a rocket.

I followed, surprised that pleasantries were apparently *not* a thing. I anxiously threw my pen and copies into my backpack and stood to meet her face-to-face. Shelly smiled and gripped my fingers hard into a handshake.

"This is the start of the rest of your career, got it?"

I stood up straighter and mimicked her grip, trying to appear just as professional, even though I was throwing a party in my mind.

"Let's have a long-running career that isn't defined by a one-hit wonder from a kid who hadn't reached puberty. Sound cool?" she said, as if she had just asked me if I wanted an iced coffee.

"A long-running career. That's the dream," I said, nodding with a shit-eating grin.

She dropped my hand and crossed her arms, her smile fading. I quickly willed the corners of my mouth to lay across my face.

"Vine, you're not big enough for a PR rep, so I have to be your everyperson. Which means, I have to be the person who asks you: Are you sleeping with Asher Reyes?"

I could feel my ears reddening as I opened my mouth to answer. "No."

"Okay, because I'm a little torn," she said. "On one hand, I don't want your career to be defined by a famous man, or by a man at all. On the other hand, I know how this machine works—you're standing in front of me *because* a very famous man put you here, and he's a good one at that. It's a cute story: 'Out of nowhere, Asher Reyes saw Maggie Vine singing and fell in love with her voice. He hired her to write original music on his movie—which she was perfect for. And then, *much later,* he fell in love with her.'"

"Well, that's not exactly what happened—"

"*Or,* we have option B: 'Asher Reyes fell in love with unknown singer, Maggie Vine. He hired her to write original music on his movie because he was fucking her, not because she was right for the job.'"

I shifted in my Converses, thrown by her blunt delivery.

"Neither of those are true," I said.

"So, tell me your truth before I read it somewhere else."

"Asher and I fell in love when we were teenagers at summer camp."

She drew her eyebrows together in a frown. "You can't be serious."

"For a few years we were a thing. And then we went our separate ways. I found out he got the rights to my favorite book, I knew I could crush the music, I auditioned for him and Amos, and they hired me. I'm not sleeping with Asher Reyes. Up until a couple weeks ago, I hadn't seen Asher since we were seventeen."

Shelly tilted her head at me. A slow smile crept up on her overlined red lips.

"I like your story the best."

"Well, it's the truth."

"Maggie, you have talent—real talent that I believe in. I've watched every live performance of yours that my intern could get her hands on. You wouldn't be standing here if I didn't see longevity. And you can string out your fifteen minutes, easily. But I want to warn you: the world loves nothing more than to form a strong opinion about a headline without reading the article. It's getting harder and harder out there to earn people's respect. My first warning here, and it's not likely, but you should know: if you're Asher Reyes's girlfriend *first*, then it's possible, if the movie doesn't do well, that that's what your brand will be. Now if the movie and music are as beloved as we both hope they will be—you'll be just fine. But there's also the possibility that you break this guy's heart before your songs are due, and his dick shrivels up and he tears up your contract, calling it 'creative differences.' I'm telling you, kid, I've seen it all, and I don't want your career to end before it's begun, nor do I care to see what a long lawsuit against the most famous man in America looks like."

I heard what she was saying. The worst moment of my past was ringing like a bell behind my ears.

"I get it. So, if, let's say, we do decide to—"

"Finish the job first. Go a month into filming, when they've already recorded your songs and can't go backward. And then, go for it. Go get that photo op of Asher Reyes making out with you on a yacht in St. Barts. Let him undress you on the yacht, for all I care."

"Sounds like a plan," I said slowly, trying to stop my imagination from painting the vivid portrait of Asher using his teeth to take my bikini off on the aft deck. *Not specific at all.*

"One last thing, my team did a deep dive into your social. Mazel tov:

you're clean as a whistle. But I don't have access to your DMs. So, is there anything regrettable on there, or anywhere else?" She folded her arms, dead serious. "What I'm asking is: Is there anything from your past that I need to know? Any lost demos floating around? Any horrible stories? Important people you pissed off?"

I went to shake my head, but the name Cole Wyan was stuck in the back of my throat, stiffening my body. I had a demo that was technically floating out there, somewhere. But it was irrelevant now, so I tucked the knowledge of it back where it belonged: into the darkest, most horrible corner of my mind. That man had taken enough of my past, and I refused to let him anywhere near my future.

I dropped my shoulders, shook my head, and painted on a smile.

"We're all good," I said.

It felt so nice that I almost believed the lie.

25

THIRTY-FIVE

THE SUN SET OVER CENTRAL Park, leaving a glittery afterglow, which poured in through Marea's windows. The long yellow-and-orange marble bar seemed to echo the sunset outside, and I sat at the far corner, poring over my script notes, pretending to be important enough to occupy a space so elegant without drooling in every direction.

All at once, the collective chatter quieted, as if the air had been sucked out of the room. I glanced up, seeing the eyes at the bar widening toward the front door. Asher stepped inside with his jet-black hair perfectly tousled. He walked tall, but his attention darted around the room and he clasped his fingers together nervously. All these years, and he still wasn't used to strangers' eyes on him. His hands went to his sides as his eyes found mine, and he approached me with a warm smile. I tried not to stare at his hard torso, which was peeking out under his white deep V-neck shirt—which he somehow made fancy with a dark blazer.

I fumbled with the straps on Summer's white silk top from the Row—running my hand over my clavicle so that I wouldn't reach out and grab him. I should have brought Elsa's blue gloves. I should have poured gasoline into my eyeballs. I should have done something to make being in the same room as Asher Reyes—both of us all dressed up and grown-up—less swoon-worthy. I needed to Act One Elsa my way through this: *"Conceal, don't feel."*

I hopped off the stool as he hugged me, and I soaked in the lavender pomade in his hair.

"So, you've had quite a last couple days," Asher said, grinning as he pulled back.

Wandering eyes hiding behind crystal-clad cocktails took us in—strangers pretending not to give a shit, while absolutely giving a shit. I was too unimportant to be looked at this way.

"Well, being in your orbit was always entertaining, why should now be any different?" I said.

He raised his brow and shot me a sly grin. "I could say the same to you."

Heat found my cheeks and I elbowed him in his side, indicating that he quit flirting with me, that he stop reminding me of the times where I stripped naked and made him follow me into a moonlit lake. Yet I looked down at my hands with a shy smile, giving him every indication that I wanted him to continue flirting with me. And *I did*. I didn't just want to nudge my elbow into his ribs. I wanted to use my hands to take off his blazer. And his pants.

Asher glanced at his watch and rolled his eyes, interrupting my maybe-reachable fantasy. He leaned down toward me, allowing the heat of his mouth to linger over my ear.

"Okay to go over there, smile at each other, and let that guy snap his one photo?" he asked, nodding to the other side of the bar, where the smarmy subway man stood outside the window, rocking back and forth on his heels, waiting.

Asher got the bartender's attention without even trying, and we ordered our drinks and made our way across the room, where the paparazzo got his money shot and scurried away like the lizard he was.

A few glasses of pinot later, Asher and I sat nestled side by side in a discreet corner booth. We had finished dissecting the themes of each of the movie's songs, and moved on to laughing over our shared memories. Namely, the time I visited him in San Diego and his parents' dachshund shat inside his mother's Valentino heel. Asher wiped a tear from his eye, holding his ribs to quiet the belly laughter.

"I haven't laughed this hard in a long time," he said, leaning his jaw on the back of his hand, holding my gaze.

Historically, Asher and I rarely laughed like this. That's what was actually funny—the puzzling kind of funny. We were two very intense people.

We didn't bring out the humor in each other. As kids, we spent more time exploring our places in the universe, our hearts, our crafts, and what we meant to each other than we spent trying to make each other giggle. "Find someone who makes you laugh" was a line I had always heard. But finding someone who made me see the world in psychedelic colors was equally intoxicating. It was a different kind of love language. I lost myself in Asher Reyes faster than I had ever lost myself in a joke, in a rom-com.

I leaned back into the leather booth, holding my stomach, my body swirling with red wine and house-made agnolotti, my eyes darting away from his strong gaze.

"So . . ." He brushed his hand over his chin, then strummed his fingers on the table. "How's your love life?" he asked, rather uncasually.

Garrett's lips flashed in front of my face—just briefly, but briefly enough to show my hand, to illustrate that my love life was a garbage fire.

"That good, huh?" Asher said, taking in my expression.

"Yours?"

Asher shook his head, indicating it was nonexistent.

"You know, my longest relationship ended when I was a teenager," he mused with a shy grin.

"Join the club," I said.

I picked up the script between us, twirling a gold brad in my fingers. He squinted, trying to discern my messy penmanship on the back of the script.

"'See You if I Get There' . . ."

"Just an idea for the first track."

"Punchy title," he said, smiling. "Speaking of, did your lawyer connect with mine?"

"Yeah, she forwarded me the contract, and she's redlining a few items, but otherwise said we can close on the big terms. I think she was supposed to be letting your guy know as we speak. Shelly said the contract was 'unexpectedly fair.'"

"Why, thank you," he said, taking a bow with his hand. "Just don't get used to that. Contracts, business affairs, lawyers, negotiations—usually takes months."

"So why didn't it?"

"Because we don't have time to go back and forth—I'd like to get this shooting in two months. As soon as you're ready, let's lay down your demo for 'Up North.'"

"Oh, I can record it in my mom's closet."

Asher frowned. "Don't be silly. My friend owns a studio. He'll let us record there."

"That's really not necessary."

"Mags, *it is,*" Asher said. He leaned in, eyes wide on mine. "Let's make this as beautiful and rich as possible. I want the demo to knock everyone out of their chairs, even if it's going to get re-recorded by another voice. I want the studio to know what they're getting with you, and I need to show our actress how high that bar is."

"O-okay," I said, stammering.

He tilted his neck at me. "Are you okay?"

I swallowed hard, realizing my face had fallen. I picked it up and smiled. The truth—that I hadn't been inside a studio in five years—was stinging from all sides. I didn't know what would happen when I walked inside studio doors, but based on the heart palpitations taking over my body, I was terrified that it might not be as easy as one, two, three.

"Yeah, I'm good. It's just"—I pointed to my brain—"there's a lot happening right now."

"Nice to see some things haven't changed," he said with a smile. He shifted in his seat, twisting the napkin in his lap, eyes on me. "Why do you have your dad's guitar, Mags?"

Asher waited for the answer, eyes unblinking, as if he already knew. I felt the tears building, and I peered up to the ceiling, willing them away. I'd rarely tempered my emotions in front of Asher before, but we were in a public place, and I was worried that if I started to unravel in front of him, I might never stop.

"Heart attack." I let my eyes come back toward Asher.

"When?" he asked, so softly that I swear I just heard him mouth the word.

"Two weeks after we broke up."

He didn't even say "I'm sorry." That, he mouthed. I could see the tears in his eyes, and I looked away from him, my chest threatening to cave in.

"I wish I could have been there for you."

His hand gripped mine, and instantly, tears jolted onto my cheeks.

"I should have been there," I heard him whisper.

I glanced back at Asher, tears swimming in his eyes.

After a few heartbeats, I realized my hand was still in his, and he looked down as our fingers parted.

I focused on a deep breath, in and out, a technique from my therapist, my attention fixed on a man and woman a few tables in front of us. The woman folded a cloth napkin in her lap, eyes out the window, watching the cars fly by. Her date dangled a forkful of his chocolate cake in front of her mouth with a grin. She tore her eyes away from the cars to take a bite of the cake and painted on a smile.

"What do you think's happening there?" I asked.

Asher tilted his head, studying the couple.

"She's about to break his heart," he said.

I swallowed down a throat full of tears, grateful to study someone else's misery.

"You think?"

"She's slow dancing around it," he decided, coming back to me with a gentle smile.

I had always loved the way Asher looked at the world. He once picked up a geode by the lake, squeezed it in his fist, and imagined an entire backstory for the rock. I was reminded of the time I visited him in San Diego after our second summer at camp. He had just gotten his license, and I remembered watching him in the driver's seat—the way his fingers carefully gripped the wheel, the way his amber eyes paused to take in the rocky cliffside, the way he smiled wistfully at an elderly couple sharing a sandwich on a bench, the way he looked at me to make sure I saw it, too: the promise of growing old together.

I stared across the room at the couple, watching the woman's clenched jaw—her happiness hanging on by a thread.

"You know . . . you broke my heart," I said softly, with eyes glued to the unhappy couple.

My lips stayed open in the candlelight as my gaze drifted back to Asher. He rolled his shoulders back, my statement hitting him like lightning, jolting his frame. He pulled his eyebrows together, staring fixedly at me.

"I thought we broke each other's hearts."

Smile and nod. Change the subject.

"Did we?"

"Are you asking me if our breakup crushed me?" He was fully flabbergasted.

"I mean, it would be nice to hear," I said, smiling and leaning in, my dimpled chin resting on my hand. I was trying to make light of something that wasn't light at all.

He mimicked me, resting his hand on his chin, just a handful of inches from my face, but his expression was pained. He took me in for a moment.

"Mags, there's some nights where I sit alone and think—" He paused, keeping his eyes locked on mine, the rest of the sentence in his throat.

My insides were humming, waiting for him to fill in that blank. He moved his entire body closer, his lips mere inches from mine.

"You were the biggest heartbreak of my life."

I blinked rapidly, my chest aching. For years I had thought that I was crazy, histrionic, insecure—but it hadn't just been me. Even as a grown adult, a part of me wondered if I had lost my soulmate as a teenager, and that thought was humiliating. It felt like an admission: *I don't know how to grow up. I don't know how to move on.* I carried it around like a weight. And here he was, telling me that he carried it, too. My heart felt like it was breaking for What Could Have Been.

"You weren't supposed to lose me," I said, tears rimming my eyes.

"You weren't supposed to lose me, either," he cracked, not even bothering to hide the emotion in his throat.

We traced each other's gazes, wistful, teary, and a whole lot of something else. He slowly inched his mouth toward mine. He put his finger under my chin, tilting me up to him.

I opened my lips, just an inch from his.

"I—I can't kiss you. Not until the work is done. And then . . . I'd very much like to kiss you."

Asher's eyes went wide against my words. My manager's advice was echoing in the back of my head, reminding me not to touch Asher before the work was done. He didn't flinch or pull back, because neither did I. We were frozen, just inches from each other, his eyes blazed on mine—a fire growing between us.

"One of us should move our lips here," he whispered, the heat of his mouth floating on my lips.

I couldn't move as his eyes scanned mine.

"Do you need it to be me?" he finally asked.

"I—I really do . . ." I said, achingly, desperate to just fill the gap between our mouths.

He leaned back and exhaled, adjusting his jeans and taking a long sip of water. He turned back to me, seeing that I was still frozen in place.

"Do you want to hear the song? I worked on 'See You if I Get There' this afternoon, and it's almost done," I found myself saying.

"Right now?"

"Tonight? Later? My friend, Summer, grabbed my guitar from my apartment, so I need to go back to her place to retrieve it, but . . ."

He shot me a warm smile.

"Mags, I'm not going to be that guy."

"What guy?"

"I don't want you to feel like I'm taking advantage of you, in any way, ever."

We had always played on an even field in our relationship. But Asher and I were in two different galaxies now—he had an Oscar, and I didn't have health insurance. When I was with him all those years ago, all he ever did was lift me up, cheer me on, and want me to succeed. This time didn't appear to be any different. I wasn't a woman feeling pressured by a big movie star who could make or break her career. I was a woman openly flirting with her big movie star ex-boyfriend who *could make or break her career.*

"I want to play you the song. Nothing more."

I want to play you the song and run my nails along your naked spine.

"I—I'm trying to figure out how to say this without sounding like a complete asshole," he said, holding my eyes. He leaned forward, speaking lowly so only I could hear, with his arm brushing against mine. "I don't know how I will be able to go home with you and pull back from your lips if you don't pull back first."

I circled the rim of my wineglass with my hand, watching his chest rise and fall under his T-shirt. I moved my hand to the stem of the glass, gripping hard to keep from reaching out and tugging him toward me.

"Are we really this bad at self-control?" I asked, my voice cracking.

"To be fair, we never had to practice self-control," he said.

"That's . . . kind of true," I said.

I took a sip of my wine to hide my reddening face as he raised his brows.

"*Kind of*?"

"I actually—" I closed my mouth.

Asher leaned in farther, eyes wide, a smile on his face.

"You *what*?"

"Last day of camp, our second year. After color war, I really wanted to—you know."

He shook his head in a laugh. "Why didn't you say something?"

"Because I knew you weren't ready to have sex yet."

He smirked into his drink. "Oh, I was *ready*."

"Shut up," I said, shocked as I swatted his arm. I shook my head at his wide smile. "You know what though, I'm glad we didn't that night."

"I think we got a lot of things right," he said, with eyes cautiously scanning mine. I nodded, my chest pounding as he shifted in his seat, sitting up taller. "Look, Mags, I don't want you to regret anything here. And the only regret I would have would be any you might carry."

I stared at him harder, trying to see the shoreline past Asher's eyes, which seemed to carry the tide. I wanted to lose myself in him, but instead, I scooted back into the booth.

"It's strange . . ." I breathed, shaking my head.

"What is?"

My eyes floated over his face, wowed by the way the amber light cast a glow over the curve of his top lip.

"You became the kind of man I knew you'd become," I said.

He tilted his head.

"Is that a compliment?"

"Asher, it's the best compliment I've ever given anyone."

He held my eyes for a long moment, then looked down at the table with a big grin. No part of keeping my mouth from meeting his was a safe bet. At the same time, sharing a room with Asher wrapped my heart in something it hadn't felt in years: a safety net.

26

ALMOST SIXTEEN

I LOOKED AROUND, MY BIG eyes taking in the most immaculate living room I'd ever seen. It smelled as clean as it looked, like Windex and ocean air. Everything inside the Reyes mid-century-modern ranch house in San Diego was stark white and glass—spotless—with the only brush of color coming from the outside—the ocean's horizon meeting the La Jolla shore through floor-to-ceiling windows. Even Asher's long-haired dachshund, sniffing my shoes, smelled brand-new.

"You've been in this home since you were seven?"

Asher rolled my suitcase past the living room with one hand, leading me down a narrow hallway. He glanced back to see my scrunched-up face.

"Yeah . . . why?"

Asher had moved to California from the Philippines when he was seven, and it was as if every object had been unboxed, set in its proper place, and never touched again. Everything in his house was just waiting to be worn well—it was unsettling.

"It just looks . . . very new," I said, with eyes on a blank white wall— where a lone, tiny hole sat at eye level.

A nail used to live there, probably holding something rich with color. Maybe art. Maybe a family photo.

"My mom likes things a certain way," Asher noted.

"Was she always like that?"

He stopped in front of a closed door at the end of the hallway, silently shaking his head.

"Oh," I said quietly.

I guess surrounding herself with emotionless objects was an easier way to live after heartbreak. I didn't know tragedy, but I surmised I'd be the type of person to make a shrine out of the memories, to wear a dead person's clothes, to hold on to their presence long after they were gone. I was one extreme, and this was another. I wasn't sure if either approach was healthy.

Asher opened his bedroom door, and my shoulders dropped. I exhaled, beaming, loving it instantly, just like I had loved him instantly. I walked inside, my hands and eyes running over the worn spines of novels on the bookshelf, a collection of shells and geodes, framed classic movie posters on the wall—*Casablanca, The Graduate*. The room smelled like Asher: musk and citrus—woods and wildflowers.

"I can't believe I'm in your bedroom," I said, standing in the center of the room, giddy. My eyes met his—then floated to the queen-sized bed behind his body.

Getting here had been seven months in the making. In September, I took an after-school job at a café on the Upper West Side. Every Thursday was open mic night, populated by undiscovered singers. While I was making minimum wage so I could afford a flight to California, I was also getting an education. In between trying not to trip over Birkenstocks while holding hot beverages, I took note of how my favorite singers sat in front of the mic like they were about to tell it the most important story of their existence, and then they'd close their eyes and do just that. They'd pull chatting customers away from their own bullshit, forcing eyes on them. It left me with a proclivity for personal storytelling. And it left me with enough money to fly and see Asher for winter break. My mother shot it down instantly—there was "no way" she was going to let her fifteen-year-old daughter "go get pregnant in California." The months that followed in our tiny apartment were ice cold—lots of slammed doors and curt answers. The joke was on my mother, because my father got me for spring break, and when I asked if I could spend the second half of break by myself in California on my own dime visiting a "friend," he didn't even call the "friend's" parents to see if it was okay. He simply said, "Of course." He trusted me implicitly. Which I recognized made him an untrustworthy parent. At this moment, standing across from Asher Reyes in a bedroom all to ourselves, I was grateful for my untrustworthy father.

"Are you sure your parents are okay with me staying in your room?" I asked, my eyes still on the bed.

Asher walked over to me and pulled me close to his warm body.

"They don't care. They both have trials going on right now—they won't even notice. I doubt they'll be home before midnight."

"You got taller," I said, measuring the top of my head to the base of his strong jaw.

He took my hand off his jaw and clasped his fingers in mine, studying all sides of my face.

"Hi," he said softly.

My lips stood ajar, my heart pounding in my throat, and suddenly my mouth was on his mouth, his tongue was on my tongue—our chests racing against each other, our hands knotted in each other's hair. He helped me remove the cotton shirt from his body, and I tugged the tank top off my chest. Lips back on mine, his fingers fumbled with the clasp on my bra, finally yanking it off me—my breasts now against his solid torso. His skin on my skin was like riding a wave at sunset—it untethered me. I felt the wooden bedpost hit my spine, and he slowly pulled back from my lips, staring down at my flushed face and sucking in air.

I sidestepped away from his disarming stare—my shaking fingers searching the CD tower. He watched, shirtless from the edge of the bed, a soft grin on his face.

"Your mix is in the CD player," he said.

Asher wasn't a big music guy, so once a month, I sent him a mix CD in the mail, hell-bent on shaping his taste in music. I turned on the CD player, to the "I Fucking Miss You" mix I had sent him two months prior. My cheeks reddened, hearing Deana Carter croon. It was kind of cheesy, but I loved it. Yet, I wasn't sure it was the *right* song for a guy to get naked to, so I went to change it on his behalf when I felt Asher's hand around my wrist, pulling me back. "Strawberry Wine" thickened the air as the heat of his mouth went onto the curve of my neck, warm musk radiating off his olive skin and into my lungs, his fingers slowly grazing the side of my breast and sending a pulse through my entire body. His hand clenched over my hip bone, spinning me around so that my mouth could find his, so that I could feel him harden against me, so that our helpless bodies could find the bed.

His lips were on my throat, his hands up the side of my ribs, my fingers knotted in his thick hair—knuckles clenched as his mouth traced my shoulder, moving all the way down to my breast. I arched my neck back—eyes closed, heart racing. We'd been here before, many times the last summer, but sex was off the table.

I could feel him throbbing against me, and my hand moved down his chiseled stomach, settling around the belt loop on his jeans. He hovered over me, arms stretched past either side of my face as my finger grazed his leather belt, as if it were a question.

"Hey. We don't have to do anything you don't want to do," he said softly.

I could feel his brother's cold necklace dangling on my chest—an antique gold medallion with a lion etched onto it. Asher wore it like a scarlet letter, so that the scar on his heart wasn't just buried underneath his skin. I knew almost everything about the guy I loved. I wanted to know absolutely everything. I opened my mouth to say three words, but his golden eyes pierced through me, and those words tightened like a knot in my throat. I was too in love to speak. I wasn't sure what made someone ready, but I wanted every inch of his body to understand mine, the same way our souls already felt like extensions of each other, and if that wasn't *ready,* I'd never be ready.

"I want to," I finally whispered.

He exhaled, a smile on his face. "Me, too."

A short while later, the setting sun poured in through his window, painting our salt-soaked bodies in a blood-orange hue. My flushed cheek lay on his racing heart, and I was bathed in peace that I didn't know my body could find. I felt my eyes getting heavier, as he pulled me tighter to his naked body.

"What's your mom going to do when she finds out your dad let you go off to California?" Asher asked. His fingers traced aimless lines up and down my spine.

"I mean, they live in two different states and she can't tell him what to do anymore. So she'll probably take it out on me."

"I'm sorry that she doesn't understand you," he said, kissing my hair.

"She knows exactly who I am. The problem is: I'm not her. I think it's upsetting to her that I'm so much more like my dad."

I shifted my body, so my chin was on his chest. He ran his hands through my hair, mouth searching for the words.

"Do you think maybe—maybe you expect your mom to be a little more like you, and she expects you to be a lot like her—and neither of you have gotten your way?" Asher asked.

I shrugged, even though the question made my insides feel heavy. Leave it to Asher Reyes to walk around in everyone's shoes. My mother was nineteen when she fell in love with my father. She was only a couple years older when she closed her heart off from ever letting another man in. She got swept away by my father's charm and was devastated by the outcome. The added weight in my chest swirled, knowing that I had also been left heartbroken by my father. But I kept going back for more, hoping the next time would be different. I was filled with hope, because the opposite was too dark and lonely. It's not the heartbreak that defines who we are, it's how we react to it. My father left scars on my mother's heart, but my mother let the pain keep her from making new ones. Norah put up thick walls—walls that made her appear like a tower of strength, when really, she was too weak to allow herself to give up an ounce of control.

Love was her kryptonite. Love was my cherry on top.

"What are you thinking about?" Asher asked, scanning my faraway eyes.

I traced the tiny white scar on his chin with my finger as I felt his hold tighten around my body. I closed my eyes, as if the admission was embarrassing.

"I've never seen a man hold my mom. Or kiss her. My whole life, I've never seen someone else love my mom. She's thirty-five, she's the youngest of anyone's mom that I know, and she's made her mind up: her future is set in stone. She's better off on her own. She doesn't want *this*. And I'm—" I went silent, thoughts strangling my throat. My mom knew how to love once. My dad told me sweeping, heart-bursting stories of the way they loved each other. Big. Epic. I could tell by the way my mom met his eyes whenever he came into the city, how she looked away all too quickly, that she was afraid of loving him ever again. How could a young woman bathe in bright sunlight, only to find her thirty-five-year-old self content with partly cloudy for the rest of her days?

I felt Asher sit up under me, bringing me up with him. I held the crisp blue sheet above my breasts as I looked away from him. He turned my face toward his.

"What's wrong?" he asked, his hand cupping my cheek, his eyes wide.

"I'm . . . I'm scared," I cracked. "I love you so much, and I'm terrified that you're going to break my heart, and then I'll decide never to do this again. I don't want to become her. I don't want to be thirty-five, with real love existing only in the rearview mirror." I felt the hot tears run down my cheek. He wiped them away instantly.

"Come here." He cupped the back of my head, pulling me toward his chest. I exhaled tears into the curve of his neck, gripping on to the back of his head, as if holding on to something that I would one day long for.

"Love will never be in the rearview for you, ever," Asher whispered. "I'll always be sitting next to you."

"You can't promise that," I said, real small, like it scared me to challenge the brightest future anyone had ever presented to me.

Asher shifted my body so my eyes were right in front of his, with his hands on both of my cheeks.

"You plan on breaking my heart?" he asked.

I shook my head effusively. "I could never."

"I couldn't ever break yours," he said.

I inhaled, wiping away tears and shaking off the panic. My forehead pressed against his, and I let a smile find my face, like an exhale.

"Promise me again?"

He gripped his hand on the back of my head, holding on to me as tightly as I was holding on to him. "You, Maggie Vine, will never be thirty-five and alone. On midnight before your thirty-fifth birthday, I'll be next to you."

"And I'll be next to you," I said, exhaling relief.

"You promise?" he asked, his lips against mine.

I opened my mouth, whispering, "I promise."

His eyes searched my lips, and then his mouth followed.

THIRTY-FIVE

"*AND THEN . . . I'd very much like to kiss you*?" said Summer, repeating my words to Asher back to me as she aggressively honked her Range Rover's horn.

"Was that necessary?" I asked, looking at Summer's hand, which rested on the center of the steering wheel, ready to honk again.

"That shithead fucking cut me off."

"Summer, we're going five miles an hour. He just switched lanes."

We were on our way to Garrett's engagement party, and stuck in horrible traffic on Route 27.

"Why have I seen no paparazzi photos of you and Asher since that dinner? I'm getting bored. Give me something to work with, Vine."

"I've been camped out at your house, which thankfully the paparazzi haven't found, *and* my manager wants me to lie low."

"You should milk this more. Build your social media following by being seen with him. You need a foundation before your career skyrockets."

I shook my head at Summer and looked to the backseat of the car, studying a giant box wrapped in lavender paper, with a huge white ribbon on top.

"What did we get them?" I asked.

A shit-eating grin danced on Summer's face.

"Something Cecily would hate."

"Towels that aren't monogrammed? God forbid."

Everything she registered for was pastel-colored and monogrammed.

It was as if Cecily was afraid they'd forget their own names in their own fucking apartment.

"A karaoke machine," Summer announced.

I stiffened.

"You did not."

Summer eyed my expression.

"I *did*. What's your problem?"

"Don't you think a karaoke machine would remind Garrett of his old life? And make him feel sad?"

"Yes. That's exactly why I got it. Because his fiancée sucks and he sucks now, too, and I want him to live with his suckage every day."

"Summer, that's not nice."

"I know. I'm not a nice person."

I reached back toward the card tucked under the ribbon.

"What are you doing?" she asked.

"Seeing if I can tastefully take my name off the card."

Summer swatted my hand away from the gift, casually swerving onto the yellow lines.

"Get a grip, woman," she said.

"Why don't you put *your grip* back on the wheel of the moving vehicle. Look, I don't want Garrett to get this gift from me and then wonder if I'm mocking him."

"Why?"

"Because . . ."

I bit my lip, and I could feel Summer's eyeballs on me, trying to put the pieces of a puzzle together.

"Spill."

"Spill what?"

Her eyes darted all around my face. "You're holding something back."

I hesitated, opening my mouth to tell Summer All The Things, but then I grabbed her chin and moved her eyeline away from my face and back toward oncoming traffic.

"What did you do?" she asked.

Summer didn't let things go without a fight, and her best friend's "something is horribly off" radar was never wrong.

"I didn't do anything," I lied. "It's just been a weird couple weeks."

Summer squinted her eyes, not wanting to show that she was hurt, but I knew she was. Historically, I always shared too much with Summer. My heavy "I bled through a supersized tampon and a pad" flow day, my hookup's "above average, so I'm gonna need lube" penis size, a new lyric I needed to try out on her, a 2 a.m. phone call to drunkenly lament about a criminally underrated Taylor Swift song which I emphatically believed should have been a single (here's looking at you, "Cruel Summer"). I shared too much because I didn't know how to not share it all with my best friend. She made me want to tell her the most important and dumbest shit ever, and she brought the truth out of me like a hostage injected with a serum.

Instead of pulling this one from my insides, Summer stitched up her disappointment, pointed her chin in the air, and glared at the road ahead.

"I'm here when you want to overshare about whatever it is you feel the need to keep from your best friend who would murder a horrible person for you *and* has never judged you."

"You judge me all the time."

"It's for your own good. You spend like a third of your day YouTubing beauty tutorials, I have to keep you grounded."

I gripped onto the handle above my head as Summer nearly missed the entrance into Wölffer Vineyard. My stomach flopped to my side as she made a sharp turn into the beautiful estate—a gorgeous Tuscan-style mansion sitting on a fifty-five-acre vineyard. I had been both a cater waiter and a singer at various Wölffer weddings. They were famous for their rosé, Summer in a Bottle—Summer loved to call it, "Me in a Bottle." In 2014, the Hamptons and Wölffer almost ran out of rosé, which was one of the most devastating misfortunes affluent New Yorkers have ever collectively endured.

Summer parked at the side of the estate and tugged her boobs up higher in the rearview, creating decent cleavage with her plunging floral wrap dress. I did the same in my mid-length floral dress, and with a wave of nerves attacking my insides, I apprehensively followed Summer out of the car.

"C'mon, let's go pretend we support this union," Summer said.

"That, I can do."

Summer paused, cackling with her head tilted back.

"What?"

"Babe, you've never been able to pretend a day in your life."

She wasn't exactly wrong.

I pasted on a smile as we made our way through the boho-chic tasting room, which opened out into the vineyard. Below us, the vines were bathed in a yellow-and-blue sunset, and a four-piece band played a folksy cover of Bill Withers under an elegant white tent. It was a perfect night to celebrate an imperfect pair.

I gazed longingly over my shoulder, eager to flee, when Summer tugged me forward. My heart thumped faster and faster as my heels dipped onto the soft grass and then found the hard glossy surface under the tent. The smell of wine and eucalyptus swirled in the air, with pastel hydrangeas and fresh greenery in the center of round-top tables. I tried my best to avoid eye contact with roughly a hundred floral-clad guests as they mingled with beaming, dewy faces and rosés in hand.

A cater waiter walked by, and I desperately reached for a glass of rosé, gulping notes of peach and citrus down with eyes glued to a ridiculous poster-size photo of Garrett and Cecily. The phrase "Meant to Be" was stenciled atop the wooden frame, taunting me like a foregone conclusion. Maggie Vine still had *questions*. I courageously fought the urge to grab a Sharpie and add "BUT IS IT?" to the frame, when all at once, an unmistakable laugh boomed behind my strapless dress.

My heartbeat found my eardrums. A familiar musky vanilla scent swirled into my lungs, tightening my insides, reminding me of my hands in his hair, his lips on my neck, my mouth on his mouth. I hadn't spoken to Garrett since our kiss. Not a text, a phone call—nothing. And now—

"Hi."

I held on to my own shoulder, hopeful that if I slapped my arm across my chest, the added layer of skin and bones would calm my heart palpitations. *Not so much.* I slowly turned to meet his face. Garrett stood uncomfortably in front of me, adjusting the lapel of his light blue linen blazer, which sat perfectly against his neck. My eyes floated past Garrett, toward his bride-to-be. Cecily was on the dance floor, aggressively using her hands and neck to compensate for her lack of footwork. A gaggle of similarly sophisticated and WASPy friends without rhythm danced frigidly around her. Cecily's tasteful tea-length blue dress matched Garrett's blazer, and I narrowed my eyes on her solid color choice. *Of course* she was the only woman *not* wearing an ode to florals. As usual, the mandated attire, "Garden Party Chic," applied to everyone *but* the bride. What kind of bride would Cecily be if she didn't treat her engagement as an excuse to wield unspeakable power over her friends and family?

"You . . . you came," Garrett muttered.

He glanced quickly at me, but refused to stay on my irises for too long, which I surmised would be an acknowledgment of the crime we had committed. Locking eyes with Maggie Vine would be like watching that video from *The Ring*: cataclysmic.

"Of course we came," Summer said.

Summer's eyes pointed down to Garrett's twitching fingers, as he nervously stirred his flowery gin cocktail. He always beamed in my presence, and it didn't take a body language expert to see that the sun had darkened. I shifted in my heels, biting my tongue and darting my eyes around the tent. I had never been anxious around Garrett. If anything, Garrett always had the opposite effect: he smiled, and my shoulders dropped. Not today.

"Wouldn't miss it," I said lowly, into my disappearing glass of wine.

He nodded curtly and scoured the room for an eject button.

"Well, you both enjoy," Garrett said, with a forced smile directed at Summer, and Summer *only*. The smile left his lips the moment his eyes brushed mine. He curved his body past me, fast-walking toward a distant group of his suit-and-tie-clad finance coworkers.

I dared to meet Summer's eyes, which were already narrowed on my face.

"What. Was. That," Summer demanded.

I shifted my body beside a cater waiter, grabbing a round, dusted chocolate puff pastry from a tray, and stuffed it into my mouth so I wouldn't have to speak.

"Real smooth," Summer said.

The pastry was hot and chewy against my gums, and then it cracked against my teeth. This was absolutely *not* chocolate. I could taste a bizarre swirl of Starbucks and something fried against my tongue. I refused to let it go down my throat, terrified that my lack of maturity had just upended twenty-seven years of full-on vegetarianism.

"What—what is this?" I asked the waiter, around a mouthful of *this*.

"A dusted espresso shell with a double-fried frog leg center," the waiter said, quite plainly, as if it wasn't the most unhinged combination ever.

I ducked behind the hydrangeas and spit double-fried Kermit's remains out into a paper napkin, directly onto the beautifully monogrammed *G* and *C*. I chugged my rosé, swishing it in my mouth like it was Scope—which honestly, was a normal thing to do at a winery. I leaned down behind the flowers, and spit out the remaining carnivorous leftovers into my wineglass.

"Come with me," Summer said flatly.

In true fashion, Summer did not give me a chance to follow her lead. Instead, she pinched her firm grip around my elbow and dragged me away from the tent, pulling me into the vineyard.

She stopped once we found ourselves with the glowing tent in the distance, both of us smack-dab in between two far-reaching rows of grapevines. Summer crossed her arms and waited for me to speak. I admired the grapes, eager to deflect.

"It's so pretty here, isn't it? Like, straight out of a party from *The Hunger Games*."

"Is he still a good kisser?" Summer asked, eyes staring me down.

She knew. Of course she did. I exhaled, relieved that it was finally Sharing Time with my best friend.

"First of all, it's completely Dave Matthews's fault."

"*Wait.* You guys kissed *weeks ago,* and you didn't tell me?"

I reddened, shrinking under Summer's shadow.

"*ME*"—she continued—"your best friend in the entire universe, the most important human in your life."

"At least your self-esteem is intact."

She glared at me.

"I'm sorry. I wanted to tell you—I *should have* told you. It happened, and I don't know what to do with it," I said, now pacing and fanning myself with my dress.

"How did 'it' happen?"

I froze, sucked in the floral air, and then opened my mouth. The words flew off my tongue like one giant exhale. "Well, so a handful of years ago I asked Garrett to spend the rest of his life with me when I turned thirty-five, and he showed up at my birthday, we kissed, but then he told me he was engaged. Super upsetting. To complicate matters, I also sort of promised that I would find Asher Reyes when I was thirty-five and he promised he'd find me—that's a promise we made to each other more than once, and here we are."

I inhaled, finally taking a breath.

"I'm sorry, do I need to break out my Google translator, or are you going to decode that run-on sentence for me?"

I opened my mouth, and I started to fill in the blanks.

28

THIRTY-FIVE

SUMMER STARED DOWN AT ME, dumbfounded, as I finished telling her everything. I twirled a grape on the vine, eager to avoid what would follow: her biting judgment.

"You're a little marriage pact whore," Summer said, her eyes wide against the dimming blue afterglow.

"I'm blanketed in the warmth of your support."

"This is worse than that movie where Julia Roberts made Dylan Mc-Dermott promise to marry her by *twenty-eight,* and then she tried to break up his wedding to a fucking *twenty*-year-old."

"Dermot Mulroney," I corrected.

"Dylan McDermott and Dermot Mulroney are two different people?"

"Yes."

"Huh . . ." Summer said.

Summer stared past my face, her lips slightly parted with the pop culture epiphany. She shook her head and pointed her eyes back to the task at hand: my self-afflicted chaos.

"Seriously. *Maggie.* How fucked-up do you have to be to ask *two different guys* to promise they'll marry you?"

"Apparently, exactly *this* fucked-up."

"At the very least, you could have given Asher thirty and Garrett thirty-five, just to space your chances out. But honestly: Why? Why did you ask Asher to marry you at thirty-five?"

I stared at Summer, holding my arms, not wanting to unload my issues.

"Your mom?" she said, reading my mind.

I nodded. Summer started to pace in front of me, like a PR shark circling a crisis.

"This is a whole phenomenon," she noted.

"What is? Marriage pacts? Being casually ruined by our parents' lack of therapy? Showing up at your soulmate's engagement party?"

"Retrosexuals," she said. "High school sweethearts who reconnect. The world is a garbage fire and nostalgia is cheaper than drugs and therapy. There was an article that said for older millennials, backsliding into your teenage hormones is a comfort—like re-bingeing a late-nineties WB show."

Well, I did embody the angst of a teenage girl holding back tears as Sarah McLachlan howled in the background. There was even a love triangle. I was living out my own episode of *Felicity,* but none of it was comforting.

Summer raised her eyebrows at me.

"You just told me Asher's been working on this movie project for *several* years. So why announce it now?" I opened my mouth to answer, but she had already formed her own conclusion. "He was waiting for that open door to walk through. A promise that he could deflect as a joke—when really, he's thought about ending up with you this entire time."

There was an undeniable swirl in my gut, shooting like a rocket up to my brain stem and nodding emphatically. Instead, I scrunched up my face.

"I don't know . . . we were babies."

"And yet, you were his longest relationship. And him, yours."

"Longest, but I doubt the most meaningful. I can't compete with Penelope Lynn," I said, referring to Asher's ex-girlfriend.

"Oh please, that was a PR relationship."

"No way."

Summer's sideways look said otherwise.

"How do you know?"

"Because it's my fucking job. They both had Oscar-worthy films to promote at the same time, and they looked good on each other's arms. Conflict-free beginning and end."

I shook my head, stunned people lived this way.

Summer stopped pacing to chew on the edge of her lip. She grinned, way too buzzy about the whole thing.

"You were always the ideal option for these two stupid boys, and now they have excuses to show up and make it real," Summer said.

"Well, Garrett's about to marry someone else."

"Debatable," she said.

I shook my head as my heart raced with the thought.

"And Asher?" Summer asked.

"My manager said I can't touch Asher until after the work is done."

My brain swirled in the other direction. The scruff on Asher's cheek as it brushed my face when we said goodbye the other night. The crisp scent of wildflowers in my lungs. How he used to study every freckle on my skin. How he used to look me in the eyes as he came—naked and unafraid of how much he loved me.

"You're thinking about him naked right now, aren't you?" Summer asked, interrupting my ode to Asher's torso.

"I'm not, *not* . . ."

"You are so, so fucked," she said with a laugh.

I closed my eyes and exhaled, defeated.

"So fucked."

"What about Garrett?"

I bitterly edged my heel into the soft grass.

"What about him?"

"Why did you ask him to marry you?"

I kept my lips together, unsure how to release the words.

"Oh, come on. Just spill it."

"I was in a bad place," I said slowly. "It was a couple weeks after—" There was a hitch in my throat, not letting me finish. Thankfully, I didn't have to. Summer nodded, letting me move past the end of my sentence.

"I felt like I couldn't begin my thirties that *lost*. When I'm with Garrett, I always feel like there's no one else. It's a cruel spell. Maggie Vine, doomed to let logic and rationale go out the window when faced with her—her . . ." I trailed off, terrified of what it would do to my body if I said the two words aloud.

"Your person?" Summer guessed.

I stood frozen with my palms open at my side. *My person.* There were years when I felt like Garrett was my person. A decade, even. If you'd asked me a month ago, with a gun to my head, I'd say Garrett Scholl was my person. But strangely, now, I wondered if Asher was my person. I thought my person would be the easiest definition in the dictionary, and Asher made falling feel like flying. Garrett made falling feel like crashing.

"If Garrett's my person, then all the fairy tales have gotten it wrong."

"What do you mean?"

"I thought our person was supposed to fit like a lost shoe. There's not even a shoe with Garrett. Loving him is like walking barefoot on shards of glass."

Summer studied me for a long while, and slowly, the sharp angles of her face softened in front of me.

"It's okay if he's not your person," she said, alarmingly delicately.

Summer spoke with a coolness, almost always. The vulnerability, the quiver in her words kept my attention on her face. Her eyes weren't on me at all. They had floated past mine, glassing over as they took in a woman chasing her giggling toddler in the distance. Summer's expression stiffened my entire body. I had only seen her hint at crying once since our freshman year of college. Summer peeled her eyes away from the mother, clearing her throat before coming back to me. I stepped closer, ready to ask if she was okay, but Summer's face found its trademark edge and she crossed her arms, able to go from teary to judgmental with the flick of a switch. A master class in deflecting human behavior.

I stretched my neck past the vines, seeing Garrett standing next to his beaming parents. His arm rested perfectly on Cecily's lower back, as he tilted his chin up in a friendly chuckle. He had become the golden child.

Cecily, the refined, pragmatic, list-checker-offer, fell in love with the amateur rock star. Cecily had dreams of working eighty hours a week as a paralegal, flaunting a sizeable emerald-cut diamond on her dainty finger, renovating an eighties Tudor home in Scarsdale on the same street as her parents, and having one child via a scheduled a C-section so as to not ruin her beautiful labia. I surmised that Garrett's parents had probably been searching for Cecily for years: someone who would tug Garrett's heels out of the creative mud and keep a smile on his face as he embraced an entirely different goal.

"I don't even recognize him anymore," I said, with a crackling sadness in the back of my throat. "And he's in love with someone else. Garrett's going to spend forever with another person."

I felt the need to verbalize the permanence of it all, equal parts reminding Summer and equal parts reminding myself of the very reason we were standing in this godforsaken stretch of wine-soaked heaven.

"He can't show up on your birthday and say all these things while being in love with someone else. You can't be in love with two people, Maggie. Not fully."

My eyes darted away from Summer in disagreement, causing Summer to tilt her bob at me.

"Oh, Maggie Vine . . ." she sang, shaking her head.

My body was able to lose its shit in the presence of two different men. Asher lit me up, like swimming in stars. Garrett tore me apart, like little paper cuts all over my skin. Both of them felt like the best and worst parts of being in love.

Summer offered up a weak grin. "We should get back there," she said. "Just smile and nod for two hours, and drink heavily."

I followed her past the vines, toward the gorgeous twinkle lights, when I felt a hand grip my arm. I turned, nearly choking on my tongue as Cecily beamed at me. Summer raised her eyebrows.

"I'm going to go get us all the drinks," she said to me, before escaping toward the bar.

"Congratulations!" I blurted to Cecily, in a high-pitched tone that screamed *"trying way too hard."* Thankfully, Cecily usually brought this level of enthusiasm to a conversation, so I knew my excessive pitch would be matched.

"*OH MY GOD!* I should be saying congratulations to *YOU*," Cecily said, smiling with a perfect row of white teeth.

"You heard about the movie deal?"

"The *what*?" She scrunched her face and leaned in, bulging eyes and cheeks turned upward. "Was it Raya?" she whispered loudly.

"Huh?"

"Did you match with Asher Reyes on Raya? They all want to know."

Cecily nodded to the high-top table behind her, where her friends gawked at me, not hiding their curiosity.

Cecily was referring to the exclusive dating app, Raya, and my new-found fifteen minutes of fame, thanks to the photo of Asher and me from Marea: Asher gazing hopelessly into my eyes, me laughing into a glass of wine. The image had spent the last week *everywhere,* leaving tongues wagging and interests high. Her friends were foaming at the mouth for any morsel of a scoop. It was a strange feeling, but for once, I was on the inside of something. I stood up straighter, feeling less like a weirdo outcast amid the privileged housewives of the Northeast, and more like the Cool Mysterious One.

I let my eyes wander toward Cecily's friends. I recognized this group as her high school buddies from Taft. I met them at a dive bar during Cecily and Garrett's first year of dating, a group of women in their midtwenties who Clorox-wiped the bar's counter before they sat down. The Taft group had all survived a prestigious boarding school together and then filtered off to separate Ivy Leagues before landing back in New York like a terrifying pack of preppy wolves dressed in Ralph Lauren linen dresses. There was a baseline of three carats on their respective ring fingers and bouncy blowouts atop their very minimal laugh lines. Cecily was the last of the women to acquire a diamond on her left hand—thanks to her fiancé taking roughly four years to get down on one knee.

"It *was* Raya. I knew it," Cecily said, believing that my silence was an admission of guilt.

"Oh, Asher? No, we know each other from forever ago. I'm not dating him. Also, I'm not cool enough for Raya."

"Yes, you are—well, *now* you are."

"I've already fucked enough DJs to last a lifetime," I mused.

Cecily laughed with her entire body and slapped my arm, hard.

"You're so funny. How are you always this funny?"

Years of rejection. Comedy is tragedy plus time.

"God, you and Garrett have this way of just saying things. *Your brains!* I wish I was like you," she said.

I pursed my lips together, fighting a sardonic laugh. Cecily wished she were like me, and a part of myself longed to be her—standing in her shoes with that ring on my finger and that gorgeous man impatiently waiting to wrap his arms around me on the dance floor. Hating Cecily would make it harder for me to hate myself, and I had tried. Her cheery demeanor was completely disingenuous—no one could be this happy for mere acquaintances. But her bubbly attitude and words of affirmation were wildly infectious to those basking in her rays of positivity. In conclusion: I hated her, and I liked her. And I hated myself during these wretched moments when I wanted to *be* her.

"So, I have a favor to ask," Cecily said, interrupting my green-eyed-monster dilemma. "Can you perform a song tonight?"

I stared at her blankly, until I realized she was serious. I couldn't sing at my unrequited love's engagement party. *I couldn't.*

"Cecily, I—I don't want to take the spotlight away from you guys tonight. I don't even have my guitar."

She clasped her fingers together and bent her knees toward me, like a child spotting an ice cream truck in front of her daddy.

"*C'mon! Pleeease?* I'm sure someone from the band will let you borrow a guitar, or a ukulele, or a tambourine or something."

"Those are three very different instruments—"

"And my friends are dying over you. *Dy-ing.* They've been listening to your songs on your Insta for a week and are *obsessed*. Honestly, you're half the reason they even came tonight—they hardly ever leave Westchester."

"They're obsessed with me because they saw some photo of me with Asher Reyes?"

She gripped both of my wrists. "Maggie, nothing happens in Scarsdale. This is all they have."

"Let's . . . let's just see how the night goes," I said, deflecting and saving my "*fuck no*" for later in the night.

"Yay!" Cecily tugged me into a swift hug and spun toward her friends with a squeal.

"That was a *hard maybe*," I called after her, but Little Miss Sunshine was already across the room, disappearing into her elite friendship huddle.

In the distance, Garrett turned away from the bar and snuck a glance in my direction. He looked away the millisecond my eyes caught his.

"What just happened?" Summer asked, sidling up to me with two full glasses of rosé.

I grabbed one glass out of Summer's hand, taking a large sip.

"Nothing good."

29

TWENTY-NINE

IF I HAD KNOWN THAT breaking up with Drew Reddy would gift me a hit song, I would have done it sooner. To be transparent, *he* dumped me two months into our New York love-bubble. While I had left that night at the bar knowing Drew and I were temporary, I wasn't yet tired of his companionship. Or the sex. It was the kind of sex almost worth living a mediocre life for. *Almost.* When our fundamental differences hit the fan, I was relieved to let Drew be the bad guy. My entire body exhaled when he tearfully and melodramatically cried, "New York is *killing* me, Maggie. I have to go home." I patted his head, telling him to go back to Los Angeles—where I knew he would find things that killed him just the same. I didn't miss Drew nearly as much as I should have. But one early morning, when I should have been sleeping, I thought about the way he ran his hand down my spine, and how nice it was to have someone who touched me like that night after night, and a song came swinging inside my brain. It was a yearning, folksy ballad, called "When I Can't Close My Eyes," and now a preteen was going to make it a hit.

Garrett tilted his glass of Veuve toward mine in a dark, swanky bar high atop Columbus Circle.

"To Maggie Vine, and her first of many hit songs."

"Fuck yeah," Summer echoed, bumping against my shoulder with a proud smile.

"Why are we making this about me? I thought these were goodbye drinks," I said, eyeing Garrett.

Garrett was temporarily moving to San Francisco tomorrow, leaving us for nine months. He was going to fully immerse himself into his father's company, starting with the West Coast branch. The only reason I hadn't let it fully break me was because I knew he was coming back.

"It's not a goodbye, it's a 'see you later,'" corrected Garrett.

He smiled at me, and under that Cheshire cat smile, there was a shift, his lips coming together into something apologetic. Garrett knew it wasn't his leaving that was a letdown, it was his reasons for leaving. When you love someone and you've seen the way their heart beats when they're doing what *they* love, it kills you to watch them extinguish the fire from their chest. He was officially becoming his father. He would come back to New York City in nine months, be promoted to SVP of his dad's company, and fold into a life he knew deep down he didn't want.

"Can we get drunk already?" Summer asked, her glass dangling in the air, waiting for Garrett and me to stop reading each other's minds. "Congrats, you superstar," she said, eyes beaming on mine.

All three of our glasses clinked as Central Park hummed outside the window.

Two months prior, a music producer had stumbled across "When I Can't Close My Eyes" on YouTube, and I had just received a nice fat check in exchange for allowing a prepubescent male heartthrob to have my song. He turned my angsty words into a candy-coated pop ballad, and I didn't mind one bit. I could feel myself inching closer to daylight. The world finally felt like my goddamn oyster. And with my ego thumping the way she was born to thump, I decided to take matters into my own fingers, starting with loosening the tie strangling Garrett's pulsing neck.

His eyes widened to the ceiling as he let my fingers unknot the thick silk. I undid the top pearl button of his collar, exposing the lump in his throat that I was aching to run my lips over. Instead, I practiced restraint, tapping my hand on his chest.

"That's better."

He rolled his eyes toward mine, and with our eyes locked, he ripped the rest of the tie off his shirt and undid another button.

"Happy?" he asked.

I was too lost in the ways he was scanning my face to answer. His expression had been playful, but now it was hardened, and a familiar heat was bubbling inside me. He looked away first.

We finished the bottle, with Garrett insisting on picking up the tab, and none of us objecting.

"Let's go dancing," I said as we stood up.

Garrett winced, looking down at his watch. "I have a nine a.m. flight," he said.

"Good news: that's twelve hours away."

Garrett shook his head at me with a grin.

JUST AS MY VOICE WAS meant to give life to lyrics, my tiny frame was made to move to a beat, *especially* a few drinks in. Tequila and lime danced on my gums and sweat dripped down my chest as a blissful buzz swirled in the back of my head, my feet and hips owning this dark, packed dance floor. The exact opposite was happening in front of me. Like a lone giraffe in a crowd of humans, Summer stiffly used her neck muscles to move her body, clutching her glass of wine, eyes darting around the room like it was a crime scene. While she had the body of the kind of woman who you'd picture gliding around a pop song like melted butter, she was too in control of a situation to let go—Summer Groves couldn't dance worth shit. I laughed to myself, tempering the urge to take a video and play it back for her in a sober light.

Summer took the empty tequila drink from my hand and slung her purse over her shoulder.

"THIS IS MY HELL," she yelled over the music, flatly pointing up to the mirrorball on the ceiling. "I HATE THIS, I'M LEAVING. BYEEEEE."

I grabbed her arm, tugging her back.

"C'MON! IT'S TOO EARLY!"

Summer raised her perfect thick brows in my direction, implying that I should understand something that my second tequila was keeping me from understanding. After a moment of blank stares, she cupped my sweaty cheeks and put her mouth up to my ear.

"YOU'RE WELCOME," she said.

Summer whirled me around, putting me face-to-face with Garrett's wide smile. He spun on his wingtip shoes, his sweat-soaked shirt now unbuttoned halfway, revealing his bare, ripped torso. He moved the same way I did, to the beat as if the bass was inside his veins—which only made me want him more. We had been dancing around each other for an hour, both of us flirtatious, but the only parts of our bodies that dared touch were our hands. He kept his eyes on me, getting low to the ground, as a gorgeous dark-haired woman moved her shoulders alongside him, waiting for Garrett to discover her hips—but he never did. With a piercing one-sided grin, he took my hand and spun me around. His other hand slipped around my waist, tugging my back to his moving body. Goose bumps enveloped my arms as his hips moved against my spine, his fingers tightening around me and pulling me flush against the heat of his body. I turned my hips with his, my eyes closing as his hand landed dangerously on the open space between my jeans and my barely-there silk crop top.

The air thickened with the velvety doo-wop of Rihanna's "Love on the Brain," and his fingers clenched around the right side of my waist, spinning me around, with two firm grips catching my body in front of his. My eyes met the veins tightening in his reddened neck, and I inhaled the vanilla musk radiating from his glistening torso. The mirrorball overhead dusted dark red and blue lights all over our bodies as my hand found the back of his neck, the other loosely around his waist. We moved with and against each other, bodies learning each other's edges as our gazes brushed past each other, but our eyes refused to intertwine. We knew what would happen if they did. Garrett Scholl went from dancing around me like a teenager at prom with a chaperone watching to dancing with me like a teenager at the prom's unsanctioned after-party. I could feel the warmth of his quickened breath above me, see his throat quivering. And then, I dared to look up.

His blue eyes swallowed me whole, hardened and hungry.

His grip loosened around me. I was still, he was still—our insides doing all the dancing. My throat went dry, my lips parting and my body melting with the light touch of his fingertips on the stretch of bare skin above my hip. His hand clenched around my side, tugging my weakened body tight against his hardened stance, while his other hand traced a line up my back, from the base of my spine, sliding under my shirt, up between my damp shoulder blades. His fingers moved slowly with the music, back down to my waist, sending a shiver all over my skin. All my senses were tied up in the way he was touching me—my hips and neck gliding with the heat of his hold. We danced against each other, and as I moved down and up his body, I felt him harden against me. I couldn't remember how to breathe, and he held me close to him, his throbbing dick against my hip. I was turning him on, and it unraveled every tightened muscle inside me. My mouth searched for air as my bottom lip brushed against the salty smooth curve on his neck, and Garrett tilted his head down, dancing his forehead against mine. The intoxicating heat of his mouth was just an inch from mine, and with a hand gripped tight on my hip bone, he led the rhythm of our bodies off the dance floor.

I closed my eyes, feeling Garrett's thumb on the curve of my neck, my spine landing against a cool wall, his sculpted body pressed hard against my heaving chest. One hand slid up my rib cage, over the side of my breast, settling on the right side of my face, as his other hand cupped my left cheek. I swallowed hard, my face in his hands, my eyes opening to find his breathless gaze scanning me like a realized dream. And all at once, his hungry open mouth collided with mine, two scorching-hot, tequila-soaked tongues lighting matches all over my body.

My chest engulfed the mirrorball above us—slippery, shining, bliss reflected everywhere. His body trembled against mine, sent me quivering in the same places the dream of Garrett had always sent me. It was like living inside my favorite line of my favorite song—a fantasy come to life. I gripped my hand in his wavy blond hair, my lips drowning on his, as his strong arm lifted my weight, my feet barely touching the ground, his hips pinning my swelling body between him and the wall. I felt him hard against my pelvic bone, and I clenched my hand rough around the back of his damp shirt, tugging him tighter against my limbs, bringing a wet, pulsing heat between my legs. His teeth softly tugged at my bottom lip, and he kissed me up my jawline, up to my ear, with the warmth of his tongue on my earlobe sending my eyes up to the ceiling with a moan. My chin came back down, just as he arched his head back to take me in. Garrett's large, firm body pressing me against this wall was all that was keeping my legs from buckling.

Eyes locked on his, adrenaline splintering my veins, I gripped my hand over his erection. Garrett swallowed hard, his chest thumping in front of my eyes, his stunned eyes watching as my hand moved upward, over his belt loop, sliding inside the opening of his shirt, my fingers tracing the sweaty lines of his ripped abs, my palm landing firmly over his chest. I kept my hand there, steady—my touch moving his insides like a racehorse. My eyes widened in the glory of it all, as his primal gaze blazed onto mine.

"I want to take you home, right now," he said, in a voice so low and husky that I almost dropped to the floor.

My humming lips parted in the air, eyes on him until the words found my throat.

"Mine's closer."

THIRTY-FIVE

THE ENGAGEMENT PARTY FROM HELL roared on as the glasses of rosé buzzed behind my eyes. Summer had excused herself due to a fashion emergency—one of her brand's A-list model ambassadors had decided he was equipped to solve the Middle East crisis on Instagram, and he wasn't. I leaned coolly against a high-top table, pretending to send and receive important texts on my phone, while actually doom-scrolling Twitter. My eyes darted to a pop-up tent yards away from the dance floor, as Garrett's laugh pierced through the air. His parents had hired a famous illusionist to come and perform magic tricks for the crowd—because an entire band at a winery wasn't enough. I chewed on my lower lip, watching Garrett pull two cards from the magician's hand. Garrett slammed his palm on his chest, stumbling back, head shaking, in total awe.

Suddenly, from the speakers, I heard, "Can Maggie Vine come to the stage please?"

Below the stage, Cecily giddily waved me over with one hand, while holding an acoustic guitar out to me in her other hand. My eyes turned big and round, and I shook my head toward the stage, plastering a "thanks, but no thanks" smile on my cheeks. Cecily cut through the scattered crowd, darting toward me like a bullet, grabbed my arm, and tugged me toward the stage.

"Cecily, look, I've had a lot to drink and I really don't want to."

"Please?"

I stared into her perfect blue pleading eyes and her pink pouty lips.

I stuck my tongue down your fiancé's throat. The least I can do is sing you a song.

I swallowed my lack of pride, grabbed the guitar, and hopped onstage. I made it a point to slowly tune the already-in-tune guitar, taking the time to figure out which song to play. My chest tightened as I watched Garrett approach Cecily, with his alarmed eyes locking on mine. His brows were pressed together, and the usual smile on his face was gone.

I could hear my heartbeat in my eardrums as he stared up at me. I wanted so badly to let my song "Let's Lie" leave my mouth, but I wasn't brave enough, for so many reasons. A handful of years ago, I wrote that song while sucking in tears, a song that would haunt me later. Just once, I had let the song go in front of an audience that didn't include the man it was meant for. Later, I recorded it in a professional studio. I had never been able to listen to it ever again after that recording session—and it wasn't just the emotional pining behind the lyrics. Every time I ached for Garrett, I could hear the blooming melody of "Let's Lie" in my head. But it always grew into something evil like a chemical reaction to a cocktail of pain, so I willed one of my best songs away like one would a dark nightmare.

I looked down to the dance floor where Cecily clung to Garrett's broad shoulder like a monkey to a tree branch. All eyes were peering up at me, impatiently waiting. I had to sing *something*. Garrett shifted nervously, wrapping his arm around Cecily and resting his chin on the top of her head with eyes narrowing on mine.

It was the crushing jealousy that did it. It was looking down on Garrett, watching him go all-in on the wrong woman. It allowed my mouth to open on a live microphone and go back to the moment we shared a stage, years and years ago—the moment his lips were inches from mine, when our futures were hopeful, when his smile lit up my entire being. I pierced my eyes into his, and out it poured.

"I've waited here for you / Everlong."

A stripped-down, aching version of "Everlong" flew out of my lungs, as if the pain of that unrequited moment had been punching my gut for eleven years, begging to break free. Just like the first time we sang it, my eyes didn't leave his, not once, and his eyes didn't leave mine.

I nailed the last note and slowly stepped back from the mic, breathless. The tent filled with tempered cheers and claps. There were some crossed brows—Garrett's and Cecily's perfect parents appeared confused by my song choice—it didn't exactly scream, *"Marriage: yay!"* I had done nothing to disguise the fact that I was singing this song to the groom at his engagement party, but thankfully, Cecily couldn't read between the lines. Instead of trying to stab me with her perfect Bubble Bath oval manicure, she giddily clapped her hands high above her head. She didn't know this song was a fixture in Garrett and Maggie's What Could Have Been Hall of Fame. Garrett's arms stayed wrapped around Cecily the entire song, so casual observers absolutely thought I was singing to the happy couple. But he knew better.

His expression was unreadable against mine, his jaw shifting under my glossy green eyes, and I knew that his head was also filled with the dizzying memory.

He knew.

He knew I wanted nothing more than to go back to that moment and do it over. I should have let him kiss me. Everything might have ended differently for us both. We could have built a chaotic, sparkly, wild, love-filled life together. The *what-ifs* stung my eyes, and slowly, I watched his expression soften. There was pain all over his face, the kind that he only let me see.

Quickly, Garrett turned away, his eyes back to Cecily, with a forced smile across his face. I felt my lips quivering, and I quickly handed the guitar back to its rightful owner and rushed offstage.

I kept my eyes away from him, but as I mazed through the crowd, I walked past Garrett, and I let the sharp corner of my shoulder edge into his tall frame. Tears sprung to my eyes as we made contact, and he arched back, taking me in for a moment.

I had to escape this party before I went full Claire Danes. Yes, I sobbed with my entire body, as if puppet strings were pulling every line of my face down to my toes. I was not a pretty crier.

I held my breath as I made it past the crowd and out of the tent, somehow tempering my bubbling emotions, which I surmised made me look like a fish gasping for air. I could feel my chest caving in as I turned to walk toward the tasting-room gazebo. I would call an Uber and hide behind one of the large trees on this Tuscan villa until I shoved my body into a getaway car.

In front of me, Summer paced in a tight circle with her phone glued to her clenched fist, her body blocking the stairs going up to the estate. I shifted away from her, unsure how to leave this vineyard before I broke down and confessed to everyone that I was helplessly in love with the groom. I glanced behind me, my heart racing as I saw Garrett making his way past the crowd—making his way toward *me*.

I was at a dead end. I needed an escape route. I whipped my head around to find freedom: the sprawling vineyard.

Suddenly, my heels were sprinting in and out of soft dirt, salt air beating against my wet cheeks, legs moving faster and faster through endless rows of grapevines. I couldn't stop running as the throbbing pain behind my eyes gave way to white-hot tears.

"Will you just slow down?" said an exasperated voice behind me.

It was him. *Of course* Garrett had followed me. There was nothing Garrett hated more than disappointing other people. I picked up the pace, running faster.

"*Really?*" he yelled.

Yeah. Really. I couldn't slow down. I was terrified of what would happen when he caught up to me. I was petrified that he would say words I couldn't bear to hear—that he wanted to be my friend, that he hoped we could find a way past that kiss. The thought of giving Garrett the closure he needed to move on and be happy with someone else was shattering.

Suddenly, my wet eyes were met with a wooden fence. I had reached the end of this stretch of grapevines. Instead of turning around and facing our ending like a grown adult, I kicked my heels off, threw them over the fence, and hurled my body upward, onto the other side.

Apparently, using my mother's Peloton bike twice a month hadn't adequately prepared me for a five-foot fence-hop. My cheek hit the sandy ground with a thud. I winced, blinking back the night's swirling blue-and-yellow sky above, which lit up a gorgeous stretch of empty paddocks and horse stables.

I stumbled upward, seeing stars in my eyes as I held my side—scalding pain stinging inside my ribs. I snatched my shoes and lumbered toward the row of horse stalls in front of me, exhaling under the dark wooden roof, which housed cooler air, with the romance of hay and horse shit swirling inside. There was a horse for each respective stall, and I was relieved to find most of them sleeping and uninterested in my presence. I leaned my back against one of the stall doors, letting the metal lines edge into my back—cold against my sweltering skin.

A white miniature pony stuck her head out of the opening in her stall, jolting my body from its moment of peace. Her excitable wide brown eyes were just inches from mine, and while the other horses were getting their eight hours of sleep, this lady was eager to party. I took in the bronze plaque on the stable door, reading: DOLLY. Under her name there was a framed newspaper article all about Dolly, who was apparently Wölffer Estate Stables' mascot, and the happiest bitch on the block.

"How's it going?" I asked her, breathless.

She tilted her head at my sandy face with squinted eyes, then looked sadly down at her hoofs.

"Yeah, me, too."

I wiped the sweat from my temple, my cheeks red hot, my fingers tingling, and my insides racing. I clenched my eyes shut, and my chest pounded harder as I heard his heavy footsteps echo on the barn's concrete floor.

"Fence hopping?"

I peered up to find Garrett panting in front of me. He caught his breath with his hands on his knees, then shook his sweat-soaked head at me as he leaned the back of his neck against the stall opposite me. I was grateful that he wasn't coming any closer, terrified that if Garrett set one wingtip shoe inside my personal bubble, it would break me. At the same time, I longed for him to come the fuck closer and throw my body against the stable doors.

I wiped the fresh sand off my arm, biting my lip, choosing to be passive-aggressive. His blue eyes apologetically searched my face as he took deep breaths in and out.

We stared at each other for a tense minute, until a beautiful black mare poked her head through the opening in the stall next to Garrett. He turned toward her to tenderly pet her nose. His eyes stayed on the mare as his lips opened.

"I shouldn't have kissed you. Not like that," he said, just low enough so I could barely hear it.

I waited for his eyes to find mine. They steadied on me as he loosened the tie around his neck with an exhale, clearing his throat and standing up straighter.

"You followed me all the way here to tell me you shouldn't have kissed me?" I asked, incredulous fire on my tongue. "You've had weeks." I held up my phone. "It works, you should try it."

"It was a mistake. I made a mistake that night, and I'm sorry."

"*Sorry?* You showed up to my birthday and let me kiss you when you had no intention of changing the state of our relationship. And not for nothing, we talked about showing up on my thirty-fifth birthday when it would mean forever—not as a way of gifting me emotional turmoil."

Garrett began to pace in a tiny circle, as if *he* were tortured. I stared directly at him, my eyes cold, my chest pounding with fury. He didn't have a right to be the one clenching his fist. He had me in the palm of his fucking hand—he always did, and he knew it.

"I don't know how to lose you, and I don't know how to be with you," Garrett finally said.

I shook my head, narrowing my eyes onto his. "What does that even mean?"

He shifted uncomfortably, placing one hand in his pocket and opening and closing his mouth.

"Just say it, Garrett. Just fucking say it."

He stared at me for a long moment.

"Maggie, it's not like you haven't turned *me* down."

I felt my diaphragm expanding with anger, with words fighting to escape from my lungs. Finally, they lost a battle with civility.

"Fuck you," I said, tears making their way from my throat to my eyes. "You've only hovered around my lips when it's been conveniently the most inconvenient time for one of us. You never go all-in when the timing is right, you just dip one toe past the line when you know the outcome can't be successful."

"That's not true. And you know it," he said.

"You can't hold my thirtieth birthday against me. That doesn't count—"

"IT COUNTS FOR *ME*! I WAS IN LOVE WITH YOU."

The words left his mouth forcefully, so loudly that they echoed against the dark stable walls, bringing surrounding horses up to their feet. The horses poked their noses through the open stall windows, wide eyes darting between myself and Garrett, as if they were waiting for my reply.

Garrett's body tightened, like I was weaving it in a knot and pulling harder and harder. His face went red, and he threw his hands in his hair, exasperated.

"We—you and I—we should have happened years ago. But . . ." He trailed off, shaking his head.

I took a step toward him, anger in my throat.

"Finish the sentence."

The vein on his neck was pulsing and he studied me as if he were staring down the barrel of a gun.

"But *what*, Garrett? You could have had me. Fuck"—I threw my hands in the air—"you could *have* me. I'm standing right in front of you telling you that I've been in love with you for twelve years," I cracked, tears falling. "Even when I couldn't be with you . . . I loved you."

He opened his mouth, with anguish pulling his face down.

"I'll never be enough for you."

He said it so softly that it took me a moment to piece the words together.

"That's . . . that's a bullshit excuse. It's like . . . like telling someone they 'deserve better,' when really, you don't want them the way they want you, and you're trying to be nice about it."

"Goddamnit—MAGGIE, I WANT YOU," he exploded.

Garrett stepped toward me, now inches from my shaking body, his wet eyes meeting mine. "I hate that I'm not enough for you. I hate that I'm not more like you—you know I'm not what you want. I gave up the things you love—and I know you look down on me for it." I shook my head desperately to argue, but he kept going, pain wrapped around every vowel. "I hate that we're not together. I hate that I can't be brave enough to just reach out and grab you and never let go. Every moment I spend with you, *I love you,* and then I go home, and I *hate* myself."

The tears strangled my throat, and I felt my heart twisting like a damp rag. I'd imagined this a hundred different ways—how it would feel when Garrett said those three words to me. The skies would part, doves would cry, it would be biblical. This was a punch in the gut. "I love you," with a qualifier.

"Well, I guess we have something in common," I said, my voice quivering.

I gulped back tears as the pain inside my chest morphed into something new. Garrett was no longer just an ache. All at once, he didn't stand on my chest like a heavy weight: the weight of yearning. This pain was sharp—a thousand needles stitching up a gaping wound. It felt like closure. I didn't know why people went looking for this kind of sorrow.

Garrett had a way of lighting up my body. He knew the adult me better than any other man—he knew me inside and out. And he knew my heart was breaking right in front of him. As I studied every inch of him, I couldn't help but wonder what the permanent void would feel like.

I exhaled into hot tears, and I felt myself crumple into his arms. While I let him pull me tight against his chest, I refused to wrap my hands around his body. Instead, my arms lay limply to the sides as tears ran down my lips, onto the curve of his neck, onto his perfectly pressed shirt. I could smell starch and vanilla on his lapel.

I pulled away from him and turned my back to Garrett with deep inhales, trying to get the scent of his skin out of my lungs. I shook my head and turned around, just to see tears find his clenched jaw. He wiped them quickly with the back of his hand, but I saw them just the same, and my lips hung open in the beautiful horribleness of it.

"I'm on this train, Maggie, and I can't get off it. It's been that way for a while now. And sometimes, when I look at you, I'm reminded of who I really am. And what I really want. And it hurts," he said, tears now falling openly—tears the back of his hand couldn't catch. "You remind me that there's a best version of myself somewhere out there, and I know"—he pointed hard at his chest—"I know this isn't him."

I swallowed, searching past my pain to find the right words. Instead, my mouth hung open, because no words could fix an ending like this.

He studied my broken face for a long moment and looked up at the beams on the barn's ceiling, as if begging the rest of his tears to stay where they belonged. His eyes came back down toward mine.

My body jolted like lightning as his eyes hardened on my face.

All at once, adrenaline prickled through my body, soaking up the pain and anger and replacing it with wanting. I wanted him so badly that it felt like my pounding chest was pulled toward him by a force out of my control.

"Goddamnit," he said under his breath.

We seemed to meet in the middle, colliding into each other as he fastened his hand around my waist and led me two steps backward. I felt my back edge onto the stable door's latch as his hand settled over my hip bone—right above the slit in my dress. His racing chest pressed hard against my breasts as my heart pounded faster and faster. He took deep breaths in and out, hungry eyes on mine as his finger left my hip, tracing a line up my ribs and slowly along the curve of my neck. I swallowed hard as he pressed his thumb against my bottom lip, with the heat of our mouths against each other. I cupped one hand around his reddened cheek, and he curled his fingers around the back of my neck, tugging my open mouth onto his.

This was not closure.

His hand slid under my dress, sending a rush of heat across my skin as his throbbing body pressed hard against mine. My legs tightened around him, and Garrett lifted me up against the stall door, with one hand clenched around my backside, his lips moving from my mouth to my clavicle. I felt him grow under me, and I tugged at his belt loop as the heat of his mouth found my ear, sending my eyes to the ceiling with a moan. His fingers moved under my dress, torturously stopping at the base of my underwear line, softly grazing it as my insides grew hotter and hotter. He pulled one corner of my thong along my leg, sending it to the floor. I shifted my gaze down, purposefully locking my eyes onto his as my hand settled under his leather belt loop.

Our mouths slammed against each other again. He tasted like bourbon and mint. I needed to feel all of him. I unclasped his belt and grabbed him hard as his fingers moved inside me, sending stars to my eyes. Suddenly, our wild-beating chests jolted against each other as a loud boom echoed from outside the barn.

Breathless, I turned, seeing sparkly gold fireworks lighting up the dark night, erupting over the party tent in the distance. The fireworks shined like a spotlight on his face, their reflections blooming in his warring eyes. I ran my hand over the red lines on his pulsing neck, admiring the traces of my fingers on his skin. The explosions roared over our shallow breaths, our lips open inches from each other, our flushed skin pressed against each other. His eyes took in my heaving chest, my dress tugged up over my hips, my hand clutching his open belt loop. The fireworks kept sounding, trying to call him back, as if they were the angel on his shoulder.

"I—I should go," he said, unmoving, as if he were waiting for me to tell him to stay and take comfort in the messy sparks roaring inside our bodies instead of the picture-perfect fireworks display meant for him and his fiancée.

Garrett slowly set me down, and my feet touched the ground as his hold left my body, bringing me back down to earth. I leaned my shoulder against the stable door, catching my breath as I aimlessly fiddled with the sliding lock. I glanced up slightly, seeing his fingers fumble to refasten his belt, missing the loophole twice. I cleared my throat and extended my foot toward my wet thong on the dusty floor, using my toes to pick it up, *like a goddamn lady*. While I wasn't born with enough tact to keep my underwear on inside a barn, I did have enough self-worth not to wear Barn Floor on my vagina. I awkwardly tucked my underwear into my purse and shifted my attention back to Garrett. He tightened the tie around his neck, like an actor getting back into character.

I studied his face as fireworks lit up the sky.

"Don't go," I said, quivering.

He hesitated, then took a step toward me, leaning his face down so that we were nose to nose, our sweaty foreheads pressed against each other. I could feel his body shaking against mine, as I undid the tie around his neck, then the buttons on his shirt, one after the other, neither of us moving.

"Okay," he exhaled.

Garrett kissed me—his warm tongue sliding inside my mouth as I pulled him closer and closer. All at once, I felt a sharp object edge into my back. Before I could turn around, a strong force sent our bodies flying to the ground.

I landed with a thud on top of Garrett, my heaving chest pressed against his naked torso. I peered upward, slack-jawed, to find tiny hoofs racing past me—hoofs belonging to the white miniature pony, Dolly. She had broken out of her stable, and was now prancing toward the open field in the distance. Garrett and I shot one wide-eyed look at each other, scrambled to our feet, and ran after her—just two traitors running side by side trying to catch a rebellious miniature pony—a pony who was barreling toward the engagement party tent.

THIRTY-FIVE

Barefoot and commando, I sprinted for my life through the dark field. Wind howled against my cheeks as Dolly ran yards ahead of me. She was the corgi of horses—tiny legs, long body—but she thought she was a fucking Great Dane. She jumped over a low crossrail with her head tilted proudly to the fireworks in the sky.

My hip slammed onto a low post, bringing my legs to a halt. I winced, holding the pounding pain on my side, unable to do anything but watch as Garrett darted after Dolly, his natural athleticism putting me to shame. Dolly inched closer and closer to the glowing vineyards in the distance—to the engagement party tent. I taught my body how to move again, beads of sweat dripping down my curls as I picked up the pace behind them.

"What do we do?" I yelled to Garrett, on his heels.

"Catch her," Garrett yelled back dryly.

"I think you need to outrun her. And then get her to turn around."

"Oh, okay, I'll just outrun a horse."

"You ran the New York Marathon. You can outrun a pony!"

"One of those things doesn't equal the other!"

Under any other circumstance, Garrett would be shaking his head at me with his devilish grin, and I would be shaking my head right back. Yet, sadly, banter while running for your life is rarely full of heart flutters and flirtatious smiles.

My chest thumped harder as Dolly barreled toward the fence that stood between the vineyard and the field. There were rows of grapevines between us and the party tent in the distance, but if one person walked out of the tent, they would see Dolly, and then they would see us. Garrett's shirt was unbuttoned, and I looked like I had almost fucked someone in a barn. It would be unexplainable on every level.

Dolly slowed her hoofs to a stop at the fence and turned back around toward me. I leaned against a high-jump hurdle, exhaling relief. Garrett quietly walked toward Dolly, just as she turned her back to him, burying her pink nose in the hay to refuel before her next 3K. Garrett cautiously tapped his hand on Dolly's back like she was a door.

"What are you doing? You're not supposed to approach a horse from behind!"

Dolly whipped her head at Garrett, her big brown eyes narrowing on him, her ears pointed toward him like she was a bull and he was a bright red flag.

"How was I supposed to know that?" he asked, as he stepped back from Dolly with his hands in the air.

"You're a privileged white kid from Connecticut," I hissed.

Dolly edged her hooves into the dirt, eyes unblinking on Garrett. I moved in front of Garrett with my palms outstretched, crouching down to Dolly's level.

"Hi, Dolly," I said, offering her the front of my hand.

Her ears softened as she let me pet the bridge of her nose.

"What do you say we get you back home?" I asked, walking in the direction of the barn.

I turned around, hopeful that Dolly would be on my heels. She hadn't moved an inch. Unfortunately, there was no halter and also no rope to lead Dolly back to her home. I glanced up to the sky, clenched my eyes shut, and drew in the dusty air. Dolly was a miniature pony. I was also miniature: standing at five-foot-two. If a three-year-old could ride Dolly without going catatonic, so could I. I opened my eyes with my heart pounding, I sucked in courage, and I climbed on board.

"What are you doing?" Garrett asked.

"The article in front of Dolly's stable—it says she loves nothing more than giving pony rides."

"To *children*," he said.

"Well, I'm improvising."

I laid my stomach along her spine, lifting my leg in the air. I was far too adult-sized to make getting a ride from a miniature pony look good, but damn, this bitch was loving it. Dolly trotted toward the stable, giddily, and I couldn't help but smile as the warm breeze hit my cheeks.

The pace was slow and steady, until suddenly, dirt started to fly in the air, wiping the grin off my face. Terror took over as Dolly's little hooves picked up speed. My eyes widened to saucers, seeing us galloping ahead, toward a low crossrail.

"Dolly, don't you fucking dare!" I yelled.

She fucking dared.

Dolly lifted her head up, and barreled toward the hurdle like Ryan Gosling was waiting for us, shirtless, on the other side. We flew through the air, and I closed my eyes, feeling my stomach slam against my ribs. Dolly thudded to the ground on her front hooves, pounding my vagina hard against her bony backside.

I patted the side of her head, screaming into her ear over the increasingly dirty wind in my face. "OKAY, DOLLY, YOU DID IT. YAY! IT'S TIME TO GO NIGHT-NIGHT NOW."

Garrett was on our heels, panicked. He whipped his head back to the party tent, making sure that we were getting farther and farther away from blowing our criminal cover.

Breathing hard, I looked up to see rows of low-jump hurdles. I tugged at Dolly's mane as she lurched over one jump ring after another, my lady parts getting hammered, and not in a good way. My cheeks flapped harder against the wind as she picked up her pace, holding on to a speed that miniature ponies shouldn't be capable of reaching.

A high hurdle was ahead of us, clearly meant for a stallion, not for Dolly, the unsung hero of a petting zoo. I guessed Dolly had bitterly looked on year after year as the big horses got to cover the tallest hurdle while she had to give screaming two-year-olds a nice little trot around a ring. Now, she would show us all.

I could hear my heart beating in my head with nausea settling in my throat. I turned my head around to look at Garrett. He was running yards behind me, with helpless wide eyes and his gorgeous, messy hair blowing in the wind. Dolly picked up the pace, and I whipped my head forward: yards away, the tallest hurdle was approaching. I squinted, realizing it wasn't just one hurdle. Dolly would have to jump wide enough to clear a triple.

Dolly's mane flew into my howling open mouth as I ducked my head to the side of her neck, unable to watch as I met my death. This was a fitting end. I imagined how the *East Hampton Star* would cover our demise: *"Dolly died heroically, a miniature pony trying to reach her full-sized dreams. Also a casualty of Dolly's high-hurdle aspirations was Maggie Vine, that rando who was last seen with Asher Reyes."*

I opened my eyes, seeing Dolly's hooves tuck under her belly as we left the ground.

"AHHHH!" I screamed, with two hands clutched behind her ears.

We arched toward the hurdle like E.T. and Elliott floating over the moon—except E.T. was clenching her glutes to keep from shitting on the mini pony underneath her bare ass.

Somehow, Dolly cleared all three high hurdles. I was strangely proud of her, but I didn't have time to celebrate her personal record, as my right boob slammed against Dolly's spine, knocking the breath from me. I lost my hold on her, flailing my arm desperately toward Dolly's mane, gripping on to her fur, and squeezing my legs around her body as she ran toward the barn. With each gallop, I felt my chest inching down Dolly's side, my chin now nearing her front leg, my sweaty palms now losing a battle with gravity.

I lost my hold on Dolly's mane just as the sandy floor—the floor that my face was about to meet—became concrete. My shrieks echoed through the barn as my body tumbled off the miniature pony, hitting the cold hard floor with a thud.

I tried to catch my breath, pressing my palms onto the floor and peeling my cheek up off the ground. Dolly stopped prancing and turned to loom over me. She nudged my trembling body with her wet nose, and I dug my heels onto the floor, sliding my ass away from the least terrifying animal of all time: a My Little Pony Happy Meal toy come to life. Dolly pointed her chin into the air and pranced to her open stall, as if she hadn't just scarred me for life.

Garrett flung himself against Dolly's door, sliding the brass lock closed so she was locked in for good. He stared at me breathlessly, with sweat dripping down his bare chest. I pressed my hand onto my neck, searching for reassurance that I was still alive.

"Are you okay?" he asked.

I pulled myself up with dark eyes on him, catching my breath.

"Am I *okay*?" I crossed my arms over my battered dress and used the stall to keep my shaking body upright. "What about any of this is *okay*?" I asked.

His eyes moved away from mine, focusing on his shifting feet.

"We were never good at timing," he said quietly.

I paused for a second, almost insulted by the truth.

"You're impatient, and I'm too patient—is that what you mean?" I finally said.

Garrett stared at me wordlessly, and then lowered his focus to his unbuttoned shirt. I watched his fingers, fingers which had just been inside me, stitch up our crime.

"You know that night—the night of my twenty-fourth birthday?" I asked.

I waited for his eyes to come back to me. They did, warily.

"When we almost kissed after karaoke?" I continued. His hands froze on the loose tie around his neck. "I was dating someone else at the time, which is why I didn't kiss you back. I broke up with him right after you left." I twisted my dress in my hands, the memory pounding at my chest. "Later that night, I showed up at your door to finish what you started, and Quinn answered the buzzer."

His eyes were soft on me, his body still.

"I think about it too much," I said, my voice getting smaller, tears forming. "About how if you had believed in the possibility of us, the way I did, that we'd probably be . . ." I trailed off, unable to finish the sentence. I didn't need to finish it. He knew.

We stared at each other until the silent tears were down my chest. His fingers were still on his tie, and I shook my head in pain, walked past him with my shoes in my hands and my heart on the floor. I had waited twelve years for Garrett Scholl to come around. Our moment had passed, like so many times before.

32

TWENTY-NINE

"Fuck."

Breathless, I stared into my shallow purse, then back at my locked door. In borrowing a bag from Summer tonight, I had failed to transfer my apartment keys to this purse—which was problematic, considering the guy I had lusted after for six years was standing at my doorstep, his body throbbing behind me, ready to fuck me into the next morning.

I turned around to look at Garrett, apologetically gritting my teeth in a straight line. My lips parted, taking him in. His shirt was hanging off his sweaty body, his blond hair an adorable mess from the way I messed it up in the cab.

He tugged me close to him and hungrily kissed my mouth, then my neck. I arched my chin to the ceiling in a moan.

"We can go to mine," he whispered against my ear.

My lips came up to his mouth, with my hand gripped on his belt loop, his hard dick throbbing against my thigh, his face flushed. My breathing quickened. I needed his lips back on mine, but not here.

I stared at him, breathless.

"Kick my door in."

It was absolutely the sexiest thing I'd ever said to a man.

He stared wide-eyed at the door, then back at me.

"Are you sure?"

I was sure. I wanted him to ruin my apartment's front door. I wanted him to ruin me—in the best fucking way possible.

"Kick my door in," I repeated, hungrily against his lips.

Garrett closed his eyes as my hand ran up his leg, tightening over the bulge in his jeans. He tilted his chin to the ceiling, sucked in air, then backed up from my body and adjusted his pants. I stood a few inches behind his strong build, my body trembling as his wingtip shoe met my door's handle. The wood splintered at the lock, sending my front door wide open.

Garrett turned to me with a devilish grin, and before I could undress him right there in the doorway, he tugged my mouth back onto his, and spun us both through the open door—as if we were one.

I lifted my arms as he pulled the shirt off my body, leaving me topless in front of him. His shirt came off in a fever, and he held me against his body, so my breasts met his chest.

We stood still for a moment, two hearts racing as Garrett traced long lines with his eyes and his hands up and down the naked sides of my ribs.

I moved back, and with eyes wide on him, I stepped out of my heels and took off my jeans, now only in a pair of underwear.

His eyes didn't leave mine as he reached back to wedge the door shut. He stared, unblinking, taking in every side of me, with just the light of the city beaming through the window, yellow hues against my sweltering skin.

"You're ridiculously beautiful," he exhaled.

I kept my eyes on his as I unbuttoned his jeans. He stepped out of his pants and his briefs, setting himself free, and in one motion, he pulled me toward him.

I kissed the curve of his neck, musk and vanilla, and I let my hand move down his abs, until I had his hard dick in my grip. His breathing thickened as my hand slid back and forth, sending his eyes to the ceiling. Garrett pulled back slightly, my hand still on him as he kissed my naked shoulder. His lips made a trail down my body, taking one breast at a time full in his mouth, my eyes going to the ceiling, his tongue down my rib cage, sending my hands off his body. The heat of his mouth hovered above my lace underwear, the tips of his fingers moving up and down my inner thigh, my legs shaking. Heat engulfed my chest, as his mouth tugged my wet underwear to the floor. I clenched my hands in his hair as his tongue went inside me, my grip squeezing tighter and tighter. His tongue and his touch weakened my legs until my vision was blurry and my trembling body turned white hot. I arched my head back in a loud moan, my body writhing.

He came back up toward me and pulled my trembling frame against him, our mouths fighting for air against each other as he lifted me onto the bed with ease—his perfect, naked body on mine.

Garrett hovered over me, hands on either side of my face, his blue eyes scanning my body the way I always dreamed they would. He encircled the small tattoo on my rib cage—a full black-and-gray moon.

"You have a tattoo," he marveled.

I smiled. "It's like . . . maybe the only thing you don't know about me," I said.

His smile faded, face stiffening, as if remembering that he knew everything about me. *Everything but this*. He tucked a strand of hair back from my face, keeping one hand on my cheek.

"Maggie, I'm leaving for nine months."

"I know . . ." My voice quivered in confusion, wondering where this was going.

"I've thought about this, about us—so many times. But I did long distance right after college and it went very poorly. . . . I don't want to do that to us." He closed his mouth, gaze on me.

I knew where he was going, but I couldn't go there, not right now. I'd overthought us five years ago, when our lips almost touched, and that moment punched me in the loneliest hours of the night, or every time he smiled at me the right way. My default was to overthink every scenario, but I couldn't live with the regret of not moving forward because of fear that it wouldn't last.

"Do you want this, right now?" I asked.

His body was swelling hard against mine, fingers tracing a circle around my hip bone.

"More than you know," he whispered, his voice cracking under the admission.

My heart raced as I took my hand and wrapped it around him, showing him that I was right there with him. I wanted this. I wanted him. Garrett's eyes closed at my touch, and his breathing quickened.

"Do you have a condom?" I whispered into his ear.

He pulled back from me with a grin, then leaned his torso over the side of my bed, finding his wallet inside his pants pocket on the floor. I watched him put on the condom, and a moment later, he steadied his naked body over mine. His eyes blazed down at me, and he pinned my wrist over my head. His lips came back down to mine, soft and warm, delicate and tender, and his other hand pulled me upward in one motion, as he sank deep inside me.

Like that time when we had sung together, we just fit. Our mouths, our limbs. We knew where to touch each other without knowing—and there was no unknowing this kind of pleasure.

I wasn't someone who prayed often, just on High Holidays, but right there, with Garrett's strong hold effortlessly rolling us over, I looked down at his grin, and I silently prayed. I prayed for the memory of this moment to hurt less than the *what-if* of it never having happened. I shifted back and forth on top of his body, his hand on my waist—back and forth, hard and soft, until pulses inside me clenched over his dick, heat moving up my throat and expelling a moan from the depth of my lungs. He rolled me back over and moved back and forth, faster and faster until he was saying my name into my ear, his hands clenched up in my hair, his body sinking onto mine, my chest collapsing against his.

Later that night, my fingers memorized his naked body as he slept tangled up in me. I felt tears prick my eyes, and staring at his sleeping calm face, I prayed once more. I prayed that I wouldn't have to pine for this moment—that Garrett and I would do this again and again, forever and ever. All I wanted was everything. What's so bad about that?

Let's lie to ourselves like new lovers do

33

———

THIRTY-FIVE

ONCE I WALKED AWAY FROM Garrett at the engagement party, I broke down and called Summer. In between tears, I told her we had to leave *immediately*. She came and rescued me in front of the sprawling entrance to the stables. I cried the entire short drive back to her East Hampton home, while she patted my shoulder with wide eyes.

When we got to Summer's house, after I sobbed in the shower, Summer and I curled up outside by the firepit in her backyard. I leaned back in the Adirondack chair with wet wavy hair, plucking my guitar, trying out a verse for the movie.

I watch you throw hope to the wolves
You shrug as they rip the dream of us apart
Why should our finale have a heart
Go ahead, burn me at the stake saying words better left unsaid
Until the ashes of our maybes become my bed

Summer gaped at me, alarmed, as the last line left my lips.

"Jesus Christ, Maggie."

"What?"

"You're make Elliott Smith seem fun."

I scribbled the chords down alongside the lyrics in my songwriting notebook. "It's for the All Is Lost moment in the movie," I said.

"I thought you said this song was supposed to be hopeful."

"It is. I just . . . I might be projecting, a little bit."

"You think?" Summer grabbed the cup of melted ice at my feet, tossed it over her shoulder and refilled it with whisky. "Babe, Garrett's a giant coward, and I refuse to let you sleep in the embers of his shitty spinelessness."

"I know. I just— *Ugh.* I wish I hated him more than I do."

Exasperated, I set my guitar down, happily trading my open hand for a full glass of whisky. The liquid burned going down my raw throat, in thanks to all the screaming I had directed at a mini pony.

An hour prior, I had exhausted all the rest of my tears into a piping-hot shower, washing unrequited love, horse, and barn off my swollen and bruised body. Garrett and I loved each other. And he was going to marry another woman. One plus one did not equal two. It would have been an easier death if our physical connection didn't match our platonic one.

I stared into the hot flames, eager for them to burn me alive. Summer nudged me with her elbow.

"C'mon, you said all the things. You can't have any regrets. He's the one who is going to go forward with a lifetime of wondering, 'What-if?' Plus, it's not all doom and gloom here. Let's focus on the positive."

"I now have a rational fear of miniature ponies?" I offered.

Summer stood up, extending her glass of whisky toward my puffy eyes. I stared back at her blankly. She rolled her eyes and lifted my whisky-clad hand up toward her.

"You, Maggie Vine, are about to make it. It's your career's turn to shine, and I won't let *some dude* take that joy away from you. And the cherry on top of your career sundae: the hottest movie star on the fucking planet has every intention of ripping your clothes off. So, cheers."

Summer took a sip and stared me down until I did the same.

"We don't know that," I said, coughing into my drink.

"*We do,* you little dipshit."

Summer plopped her body back down on her chair, her smirk lit up by the moon. I looked down, seeing her phone brighten. She clicked on a text message, and a photo popped up on her screen: Valeria making a kissing face into the camera. Summer beamed, taking in the photo of the woman she loved. I shook my head at my best friend, jealous of how their union came together so effortlessly.

"What?" Summer asked, studying my expression.

"Nothing. It's just . . . you found your person, and it *works*. You don't have to turn the world upside down to be together. You don't have to blow up your lives to exist. I'm such an idiot, Summer."

"No, you're not."

"I am. I believed Garrett was my person for *so* long, even though I didn't have one claim on him. It was idealistic and stupid, and I know that—yet, here I am, still crying over him. I took one look at that guy, and I believed in All The Things, and then life kept him from me the way I wanted him, which frankly, sucks. It sucks. You're lucky. Your person is just your person, without all the suckage. I want that."

"Mags, it's not all roses and caviar."

Summer turned her head away from me, examining the deer darting along the stretch of deep woods on the other side of her property. I leaned forward, trying to read her expression.

"What do you mean?"

Summer kept her eyes on the deer.

"I love my wife. She drives me wild in good and bad ways. I couldn't love her more if I tried. But I don't know if we're going to make it." Summer let the statement leave her mouth emotionlessly, so blankly that I was sure she was joking.

Her eyes floated back to mine, and all at once, her whole face appeared heavier. I scooted in closer to Summer, trying to read the newfound pain behind my best friend's eyes.

"Summer, what's going on?"

She looked away from me, studying her wedding ring.

"My wife wants children. And I don't want children."

I clenched my jaw, trying to keep my chin from hitting the pavement.

"I thought . . . I thought you did," I said gently and quietly. "I thought you guys were about to start the process?"

Summer etched her nails into the bottom of the crystal whisky glass in her hand.

"Me, too. But the last year I keep waiting to feel it, and . . . I haven't."

"Haven't felt what?"

Summer locked her eyes on me.

"That pang. I look at kids, and I don't feel any ache in my chest. I don't feel like there's a missing piece inside of me, waiting to be filled with ten little fingers and toes. I actually—I feel the opposite. I'm so goddamn happy. I love my life, just the way it is. I don't want children. Valeria, she *needs* and she *wants* a child to feel whole—she wants one badly. And I'm going to lose her because of it. I'm going to lose my person over this. And I know I have to tell her, but . . . *fuck,* I don't want to."

Tears hit Summer's eyes, and shockingly, she did nothing to temper her pain. I had only seen Summer cry once, and my heart did flips as she let tears fall without a fight. I scooted my chair closer to her and folded one of her hands into mine, and just like a grief time machine, I was brought back into my seventeen-year-old body, to the day I lost a father who was barely mine to lose, and gained a best friend.

Seventeen-year-old Summer aggressively sprayed Angel perfume in the middle of our tiny dorm room and stormed through the wet air with her platform sandals, just as I fell to my knees below her, tears breaking across my face. She stared at me blankly, not saying a word—as I sobbed into my cell phone while my mother all too calmly told me my dad had died of a heart attack. I theorized my mother was remaining stoic so she wouldn't break down. But her delivery made me feel like I'd been punched in the gut and left on the curb with no one there to mourn alongside me. I was glued to the floor for hours, frozen in unimaginable grief. Summer left my side only once, to go to the vending machine in the lobby. She brought me back a vanilla Coke and peanut M&M's. I was embarrassingly touched that Summer knew what my favorite snack was, even if she'd never cared to know one thing about me up until this point—and we had been freshman-year roommates for three months.

"I thought you hated me," I said, blubbering, my face turned upward to Summer.

She looked dismissively out the window, sucking in red cheeks.

"I could still hate you *and* know your vending machine order. I mean, we're roommates. I have eyes," she said, biting her bottom lip in flimsy deflection.

Along with emotional intimacy, Summer was not a fan of receiving praise.

I cracked a peanut M&M between my teeth. The candy was bitter against my tongue, and the chocolate shell moved down my throat like a chain saw. I remember wondering if all the things my dad and I loved together would become a casualty of his death.

"I have to go to Boston tonight," I said to no one. I didn't know how to move my legs. How was I going to board a train to face my father's side of the family?

Summer shrugged. "I'll come with you. I like Boston."

Years later, I learned that Summer actually hated Boston. She held a sizable grudge toward the entire state of Massachusetts, because she didn't get into Harvard. Summer Groves was not someone who lost gracefully.

Later that afternoon, Summer and I shared a train car to the city she secretly hated. I cried the entire time, while Summer stared wide-eyed at every other passenger but me, searching for an eject button like a frat bro in the same room as a screaming infant. Finally, thirty minutes away from our Back Bay Station destination, Summer decided to throw me a bone.

"My mom died three years ago," she said. Summer's eyes stayed on the moving trees out the train's window, refusing to look at me, refusing to hold up a mirror to her own grief. She continued, "You'll be okay. But . . . it's going to be shitty for a while."

I was desperate for a grief timeline, but I was too new to grief to recognize that no such thing existed. I wrongly assumed that my mysterious roommate was a professional.

"For how long?" I asked.

Summer shrugged her shoulders to the train car ceiling. My stomach flipped as I watched tears fill her eyes to the brim. If you'd told me Summer Groves had never cried, even as an infant, I would have believed you. More accurately, no one had seen Summer Groves cry since she was a little kid. She hadn't even cried at her mother's funeral.

I grabbed Summer's hand from her lap, and I squeezed hard. I was less surprised by the fact that Summer let me hold her hand, and more surprised that when I unclenched my fingers around hers, she pulled my hand back and gripped tighter. Misery loves company, but even more so, misery loves understanding.

She understood.

Instead of pretending that I never snuck a glimpse past her armor, Summer kept me on the inside. From that moment forward, I was in on a secret: Summer Groves was terribly human.

HERE WE SAT, EIGHTEEN YEARS later, navigating heartbreak, but a different kind. I squeezed Summer's hand tighter as she wiped away falling tears.

"You don't know that you're going to lose her," I said. "Love is about compromise, right? And sacrifice?"

"Says the woman who kept expecting Garrett to pursue her? You're mad at him because of shitty circumstances. You're blaming him for something that's not entirely his fault. Bad timing and holding back on true feelings goes both ways. Where's the compromise there?"

I pulled my head back, stung by Summer's words.

"I thought you said he was a giant coward."

"He is. And there's been a couple times where, when it comes to Garrett, I could have said the same thing about you."

"Ouch."

"Sorry," she said quietly.

"No, you're not."

She was never sorry about being brutally honest.

"No, I'm not. Mags, when one person has an idea of what their dining room table looks like ten years from now, and the other person's vision looks a lot different—that's a hard one to meet in the middle on. Valeria wants a loud, messy future full of sticky jam hands. She wants to sit at a full table. I love being the irresponsible one on a school night. I want to travel, and I want to build a career without the guilt. I want to sit at a hundred different tables all over the world with the same woman pulling up a chair beside me."

Summer started to choke on her words. I got up from my chair and crouched down next to her, holding her hand.

"I'm not who she thought I was, Maggie. And I'm not who *I* thought I would become. This is my fault, not hers. And it's going to break both our hearts. This is the first time—Mags, the first time in my marriage—that I haven't been able to say exactly what's in here," Summer said, gripping the cotton shirt around her chest, tears effortlessly falling down her neck.

Summer was blunt. Her offhand candor was often mistaken for cruelty, even though she was not cruel. Through the years, she'd learned to soften her delivery—but she rarely had enough forethought to bite her tongue completely. It crushed me that Summer couldn't uncage this truth—one that her partner deserved to know. For the first time, Summer's entire heart was wrapped up in one of her beliefs. No matter the delivery, the truth would leave her heartbroken.

She stared at me, words falling out of her with tears. "No one tells women this when they get married in their twenties, you know? What we think we want at twenty-eight, it's not always what we want at thirty-five. The things that make you feel safe and the things that set your heart on fire aren't set in stone. I love my wife more than the day I married her, but, our ideal futures look very different."

Maybe if I had spent more time planted on my own two feet and less time chasing a dream, I would have had ever-changing opinions about how I wanted my future to look. Instead, at thirty-five, I still wanted so many of the things I wanted at thirty, at twenty-three, at fourteen. I even wanted the same men. I was as afraid to die alone at thirty-five as I was at seventeen. I was as emphatic about my career today as I had been at fourteen.

Suddenly, there were waves of heat slapping my sunken chest, and I was bathed in compassion for the man who was breaking my heart. I wanted the pain to go down easier—for me to place the blame on his broad shoulders—but it wasn't all Garrett's fault. Garrett hadn't betrayed me, he had simply grown out of the dreams I was still clinging to. I finally understood how Blink-182 could speak to someone's heart

Well I guess this is growing up.

"Love is hard," I whispered.

"It fucking blows," Summer said, doubling down as she pulled her hand from my grip and angrily wiped tears away from her eyes.

I sat back down next to Summer, and I felt her hand grip mine. I squeezed back harder as we sat side by side, the whisky warm in our bellies, watching the fire burn the logs down to ashes. I studied my best friend—wet, puffy, red eyes atop her strong oval face. She was that beautiful Bob Seger song. Summer was always my rock. She didn't have the patience or emotional capacity to crumple and overanalyze every little thing. She could pull back from my tornado of confusion and boil it down to one or two truths—a straight shooter. I sent my arrow on an emotional roller-coaster—twisting into dark woods, busting through a couple wrong targets, until finally finding the bull's-eye—and even then, I questioned the bull's-eye. Summer's jaw was clenched with her chin pointed to the sky—a rock among her own personal rubble. I appreciated how intense I was about my feelings, but I envied what it must be like on the other side—the ability to close one's eyes at night and not hear sirens running through your head.

I glanced down to my brightening phone, my heart jumping as Asher's name flashed upon the lock screen. Apparently, amid all the breaking, there was still room for butterflies to come alive inside my chest—flutters for another man. If only I were a simpler person.

Summer watched the corner of my mouth turn upward. She let out a slow smirk and snatched the phone from my fingers before I could read the text.

"Sure. Take my phone," I said flatly, with my empty palm open in the air. "Thanks so much, I will."

I glared at Summer as she entered in my passcode, shaking my head, thankful that at the very least, my complicated life could cheer hers up.

"What do you have to say for yourself, Mister Jawline?" Summer asked, before reading out Asher's text message aloud.

> Hope the engagement party is a blast. So, it turns out I'm the only person left in Manhattan this weekend, and I'm getting restless over here.

"I bet you are . . . *restless* to put your dick inside my best friend."
"Summer, gross."
"What?" She shrugged with a smirk, then continued reading Asher's text.

> I'm going to be That Person and helicopter it over to EH tomorrow—my friend Mike is in Ibiza, so I'll be staying at his place on Lily Pond. If you have a free afternoon, any chance you want to drink on lawn chairs and listen to nineties music?

I set a new piece of firewood into the flames, my brows crossed.

"For such a popular guy, he seems really lonely—right?" I asked. "You'd think he'd have a million friends in New York City."

"Babe, Asher Reyes isn't lonely, he just wants to spend all his free time with you."

I paused, oddly delighted by the thought. My delight found my stomach as I saw Summer typing on my phone. Before I could snatch my cell out of her speedy hands, she hurled it back into my lap like a hot potato. I looked down daringly, terrified to see what kind of damage she had done.

Me: Hell yes.

I swatted at her elbow. "SUMMER," I yelled.

"Yeah?"

"Was the 'hell' necessary?"

"Hell yes."

"I don't think heartbreak, alcohol, hot sun, and Asher Reyes are a safe combo."

"I really do. I think you should be half-naked, tipsy, and sweaty all over his body."

"My manager said—"

"Apologize later. Look, I know what she's trying to do, and I get it. But it's overkill. If you were starring in the movie, that would be one thing—but you're not. You're the brains behind the music. People are going to form an opinion about you no matter what, and the music is going to be incredible, so by that point, it won't matter. Plus, I have an *itty-bitty* Marysia bikini that's going to look killer on you."

"Stop trying to persuade me with fashion."

"Stop pretending you're not that easy."

"What color?" I asked, through gritted teeth.

"Indigo."

Fuck. That was my color. It made me feel less pale—and brought out the best in my cool skin tone, light eyes, and dark brown hair.

I screeched my chair back and stood up, grabbing my guitar and holding my whisky tight to my chest.

"Goddamnit, show it to me."

Summer grinned and snatched her drink, walking tall toward her glowing, modern ranch home yards away. I followed Summer toward the back door, glancing over my shoulder to take in the dying fire. The smoke bloomed upward, dulling the crisp stars in my eyes. One dream was a pile of ashes at my feet. But here I stood, still eager to play with fire.

THIRTY-FIVE

I HAD SEEN IT ALL as a cater waiter working summers in the Hamptons, but I had never made it past the gates of a Lily Pond mansion. Lily Pond Lane was one of the most exclusive streets in the Hamptons, and I gawked behind the wheel of Summer's car, a classic diesel Mercedes, taking in the sun pouring down on Martha Stewart's quiet street. I soared past the towering beech trees, with oceanfront estates on one side of the street and a variety of privacy hedges along the other.

Mike Emblem was a beloved action movie star who happened to be Asher's best friend, and who also happened to own a home on Lily Pond. I squinted at the address on a mailbox in front of two thick rows of perfect green hedges sandwiching a stark-white privacy gate. A moment later, the gates opened, and I had access to a three-story, classic shingle-style cottage.

I hopped out of the car and adjusted my high-waisted jean shorts, feeling smaller than usual against the towering oceanfront home. It was one thing to work inside a home like this, it was another thing to pretend like I belonged here. I squinted to read a note taped to the doorbell, written with Asher's horrible handwriting, which was still barely legible all these years later.

"Come straight on through to the pool," the Post-it read.

I creaked open the front door, and fresh ocean air hit my face as I took in the coastal foyer—studying the high ceilings, which were made of thick, white beadboard. The white-on-white home was sprinkled with vibrant blue accents, and straight ahead through open French doors, a turquoise pool glittered back at me. Behind the pool, there was a stretch of dunes, where an ocean casually hung out in the backyard.

I walked past the wraparound deck, and I felt my heart thump wildly as Asher came into view—glued to a thick novel by the pool, looking every bit like the movie star that he was: damp hair brushed to the side of his face; chiseled, olive torso; lime-colored board shorts wet against his thighs.

I swallowed hard to keep from tugging his body onto mine, and then I cleared my throat, making my presence known. Asher met my eyes and took off his sunglasses as I waved and walked toward him. He set his book down and stood up so that I could fold right into his open arms.

"Hi," he said into the curve of my neck.

I felt every muscle in his body constrict around me as he hugged me tight. He smelled like an intoxicating swirl of nostalgia, bringing me back to summer camp. Wildflowers, sunblock, and young love.

We held each other's grins for a moment too long, making the tips of my ears burn. I tugged a bottle of cold rosé out of my tote bag and thrust it in front of his mouth to keep from falling onto his lips.

"I want you to do something before we drink," he said, trying to hold back a grin.

I stared back confusedly as his smile widened—a full smile—one I almost never saw from him.

Before I could say a word, Asher's hand gripped mine, leading me past the French doors, down a flight of stairs, landing us in the chilly basement. We walked past the home gym and through the doors of an enormous, high-end recording studio.

"This is Fin Bex," Asher said, his arm stretched out toward the boyishly handsome man sitting behind the audio mixer. "He's co-producing *On the Other Side*'s soundtrack."

"I know who he is," I said, stunned.

Fin flashed an energetic grin in my direction and reached out to shake my limp fingers.

"Hi," he said.

I tried to pick my jaw up off the floor as I shook hands with one of the biggest music producers in the business. Fin Bex was a small-town kid from Pennsylvania who was now crushing it in his late twenties. He talked a mile a minute and produced number one hit after hit, also at a mile a minute. I'd known that Fin was producing the soundtrack, but I didn't know I would actually be coming face-to-face with him. It would have a been a dream, but in my dream, I wasn't wearing a see-through tank top with a barely-there scalloped bikini underneath, leaving significant side-boob sticking out.

Fin pointed to the other side of the glass where, inside the isolation vocal room, a cool-as-fuck woman with a tattoo sleeve and pink hair adjusted the cord on the microphone.

"And that's my sound engineer, Lila Corr."

I knew her name as well. These were my celebrities: the people I dreamed about working beside.

I tried to keep my attention on Fin, but I had no control. My eyes drifted to the empty, little black stool next to Fin, like a moth finding its flame. My heart began to race, and the room was suddenly thick, muffled, and hot. The walls were closing in around me, until I felt a hand on my shoulder. Asher led my body out of the studio, as I blinked back white spots clouding my vision.

Asher crouched in front of me in the basement hallway, with his eyes narrowed on my face.

"Can I get you some water? Are you okay?"

I opened my mouth to say I was fine, but no words escaped. My eyes shifted down to his gentle hand on my arm.

"I'm sorry," he said. "I should have asked you beforehand. I thought this would be a cool surprise—but now I'm thinking: *not* actually a cool surprise."

I slowly looked up at Asher, as he attempted a weak smile. It was plain as day that he felt horribly responsible for something he was not actually responsible for. He was the most sensitive human that I'd ever encountered, which was saying something, considering I overanalyzed every human interaction.

I was relieved to feel words escaping my throat. "This isn't your fault," I cracked. "It's just—it caught me off guard, is all. I—I don't have my guitar, or my notebook," I stammered, searching for an escape route.

"We were just going to lay down your vocals. I printed out the lyrics and notes for 'Joyride,'" he said. "I actually wanted to surprise you. We decided you would sing it for the end credits on the film."

I stared at him, blinking rapidly.

"Me? Not to be recorded over?"

"You. *Just* you," he said with a warm smile, which faded as he took in my expression. I was swallowing hard, trying to clear the terror boiling up to my throat. He crouched lower to my eye level with his hand still on my arm. "But none of that's relevant. We don't have to do this today."

The AC grate was below my feet, blasting air into my lungs, cooling my insides. I found my mouth moving, letting out an exhale of words as his hand ran up and down my arm, softly.

"I had a bad experience once, in a recording booth."

I could taste bile in my throat, reliving something horrible just by hinting at it. Asher's face pinched together, and I watched his chest rise and fall, right in front of me. He placed his other hand gently on my arm and turned his head to both sides of my face, so he could try and understand what I was saying. After a moment, he seemed to understand, because his eyes darkened and his neck tightened.

"Go back upstairs and lie by the pool, and I'll be there to join you in two minutes. And we'll forget all about this."

I nodded and took a step back from him, slowly walking toward the steps, my head heavy. I stopped at the base of the curved banister, glancing back at Asher. He smiled quickly at me, a reassuring smile, but I could tell there was a soft pain behind his eyes—and I knew what kept the pain there—even when there was pure bliss, there would always be sadness. All at once, I didn't know how to walk upstairs with nausea weighing me down. Even more, there was an adrenaline running through my veins, pumping blood and thumping my chest against my ribs—a reminder that I was alive. I couldn't do it anymore—I couldn't let my past keep me from opportunities that would open the doors to my future. I needed to rise out of the ashes instead of letting them darken my insides. All of them.

"No," I blurted, standing taller in my own skin, walking toward Asher. "I'm going to lay that song down. Today."

He arched his eyebrows up, staring wide-eyed into my face. He waited for a moment, as if halting to make sure that the terror inside me had been replaced with fire.

"Okay."

"I'm going to need a cup of boiling water, a cup of warm salt water, and about thirty minutes to warm up."

Asher put his hand behind his back and bowed his head down to me with a silly grin.

"At your service, my lady," he said in a flawless British accent.

I charged up the staircase.

"Where are you going?" he asked.

"To grab the Throat Coat tea bag from my purse."

Thankfully, I was used to singing at the last minute. I had a routine that I refused to break—no matter what. While I had consumed an excessive amount of alcohol yesterday, I made sure to cap off the night with a liter of water, and saltwater spray in my nostrils. Nothing kills high notes like dehydration, and water lubricates the vocal cords. I didn't have a raspy voice, so I couldn't have an off-day or hide behind a hoarse howl.

Thirty minutes later, after gargling a mug of warm salt water, I stepped back into the dimly lit studio. I made my way past Asher, who sat reading a script on a navy tufted sofa in the back of the room. In front of him, Fin twisted chords and pressed button after button on the audio mixer, as if he were a pilot about to take flight.

The sound tech, Lila, followed me into the vocal booth as I approached the microphone. For the first time, I really took in the room. I was thankful that it didn't have a personality—the studio felt unlived in, which meant that I could create my own memories here without old ones tugging me back to another place. There were no platinum or gold records cascading down the wall. The walls were papered in a black Gucci fabric, with wildly expensive guitars hung across them, and that was it.

I adjusted the vocal mic and placed the large headphones on my ears. After a few warm-ups, from behind the sound board, Fin nodded at me. I swallowed hard, my eyes wandering to the stool next to Fin, which thankfully, Lila now occupied. Asher grinned at me from the couch, leaning forward with his elbows on his knees.

"Joyride" left my lips in a hurry. It was as if I needed to get the song off my chest before a terror crept up my lungs and strangled my throat.

The terror never came. In its place was a rush of adrenaline. "Joyride" felt like letting go, like drifting along with the moody bridge as gravity seemed to leave my chest. It usually felt this way when music came out of my mouth, like my soul was skydiving. But today it also felt like my insides were mending, my voice reminding me that it existed to tell stories other people couldn't tell, in a way other people could never tell them. By the time the song ended, my white knuckles held the microphone shaft and my limitless smile exhaled over the windscreen.

I finished the song and looked up, seeing three wide grins shining back at me. Fin pointed at his ears, indicating that I take off my headphones.

"Fucking beautiful," Fin said. "Let's do it again, but this time, sing it like the world is ending, but you have plenty of time before it ends."

"So, slower and sadder?" I asked.

"Exactly. And can I hear a key change on the bridge? On *'We've got scars we can't leave behind.'*"

"We've got scars we can't leave behind," I sang, in a minor chord.

"Fuck yeah, but bring down the tempo—painfully slow."

I sang it back to him slower.

Fin whipped his head behind his back to meet Asher's eyes, both of them trading wide smiles before Fin's attention came back to me. He arched his body up from the stool and leaned over the board, beaming in my direction.

"You know your voice isn't fair to other voices, right? 'Cause if you don't know it, you should."

I chewed the insides of my reddening cheeks, my ego thumping. Fin sat back down and raised his finger up to the air, frenetic energy running through his body.

"Let's fucking go," he said.

And I fucking went.

It's a joyride
And it feels like home
Flying down this open road
I remove the safety belt wrapped around my seat
If we go crashing
Let the blow break me

THIRTY-FIVE

I DIDN'T WALK OUT OF the recording studio, I floated. I was high on a warm glow that always seemed to slip through my fingers: success. But something about this time felt different—like I could hold on to this feeling for a while. "Joyride" was going to the producers, the studio, and the lead actress so she could get a feel for the film's sound—and it was fucking perfect—and it would play at the end of the movie with my voice and no one else's.

After Fin and Lila left, I followed Asher out to the pool. I couldn't hide my giddy smile, and he couldn't hide the way he was looking at me. I caught his eye as we walked down the slate stairs, a raised eyebrow behind his golden shades, pointed in my direction as the sun beat down upon our bodies.

Asher took a seat on a lawn chair and patted toward the empty one next to him, indicating that I join him. My skin felt like it was on fire, and the last thing I wanted to do was sit still. I hesitated, then with eyes locked on him, I tugged the tank top off my chest, and stepped out of my shorts. I stood above Asher in the scalloped bikini, as he gazed openly at me, his mouth slightly parted. I tossed my clothes playfully toward his chest, and he caught them with a wide smirk. My insides were screaming, and the calm, turquoise pool below me felt like much too placid a place for the flames in my chest to land. And so, I turned my back on pleasant waters, and I ran.

Sandy wind hit my cheeks as I flew past the shaky wooden slats that bridged the mansion with Georgica Beach. I let the stretch of dunes tickle my arms, with a building heat in my chest and a widening grin on my face. My toes found hot sand, and I sprinted past the quiet shoreline. I let out a loud shriek as I slammed my pale shoulder into a booming wave.

I plunged into the icy ocean, letting it cool me from head to toe. I shot up out of the water, cold waves splintering around my skin. It was a rush of adrenaline that only made my heart beat faster. I whipped my head to the shoreline as the waves crashed against my back. Asher stood with his arms crossed on the shore, staring at me for a moment. He walked forward, planting his bare feet where the ocean foamed at the sand.

"THIS"—he shook his head at me, his grin widening—"THIS FEELS FAMILIAR."

That's because it was.

I couldn't help it. Asher Reyes brought out my daring side. He had a way of sprinkling fairy dust all over ordinary objects, cracking my universe wide open with a slow, long stare. He made me feel as though we were trapped inside a wild, hyperbolic, neon wonderland—a place where I had the audacity to get away with anything.

I always jumped in first during those last two summers at camp. We snuck out of our respective cabins and met at the gazebo, finding a soft patch of earth to roll around him. We'd lay with our limbs folded around each other as we took in the stars. The way he spoke about the world filled my mind to the brim. When Asher was midsentence, musing over the philosophical wonders of nature—saying that *one thing* that made me want to drown inside the corners of his brain—I sucked in air and stood up, springing away from him, bare feet on wet grass, running faster and faster, leaving my muse sprinting on my heels. I dove off the salty dock, fully clothed, headfirst into the warm moonlit water, and I waited for him to join me. It was a game of cat and mouse. Night after night.

Here I was eighteen years later, waist-deep in water, gazing up at Asher, my wide green eyes unblinking. The smile faded from his lips as he took his shirt off, tossed it forcefully behind his back, and walked straight toward me, into the water without flinching.

The waves crashed around his bare torso as he dove headfirst under a wave. Asher stood up right in front of my body, shaking his straight jet-black hair onto my face, like a dog. I playfully pushed him back, letting my hands tingle against his bare, wet skin. I watched the salt water roll down his jawline, his lips, his beating chest.

"The lake was warmer," he said, grinning.

"Wimp."

I splashed his face, and he leaped toward me, folding his arm around my waist, tugging me under a wave with him. We came up for air, laughing, and I edged my shoulder into his.

Suddenly, distant laughter matched ours. We shifted our attention yards ahead to the shoreline, where a little boy—no more than five—ran along the sand, gleefully piloting a whale-shaped kite in his hands. His big eyes were glued to the kite floating in the cloudless blue sky.

"If only we could go back to a time when the best day ever was flying a kite," I said, watching the boy.

"Before the world got its hands on us," Asher said quietly, with sorrow trembling behind the words.

Asher's eyes seemed to have swallowed a dark cloud, and looking at this little boy, on this very day, I knew why.

We stood there shoulder to shoulder, neither of us saying a word as we took in the boy's awed smile. Finally, I felt Asher's eyes on me.

"Hey," Asher said, softly.

I turned to look at him.

"I think—" He stopped, hesitating to continue, as if he didn't want to upset the rush of our bodies side by side in a body of water. "I have a feeling that some part of today wasn't easy for you. I don't *exactly* know why, I mean I can guess, but I'm here for you, if you ever want to talk about it."

I felt a sinking weight in my pounding chest. I wasn't sure if it was the ache of a bad memory, or the fact that a man I had once loved was making me fall in love with him all over again. Maybe it was a little bit of both. My mouth was open as waves thrashed around me. I couldn't find a way to deliver the words. While this afternoon's studio heroics left me buzzing—plucky and brave—some part of my past still felt too delicate for him to hold. I sucked in the salty air as Asher shifted his hard jawline.

"Same," I found myself saying.

"What?" he asked, tilting his head at me in confusion.

"I know what today means for you. I'm here if you want to talk about it."

Asher put his hand over his jaw and flicked his eyes away from mine.

Today was his late brother's birthday. July fourteenth. His brother should be turning thirty-eight. Instead, he was a weight inside Asher's chest. I knew his brother's birthday was the reason Asher had flown to the Hamptons for the weekend. It was the reason Asher had assembled a team in a recording studio on a Sunday. He hated sitting quietly with his own pain on this painful day. Strangely, it was also one of the reasons I was able to sing earlier in the afternoon, when all I wanted to do was crumple to the floor. Asher's brother would be seventeen forever. I was alive with the ability to rise and grow out of my own trauma. I refused to be stuck in a moment when I had a lifetime ahead of me.

After I found out about Asher's brother during our second summer at camp, the July fourteenths that followed went the same way: I didn't dare leave his side until the sun came up. I wondered if this day would be any different.

"You remember? You remembered that today was his . . ." Asher trailed off, wide eyes taking me in.

There was pain and longing stuck in my throat as I opened my mouth.

"Everything about you is impossible to forget," I said.

He tilted his head at me, his body inching closer to mine.

"Do you want to forget?" he asked in a soft voice.

I shook my head.

"Me, either," he said, exhaling with his full body.

He stood above me with ocean water dripping down his parted lips, his arms at his sides, and his palms facing me. I was his, if I wanted. If I wanted to wrap myself around his body, I could. I stared at the shape of my figure reflected in his gold shades: a blue bikini tight against my wet body, long curls dripping water down my chest. I looked like a vintage photograph of myself, like I was alive inside a real dream, with my heart beating outside my chest. The waves broke over and over against our naked spines, but we didn't dare move. I looked down at my shaking fingers—as if I was losing solid ground by not holding on to him. Asher swallowed hard and took the sunglasses off his face. His eyes were somehow both hungry and tender, and I watched them scan every line on my face.

I took a daring step toward him. We stood inches apart, his body shielding me from the incoming waves. I lifted my hand up to his cheek and ran my trembling finger over the tiny white scar across his chin. Asher's eyes closed at my touch, with his mouth parting. I settled my hand around the back of his neck, holding on to warm, familiar, solid ground. I took one step forward, letting my racing chest pound against his. He kept his eyes closed for a moment, as if the wonder of our bodies pressed against each other was too much—as if it had overpowered his ability to activate his other senses.

The air thickened around us as the heat of our mouths exhaled onto each other, lips unmoving. I felt his chest rise against my heaving breasts as he opened his eyes onto mine. His hand moved up the curve of my neck, sending a pulse through my entire body. He knotted his fingers in the back of my wet curls, with eyes on my lips.

All I could do was pull his mouth onto mine. The taste of salt water on our lips disappeared over and under our hot tongues. We held each other tighter and tighter in the cold water, wet limbs throbbing against each other. Asher Reyes lit my shivering body up like fireworks in a rainstorm.

In some ways, it felt a lot like our first kiss. Instead of a dock above the lake, there was an ocean, but the fervor and the romance swirled inside me the same way. Kissing Asher Reyes felt like exhaling sparks from my lungs. It felt a lot like *"I found you."* Except this time, I knew what it felt like to let go.

I didn't want to let go.

THIRTY-FIVE

SOMETIME LATER, MY WET BACK slammed against the tapestried wall of the sunny pool house. The guest bedroom was stark white on cream, with a view of the ocean in front of us. I wanted to mess up the entire place with Asher by my side. He kissed me hard, and I kissed him back harder.

I clenched my hands around Asher's drenched hair, tugging him closer as he throbbed against me. His lips left mine, and I opened my eyes to the ceiling as the warmth of his mouth went around my ear, sending a rush of heat down my spine. His lips found mine again as his fingers etched up my rib cage, stopping at my bikini top. He pulled his mouth off me, kissing the sand on my clavicle, kissing me until his mouth was over the thin fabric separating my breast from his lips. Asher tugged at my nipple through the cold, wet fabric, weakening my knees. I felt his hands untie the bikini behind my back, effortlessly sending it to the floor. Before I could catch my breath, his warm mouth found my breast, and he kissed me down my rib cage, to my hip bone, biting the inside of my thigh as I leaned back against the wall, gripping his hair with trembling hands. He looked up at me, pulling back slightly with his mouth near my bikini line.

"You're shaking," he said.

I admired my legs, which were shivering. All of me was. I wasn't sure how long we had been out in the ocean, but it felt like we had kissed until our mouths were numb—and maybe we had kissed until my body was as well.

He slowly appeared at my face, with his hands on either side of my arms—cold wet skin against cold wet skin.

"Come here," he said, against my chapped lips.

I exhaled as he clasped his fingers in mine and led my body to a stone fireplace in the corner of the bedroom. I watched him toggle with a smart pad on the wall. Suddenly, I blinked back a roaring fire, which seemed to melt the outside of my cold, wet skin—catching up with my insides. Asher pressed another button, and the thick, blackout shades closed, turning the harsh afternoon light into a midnight.

He ran his two strong hands against my arms, watching me thaw as the fire blazed in his amber eyes. It was the way he looked at me, from every angle, that warmed every blue inch of me. I set my palm on his thumping, wet torso, letting my nails run over the sun-kissed hair on his olive chest. I inched my hand down one side of the deep V line at the base of his stomach, and I kept going until my hand was under his swim trunks. I wrapped my fingers around his dick as he bit his lip, swallowing hard. I let my other hand tug against the elastic, and his eyes didn't leave mine as he stepped out of his suit, with his throbbing dick hard inside my hand, and my naked chest pressed against him. His hand clenched around my waist, and his hot tongue filled up my open mouth.

We both crashed backward, bodies against a new wall: the warm fireplace tile. He grabbed my wrist and pulled my hand off him, pinning both my wrists above my head, holding them against the wall as he kissed me hard. He kept my hands above my body as his tongue found the curve of my neck, inching down around my breast, until he took my breast full into his mouth, with my nipple between his teeth, my body writhing in place. His lips continued downward, finding the fabric of my bikini. The heat of his mouth against my insides sent my throat to the ceiling in a moan, my back arching against the wall, my arms itching to go free. His hand let my wrists go as he dipped his finger inside me. I felt wet and hot against his touch, my heart racing faster. All at once, his fingers left my insides and he used them to pull the bikini bottoms off my body, leaving me fully naked, wet, and panting against the firelight. He kissed the inside of my thigh, and then looked up at me with a grin.

He stood up, kissing my mouth, leaving me hungry for him to go back down on his knees and finish what he had started. Instead, he put his strong hands around my waist and tugged my body upward, into his arms, lifting me and spinning me onto the edge of the bed. Before I could come up for air, he parted my legs with his face, and set his hot tongue inside me. I clenched my nails into the silk sheets, fire inside my body. I arched my neck to dare and look at him. His eyes floated upward to harden onto mine, with his lips between my thighs. He placed his strong hands against my thighs, keeping my trembling body tight against the bed. I tugged my shoulder blades together as wild heat engulfed my insides, until I was exhaling his name breathlessly to the ceiling, with gold spots in my eyes.

I panted, holding my hand over my pounding chest, as if trying to keep it from leaving my body. He softly kissed my pelvic bone, his lips moving all the way up me, over my stomach, my clavicle, my throat— lighting tiny fires against my skin until his mouth landed tenderly on my lips. He pulled his neck back from mine, and his smile came into focus above me. He kissed me again, warm and salty, skin against skin, his dick hard against my leg.

"I'll go get a condom," he said softly into my ear.

I shifted myself up on the bed, watching as Asher's perfect naked body walked away from me like a *Men's Health* cover come to life. I took in the definition on his olive torso, his runner calves, the deep line from his pelvis to his dick, every inch of him bathed in firelight. A moment later, he came back into view from the bathroom, ripping the condom wrapper open with his teeth and putting it on.

His mouth found mine again, his body sending the back of my head onto the soft duvet below me. He parted from my lips, staring down at me for a long, quiet moment. He wiped a curl away from my face, keeping his hand on my cheek. His eyes were soft and wide, as if he knew he was about to dive into a warm, safe place, but he couldn't believe it all the same.

"Hi," he said.

I opened my mouth to say it back, but his body was trembling against mine, so wondrous that I couldn't make a sound. He widened his eyes and took me in. Tears were stuck in my throat, and I felt them sting my eyes.

"Hi," I slowly cracked, as his thumb wiped away a tear falling down the corner of my eye.

I smiled, my chest bursting. I wondered if this moment—this moment right here—was what all the pain and all the heartache had been for. This was the exit off the harsh road—the turn that I had been waiting for: a life with Asher Reyes. He was the other side of trying. Being in his arms made me feel like I didn't have to hope anymore. He was a boomerang, leaving me years ago like a sharp inhale, and coming back to me like an exhale. I could breathe now.

I ran my hands through his wet hair and brought his mouth onto mine, and slowly, I led him inside me.

"Fuck," he said, burying his face into the heat of my neck as he moved over me, back and forth, hard, hot, perfect.

He brought his eyes back onto mine, kissing me tenderly, rolling us both over, so I was on top of him. I grinned. *He always did like me on top.*

"What?" he asked, coyly.

"Glad to see some things never change," I said, raising my eyebrows.

I moved on top of him with ease as his hands tightened against my hips. He sat up suddenly, pressing his mouth against my ear.

"Turn around," he demanded.

He spun me around, his heart racing against my spine. He hugged an arm around my breasts, pulling my spine closer to his chest as he pressed his finger hard against my clit and thrust himself inside me. I felt my breathing quicken.

"Okay, that's new."

I exhaled with eyes to the ceiling fan, until suddenly, I couldn't see anything at all. I felt my body clench hot and wet around his dick, waves pulsing through me, and he tugged me closer to his chest as he came.

I leaned my head back against the curve of his neck. My damp skin against his skin felt like finding the lost piece of a puzzle. It was almost like the last eighteen years had been nothing but a bad dream.

Almost.

37

SEVENTEEN

"My mom is going to murder me," I said with a huge grin.

"Are you *sure* you want to do this?" Asher asked, raising his eyebrow.

My jaw dropped as I shook my head.

"You're chickening out, aren't you? I can't believe I got a fake ID for nothing," I huffed.

Asher looked at me hard, and with the streetlights adding fire to his eyes, he grabbed my hand and pulled me past the doors of the only space alive in this barren strip mall: the tattoo parlor.

This had, not shockingly, been all my plan. The idea of putting art on our bodies came up a few months ago during one of our nightly phone calls. "We should get matching tattoos," I said with a shrug—without honestly thinking it through. It felt like something two people in euphoric love could do—like a promise of forever without a rabbi. I knew he wasn't the type to fold into a dare that would leave a permanent mark—Asher would obviously just laugh on the other end of his new cell phone. Instead, what followed was long silence, his breath in my ear from thousands of miles away. "How about the moon?" he finally said. Then it was my turn to be silent. My eyes widened, a smile curled around my lips, and the idea of sharing a tattoo with my favorite person became all I could think about.

As junior counselors, we had use of the camp car this summer on weekends, and we both requested the same Saturday night off so that we could carry out our innocuous crime. We rode to the tattoo parlor in silence, our hands clasped over the center console, the quiet woods around us making the air feel heavy. The end of camp was nearing, and if one of us brought it up, it'd break us both.

Asher insisted on going first, mostly because he knew how I felt about blood and needles.

"Can I hold your hand?" I asked, sitting on the stool below the tattoo chair, holding his hand before he could even answer.

His eyes were on me the entire time, without a hint of pain, as the buzzing single needle pressed dark ink into the underside of his perfect, hard biceps.

"Why the moon?" asked the tattoo artist, as she set the needle down, the full moon in beautiful black and gray staring at me. It was small, but it felt real, like we could live there.

"I want to be more than the moon on your bones," Asher said, eyes unblinking from mine.

"That's pretty, what's that from?" the tattoo artist asked.

She picked the needle back up and went over a few spots in a lighter gray.

"It's a song I wrote," I said as Asher's hand gripped harder.

A few minutes later, after securing his tattoo in plastic wrap, the tattoo artist tilted her head at her handiwork, then let a slow smile find her lips.

"You're all good, Romeo."

Asher lifted his arm, admiring the moon with a quiet grin.

"Where do you want yours, Juliet?"

I raised my tank top, drawing a small circle over the right side of my rib cage.

"You sure? That's directly over the bone, *and* thin skin—one of the most painful places my needle can go."

Let's set this summer fling in stone
I want to be more than the moon on your bones
'Cause when you wrap your arms around me tight
It's a galaxy come alive at night

Long distance hurt to the bone. That was the whole damn point.

"I want it right here," I said, keeping my finger pressed on my rib cage with my song echoing in my ear, the lyrics ripping me apart.

Asher tilted his head in my direction as my eyes watered like a tidal wave—an ache I'd pressed down the entire week. He leaned forward and gripped both my hands in his.

"What's wrong?"

"I hate this," I cracked, hot tears rolling down my cheeks.

The tattoo artist widened her eyes and pressed her lips together. She tiptoed to the back of the small studio, clearly not wanting to get in the middle of a teenage meltdown.

Asher cupped my wet cheek and pulled my forehead onto his.

"Mags, we have two more nights. Let's not do this until we have to, okay?"

I felt his chin quiver.

"I don't want to do this at all," I whispered.

"Me, either."

The tattoo artist reclaimed her stool, with the purple stencil of the moon in her hand.

"You two done having your *Armageddon* moment, or do you need more time?"

I sucked in tears and traded places with Asher. He squeezed both my hands, knowing my threshold for pain was pitiful.

"No boy is worth crying over," the tattoo artist said, smirking directly into Asher's glassy eyes before turning back to me.

I looked at her softly, with sympathy, studying her hardened edge—an edge that my mother embodied. This tattoo artist had either never met a guy worth crying over, or she'd made sure no guy would ever bring her to her knees again. All I knew: Asher Reyes was worthy of every tear stuck in my throat.

She leaned over my rib cage, placing the stencil paper on my skin and wetting the other side. She pressed down, dried it, then pulled the stencil back, smiling at the placement—a little temporary purple moon that would become gray and black and beautiful. She pointed the needle sadistically in the air.

"Save the crying for what my little friend is about to do to you."

I held the tears inside. My body turned numb, preparing itself for the undertow that would engulf my skin in two days. Asher and I had gotten good at goodbyes, but this one coming felt like a question mark, not an ellipsis.

38

THIRTY-FIVE

THE BACK OF ASHER'S HAND traced my rib, fingers on my tattoo as his legs held my body. I had no idea if it was the middle of night, or the break of dawn. Our skins were salt-soaked and flushed; our bodies tangled up around the silk sheets. My stomach rumbled, a reminder I had burned thousands of calories over and under Asher, and eaten absolutely nothing.

"How do you like your eggs?" Asher asked, with his mouth against my ear.

His beachy hair stood straight up, making him look sillier than he could ever be.

"Sunny-side up," I said against his top lip, as I ran my fingers through his hair.

He kissed me hard and fast and rolled off the bed with a wink.

I studied his gorgeous naked body, bending over a leather Louis Vuitton weekender bag. He pulled cotton briefs out of the bag and tugged them over his toned glutes. I clicked the smart pad next to the bed, finding a button for the blinds. A purple sunrise lit up the room. It was morning.

I grinned like a giddy child, tugging the duvet over my reddening cheeks, as if it was the first time I had seen another person naked.

Hours later, as he walked me to the car to say goodbye, Asher tugged me back to his chest for one last kiss. Our lips parted, and we stood with our foreheads pressed together in front of Summer's car in the front yard.

"So, any chance you don't want to leave?" he asked, smiling.

I want to stay forever.

"I mean, I don't *want* to leave, but my sheet music, my lyrics, my guitar—everything is back in the city." I sighed, hating being rational. "And I don't exactly have a lot of time left to deliver you perfection."

He delicately tucked a stray hair behind my ear. "Fair. I'm going to head back into the city Friday. My co-pro is organizing this thing at his townhome in Brooklyn. A bunch of people who are involved in *On the Other Side* will be there." He tugged me closer to his body. "Come with me? Schmooze, meet some music people? Raini will be in attendance, and it would be nice to put you two in the same room."

I went to say yes, but then I hesitated, hearing my manager's words echoing in my head—a reminder that my career was in Asher's hands. As swiftly as Asher had given me my dreams, he could take them away.

"Are you sure that's a good idea?" I asked.

"What do you mean?"

I shuffled, uncomfortable with the direction this conversation was going—bringing up distrust toward a man I had only ever deeply trusted.

"I don't know if we should be seen together in public . . . or if this is a good idea while we're working together. I just . . ." I trailed off, silenced by the way his brows pressed together.

Asher was visibly stung, and he had every right to feel that way. I had kissed him in the water, I had pulled him closer to me, I had taken off his clothes just as he had taken off mine.

"Well, you really are being managed by the best, aren't you?"

He kicked the gravel below his feet, keeping his eyes on his tennis shoes. I took his hand in mine, and he didn't squeeze my fingers back.

"I have everything to lose here, Asher."

"And what makes you think I don't?" He stared directly into my face, waiting for my answer.

"Asher, you've made it. You're an Oscar winner. You have an entire career to rest your decisions on. I don't. What if we move forward and this doesn't work out, and you . . ."

"And I *what*? And I ruin your career out of spite? *Really?* This movie is going to put you on the map. With or without me in your bed, you're going to make it, Maggie Vine."

"You don't have to phrase it that way."

"How else would you like me to say it?"

He put his hands on either side of my arms, holding my body steady, so that his statement would soak in through my bones, so I would believe it.

"You're going to make it. I'd like to be by your side when you do, but I wouldn't dare stop you from succeeding if I'm not. I don't know how many times I need to tell you this, but a career win for you on this movie is a career win for me. I'm up against the clock, I hired you for a reason, and no one else is taking your place. I know you have the best team, and I know you've heard horror stories, but Mags, I wouldn't take this away from you, not for the world."

I wanted to tell him the truth, that I hadn't just "heard" horror stories. I had lived one. Truthfully, the idea of someone who was so deep inside my soul hurting me—the idea of Asher Reyes turning on me—it felt impossible. I had tried to leave hope in the rearview so I could focus on reality, and it was possible that believing in Asher's good nature was too optimistic, but trusting him felt more realistic than hopeful.

"Mags, I've spent so much time trying to hide what's going on inside. Something about you, about the way you always made me feel, about the way you *make* me feel—it feels like *everything*. In the ocean yesterday— that's the most alive I've been in almost twenty years."

I gazed up at him with wide eyes.

"Why didn't we do this sooner?" I asked, my voice trembling with regret.

Asher's eyes flickered down to his hands as his mouth searched for the words.

"I didn't know if I meant something to you, the way you meant something to me. And then, the cards fell into place on this movie, and it felt like a window I could open."

"And if that movie hadn't come together the way it did, exactly when it did, would we be standing here like this—you and me?"

He looked me dead in the eyes. "I would have found you, because the question mark was killing me," he said without hesitation.

I took a step forward, my hands on his hips, my eyes locked on his.

"You meant something to me. You know you did. And you still do," I said.

He exhaled into a smile and pulled me tightly toward him. I wrapped my arms around his neck as the ocean air swirled around us. There was a silly grin on my cheeks. It felt like letting go and holding on, all at once; like watching every piece fall into place.

SOMETIME LATER, I HELD THE same expression as Summer drove me back toward the city, her usually aggressive driving tempered by her wavering attention—which was half on the road, and half on myself.

"So, did his penis grow since the last time you saw it?" she asked, as we passed by a vegetable stand.

"*Summer.*"

"What? My boobs didn't stop growing until I was twenty-one. How am I to know if penises work the same way?"

"His penis was great then, and it's just as great now."

"Boo, you're no fun. I want the dirty deets."

I shifted in my seat, my vagina pounding and sore underneath me, a reminder of all of last night's heroics. Prior to that night, I hadn't had sex in four months. Clearly, it was advantageous to have gone this hard, but baby steps weren't my forte.

"Okay, maybe he was a little thicker," I offered.

Summer made a vomit motion with her mouth, and I slapped her arm as her shit-eating grin grew into a laugh.

"I hate you," I said.

"I know, I'm the best. Did you two retrosexuals talk about what all this means?"

I stared out the blurry windows, watching the cornfields fly by as the cloudless afternoon sky beamed down. The answer was not a yes, and not a no. I hoped that we didn't feel the need to define it, because it was clear as day that it meant a lot to us both. We were the kind of kids who said "I love you" to each other before we gave ourselves a label. We believed in big feelings, we let our hearts guide us, and I was certain this time was no different.

"Sort of. I think it means something kind of . . . big."

"*Big* like his penis? How big?"

Summer made a gesture with her fingers, and I slapped her wrist. She put her hand back onto the steering wheel with a squeal.

"I love this," she said.

"You have too much serotonin up there right now, it's unsettling," I said.

Summer grinned as I felt my phone vibrate. We both looked down, and instantly, Garrett's name on my lock screen sucked the buzzy air out of the car. I pressed ignore and slumped in my seat, resentment brewing inside me.

"How do men just *know*?" I asked, bitterly.

"What do you mean?"

"They just *know*. Men know when you're on the verge of moving on, and they swoop in to remind you that they still exist. They have a 'she's fucking someone else and happy' sixth sense."

"Come be a lesbian. We stay friends with our exes, like one big happy passive-aggressive family."

"Tempting."

I felt my insides darken as I stared out the window, watching the horse fields pass me by. Garrett's name was a brushstroke of black paint on my glowing heart, and I hated that I had so little control over his effect on me.

"Garrett who?" Summer sang, trying to brighten my face back to its happy place. "By the way, you can stay with me the rest of the week, if you want," she added.

Summer kept her eyes ahead and nonchalantly strummed her fingers on the steering wheel. I knew what she was doing, and she *knew* I knew. She was stalling. Summer wanted me to stay in her condo for another week so that I could be a buffer for her and Valeria's soon-to-be complicated future. She was desperate for an excuse to keep from having The Conversation with her wife.

"When is Valeria back?" I asked cautiously.

Summer tensed. "Tomorrow afternoon."

"I should probably get out of your hair tonight."

I could only hope that the paparazzi had grown tired of not seeing me at my front stoop.

"Are you going to talk to Valeria about—"

"I don't know," Summer said, answering my question before it could fully leave my lips. She let out a labored exhale as our car slowed, entering a traffic pileup on 27. "I don't know . . ." she repeated.

Just weeks ago, I had envied every part of Summer's life. It was effortless and shiny, with a world of opportunity at her oval fingertips. And now, she was driving straight into confusion and heartache, maybe even into a dead end. I inhaled the scent of Asher's lavender pomade on my shirt, as if it was my finish line. My body was fighting like hell to make the green light ahead, while Garrett was tugging me backward. I had let Asher kiss Garrett's heartache off my body, but it wasn't an instant cure.

My entire life, the *what-ifs* never disappeared. What if Asher Reyes and I had never broken up? What if Garrett Scholl and I had kissed the night of my twenty-fourth birthday? What if Cole Wyan hadn't been at my show at the Bowery Electric five years ago? *What if . . . ?*

A lengthy honk interrupted my ode to the road not traveled. Summer released her hand from the horn and flipped off the BMW merging into our lane. I grinned, relieved to have some semblance of normalcy back inside our vehicle.

"You got a text," Summer said, eyeing my brightening phone sitting on the console between us.

I held my breath, bracing for the worst as I peered down toward my phone like it was a horror movie. I exhaled relief, seeing it was a text from Asher.

Not NOT thinking about you xx.

My heart fluttered and a silly smile broke across my face. The finish line was coming into view. I could live without the object in the rearview. Not just live without—I could soar without it. For the first time in so long, the *what is* was better than the *what-if.*

THIRTY-FIVE

I HID BEHIND A CONSTRUCTION pole, my eyes scanning the area around my tiny, charming, five-story walk-up. As far as I could tell, there wasn't one paparazzo in sight, but just in case, I sprinted toward the building like I was running to rescue someone from a fire.

I spent the entire week back in my apartment, watching the sun rise and fall as I sped to finish the rest of the tracks for the movie. By Thursday night, I hated both the final song *and* the ending of the movie, and I knew exactly why I'd turned on my heroine—my heart was just too delicate to unpack it. Asher stayed patient with me on FaceTime—and I think he could tell I was losing it, as I pushed back on his character arcs and creative choices, something no one should ever do to a writer/director who has a studio-locked script. My fingers were swollen and nearly bleeding from the guitar strings, and my mind felt the same way—inflamed from the music and lyrics swirling around it.

"You've lost perspective," Asher said over FaceTime.

He wasn't wrong. I had gone from championing our movie's protagonist, Yael, to going to war with her decisions. Yael longed to move planets for a man who wouldn't commit one crime to be with her. She wanted to turn her life upside down for someone who was too afraid to meet her in the middle. Heartbreak historically fueled my art. Garrett almost fucking me at his own engagement party should have birthed some of my best lyrics. Instead, it had stifled me. I built a panic room inside my brain, where only Maggie Vine and *good vibes!* were allowed to exist inside the padded walls. To cling on to a bright future with Asher, I couldn't muse over the moment where a taken man's body trembled hard against me as fireworks lit up the night. But I was holding a brushstroke, being paid to use someone else's color palette. It was my job to paint hopeful bright hues for a future I didn't believe in. *Not everyone ends up with their Garrett.* Giving Yael that kind of happily ever after required me to grieve one of my ugliest endings. Yael was supposed to end up with this man, *her* Garrett. He eventually becomes worthy of her plight, and the movie's climax made complete sense the first time I read the script. I even ugly cried, clutching my chest. But rereading the script after the engagement party, I hated Yael for clinging to hope—I likened it to worshiping a false God.

I sat on my bed tugging cold sesame noodles out of the to-go container, shoving them into my mouth, and washing them down with room-temperature coffee while I sneered, listening to my voice sing the final song back to me on my phone. Suddenly, I heard a knock at my door. I furrowed my brows, twisted my hair into a messy topknot, and hopped off the tiny bed, edging my body past the gap between the bookshelf of records and the bed frame. I opened the door and nearly choked on the sesame peanut noodles in my mouth.

Asher stood in my doorway looking like a goddamn movie poster. He had the audacity to lean on one side of the doorframe, tucking his aviators into his fitted V-neck.

"Hey there," he said.

My heavy eyes blinked him into focus, not 100 percent certain if he was a mirage—a combination of my lack of sleep and caffeine consumption—or if this beautiful man standing in front of me was, in fact, real.

He was real, and I was a *real* hot mess. I quickly wiped sesame paste off the corners of my lips, horrified as I scanned the messy dishes piled up in the sink.

"I—I thought you weren't due back until tomorrow," I said.

He fought a grin, watching as I non-stealthily grabbed a stray bra from the floor and tucked it under the messy duvet.

"I've come to save you from yourself."

I crossed my arms over my oversized wine-stained T-shirt. "Is that so?" I asked, playfully.

"I'm worried that if I let another day go by, you'll declare that you don't know how to write music anymore. I've been where you are right now: too deep into the material. What you need is to get the heck out of your bubble."

I smiled for a long moment, taking in his soft smile, his perfect cheekbones.

"Are you going to kiss me, or what?" I asked.

Asher raised his eyebrows and the corners of his lips, and then filled my grinning mouth with his tongue, the taste of fresh peppermint thankfully overpowering the taste of day-old Chinese food. We spun together onto the bed, our mouths barely parting as our shoulders hit the mattress. All at once, I felt something cold and wet on my cheek. I lifted my hand to my face, finding half of my hair swimming in a bed of sesame noodles.

"Fuuuck," I groaned, pulling a handful of noodles out of my hair.

I turned to frown pitifully at Asher. He picked a noodle off my cheek and stood up, offering two hands out to me. Begrudgingly, I let him tug me upward. Asher stepped back with a grin and took his shirt off. Then his jeans. Then his briefs. Naked, he walked right into my bathroom. I craned my neck to see him turn on the shower.

"You coming, or what?" he asked.

AN HOUR LATER, I GOT dressed, letting my beachy waves air-dry and my naturally flushed face count as makeup. Asher told me to bring my guitar and my writing notebook, and so with both those in hand, I curved my neck out of the town car as we rolled up to a gate at Teterboro. Asher rattled off a tail number into the call box, and a minute later, I was ascending the stairs of a sleek private jet.

A bubbly flight attendant handed Asher and me cold glasses of champagne as we sat alone, side by side in a plane meant for eight humans. I studied the light taupe leather seats and cream-colored wood accents, with Hermès blankets on the backs of each seat. For a moment, I tried to keep my jaw attached to my cheeks—to act like I'd been there before—but I had never been *here*. I gave way to reveling in fuck-you money, my mouth open to the thick fog on the floor (water vapor, caused by the humid outside air mixing with the cool AC). The jet door closed, and after flashing our IDs at our two pilots, we took off. I gaped at Asher, and he grinned back with a sly smile.

"Flight time to PDK is one hour and fifty-nine minutes," said the flight attendant, as she handed us warm lavender towelettes for our hands.

I turned to Asher and leaned into his ear. "*What* is PDK? And *what* is happening?"

"Peachtree-Dekalb. Atlanta," Asher answered.

"Atlanta?"

I had never been to Atlanta. And as far as I knew, Asher had little ties to the Peach State. I couldn't wrap my mind around how one minute I was eating stale noodles in my hot studio apartment, and the next minute I was learning about the curious mist coming up from the floor on a private jet. My usual air travel experiences involved a thorough pat-down from an unamused TSA agent, sharing space with the worst of the worst on a plane: a screaming child with a newly diagnosed ear infection, a man who didn't understand that the armrests belonged to the middle seat holder, people who thought that taking off their shoes in public was acceptable, and That Guy who decided to belly laugh to his favorite episode of *The Office* without headphones on.

This was the opposite. The flight attendant unclasped a wood table in front of us, and suddenly, a charcuterie board, chips, guacamole, and a fruit plate was in front of me. I widened my eyes on Asher as he offered me a chocolate-covered strawberry with his hand outstretched to my mouth. I took a bite without blinking.

"How does one go back from all this?" I asked around a mouthful.

"The goal is not to."

"So, keep making enough smart decisions so that dropping twenty-K on a two-hour flight is just another casual Thursday?"

He took my hand and pulled it toward his mouth, biting my knuckle playfully.

"It's cute that you think this flight is twenty-K."

I nearly choked on the thought of this costing as much as my yearly rent.

"I don't want to know," I said.

"You really don't."

The golden sun swooped in through the windows, and I looked past Asher, leaning forward to watch the sun set along the purple sky and the wing. He put his hand on my cheek, and tilted my face to his, staring at me. His eyes seemed to swallow up the color of the setting sun, and it was as if I could look at him and see a world full of golden light—the kind of world you could only dream of. He grinned and leaned forward to kiss me. The warmth of his mouth on mine melted the sweet chocolate against both of our gums.

I pulled back and stood up.

"Where are you going?" he asked.

I grabbed his hand and tugged him away from his seat.

"*We* are going to induct *me* into the Mile High Club."

He shook his head at me with a grin as I pulled him toward the bathroom door.

"God, you're romantic," he said with a smirk.

A couple hours later, Asher pulled a hat down over his eyeline and ushered me past a dark alleyway behind the BeltLine, which reminded me a lot of the Highline. Asher had my guitar slung around his back, for some reason he'd said I "had to" bring it. I could see a walkable stretch of bars and restaurants come into view, just as a tall older gentleman met us at a side door in the alley and led us through a modern, neon-lit lobby.

"Welcome to Illuminarium," Asher said.

We entered a giant room with not one right angle. The white walls were curved, and there was a vast amount of state-of-the-art projectors beaming down on us from the ceiling. Asher and the man exchanged pleasantries, then the man left. Suddenly, Asher and I were alone in a room meant for a couple hundred people. The lights dimmed, and my heart pounded against the bleak darkness. I felt Asher's elbow brush against mine as the projectors above lit up. I spun in a circle, seeing video footage of outer space towering around me. It was as if someone had pressed play on a trip to the moon, inside my brain.

"Look down," Asher said, smiling.

I glanced down to my sneakers, which were now walking on the rocky surface of the moon. I dared to take one step forward, and my heart fluttered, seeing that I was kicking up moondust as I walked. I could feel a rumble against my heels—optics coming from the floor. It was virtual reality without the glasses.

"Welcome to space," Asher said, with arms outstretched as the galaxy shifted in front of us.

I took in the atmosphere around me, as if I were really there.

"What is this place?"

"I thought you'd have an easier time writing about a woman lost in the Milky Way if I could take you there."

I sat down on a seat in the middle of the room, letting my ears take in an empty but loud sound—what it was like to float through the stars. I could feel it in my chest. Asher handed me my guitar.

"Play it for me," he said.

"'Bonnie and Clyde'?" I asked, referring to the song that had given me the most trouble, the song that would follow the All Is Lost moment of the film. The lyrics were supposed to be heartbreaking but hopeful. Instead, they were clawing for the shore in moments of anger.

I studied Saturn, her rings floating in front of me, and I kept my eyes on her lonely planet with my fingers on the G chord.

I grew up looking down
Held my hands against my ears, silencing siren sounds
I flew out the screaming back door every time
Hugged my shoulders until I found your street
Said I was just walking by
But you knew to hold me till I cried

Now I watch you throw hope to the wolves
You shrug as they rip the dream of us apart
Why should our finale have a heart
Go ahead, burn me at the stake
Say words better left unsaid
Until the ashes of our maybes become my bed

I left the sirens behind
Ran past your street without stopping for our goodbye
Didn't slow down until my skin was bathed in bright hues
Sandy shores at my feet, feeling golden and blue
I didn't miss running
I missed having someone to run to

Now I watch you throw hope to the wolves
You shrug as they rip the dream of us apart
Why should our finale have a heart
Go ahead, burn me at the stake
Say words better left unsaid
Until the ashes of our maybes become my bed

You blew through my door like I was your partner in crime
The Bonnie to your Clyde
I told you I was taking flight
Your lips didn't seem to mind
But you weren't the type to let me drive
Don't save the passenger seat for Clyde
To the moon and back, what a lie

You were never the wind beneath me
You were never my alibi
You were just someone to run to
I built my own wings when I was five
Watch me leave the ashes of our maybes behind

I finished the song and set my eyes on Asher. A million stars floated behind the smirk on his face.

"So, this is supposed to be the moment in the movie where she regrets the way they left things—not where she's livid at him for letting her go," he said.

"But she *should* be livid. She started a new life, he had the balls to show up at her door and sleep with her, and then he decided that he couldn't be a part of her journey."

"Sure, but it's circumstance. Neither are really at fault here, and you're putting all the blame on his shoulders. And if *he's* not likeable, we won't root for *them*."

I scrunched up my face. Asher exhaled and walked behind me, turning my shoulders to another wall. It was a jet-black sky, with the moon slowly coming into focus. He kept his hands on my shoulders.

"Breathe in," he said.

I inhaled. The room smelled like gunpowder, like moondust. Somehow, they had piped in outer space through the HVAC unit.

"Now, keep your eyes fixed ahead."

I drew in the blurry moon as it came into focus, dead volcanoes and craters swirling into view. I felt the heat of Asher's mouth on my ear as his chin rested on my neck, bringing the stars on the wall under my skin. He pointed to the moon, and I knew exactly what would follow. He was going to paint a picture for me. He'd done it so many times before, staring up at the sky with me during those Connecticut summers, making up stories about wild people who lived in the clouds.

"Okay, you're Yael. Now, the only person who understands you? He can't join you up here. It's lonely, dark, new, and getting here was the most important moment of your life—which is complicated, because you can't enjoy it the way you want to. *Yes,* he threw hope to the wolves, but maybe you did, too. You chose this life. You could have stayed with two feet planted on earth and had a nice life with that guy, but this is the first time in your existence where you've been the wind beneath your own wings, right? And we can keep some of the early verses, but let's be fair here, and let's hold on to hope for these two crazy kids. Sometimes circumstances change. Sometimes people make big sacrifices. And sometimes"—he tugged me closer to his chest, the warmth of his heart fluttering against my back—"sometimes, lovers follow through with the promises they made," he whispered into my ear.

I wanted to turn around and kiss him, and I wanted to hold Garrett at the same time. The last thing this moment needed was my boundless mind floating back and forth between these two men. His words seemed to wrap Garrett inside a blanket of possibilities. I preferred the unrequited *what-if* to stay safely behind heavy doors—inside the dark, devastating corners of my mind. I needed only Asher to occupy the warm, golden parts inside me. A sparkly swirl of those two men made me feel like I was walking into a sunlit room, where Asher and Garrett were seated at two separate tables, both of them holding a chair out toward me, expectantly.

I had always embraced my emotional state with such vigor that it was absolutely impossible to separate my heartache from my lyrics. My songs were specifically autobiographical, which was never problematic because no one had paid me to write someone else's story. It wasn't that I was fighting artistic growth with the stubbornness of a child, it was that I didn't know how to embrace hope for a hopeless man after Garrett had put his *loving you makes me hate myself* card on the table. I needed to untangle the corners of my mind so I could dive into the stars with my palms outstretched and my eyes closed. If anyone could get me there, it was the man whose warm arms were wrapped around mine.

Asher tilted his face, just a few inches from me as he watched my expression tighten to concern.

"Mags, think of this as a privilege—a privilege to walk a mile in someone else's shoes. We're all built different. We don't feel the same. I remember the struggle I went through when I started acting, how I was terrified that if I felt loss, I would step out of a role and feel like I was losing my brother all over again. Sometimes it felt that way, but mostly, it felt incredible to have that gift—to be able to step into other shoes. I know you have it. I see the way you look at the world. It's going to be uncomfortable, but if it isn't uncomfortable, then you're not doing it right."

"Kind of not fair to give an Oscar-winning actor the opportunity to change my mind."

He smirked at me.

"But it worked," I added, squeezing his hand in mine.

I stared past Asher at the moondust, studying the expansive, chalky craters. Making it in this industry felt like walking on the moon. Impossible, otherworldly, floating, lonely, something you couldn't explain to anyone else. And getting there without anyone in the passenger seat sure seemed like a hollow victory—one I didn't want to embrace. I stood up and walked, with him a few yards behind me. I watched my feet create moondust on the floor, my throat humming the shifting chorus as I approached Saturn, then Jupiter. The loneliness and the majesty of it all swirled around inside me, until hope for the hopeless was a fully formed chorus—until I could find a silver lining without it being about Garrett. I roamed the room until I was able to become Yael. I felt my shoulders drop as I floated on, and I let the stars in front of me splinter back into my soul—piercing and uncomfortable at first, but then warm and familiar.

Sitting down at a far bench that was splattered with a projection of a million stars, I furiously typed lyrics into my Notes app.

Asher peered down at me as I finished writing the chorus. I grabbed my guitar and gazed up at him, and then, with good old-fashioned hope inside my soul, I sang Asher the new chorus. It looked golden and achingly shiny—it tasted like Pop Rocks, but with a bitter sour landing on my gums—an explosion of wild energy that needed a palate cleanser.

We threw hope to the fire and now I'm floating past Mars
I should know better, but I don't see no harm
The ashes of our maybes will keep me warm
Floating through Saturn remembering you tangled in my bed
A time before we said words better left unsaid
I float through Jupiter but I still want the moon
I should know better
But darling, it'll always be you

I exhaled the final note as if I had untangled the last clue of an escape room—with relief and pride.

"You made that look easy," Asher said, shaking his head with an awed grin on his face.

I stood up and slung my guitar around my back, taking his fingers in mine. He pulled me closer to him with his hand around my waist.

"Well, you flew me to the moon. The least I could do was deliver you a chorus."

"Deliver *us* a chorus," he corrected.

"Us," I said, liking the sound of it.

Us. Midnight blue. Hot chicken soup.

"Do you still think the movie's ending is a 'wild disservice' to our lead?" Asher asked with a smirk.

He was referring to my frantic FaceTime the night before, where I hosted my own TED Talk: Why Yael *must* end up alone at the end of the film.

Truthfully, I understood the movie's ending, and at the same time, I felt betrayed by it. Yael, our movie's protagonist, refused to cling to anything besides a fantasy, and her fantasy came true because of a relentless eyes-to-the-sky mantra. Music and hope were her drugs, her bridges to a better life and her lifeline back home, when she recognized that the real thing she'd run from—the love of her life—was back on earth. She was a ball of sunshine who'd rolled around in some dark shit . . . and remained a ball of sunshine. After feeling the warmth of hope again, I didn't want to let it go, but I was afraid of what would happen this time if it didn't amount to something real.

Asher tugged my warring soul upward.

"Thanks for taking me to the stars," I said against his lips.

"Only the best for you."

He kissed me like he meant it, like he would send me to the moon just to watch me bathe in its afterglow. I kissed him like I would only fly to the moon if he was by my side.

We jetted home that night, and after eating an extravagant Italian dinner somewhere over the Atlantic, I fell asleep on Asher's shoulder. He woke me up when we landed at Teterboro, with a car and driver scooping us up the moment our feet hit the asphalt.

The next morning, I woke thanks to the yellow sunrise pouring in through Asher's bedroom ceiling—the downside to having an "airy" loft where the owners thought a rooftop skylight was the key to getting a daily dose of vitamin D. I rolled over and studied his olive skin wrapped peacefully in crisp white sheets. He even looked gorgeous when he slept. Beauty stitched with an aching sadness. My phone vibrated—pulling my attention away from the freckles on his arms. I read a text from my manager, Shelly.

> Just heard your end credits song from Bex last night—the producer sent it over. Babe, you are going to be a goddamn star. BUCKLE UP. Also, call me the second you get this text.

I dialed Shelly's number immediately, not even bothering to put on pants or a bra, as I hopped out of bed and slunk into the golden living room.

"Bex wants you to meet him at his home studio in Brooklyn, like, this afternoon," Shelly said. "So whatever plans you have, cancel them."

"Umm, okay. *Why* does he want to meet me?"

"Super vague, but he wants to have a 'convo over tea,' and I don't let my baby clients have convos with music producers without me present, so I'll be there."

I had never heard an American twentysomething use the phrase "convo over tea," but I would meet Fin Bex for a conversation over luke-warm Florida tap water if he wanted.

I ADJUSTED MY LEVI'S SHORTALLS over my black tank top, squinting at the address on a beautiful redbrick brownstone, which sat on a sleepy street in Brooklyn Heights. Bex lived on an idyllic street where strollers occupied the sidewalk, and you could hear birds chirping instead of taxis honking. Shelly sat on Bex's floral stoop with her nose buried in her phone, her chunky jewelry rattling with the banging of her acrylics. I tugged my windblown curls into a tight topknot, wiping the summer sweat off my forehead before I made my presence known.

"Hi," I said.

Shelly stopped typing and stood up, patting me on the shoulder.

"This is cute. It's refreshing to have a client who can pull off toddler-wear in her midthirties."

I adjusted the strap on my overalls, wondering if she was being serious or sarcastic.

"Listen. Do not commit to anything, no matter what he says, got it? Wait for my lead, if I ask for your opinion, give it honestly. Otherwise, let me do the big talking." I nodded as Shelly rang the buzzer.

A moment later, Fin Bex opened the door, hugging us both and ushering us into his partially gutted three-story brownstone. He gave us a quick tour of the first floor, which felt like a melding of the Old World with a colorful edge: original dark-wood Victorian wall panels and matching coffered ceilings from 1910, surrounded by modern light fixtures and bold furniture choices. My jaw dropped as I stepped past a built-in bookcase in the sitting room, which was home to the grandest record collection I'd ever seen outside of an indie record shop.

Bex led us to the garden-level dining table off the dreamy kitchen, where Lila, his sound engineer, stood up to greet Shelly and me. Bex made us our respective cups of black tea, and then sat down across from me. He folded his jittery arms across the table and sat still for a handful of seconds, staring at me with wide hazel eyes.

"So, you're probably wondering why I asked you here. Look, Maggie,

I've heard all your demos for the movie. And this stays between us, but I think you do each demo better than Raini—and that's not an insult to Raini—who is fucking outstanding—it's simply a compliment to you— you are *more than* fucking outstanding. I'm blown away, and you can ask Lila, it takes a lot to knock me off my feet," Bex said.

"His standards are obnoxious, honestly," Lila said. She rolled her eyes with a smile, stuffing a tiny scone past her magenta lips.

"Your work ethic, how quickly you turned around these songs, how you sang them, how working in a studio with you was like wildfire: you're a dream. So, I want to produce your EP, with Lila here as the sound engineer."

My eyes widened.

"Are . . . are you serious?" I asked.

Shelly whipped her head at me with pointed eyes, as if telling me to keep my enthusiasm to myself.

"Why should she go with you, instead of waiting to go with one of the big guys after the movie comes out, get a studio record deal, and then pull you on as producer?" Shelly asked.

"Shells, c'mon. They'll make her promises, let that *one* single run wild, and the second it stalls on the charts, they'll pull her deal. You know how the big guys operate. Plus, she doesn't need them. She's going to have a platform to launch her—she's going to have the movie. Geffen will find her, Columbia, Sony, they'll come. But I think we should make them beg, make them put their money where their mouth is, and I can help her do that. And after the EP, we'll produce your big studio album with a shiny label behind its release."

Shelly could hardly hold her poker face. I could see her lip twitching upward as Bex tilted his head at her. These two clearly had circled around each other for years.

"What's your plan for Maggie Vine?" Shelly asked.

"We record four tracks in my home studio, and we release her first single after the movie wraps and before it premiers, just as the promotion for the movie starts. *On the Other Side* is a two-month shoot, and I think post will be a couple months, and then, we can time it just right. She'll have that end credit song already, which will get people clicking to see who this woman is, to see the kind of artist she is, and what the rest of her

EP will look like. And I think we hold off on releasing the rest of the EP until after the movie premiers."

Shelly grinned and looked at me.

"What do you think?"

I smiled too widely.

"I think . . . *fuck yes*."

Giddy heat blanketed my cheeks, and I clenched my mouth shut to keep from squealing.

"Look at you, a thirty-five-year-old overnight sensation," Shelly said.

Knocking on the back of my mind was the real truth: I should have been a thirty-year-old overnight sensation.

40

THIRTY-FIVE

RAINI TUCKED HER LONG, WAVY hair behind her ears and stared at me with wide brown eyes, waiting for my opinion.

"He said, 'You remind me of my mom,' and then stuck his tongue down your throat?" I winced.

"So it's bad?" she asked.

"I mean, it's weird, but maybe that's just because I have complicated mom feelings."

I leaned forward under the window canopy in Asher's meditation area, grabbing my coffee from the table in between Raini and me. Over the last few weeks, I had become close with Raini, the lead actress in the film—the young woman who would bring Yael to life. She was a former child star who was born with fire in her belly and a good head on her shoulders. Her childhood could have been a cautionary tale, but instead, it was a road map for young realized ambition. She was a bit like me—me if I had made it like three decades prior.

"He's just . . ." Raini's eyes found the blue sky, with a giddy smile plastered on her cheeks.

"I know that look," I said, shaking my head. "That right there is the best and worst feeling in the world: love and uncertainty."

"You're so lucky. You have love without any of the confusing parts."

"How do you know that?" I laughed, tickled by the way she spoke so surely about situations she'd only taken a peek at.

"I see the way Asher looks at you, and the way you look at him. It's like . . ." She studied her open palms, carefully finding the words.

Okay, maybe she wasn't so much like me. I'll tell you who Raini was like: Raini Parish was like Asher Reyes.

"It's like watching two people just exhale," she added.

I felt my chest warm with the truth. Asher and I had exhaled around each other for the last few weeks. In so many ways, it felt like we'd picked up where our teenage selves ended. But neither of us had outright said "I love you," or asked the other to define the situation. That being said, we were bathed in bliss—and something about feeling this secure left me perfectly happy in the undefined gray area.

"Well, not every man has been like Asher," I said, smiling and marveling at the fact that Asher brought me fireworks without question marks. "If possible, try and find someone who lights you on fire without leading you down a dark, torturous smoky maze of unrequited love for twelve years."

"*Twelve years?*" she asked, eyes wide.

"Oh girl, I have a master's—no—I have a *PhD* in pining," I said.

I felt my throat tighten with the realization that Garrett was getting married in two months. I wasn't going. I was leaving masochism in the rearview, but the reality was still a little gut punch. Our ending wasn't wiped clean from my heart, but it wasn't screaming in my ear, either.

Raini smiled.

"Honestly, I've met a lot of creepy dudes who are older and . . . Asher is just . . . he's the nicest person in this business—the kindest I've ever met."

"He's been through a lot, and I think he actually does treat people the way he wants to be treated, which is rare," I mused.

"What do you mean?" she asked, taking a sip of her tea.

"I mean . . . his life hasn't always been easy."

Raini shrugged, setting down her tea bag.

"I guess I don't know much about him, like, personally? He's super quiet."

I grinned.

"What?"

"Around me he's not quiet. Not at all," I said.

"Like all I know about him personally is what I read before the audition—that *Rolling Stone* interview from a couple years ago. But it's sort of sexy that he's an enigma. I wish Josh didn't have Instagram—God that would be so hot," Raini said, referring to her current crush who was keeping her up at night—a young heartthrob not worthy of her heart.

"Okay, you little sneak, stop trying to deflect from the fact that you hate my bridge," I said, picking up my guitar.

"I don't hate it, it hates me."

"Neither is true, but what if we do a key change?"

"Then you'd be my hero, because I can't do that low-register shit the way you can," she said, with a big smile.

A little while later after Raini left, I sat on the Barcelona chair in Asher's living room, poring over the *Rolling Stone* article Raini had been referring to. It was surface at best, or at least I thought it was, because I knew most of the corners of Asher's brain. I pulled my neck back, shocked as I read the end of the article. When asked about what his family thought of his fame, Asher joked about how his parents wished their only child was doing something they could brag about to their friends—like becoming an attorney. The phrase "only child" twisted my heart. I checked Asher's Wikipedia page, seeing in plain black type that there wasn't a sibling listed.

Asher walked into the kitchen as I set down my phone, and I hesitated before standing up and leaning against the kitchen island. I watched him open the cupboard above the stove and grab a bottle of tiny lime-green pills. He put the pill on his tongue and swallowed it down with running sink water. I looked away, not wanting to be intrusive. We had been doing this for a few weeks, occupying our own corners of our creative universes under one roof—keeping our relationship secret. And then at night we would collide—bodies discovering ways to light each other up that our teenage selves were too modest to try. Every morning I looked at him, at the stillness of the room and the calmness of his body, at the new life outstretched before me, and I thought, *I could get used to this*. But I couldn't escape that we both had pasts that were treacherous, pasts that made us who were today.

"Can I ask you something?" I said.

He leaned forward across the marble, smiling warmly at me.

"Anything."

I searched for the words, and he tilted his head, waiting.

"You don't talk about your brother. Not to me . . . not to anyone . . ."

He froze. "What's your question?" he asked, eyes unblinking.

"Asher, are you okay?" I asked quietly, my throat quivering under the possibility that he wasn't.

Asher exhaled with his entire body. He looked back down at his hands as they twirled the orange pill bottle against the counter. They were likely the same pills he took when we were teenagers. I was relieved he was still taking them—I was relieved he was getting help for the pain that life put on his shoulders—pain that he shouldn't have to fight by himself.

"It's easier this way, Mags," he whispered.

"That didn't really answer my question," I said. "Ash—if I've learned anything over the last few years, it's that hiding all your pain . . . well that just causes more pain."

I swallowed a past punching at my throat, and he met my eyes, seeing it.

"I don't keep him a secret for me," Asher said.

His eyes seemed to swallow a new kind of sadness. I walked over to him, gripping my hand in his until his brown eyes met mine.

"My parents didn't want to relive it. They didn't want every interview I gave to be about their greatest loss. You know my mom, she's . . ." He drifted off. "When my career took off, they asked me not to offer it up."

Asher's parents were cold people. I couldn't judge them. They had lost a child in the worst way. But Asher needed warm arms that would hold him tight. At camp, Asher told me that I came along at just the right time. That feeling was mutual. He said I taught him how to let someone love him, which broke my heart. I knew how to love before I met him, he just became the first thing in my life worthy of loving.

"Do *you* want to talk about him?" I asked.

"To pretend he never existed—to pretend that the person who made the biggest impact on my life never lived—it fucking kills me, Mags," he said, letting tears envelop his eyes. "But . . . sometimes I don't know where to start."

I gripped his hand harder.

"If you want to, you should tell his story, Asher. You loved him—I don't want you to be afraid to tell people how much you loved your brother."

"It would—it would kill my mom."

I studied the pain written all over his face.

"I think it's killing you."

He swallowed hard and rested his hand against my cheek. He took my other hand up to his mouth and kissed it.

"Thank you."

"What for?" I asked.

"I—I haven't dealt with my own stuff in a while. And being around you, it reminds me of the first time I cared enough to try. So, thank you."

"Thank you," I said, my eyes locked on his.

"For what?" he asked with a grin.

"Everything."

He hesitated for a moment, then scanned my eyes.

"Mags, do *you* want to talk about it?"

"About what?" I asked brightly.

"I feel like . . . maybe something happened the last few years. You've hinted at it, but . . ."

My throat grew hot and tight, and I felt my chest swirl. His eyes widened upon my expression, and he bent down, his warm face right in front of mine.

"Not yet," was all I could manage.

He pulled me tight to his body, kissing my forehead hard, as if shielding me from a bullet. I hugged him back, trying to hold all his pain.

He had the kind of pain I couldn't hold.

And the bullet was already inside me, sitting in my gut.

41

THIRTY-FIVE

A HANDFUL OF WEEKS LATER, I rolled over at the sound of my phone ringing, edging my arm delicately past the gorgeous man quietly snoring in my bed—well, *his* bed.

"Who is it?" Asher grumbled, a pillow covering his face, half asleep.

"I got it," I said as I reached for my phone.

I squinted my eyes, seeing that Summer was calling me at five thirty in the morning, which was something I usually did to her.

"Hello," I said, my voice hushed as I tiptoed out of the dark bedroom.

"I told her," Summer said, her voice trembling.

I froze and leaned on the kitchen island, my eyes blinking back the sun rising atop the brownstones in the distance.

"You told Valeria you don't want kids?" I asked softly.

"Late last night. And—and she told me..." Summer paused with a thickness in her voice, as if she was being strangled by her own emotions. "She told me it was nonnegotiable." Her words were barely audible amid the tears.

I felt my heart thumping against my chest as my spine grew upright, as if the child had become the adult. It was a strange feeling, a role reversal.

I once read an article about relationships. It stated that some of the best partnerships existed because someone was the rock, and someone was the kite. In my love life, I preferred two kites. But as far as friendships went, Summer and I were a rock and a kite. Summer was my rock: my rational backbone, a logical thinker, the person I could untangle all my warring questions with without her crumbling under my chaotic spiral. I was Summer's kite: full of wanderlust and consumed by matters of the heart, floating through the clouds, swayed by my surroundings, allowing emotions to tug me toward another corner of the universe without a stable force below. I was the place Summer went to lighten her load, to dream a little, to chase the stars among the harsh light of day.

Suddenly, the rock was calling the kite for advice.

I rushed back into the bedroom, pulling my T-shirt and distressed jeans off the Eames lounge chair in the corner of the room—the chair I had made my clothing pile—much to Asher's amused dismay.

"I'll be right over," I said into the phone as I tugged my jeans over my hips.

"I'm standing outside your boyfriend's loft."

I snatched the electronic key off Asher's console and flew into the elevator.

Seconds later, I opened the front door of the lobby as the sun rose behind a puffy-faced Summer. She was sucking her cheeks in, her eyes red, but momentarily dry. She had clearly just been crying, but didn't want me to notice. I took her into a hug, feeling her body shake against mine, an exhale of silent cries thumping against my chest.

"*Boyfriend's* loft? We don't use that word," I said, trying to lighten her load.

"I hate this," Summer said as her tears fell on my neck.

My heart sank, and I pulled her in closer. The sob of heartbreak is primal and universal, and if you've ever been there, just thinking about the moment your heart broke makes your insides heavy, leaving you with a need to clutch your chest, as if to marvel over the fact that you survived. Tears prickled my eyes—the memory of all the little and big heartbreaks punching the scars on my chest—it killed me that my best friend would have a scar like this—one that would take so long to heal, and one that would sting every now and then, even decades later.

"I hate this for you, too," I whispered.

I hugged her tighter. Summer pulled back, and I slung my arm around her waist, leading her into the building.

A few minutes later, I handed Summer a piping-hot cup of PG Tips tea as we sat under a flowing canopy in Asher's meditation area.

"What the fuck is this place? I feel like Sting is going to pop out at any moment and teach me how to have long, boring sex sessions."

Summer was always wonderful at delaying an emotional reaction, and it brought me joy to see her embrace her wicked side before we dug into her heartache.

"Yes, this is the tantric sex area," a distant voice said.

Summer and I whipped our heads to the door and saw Asher. He looked like he had rolled out of bed in just a pair of athletic shorts. There was a slight smirk on his face, his hair was untamed, and his arms were crossed over his bare torso. Summer gawked at him, taking in his perfect body.

"I woke up and you were nowhere, just wanted to make sure you were alive, since I've never seen you wake before nine," he said with a smile. "Didn't know you had company, sorry to interrupt." He gave Summer a shy wave.

"Asher, this is Summer, Summer this is—"

"I know who the fuck he is," Summer said, rolling her eyes. I hugged her tighter as Asher walked over.

"Sorry, I would get up and shake your hand, but I feel like I'm dying, so . . ."

Asher nodded as I stared at him wide-eyed. "Sorry," I mouthed.

"Can I get you anything?" he asked Summer, rather sweetly.

"Yeah, salty snacks and a goddamn time machine," Summer said.

I raised my eyebrows to Asher. I had told Asher nearly everything he needed to know about my best friend—minus the child dilemma, which wasn't my story to tell. I spared little detail when it came to Summer's bluntness. Asher had the sense to smile and nod nicely in Summer's direction.

"Sorry, I'm having a crap day. Nice abs," Summer said.

"We'll be inside in a little while," I said.

"Take your time."

He leaned down and kissed me on my cheek as Summer watched, and then he disappeared back down the stairs.

"He's fucking *into* you. Why haven't I seen a photo of you both? Why haven't you DTR'ed? Also, you better let me pick the bridesmaid outfit—and I'll have none of this empire-waist bullshit."

I knew what she was doing. Now would be the moment where Summer would try and distract me from her own pain, just to unravel what was going on inside me. I decided to throw her a bone.

"We're actually venturing out for the first time tonight, but the goal is to not create a media frenzy. We haven't defined anything because we don't feel the need to, and you made me wear an empire-waist bridesmaid dress at *your* wedding."

"Oh, nice job, Maggie. Way to bring up my wedding the day my marriage falls apart."

I stared down Summer, shaking my head.

"*Summer.* No more fucking around. What happened?"

Summer exhaled, staring out at the cityscape. I watched her hard exterior soften in front of me, her spine folding forward as tears rimmed her darkened eyes.

"I told Valeria that I didn't want kids, and she called me selfish. She said I was a liar, and that when we met, I presented this whole 'I see myself with a child' narrative to her, just so I could be with her for the moment, and that I'm changing my mind just so I can get out of the marriage. I told her I loved her, and I wanted to stay with her, but she really thought this was me wanting a way out of our marriage."

"Summer, make her understand that you aren't lying. Talk it out. Explain to her how this wasn't a decision that came to you slowly, or one you take lightly. It's one you've been wrestling with, and you were terrified to tell her once you'd come to the conclusion, because you didn't want to lose her."

"I tried, but she kept cutting me off. It doesn't matter anyway."

"*Of course* it matters."

"Maggie, how I came to this conclusion won't bridge the gap between what Valeria and I want. I don't want kids, and she wants them—full stop. Marriage is about compromise, and this isn't a place we can compromise. We're done. Our marriage is done."

Summer buried her head in her hands, and her entire chest heaved with thundering sobs. I pulled her body to my side and folded two arms around her, holding her tightly, as if compression would heal the swelling wound of deep loss.

We sat side by side as the sun rose atop our bodies, until Summer inhaled and shook her head. She wiped the tears from below her eyes.

"I need to move out. I can't . . . I can't live there anymore. I mean, it's our place, but technically, it's her place."

"You can stay in my apartment. I'm hardly ever there."

"Your little shithole? Oh God, I'd rather die."

Summer started sobbing again. Apparently, for Summer Groves, the thought of existing in a peeling two-hundred-square-foot studio apartment with faulty window AC was just as horrifying as losing the woman she loved. I rubbed her back as Summer slowly swallowed her emotions back in.

"I'm going to fly home. I booked a flight on the way over here. I leave tonight."

My eyes widened in alarm. "To Florida? Really?"

Summer nodded.

Summer hadn't been home to see her dad in nearly a decade. Summer and her divorce-attorney father had a historically prickly relationship, one that she couldn't bring herself to mend, even as her dad desperately tried. When Summer was a teenager, her father had buried himself in work and younger women to escape his wife's untimely death. Along with not being crowned Single Father of the Year, her dad didn't exactly embrace Summer's coming out with open arms. Instead, he brushed off Summer's "I'm gay!" as "just a New Age phase." It didn't help that these two events occurred during Summer's sophomore year of high school. So by the time she left for college, Summer held on to a rightful grudge—one she could never let go of.

"He keeps begging me to visit. Apparently, I'll *love* his new wife because she's 'a bisexual,'" Summer said, rolling her eyes as she quoted her father.

His new wife was forty, just five years older than Summer—which we counted as a blessing—the previous one had been a year younger than us.

"What is Luca? Wife number four?"

"My dad says three, because Britney's ended in an annulment."

"He can help with the legal stuff at least. Right?" I said, trying to find a silver lining amid the pile of shit.

"We have a prenup. So . . . it should be easy. Like—" Summer snapped her fingers. "Like it never happened," she said quietly, her voice growing small under such a huge blow.

"What can I do? Want me to go to your place and pack up a suitcase for you?"

Summer shook her head. "No, Valeria's going to stay at her parents' place while I grab my things."

"I'm coming with you to help you pack."

"That's stupid," she said.

"No, it's not."

"Be honest. You never really liked her anyway."

I went to agree, but I hesitated with my mouth slightly ajar. I knew better than to bash a soon-to-be ex. As easily as a relationship could end, it could begin again. Unfortunately, the mud you hurl at your best friend's ex can never be un-hurled—words are forever.

"What do you want me to say?" I asked.

"Say how horrible she is. I mean, she can't cook worth shit. And Valeria . . . she does this annoying throat-clearing thing when she's nervous. Drives me nuts. And she never cleans up after her messes. How hard is it to put gum wrappers in the trash? And she's *so* loud when she walks—she walks like a giant, like there's lead inside her shoes. . . ."

Summer stopped speaking, tears back in her throat with a realization that all the little things that annoyed her about her wife would become things she'd miss. The spaces that were obnoxiously loud and messy would become even worse: quiet and empty.

"I'm a failure," Summer whispered. "I'm thirty-five, and I'm getting *divorced*."

She said "divorced" like it was a dirty word.

"You're not a failure. You met Valeria, and you learned how to love someone with your whole heart. I had never seen you love someone before her. You might have a divorce to show for it, but I think . . . I think you're going to make someone else so happy one day with all the love you learned how to give and take. And it'll be the right person, who wants the kind of life you want, because now you know who you are. We can't be bashed for growing up and changing. Summer, most importantly, you love yourself enough not to sacrifice your future just to hold on to someone else. We see divorce as a failure, but sometimes it's not. Sometimes we have to wave a white flag in order to save ourselves, or *be* ourselves. You love Valeria too much to hold her back from a life she deserves, and you love yourself too much to fold into a life you don't want."

I thought of my own mother, who filed for divorce from my father when I was just learning how to form words. I had grown up clinging to the fantasy that they would find their way back to each other, but as I got older, I couldn't comprehend how they even withstood existing in the same room together. My mother knew that there would be success in letting go of my father. She knew that tethering herself to him would end in wild disappointment. He would only ever let her down. I knew this to be true because I was his daughter, and he let me down every time I thought he would prove my mother wrong.

I felt a newfound heaviness tug at my heart. Guilt. I felt the urge to vomit and call my mother. Summer thankfully put a stop to both.

"I just wish I could be like everyone else. I wish I could want what most people want, and hold on to the person I love," Summer said.

I slung my arm back around her.

"Summer Groves, you know what? This is probably the first time in your entire life where you're just like everyone else. You've always known exactly who you are, unapologetically. And this time, it took you a moment to figure out that something you thought was for you, isn't. Don't apologize for being human. And don't you dare apologize for not wanting to be a mother. Ever. If you had decided to disappoint yourself in order to make someone else happy, then you'd have something to be sorry about—then you can apologize."

Flashes of Garrett entered my brain—the man who folded into other people's vision of what his life should be, just so he could pacify them, all the while failing himself.

A spark of wild energy shot through my veins, and I sat up straighter. All at once, I realized why Summer and I were so close. She was authentically herself, in every way. It was why I loved her. It was why our relationship felt more like a soulmate connection than a friendship. Summer was a rock and I was a kite, but most importantly, we were both unabashedly ourselves. Maybe, when it came to love, I had it all wrong. I thought I would end up with a kite—with a creative who was a wild dreamer, who could light up my nights. Really, it wasn't about who was practical and whose head lived in the clouds. It was about finding another soul who was unapologetically himself. I needed a man who was confident enough to play his own music, regardless of what the critics threw at him.

I stared directly into Summer's teary eyes. "You're my kite, and my rock," I said to my best friend.

"You're a fucking weirdo."

She glared at me, and then Summer turned her eyes away from mine. I watched her chin quiver—emotions coming back like a boomerang. She shook her head, tears falling down with ease. Suddenly, Summer turned around toward me and tugged my body into hers, holding on tighter than she ever had.

Success doesn't come easily for women who dare to be themselves. It's a painful road, and Summer and I had already let down a few people along our chosen paths, and we'd let down more. But if we were lucky, at the end of our roads, we'd look back and smile, realizing that we'd made ourselves proud.

42

THIRTY-FIVE

AFTER I PACKED SUMMER'S LIFE up into a few suitcases and got her off to the airport, I came back to Asher's loft with a hurried realization: I had just thirty minutes to get ready. Normally, I could go from a braless mess to "not so bad" in twenty minutes, but tonight, Asher and I were venturing out into the real world for the first time since our photo had been snapped at Marea. I needed to go from a braless mess to "fucking hot" in thirty minutes. It was a stretch, but I had spent my entire life preparing for this moment. Or at least I had spent the last few years YouTubing too many beauty tutorials to prepare for this moment.

Asher and I had made a deal to keep our relationship—or whatever we were—under wraps until I could turn in every track on the movie. I had stayed in a few nights when Asher went out over the last few weeks, not because I didn't want to be by his side, but because I wanted to give the utmost respect to the thing I'd nearly killed myself for: my career. My manager had her point of view—she didn't want to see us together until my work was finished. It was a bad idea to piss off my representation at the start of my career. I wanted her to trust me. Meanwhile, Asher wasn't the type to flaunt a relationship, so he didn't push it.

Asher was already in the shower when I got home, a sudsy mohawk on his head, and I disrobed as I opened the steam shower doors, the cool outside elements barreling in and completely disrupting the entire steam situation going on.

He turned to me with raised eyebrows as I grabbed the bottle of Le Labo mandarin shower gel.

"Well hello there," Asher said.

He pulled me in to his wet, naked body, and I could feel him harden against me.

"I will *totally* make this up to you later, but I only have thirty minutes to become a person."

"I pushed the dinner to eight thirty."

I put my hand on my chest and batted my eyes at him.

"For *me*?"

He tugged me back to him with his wet hand on my waist, the hot rain shower now pouring over us both. He leaned in and kissed a slow, warm, wet trail from my neck, down to my clavicle, in between words.

"You texted me saying you might be cutting it close . . . and that you wanted to stay to get your friend into a car . . . and that you wouldn't be back until seven." My heart beat faster as he turned his head, kissing the other side of my neck. "What's the use of having fame if I can't use it to secure a later table at Carbone?"

He stepped back and raised his eyebrows at me as the steam clouded my vision of a perfect, beautiful man. I wrapped my arms around his neck. The thick body wash on his chest sent the smell of crisp geranium into my lungs, and he lifted me with one strong hand, pressing my back against the cool Carrara marble tiles with my legs wrapped around him. I clung onto his shoulder blades, arching my neck to the sky as he guided himself inside me.

I clenched my hands behind his head.

"Touch me," I whispered into his ear.

He kissed me hard, water raining down on us both, his fingertips moving from my ear, tracing a line down my throat, encircling my wet breasts—one by one—achingly slowly, as I breathlessly exhaled his name to the flowing showerhead.

An hour later, with dewy, flushed faces, we sat inside Asher's town car, in dead-stopped traffic on Thompson Street. Asher curved his head out the window, surveying the traffic.

"We're going to get out here, Joey," he said to his driver.

"You sure?" Joey asked, with eyes raised.

"We're already a couple minutes late, it's right there." Asher looked at me. "C'mon." He nodded as he opened his door.

He held my hand as I expertly folded my body to the side, so as to not show my vagina off to any passersby. Exiting a vehicle in a minidress should be an Olympic sport. *Men could never.* I exhaled as my heels hit the pavement, tugged my dress back down, and Asher wrapped his hand in mine. Like clockwork, he put his chin down, walking forward toward the red neon CARBONE sign as if he were a bull. Suddenly, I understood why he walked that way, as huge camera flashes lit up my face. Asher's arm instinctively went over his own face, and he shielded me behind his body, leading me into Carbone as the flashes disappeared.

He tugged me far past the front doors and pulled me close to his chest as we approached the hostess stand. The restaurant was dimly lit, and all I could see were flashes behind my eyes. Asher held me against his body, his hand on my cheek as he took me in with concern. I knew he could feel my chest racing against his.

"You okay?" he whispered.

He studied me like no one else was watching, even though I knew that everyone else was watching. I could get used to the way he was looking at me. Which I guess meant that I would have to get used to strange men shoving their lenses in my eyes.

"I'm fine, I promise."

A hostess tapped her hand on Asher's arm, with a bright, red-lipped smile. "Mr. Reyes, can I show you to your table?"

Asher nodded, and he locked his fingers into mine as we made our way through the old red-and-black square-tiled room. Carbone was a New York institution. Red-and-brown brick walls, dark woods—the kind of restaurant that the Mob would lust after. I could smell the red sauce and garlic pouring out from each dish as we passed the tables, and we entered into a private corner, with a packed long table taking up the entire alcove.

I saw Raini immediately, and hugged her tightly, thankful to have a friend at the table. Asher introduced me to three different producers. I recognized one of them as Amos. Then, he introduced me to the film's first AD (assistant director), the DP (director of photography), the PM (production manager), and person after person who had acronym after acronym—people who were going to make Asher's movie something beautiful. The phrase "it takes a village" absolutely applied to filmmaking.

Around the first course, Amos leaned back in his chair across from me and Asher, with his indifference slightly waning now that it was buried under a second glass of red. Asher was engaged in conversation with Raini about the movie's sex scene—him assuring her they'd hired an intimacy coordinator, and that the crew assembled that day would be minimal. Asher's hand was casually around my shoulder, and in between their conversation, he looked back at me and kissed my cheek. I watched Amos stare at Asher and then myself. He grinned like a little kid.

"So, when did this happen?" Amos asked, not so subtly and not so quietly.

I swallowed my forkful of eggplant-and-zucchini scapece with a large sip of a terrifyingly expensive glass of Barbaresco, wide-eyed. Each head at the rectangular table quieted and shifted in my direction. I looked to Asher, seeing his hard jawline soften into a slight smile.

"Twenty-one years ago?" Asher asked.

"Yes and no," I said.

Amos bunched up his eyebrows and leaned in.

"You lost me," Amos said.

"They're the cutest," Raini said, with puppy dog eyes staring at us both. "Do you guys know they fell in love when they were fourteen? *Fourteen*."

Raini loved this story. I told it to her one morning over tea, and she couldn't stop idealizing it. I wanted to tell her to stop—to darken her sunshine just so that she wouldn't go looking for this kind of rare fireworks, because, again, I was still a little stung from He Who Shall Not Be Named. But I didn't. I let her bathe in my love story, because even after experiencing heartbreak, I believed coming out the other side was worth celebrating.

Raini beamed at us, her body close to the maybe-boyfriend seated next to her, the guy she couldn't get enough of, Joshua Carlyle. He was a nice enough Ken-doll actor whose fame had recently exploded in his early twenties, but Josh could play sixteen, and so he had been cast in every young-adult movie that Netflix spit out over the last two years. Sure, he was a vulnerable actor whose sad eyes made your insides hurt, but I was certain that he had to know where Netflix buried their bodies. Josh was good, but not five-movies-and-two-TV-shows *good*. He was also a man-child, with his eyes glued to his overactive Instagram account. Raini pursed her lips and put her hand over Josh's cell phone. He looked up and smiled brightly, tucking his phone away as she pulled him close to her chest and nodded at Asher and myself, as if showing her boyfriend what she wanted out of their relationship. She wanted him to look at her the way Asher looked at me—like I hung the moon. My body lit up and my cheeks reddened, realizing how fucking lucky I was. It wasn't every day that a man looked at a woman this way.

"Well, you just made the studio's PR team very, *very* happy," Amos said.

Asher tugged his eyes off me and took a sip of his wine with an eye roll.

"That's not what this is," Asher said.

"Just, please plan the messy breakup for after the movie comes out," said Amos.

Asher turned to me, eyes unwavering on mine. "I don't plan on a breakup of any kind," he said, following the statement with a wide grin. I couldn't speak, I just let the words comfort and warm every inch of my body.

"Jesus Christ, I don't think I've ever seen you smile in public before," Amos said as Asher's gaze stayed locked on mine. "You usually save the smiles for the camera." Amos turned to me, alarmed. "What have you done to him?"

I shrugged, because this was always how we were.

"Alright, enough already. Stop interrogating my girlfriend," Asher said, putting his arm around me, as if to shield me from their stares.

The word "girlfriend" shot through me. I hadn't heard someone refer to me as their girlfriend since I was . . . seventeen. Drew Reddy and I hadn't even put a label on his love for me. I had never been anyone else's anything as an adult. I had dated different types of unstable men for months at a time. My relationships were tiny love bombs—men whose instability gave me a high level of anxiety. With the uncertainty came the sweeping fireworks. When I had their attention, I coveted it. When I wasn't in their presence, I stared at my phone like it might eat me alive. These men were gorgeous, emotionally unavailable, unable to look at the future, and/or terrified of commitment—I had never gotten myself past the DTR finish line. So of course, the first kid to call me his girlfriend would be the first adult man to call me the same. Somehow, unwittingly, Asher Reyes had marked the stability territory, and I had been waiting all this time for him to come back around and be my rock.

Suddenly, Amos and Asher shifted out of their seats, effusively greeting a man who approached our table. I couldn't see his face, his back was to me, but he used his hands aggressively as he spoke, with a loud Jersey accent. My chest thumped, faster and faster, and I bit down hard, tasting blood and metal in my mouth. Asher gestured in my direction, and the man turned toward me with a wide smile. He looked the same, like he'd rolled around inside a vintage shop, but an expensive one. My mouth parted in the air—my throat strangled with heat. A loud ringing blared in my ears, and my heart pounded inside my skull.

The paparazzi were camped outside Thompson Street, and I was the other half of their target. Tonight was a super-problematic time for PTSD to pop on by for a visit, but I didn't blame her. I could feel every inch of my body wrapping itself up in distress, like a siren sound warning me to hide, to hold myself under the table, to exhale horrifying screams so that others could save me. Instead, I gripped one hand over the other with white-knuckled fists, letting my nails etch onto the backs of my hands—an attempt to feel physical pain, an attempt to keep my body upright and glued to my seat instead of folding into a panic attack.

"Maggie, this is Cole Wyan," Asher said.

Cole smiled in my direction, and his eyes widened the moment he met my face. His expression shifted back to neutral just as quickly, and with a sickening smile, he extended his hand down to mine.

43

TWENTY-NINE

I STOOD UP ON THE stage at the Bowery Electric—making it to the stage of my dreams at twenty-nine. I was uncharacteristically nervous at first—but there was pressure on my shoulders—my chest thumping against having the largest crowd that had ever gathered simply *for me*. Just hours prior, Garrett had texted me that he couldn't make it—there was a burgeoning medical supplies company in San Francisco that his dad wanted to acquire, and Garrett needed to stay there. I texted him back that it was fine, in lowercase, without an exclamation mark, which, if you're listening (men), means the opposite of fine.

Over nine months ago, we had parted with a long kiss before he left at five in the morning, neither of us knowing what our bodies wrapped around each other meant. We texted often, but neither mentioned that night. He had been in San Francisco longer than he was supposed to, working eighty-hour weeks, and he was due back in time for my show. I had put too much pressure on the idea of seeing him again, so even as my career was about to take flight, on this big booming stage there was a large ache in my heart.

The song I had written for Garrett, "Let's Lie," left my lips, fueled by a newfound bitterness in my veins. As I finished the song, the air got sucked out of my angry lungs. My wide eyes blinked back a famous face, a genius whose indie-folk lyrics had inspired many of my first songs. Cole Wyan. I owned all of his CDs. In high school, I downloaded his demos on LimeWire. This was the extent to which I worshipped Cole's music and his melancholic indie-folk vibe: I risked being caught by the FBI to hear his rarities and B-sides. He was a vulnerable and prolific singer-songwriter, who also produced a handful of artists under his Power Groove label— many of them female artists who I admired.

He carried himself with a Venice Beach vibe: *I might look like I don't embrace personal hygiene and I shop at Goodwill, but if you look closer, you'll see I'm wearing a $500 beanie.* He had a cherubic face with a wild mop of sandy-blond hair, with gold and leather bracelets hugging his tattooed wrists.

Cole grinned up at my glittery, wide eyes like he was Moses and I was the Promised Land. Finally, right place, right time—chest pounding, perfect out-of-this-galaxy vocals, yearning lyrics, someone important watching. It had only taken me twenty-nine years.

Cole waited for me after my show, nervously chewing off his chipped black nail polish with his face hiding behind the glow of his phone. He knew that I would approach him. And the second I did, he looked up from his phone with a dry smile.

"You know what you are?" he asked, fully prepared to tell me. "You're like a manic pixie dream-girl version of Fiona Apple. And I'm going to change your life."

He said it, and I believed him, wholly.

Over the next few months, Cole's enthusiasm for me only grew stronger, which made me feel like the most talented woman alive. What followed were writing sessions, incessant text messages, and FaceTiming at all hours of the night—his nervous gusto, 5-Hour Energy drinks, microdosing on shrooms, and Adderall consumption keeping him and me up while the rest of the world slept. Cole inspired me to leave a little bit of my softer folksy side behind and lean into heavier sounds that I had previously shied away from. He inspired me to experiment with my sound. I would spend nights in front of my computer, layering my demos with a grungy edge, bringing angry instruments into the once-quieter spaces of my favorite tracks. He came to watch me play at my usual dive bar, sitting in a corner while eyes floated toward him. He would react with his hands in the air—a *"you CAN'T be real"* sort of exclamation—as I played every song I'd ever been proud of. There was a safeness that I felt with him. Cole was married to his gorgeous high school sweetheart, so the knowledge that a man simply appreciated a woman for her talent allowed me to drop my guard. I had roamed through the music world without a mentor, and finding one this late in the game was like being rescued after nearly thirty years on a desert island.

After a few months of being emboldened by Cole's guidance, he let me know that I would record his favorite song, "Let's Lie," in his studio, and then another two tracks in the weeks to come—so we could get my EP out into the world as soon as possible. There was even a cherry on top of this life-changing news: I would open for Cole Wyan on his North American tour. Gone were the days of playing half-empty dive bars. This was the birth of Maggie Vine, the professional singer-songwriter.

We recorded "Let's Lie" in a real studio a few weeks before my thirtieth birthday. A stupid smile stayed on my face as my guitar was mic'ed separately from my mouth in the vocal isolation booth. There wasn't pantyhose tugged onto the mic's windscreen. My body wasn't hunched inside my apartment's tiny closet in an attempt to get a semiprofessional sound. This was the real deal. This was Making It. Cole was making the real thing happen the way it was meant to. When other producers would pop their heads in to say hi, Cole would tell them that he had just discovered the Next Big Thing, pointing to me.

But he said it in a way that put no attention on me, and all the attention on himself. I started to see another side of him, and I started to see him as human. His imposter syndrome was the amalgamation of an insecure kid who became the most powerful person in a room.

After his sound engineer stepped out of the studio to go on break for lunch, I sat with my bony knees pointed inward as he played back "Let's Lie." Cole sat across from me on a black stool in front of the mixing board, his eyes shining at me as the pre-chorus to "Let's Lie" swelled. I tugged at a loose thread on the tufted couch below me, a mixture of self-consciousness swirling with thrilling pride—I had never heard myself professionally produced. This was the one song that I didn't layer with a heavier sound—it was delicate in all the right places, with the quiet swelling of acoustic guitar and tambourine, using reverb to give the song a dreamy, thickening air of romance. It was perfect.

Cole leaned back, pinching his eyebrows together. He energetically toggled with the sound effects on the board in front of him.

"What if we try this?"

Inside the chorus, there was now a gunshot in a space where a sparkling tambourine had once sounded.

I shook my head no, emphatically.

"Really? I think it gives the sound some mystery. Brings Mazzy Star into a gunfight."

"I don't want mystery here. I want hope. This song has to sound like a dream, and a gun cuts through it—it's like a pointing a middle finger and saying, 'This dream will never come true.'"

"Let's Lie" was a song about Garrett, and darkening it for public consumption felt like stabbing myself in the chest. I didn't want to add a grimness to the very hope that I was desperately clinging to. I was consumed by the fact that in two weeks I would be seeing Garrett, on my thirtieth birthday, in person for the first time since we slept together. I needed to roll around in hope so that I could take matters into my own hands and finally tell Garrett my feelings—tell him I was in love with him, tell him I wanted us to start right fucking now.

After a few minutes of back and forth on the song and the gunshot, Cole shook his head and smiled.

"You're a pistol, you know that? I love that you believe in your music. Point, Maggie," he said as he removed the weapon from my song. I looked down at my buzzing phone, silencing a call from Summer.

"You should be proud of this," I heard Cole say.

I exhaled and smiled, as I found his face just inches from my face, and his hand on my knee. My heart raced furiously, and I held my breath. Instead of arching back, I froze with every muscle in my body squeezing inside itself. Suddenly, Cole's sweaty palm was on the back of my head, and his mouth was on my neck.

I had not gone thirty years without being touched against my will. I was a woman in New York City who dared to ride the subway. Having a stranger purposefully grope my breast or my ass before he slipped out at his next stop had happened more than once. And those moments had fueled an anger inside me. I was tired of feeling like self-control was slipping through my body just because I needed basic transportation. This led me to take self-defense classes at the 92nd Street Y, hell-bent on the possibilities of publicly annihilating a groper in front of half of Manhattan. I wanted to hurt my assailant so badly that it would land me inside the "Everyday Heroes" pages of *People* magazine. I would no longer be a casualty of men offhandedly taking what they wanted from me in public.

But in private? In private, I had been lucky. A man had never touched me against my will behind a closed door. I knew this fact was good fortune and nothing more. I had gone nearly thirty years.

A supercut of the last couple months cascaded behind my eyes, which were the size of saucers. Had I given this man the green light to touch me in a place he absolutely needed permission to touch? And how could I politely say "thanks but no thanks" to a man who could make or break my dream? He was handing me something that had taken me too long to get, and I wasn't sure if I could brush Cole Wyan off my body without ruining my career.

I slowly backed my body up on the couch, inching my neck away from his lips and his hands. He leaned back with wide eyes, as if he was shocked that I didn't want his hands and his lips on my skin. He tilted his head to one side with a smile.

"C'mon," he said. "I know what you're afraid of . . . but we can still have a working relationship."

He did not know what I was afraid of. Or he knew and couldn't care less.

"I—I'm sorry. I just—I take all this seriously, I really value working with you. And—you have a wife, right?"

I knew none of these reasons mattered. All that held value was my no—my body language, which told a man to stop, no questions asked. I wanted to say, *"Don't fucking touch me, ever again—NO."* Women have to mollify broken, cruel men with outside excuses and apologies as to why taking pieces of our soul isn't a smart move, for *them*. We are wired, even in moments of screaming terror, to deescalate a situation that could kill us. I knew this to be true. I also knew another truth: monsters don't care about consequences. I wasn't sure if there was a monster sitting in front of me. I was praying there was reasoning inside Cole's brain.

He stared at me blankly, a face I worried lacked reason.

"We have an open relationship," Cole said flatly, referring to his wife.

The wheels of his stool creaked slowly on the carpet fibers, rolling toward me. Sweat prickled on my forehead as I tightened.

"I want you to respect me as an artist, and I don't want to cross this line with you, okay?"

Cole's eyes darkened. The red light over the door lit up half his face. In that moment, a man I had once felt comfortable with suddenly looked like a horror movie come to life: a monster.

"Oh, so you're that kind of girl? You think you can just lead me on, take what you want from me, and I'll sit back and be satisfied?"

I shook my head effusively as my heart raced faster. I blinked back a dizziness behind my eyes. I couldn't quite understand how in the span of two minutes, my world seemed to turn upside down.

My voice was as shaky as my insides. "No. No, I thought we were going to work together—that you saw something in my music, and that was that. I didn't know you had feelings for me. I'm sorry if I made you feel that way, I didn't know."

The sick part was, that in this moment, I was sorry—sorry for something I had never done. Sorry for a man's inability to understand the very simple meaning of a very simple word: no.

He squinted at me, turning his head to study both sides of my cheeks, as if trying to read me. It made me want to run, but I was still hopeful that there was no reason to run.

"Is this a *hard to get* thing? Like, you're trying to pretend you don't want me so I'll think you're not like the other fangirls? 'Cause I get it, you're special. Congratulations."

I shook my head, no longer able to hide my shock. My jaw was open and my eyes were wide. "I would like to keep this strictly professional, Cole."

"Kiddo, I'm going to give you a few seconds to really think what you're saying through."

It was a threat. A powerful man was threatening me, alone, behind closed doors. I looked down to my leg as I felt his hand back on my knee-cap. He leaned his face in to mine, staring directly into my eyes. I could feel his fingers circling below me as he raised his eyebrows. I could feel the tips of his fingers moving from my knee, all the way up my skirt. I had said no, and nothing I had done up to this point gave this man the right to know that the inside of my thigh was soft and warm.

There is an oval-shaped gray mass inside our brains, directly responsible for how we process fear: the amygdala. Mine was sending a signal to my brain stem, asking it to paralyze my body. My body didn't want to be present, but there was a fighter in me that did. I could feel the struggle as my hands went numb. I could hear his heavy breathing grow louder, as if it were inside my skull. My cross-wired senses had multiplied, and nothing worked the way I needed it to. I closed my eyes tightly and found the rhythm of my own breath. I opened my eyes on his lips coming for mine, with his finger inside me.

Boiling rage itched through my bones, and all at once, I lifted my body with the force of two women, edging my elbow into his nose. He shot backward off the stool, hitting the floor as blood gushed out of his flaring nostrils.

"FUCK," he yelled, seeing the blood all over his white crew neck.

My entire body sat shaking on the couch. I had undoubtedly broken his nose.

"You cunt," he growled. "You can fucking say goodbye to your career," he hissed, holding his body in a circle on the floor.

I was terrified that he was right. I was nearly thirty, and thirty-year-olds in the music industry didn't get first chances to succeed, let alone second ones. I watched as Cole started to unfurl his body. He was about to stand, and I didn't know what would happen when he regained use of his limbs. Would he use them to pin me down and take even more than my career from me? This was the flight part—the part where my self-defense instructor had told me to "fucking run." Fight *and* flight. Both were prominent factors in survival.

I scuffled off the couch, away from his standing frame. My shoulder slammed past the door, sending a seething pain through my upper body. I held my arm across my pounding shoulder as I flew out of the studio and into the empty, dimly lit hallway, inhaling industrial carpet cleaner—a smell so pungent that it punched the back of my throat. I could taste the bile against my tongue—nausea rushing out of me like a volcano. Tears in my eyes, I stumbled past the shiny platinum records that lit the walls. When I had walked into the studio hours earlier, I had beamed with a giddy hope, seeing these records as aspirational: *this'll be me one day.* They had lifted me up and floated me into the sound booth with heart-fluttering, glittery promise. Now, one after the other, they seemed to taunt me, illustrating how a mountain of possibilities had died inside a shitty man's hands. The impossibly long hallway started to swirl slowly around me—the air thickening like molasses. My vision was hot and blurry, and I wasn't sure if I was on a moving sidewalk, or if my legs were doing the moving. I looked back, seeing Cole open the studio door. Heart pounding in my ears, I flew toward a neon-green sign atop a door, just yards ahead of me. EXIT. Somehow, my feet tugged my entire weight outside.

I blinked back the harsh afternoon sun, gasping for air. The sounds of cars honking and teenagers laughing and mothers yelling and babies crying. The smell of burning rubber and cement and sewer and body odor and perfume. The pressure of a strange woman's fingers against my bare shoulder. The words "are you okay?" echoing over and over as white flurries filled my vision and hot pavement scraped my knees.

He had turned my dream into a nightmare.

44

THIRTY-FIVE

I COULD TASTE THE MEMORY—ACID rising up from my throat inside Carbone. There was a terror roaring through my body—a dizzying, red-hot alarm swirling inside my veins, warning me that I was in danger. I held my breath and clenched my stomach inward—desperate to keep from emptying my insides out on the crisp white tablecloth in front of me.

The room moved in slow motion. I was a deer in headlights, watching the man I loved converse joyfully with the man who'd tried to rape me. I couldn't hear a word they were saying—all I could hear was the loud beating of my own heart pounding in my eardrums. Asher nodded and grinned toward me. I guessed he was lavishing praise on me. I did my best to force my lips into an upward curl—a tiny hint at a smile. But then, Cole's smile beamed in my direction, like tiny knives under my skin.

"Excuse—excuse me," I said, the words trembling.

I stood up too fast, and white-hot flurries flew behind my eyes. I pushed through, edging my way past Asher, then I picked up my pace, as if running for my life. I needed air. I needed the exit. I didn't stop to con-sider who was outside—I couldn't wrap my head around my own reality. I pushed my way out of Carbone's front door, and the white flurries in my eyes were replaced with flashing cameras—more than I could ever count. *Fuck*. I could feel the bile rising, and suddenly, an arm linked in mine and pulled me back into the restaurant. My vision was blinded, but I felt my legs moving, I felt someone leading me a few steps away, past a door, and into bright fluorescent lighting. I slung my body into the open bathroom stall, emptying my stomach into the toilet in one swift move.

I leaned my back against the cold door, inhaling and exhaling deep breaths. My hands were shaking. For five years, I had worked tirelessly in therapy to alleviate the unfounded guilt that mounted in regard to Cole. He was the guilty party, but it was hard for my brain to conceptualize how a man who had my best interests at heart one moment was a man refusing to take no for an answer the next. And so, I filled in the blanks, blaming my ebullient energy for the reason why Cole heard yes when I said no. I was racked with specifically horrifying guilt for breaking his nose—even though I should have been patting myself on the back for defending my body. I'm not sure what would have happened if I hadn't fought back. It was a thought that crept into my brain every now and then, and it took two edibles and a *Friends* marathon to make the nightmare leave my mind.

"Maggie?" a voice said.

I suddenly remembered that I wasn't alone. That someone had tugged me into the women's restroom. I peered down at the penny-tile floor, seeing Raini's suede pumps.

"Are you okay?" she asked.

I looked up at her face—her eyes were wide, and her hands were open, as if she was ready to catch me if I fell to the floor.

"Yeah," I lied.

I moved slowly, uneasy as I found the sink. Raini watched me in the mirror, studying my ashen face for a long moment. I wasn't sure how long it was, maybe a minute or two, before Raini put her hands on mine. I looked down, realizing that I was scrubbing my hands under scalding water—hands which were now raw and bright red. Raini grabbed a towel and dried my hands as I stared wide-eyed at her.

"Did he do something to you?" she asked, her voice small.

"Who?" I cracked, looking away from her Disney princess eyes—doing a bang-up job of playing dumb while my insides ran a traumatic marathon. My pulse was racing. I knew very well who Raini was referring to, but I did not want to acknowledge it aloud—especially not to someone who I didn't know like the back of my hand. In five whole years I had told only three people about the day my career started and died—and one of them was my therapist.

"I've heard things about Cole. From my older sister's best friend."

I looked up, seeing Raini raise her thick brows at me, as if telling me it was okay to speak freely. Instead of taking horrified solace in knowing that I wasn't the only human Cole Wyan had ever attacked, instead of letting Raini in, I felt armor move around my body. In this moment, I didn't know how to relive it aloud without being carried out of here on a stretcher.

"I'm okay. I just got a little dizzy—I drank too much before the appetizers got there."

"You've had like one glass of wine."

Who was this kid? Fucking Sherlock Holmes?

"Just wait until you get to be thirty-five. One glass is enough to trigger a three-Advil-and-Gatorade morning."

"What did he do to you?" Raini asked, wide eyes on me, voice small.

It was the way she held herself in front of me that made me grip her hand tight as tears fell down my face. She shuffled in her beautiful pumps with a fragile brokenness, as if her road hadn't been all rainbows and sunshine. I let my shoulders fall, a dropping of my guard. Instinctively, I hugged her. She hugged me back. We both held on to each other, acknowledging some sort of different but shared nightmare.

"Can you look out there, and tell me if he's gone?" I whispered.

She pulled back and nodded, and then poked her head out the bathroom door.

"He's gone," she said, coming back to me.

Somehow, I made it back to the table and forced a smile on my face all night. Every few minutes, Raini's warm eyes studied mine with a tilt of the head and an arch of the eyebrows, as if to acknowledge that I didn't have to pretend to be okay. I held my own, but the knowledge that I could break down and have someone catch me? Especially a woman? It was a comfort I could not put into words.

A few hours later, Asher tossed his wallet on the console as we entered his apartment, and his eyes narrowed on me as I held the side of my stomach. Just a couple hours ago, Raini and I had laughed off how I walked out to the paparazzi—how I mistook the darkened front door for the bathroom door—clearly the glasses of wine went to my head. I thought Asher had bought it, but his gaze told me he was calling bullshit. Historically, I was the person you wanted to bring to a dinner party. I could talk to a snail, I had amusing stories, I was a feisty ball of energy. This night, I had kept my mouth occupied with a plate of heavy pasta, a decision that I was starting to pay for, physically. I felt the red sauce burning in the back of my throat.

"What's going on?" he finally asked.

"Nothing. I'm good," I said enthusiastically. "I mean, I could use an IV of Pepto, but seriously: all good."

Asher could see right through me. He always could. I knew it by the way his eyes had searched mine all night. I was rigid in places I was usually soft. I had been trying to stay engaged in each of the conversations tonight, but with Asher, I never had to try. Fortunately (and in this moment, unfortunately), Asher wasn't like the average straight man: he picked up on a woman's subtle hints.

"This is too much for you, isn't it?"

He spun his Rolex around his wrist, pain softening his strong jawline. I stepped out of my heels, shaking my head at Asher.

"What are you talking about?"

"The paparazzi, the fame—it's chaos. You accidentally opened the wrong door and a thousand flashes hit your eyes. I have a life where I can't go to a restaurant without a circus meeting me. It's a life you didn't choose."

He looked at me like I was pouring salt into his open wound. I walked over to Asher and clasped my fingers inside his hand, standing upright in front of him.

"Hey. Look at me," I said as I gently nudged his face into my view. His eyes drifted from his fingers up to my face. "Ash, it had *nothing* to do with you."

"Then what was it?"

I opened my mouth, with the truth sitting on the tip of my tongue. There was a wall up between one of the scariest moments of my life and the person I could picture spending the rest of my life with. In some ways, being around Asher made me feel like the girl I had been before—that girl with her palms outstretched to the world at summer camp. Before the trying was met with wall after wall. Before loving someone was bursting bright red and left me bleeding out. Before a man who promised to lift me up tore me apart with a wave of his hand. I didn't know how Asher would look at me after I told him about Cole, but deep down, I knew it wouldn't change how he saw me. That wasn't why my feet were shifting—why my mouth was pressed shut. I was keeping this from him because I didn't know how *I* would look at Asher after I told him. We weren't teenagers anymore. We didn't only exist inside the trappings of young love, but he brought me back to a place that was warm and safe and unspoiled. In Asher's hold I felt innocent, and this truth would bring me into reality—into my complicated adulthood right in front of his eyes. It would be an admission that our lives had shifted when we fell apart, an admission that we weren't the same people who'd held each other naked on that dock.

I chewed the insides of my cheeks and flickered a tiny smile his way.

"I . . . I honestly started to feel not so great. Major period cramps." I smirked with a little exhale. "I have a very sensitive reproductive system, and I was trying to spare you the details."

If you want to end a conversation with a male, the word "period" usually gets the job done. While Asher was completely above average in so many ways, he was also an average male when it came to discussing women bleeding out of their vaginas.

"Okay," he said with a tiny smile, nodding and putting it to bed.

"Ash, I'm in this. You, me, the circus, the flashy lightbulbs, outrunning shitheads holding cameras—all of it. Yeah, I'm not super pumped that my every public move might be caught on camera. But hey, I plan on being more famous than you one day, so I may as well get used to this."

His smile cracked wide, and he tugged me toward his body so my bare feet stood between his shoes.

"Oh, well, I'm glad I could be of assistance," he said, his nose touching mine.

I grabbed the back of his neck and pulled him onto my lips, a silent reassurance that he had nothing to worry about, that I was all-in on all of Asher Reyes. But there was a mounting voice inside my head, a question that got louder and louder even as I kissed him harder and harder: if I was all-in on Asher, then why was I afraid to show him all my cards?

Even after all the extensive work I had done during therapy the last few years, there was still a thread of shame stitched around a moment where I carried no culpability. I hoped one day I'd be able to untangle it in front of the person I loved. Maybe it would come out in sobs, the way the truth about Asher's brother's death came out in guttural cries. I got it now. Asher holding on to that horrible truth wasn't about me, any more than me holding on to this horrible truth was about Asher. My deflection was about my pain, and my need to release it to the universe when I was ready.

But sometimes, the universe gets its claws on you and shakes the truth from your bones before you're ready.

45

THIRTY

"Tonight . . . tonight when I blew out the candles, my birthday wish was for us to end up together."

Garrett and I sat side by side in this tiny Nolita bar on my thirtieth birthday, as the maybe horrible truth fell out of me, and I couldn't put it back in. He studied me like he was dropped inside a play without knowing any of the lines. My lips stayed parted in the air—stunned by their own handiwork. There was a familiar white-hot adrenaline coursing through my body, the kind of bravery I only felt when I sang under a spotlight. Which is why I kept going, even as all rationale screamed, *STOP SAYING WORDS, MAGGIE.*

"If we're not married in five years, promise me you'll show up at my door and marry me," I heard myself say.

"You . . . you want me to marry you?" he asked slowly, as if he needed to say the sentence aloud to understand it.

I shook my head. "Scratch that."

"You don't want me to marry you?"

"I do. But *I'll* show up at your door—you're horrible with timing."

Garrett opened his mouth, but no words followed. His brows pressed together for a long moment as my breathing became more rapid. I couldn't feel my fingers, and there was a ringing in my ears.

Did I just spring a marriage pact on Garrett Scholl?

I knew I was in a bad place, but I didn't know I was in a reckless one. I bent my neck forward with my hand around my throat, fighting the wave of humiliation rising up from my stomach. I turned toward the bar, staring hard at the freshly washed glasses as if they were a time machine. Garrett reached his hand down to my seat, twisting my barstool toward him and bringing us face-to-face. My heart thumped as his eyes scanned every line on my face. And then, he leaned forward, the heat of his mouth against mine.

"Why do we have to wait until we're thirty-five?" he whispered against my lips.

I hadn't seen Garrett since he got back from San Francisco. Two weeks ago, the idea of seeing him after ten months apart consumed me wholly. But then—Cole Wyan happened to me. But here I was, my lips just inches from Garrett Scholl's mouth, a fantasy come to life.

"Maggie, all I've been able to think about the last few months is . . . us . . . *this* right here." His thumb moved along my chin, like a question waiting to be answered.

His eyes didn't leave mine, and there wasn't a hint of playfulness anywhere in his jaw. I felt warmth envelop me. *Here it was.* Right person. Right time. All I wanted to do was lean into his lips and start the rest of our lives together, *right fucking now,* but his hand—his hand was on my thigh.

His hand.

My thigh.

My breathing quickened and I clenched my eyes shut, my chest growing hot, my mind boomeranging back to two weeks ago, when Cole Wyan's hand had been right there, right on the soft spot of my skin. His hand gliding up my body. An intruder in my home.

"Maggie?" I heard Garrett ask. I felt his hand leave my thigh.

"I should—I should go," I said quickly, eyes still shut, body frozen.

"Did I do something?"

I swallowed hard and blinked my eyes on Garrett's hurt face. His hand was on my arm, his eyes were wide, searching for an answer.

"Garrett, I'm not in a good place right now—not for this."

He scrunched up his face.

"Okay. But . . . then why did you say what you said? That you wanted us to end up together?" he asked, baffled, maybe even a little stung.

I searched for words amid the sound of my heart pounding in my ears.

"I meant what I asked you. I meant it. I just—I can't be with anyone right now."

I edged my body off the stool, but my legs were numb, and I felt my chest dropping to the floor. Garrett caught my side with one strong arm, quickly steadying my body against his. He put his hand around my waist, looking at me, panicked. I'd never seen him look at someone like this before. I darted from his view, focusing on my shaking hands.

"Let's get you home, okay?" he asked quietly.

I felt tears in my throat as I nodded.

I was in pieces, with no instructions on how to glue myself back together. My hopes, my dreams, my body—broken. Three weeks ago, Garrett saying he wanted to start a life with me would have gone down as some of the greatest seconds of my life. And today, my body and my mind wouldn't let me go anywhere near bliss. My happiness was frozen behind a moment of terror.

Garrett took me home instantly, made sure I got under the covers, and left me Advil and water by my bedside. He watched me for a long moment, and right before he left, I could see his expression out of the corner of my eyes. He was bathed in confusion.

I stared at the ceiling, limbs shaking until the sun rose. And I did it again the next day. And the next.

46

THIRTY-FIVE

FOR AN ENTIRE WEEK AFTER my encounter with Cole at Carbone, I crushed a Xanax between my teeth every night, quieting my racing mind. It had been a full seven days, and Cole hadn't touched my future or called Asher to warn him that I had a mean right hook.

I exhaled, letting the sun bathe my freckled shoulders as I walked up West Thirtieth Street. It was time to let that encounter go, and starting today, I would carve my own path—or that was what I was saying to the sky, during my morning mantra. I told myself I had merely seen a ghost at Carbone—one that no longer posed a threat. I adjusted Asher's aviators over my eyes—large frames that didn't fit my narrow bone structure, but dulled the paparazzi camera flashes. His shades also hid the fact that I refused to apply makeup before an aggressive amount of caffeine was coursing through my blood. The glasses quieted the online trolls who expected all celebrity girlfriends to roll out of bed with contoured faces.

There was a wide grin on my face as I ducked my head down past a stray paparazzo, fingers pinching my AirPods farther into my eardrums. My homemade demo, "Full Circle," lit up the street with an ethereal, folksy sound—a sound that was about to get the studio-produced treatment. In a handful of hours, I was set to record the track, my very first single, in Bex's studio.

I felt my phone vibrate in my fanny pack as I flew inside my favorite coffee shop, inhaling caffeine and fresh blueberry scones—a combination that my body desperately needed. While the paparazzi had discovered my morning routine, there was no "money shot" if Asher wasn't in the frame. Thankfully, my solo presence made the paparazzi scatter once I was inside, leaving me to order an oat milk latte in peace.

I sucked in the caffeinated air, calming my anxiety. I had been expecting a phone call from Shelly ever since Asher and I took our relationship public at Carbone. His arm was tight around my waist when we left the restaurant later that night, his hand holding me in a completely intimate way, leaving nothing left to wonder about the state of our relationship. While I had waited until after the money went into my bank account and for all the songs to be turned in before I took our relationship public, I knew that Shelly probably would have preferred we wait a bit longer, or at least give her a heads-up.

"Hi," I said into the phone as I shuffled to the back of the obnoxiously long line. There were a few head turns, likely people trying to figure out why a nondescript, tiny woman wearing a pink fanny pack and a Nap Dress was being followed by flashing lights.

"So, remember that time I asked you if you had any demos floating around, and you said no?" Shelly asked.

"Yeah . . ."

"Well, I just got off the phone with Cole Wyan's manager, and it would appear that you not only have a demo floating around, you have a *Cole Wyan*–produced demo. And the world's about to hear it. So, I'd like to know why you straight-up lied to me."

My heart rate quickened, and my hands started to shake.

"Hold—hold on for a second," I said, wide-eyed and stammering.

I tugged my body out of the line, walking back outside the coffee shop. I darted across a break in traffic, and ducked past the doorman, running into Asher's building. Heart pounding in my ears, I exhaled as my body found a leather chair in a windowless, private corner of the opulent lobby.

"Maggie? Are you still there?"

I tugged my AirPods out of my ear and threw them in my fanny pack, grabbing my phone and pressing it up to my mouth.

"Can he do that? Can he just release the song, whenever he wants?" I whispered.

"You signed a release. I'm staring at it right now."

"But that was . . . that was over five years ago. I signed something five years ago—"

"Unfortunately, you signed it in perpetuity. Cole could release your song in twenty years if he wanted to. Look, obviously this guy found out you were about to become a success, he's seen you online, he learned you were doing the original music for Asher Reyes's buzzy film, *and* most significantly—he heard that you were recording with Fin Bex. Cole feels the need to engage in some sort of pissing contest with Bex at every turn—as Bex's producing career has eclipsed his."

I tucked my knees into my chest, holding my body to keep from falling apart in public.

"Cole's going to take credit for my career, isn't he? He's going to get to profit off me, forever?"

I already knew the answer. Angry, hot liquid masked my vision.

"Yes, to both of those questions," Shelly confirmed.

In the fairy tale, the villain doesn't profit off the underdog until her dying day. The villain doesn't get to take credit for discovering the underdog. The villain doesn't loom large until the underdog draws her last breath. But now, my villain would get to do exactly that.

"When's he releasing the song?"

"It's Friday, Maggie."

"What does that mean?"

"It means check your Spotify. Apple Music. It came out at midnight. Across all platforms."

I went silent. I couldn't bring myself to even move a finger.

"Do you want to tell me why you kept this from me?" Shelly asked.

I opened my mouth to explain, but shock strangled my throat.

"Maggie, before I lay into you, just know this: it's a phenomenal single. The song is nothing to be ashamed of. But the timing, unfortunately, couldn't be worse. I'm trying to do some smoothing here, which is why I need you to start talking. I don't think Bex is going to want to produce you five seconds after Cole Wyan releases your first studio-recorded single to the world. Fin Bex is the most honest guy in the business, and all he expects in return is transparency. He called me pretty pissed off this morning. Angry I kept this from him, angry you kept this from him. He wants to press pause on recording today."

Cole Wyan had stifled my career five years ago, and he was about to do it again. Silent tears started to fall, and I wiped them away quickly with the back of my hand.

Shelly let the sniffles linger between the phone lines.

"Maggie, why don't you call me back later with the full story?"

"Okay," I finally cracked.

I set the phone down on my lap, my eyes wide with tears, until I clenched them shut. I could feel the panic rising, the walls around my body closing in, my past and present swirling together to suffocate me in this beautiful marble lobby with the paparazzi waiting outside. I took labored breaths in and out, trying to get my heart rate to slow. Instinctively, I pressed hard on Summer's name on my phone.

For the first time, a call to my best friend went straight to voicemail. Historically, I had never enjoyed sitting by myself with horrible news. Summer was my first phone call, my lifeline, the person who would come over and hold me for a brief moment, and then clap her hands and form a game plan for success. Unlike myself, Summer preferred to sit with her shit quietly—she did not enjoy a group project—which is why her phone was off. Yesterday, she sent an email to all her friends, letting them know that she and Valeria were getting a divorce. It read like a stone-cold PR statement, which was of no surprise to me. Summer turned off her phone after sending the email. She wanted people to know her truth, but she didn't want to talk about it—especially while untangling it herself.

My rock was crumbling in South Florida—I was without a lifeline, crumbling in New York City. I glanced down at the electronic key fob in my hand—the key to Asher's loft, a reminder that I actually did have a rock.

I uncurled my limbs from my chest, slowly standing up as dizziness shot behind my eyes. I drew in air, my heart pounding as I watched my scuffed Converses take labored steps forward. I put one foot in front of the other until the balmy morning air was howling inside my lungs and my feet were planted on a cobblestone street in the Meatpacking District. I felt my finger dial a name on my iPhone's "Favorites."

47

THIRTY-ONE

I INHALED THE HARD SUN with my eyes closed—the aroma of freshly cut grass swirled with the stench of hot pretzels. It was the first warm day of spring—sixty-two degrees—which after surviving a winter in New York felt like the equivalent of a scalding summer day. I was grateful to have warmth on my pale shoulders—shoulders which were feeling the sun's rays for the first time since fall's harsh turn. It was honestly the only thing I was grateful for today.

I opened my eyes on Sheep Meadow, just as a red flat object came spinning toward my face at lightning speed. I slapped my hands together around the Frisbee before it could slice my face in two.

"Heads-up," Summer said, deadpan.

She stood above a blanket, and I glared at her, throwing the Frisbee back with too much force. It soared over Summer's straight long bob, landing in the hands of a woman standing a few yards behind Summer. The mystery woman was my age, maybe a little younger, twirling in the breeze, not even bothering to see where the Frisbee had come from. She wasn't one to question why something fell into her hands—life just did, and you knew it by looking at her, the way the harsh sun bathed her face gently, like a soft light box on a beaming smile. Effortless. Her blond hair was perfectly pinned up to the side, her lips were a matte red, her long legs stood tall in a white linen dress. I swallowed hard as Garrett came into view, his bare torso folding around this mystery woman, swinging her giggling frame into a dipping kiss that made her chin go all the way to the sky.

Over the years, I'd watched Garrett enjoy the company of a handful of other women, but I had never seen him do it so . . . freely. So openly. They shared a look you could recognize almost anywhere. I had never seen Garrett Scholl in love. Scratch that. I had never seen Garrett Scholl in love with anyone who wasn't me. It was like a chain saw running down my heart. I pressed my hand to my chest, trying to mend the hot, sharp pain. They held each other's gazes for a moment, and then Garrett kissed her neck and she danced herself out of his hold.

"Earth to Maggie Vine."

I broke one-way eye contact with heartache, meeting Summer's hand waving in my face.

"Are you going to come sit with us, or do you need more time to stand here like a weirdo?"

Yards in front of Summer, I saw Valeria sitting on a blanket, eyes down on her phone. Summer and Valeria had been married for a few years now, and I was trying to warm up to her since my best friend loved her madly. Call me selfish, but while I loved that Summer had found her person, I wished it could be with someone who more than tolerated my presence. I got the sense Valeria was always concentrating on something else when I was around—like I was a person worthy of flicking your eyes at every now and then. I think she understood that Summer and I had our own language, and instead of trying to join in, it was easier to disengage.

I looked back at Garrett, who threw the Frisbee straight into the mystery woman's arms.

"Who is that?" I asked, eyes on the woman.

"Cecily," Summer said.

"How long's that been going on?"

"Four months," Summer said, confusion on her face as she watched me.

"How'd the showing go yesterday?" Summer asked.

A month after my thirtieth birthday, I'd quit performing altogether. I was stifled every time I got onstage—terrified that I would see Cole's face in the audience. After bailing on three gigs in a row—bathed in panic attacks behind stage curtains, I threw in the towel. There was no fighting this kind of monster—he stood too tall on my chest, and I didn't know where to start, or how to pick up a sword against a powerful man who had touched me against my will and threatened my career. It was easier to lock everything up and throw away the key. The music died. I took the real estate license exam, made my mother's dreams come true, joined her firm, and started making money. Real money. I was phenomenal at selling beautiful places. My soul died, too. I could barely look at myself in the mirror as I got dressed in the morning, I didn't want Maggie Vine seeing what she'd become.

"The three-three in Gramercy?" I asked, referring to my biggest listing yet.

"Yes . . ."

"I got an offer. All cash," I said flatly, my eyes on Cecily and Garrett.

"Shut up!" Summer said, beaming at me.

Cecily's fingers running up the lines on Garrett's stomach. His hand wrapping around her waist.

"Maggie."

Summer's voice was forceful, and I tore my eyes off Garrett as she stared at me.

"You just made your biggest sale."

"And?" I said, emotionless with a tiny shrug, my eyes leaving hers.

Garrett tugging Cecily's body tight against his. Their lips brushing. Matching cackles. Sun on both their smiles.

"And?" I heard Summer say, mocking my indifference.

It was strange, what was happening inside me as I watched Garrett dance his body around a woman, the way he'd danced his body around mine. I brought my attention back to Summer. Her eyes widened, taking in my face, which had darkened to something angry. I felt spite, the spite I housed for myself, come barreling out my throat, burning my tongue on its way out.

"I don't give a shit about anything," I said, the words caked in venom.

Or, I think I said that.

That's what I meant to say.

I'm not sure what came out of my mouth, because all of a sudden, every emotion I had buried for the last year and a half after Cole Wyan ended my career, after I couldn't get onstage again without having a panic attack, after I quit picking up my guitar, after I stopped writing music, after I took the real estate exam, after I made my mom's dreams come true, after I had a hard time being in the same room as the guy I loved—all of a sudden, something white hot was strangling my throat. I felt my shaking hands go to my neck, but Summer's arms were already around me, leading me under a cool patch of shade—a tree out of sight.

I couldn't catch my breath, and the splintering inside me turned to a heaviness, as tears rained down my throat. At first, the words came out in a jumble of sobs, between gasps for air. I knew Summer couldn't understand me at all. As I caught my breath, she made me repeat it to her, slower. My horrible truth escaped my throat like a prisoner set free, one who was terrified to step out into freedom. One who was innocent. One who didn't know how to look at the world after being locked in a cell for so long. I was coming apart enough for us both—and so, Summer quieted her quivering chin, remaining as steady as that Bob Seger song—my rock.

I finished telling her everything. From Cole Wyan, to how I pushed Garrett away, to how I hadn't been hungry for much of anything in over a year—food, sex, music, happiness. How like a light switch, my soul went gray, and I didn't know how to find the sunshine anymore, nor did I think I was deserving of it.

Summer sat with it for a while, wiping away my tears and inhaling the wind.

"So, here's what we're going to do," Summer finally said, her hands on my arms.

"First, you've got a fancy job, and it has fancy health insurance, so we're going to find you a fancy therapist. And if I have to walk you to an appointment every week, I will. But you're going to get some help."

I nodded, tears streaming down, realizing that my insides weren't on fire. Somehow, the freedom—the ability to exist with a brutal truth living outside my lungs—was as terrifying as I could have imagined, but I could inhale without smoke. I was no longer suffocating.

"Second, and this is going to take a while, but Maggie Vine, we're going to get your career back to where it's supposed to be."

I shook my head, feeling the weight of the impossible. She gripped my chin in her hand and lifted it to her piercing eyes.

"Don't you shake your head at me. It won't happen overnight, but it will fucking happen. Maggie, you are not allowed to close the door on something you were born to do. That man isn't always going to stand in front of your door. You will be bigger than him, stronger than him, and you will eclipse that monster in every sense of the word, and you will stomp over him on your way to success. And I will be there right by your side the entire way."

She stared at me, waiting for me to nod, the breeze not even making her big eyes flinch.

"Okay," I said, real small, as silent tears kept flowing, my hands now gripped in hers.

"Third: you will, when you're ready, and this might take a while, too— but you will tell Garrett how you feel about him."

My eyes floated to see the way Garrett's large hands were running down Cecily's arms. The way his eyes studied the freckles on her back like they were a map. Like she was his North Star.

"What if it's too late?" I said quietly, wiping tears from my nose.

Summer laughed softly.

"Babe, I'm going to tell you something you already know. Despite what happened to you, you are madly in love with Garrett Scholl. And despite what's happened in the last year, Garrett remains madly, madly, madly in love with you."

"I don't know that. You don't know that." She glared at me like she knew. "How do you know?"

"A little while ago, I saw you walking along the fence, yards and yards away, approaching us. And I said, 'Maggie's here,' and then Garrett looked over at you. And you know what he did? He swallowed really hard, and he turned away real fast."

"So he can't even look at me?" I felt different kind of tears welling.

Summer steadied her hands on my arms.

"Maggie, he's so in love with you that he can't even meet your eyes because it hurts too much."

"I'm the type to look at something harder when it burns."

"He's a man. Men look away. It's how they go through life— compartmentalizing and putting what hurts them in boxes. You're in a box right now. But let me tell you, when you're ready to open yourself up again, when you stand in front of him and pour your heart out, he won't be able to look away."

I liked the idea of that. I hated the idea of what I would have to put myself through to get there. But I wanted to get there so badly, and I wanted to start now. I nodded, a soft sad smile on my chapped lips.

"Will you help me get home?"

"Fourth thing: you're going to come live with me for a little while."

I tilted my head up to the sun, lashes wet and closed, face red, and I inhaled something new. Summer held me closer as I exhaled tears on her shoulder—pain and relief leaving my body. No one can hold you quite like a best friend.

I was grateful for much more than the sun. And that was a start.

48

THIRTY-FIVE

I FELT LIKE I COULDN'T breathe, and I flew from the cab into my studio apartment like it was a goddamn oxygen tank—in a way, it was. I pressed my shoulder blades against the back of the front door, and with one exhale, I felt my chest cave in. It was the first time I had been really, truly alone since I saw Cole Wyan a week prior. And finally, I could scream.

I let out a bloodcurdling yell, not realizing I had been hiding so much anguish and trauma inside my tiny frame for seven whole days. And all at once, I was *throw something* angry. My white-knuckled fists snatched a porcelain plate holding a stack of bills, and I threw the plate against my wall, watching it break into scattered pieces. I held myself amid broken glass and shattered dreams, frustration and pain pouring out loudly as my body slid down the side of the door. I had been clenching the trauma of seeing Cole again inside me—playacting *fine* so that I wouldn't hit rewind on the nightmare that I was desperate to keep on the left side of the tape. Sidestepping away from my feelings—a practice I rarely embraced—had taken more of a toll on my body than leaning into them.

I made it atop my unmade floral quilt, my body sending records and open journals to the floor. I stared at the dark wooden beams above me, eyes wet and red, chest quieting under the catharsis of coming clean with myself.

HOURS LATER, I WOKE UP with the covers tucked around me, my tired eyes frozen on the ceiling fan. Breathing felt like inhaling smoke, and my dad's guitar in the corner of the room wouldn't stop making eye contact with me.

My studio was suddenly claustrophobic and inescapable. I forced my body off the bed, legs both heavy and numb, and I lumbered outside of my apartment, inhaling the musty dark old Victorian wood surrounding me inside this hot, shitty place I could now more than afford. I plopped down on the top of the stairs, clamming my eyes shut as I inhaled and exhaled deep breaths.

"Hey," a voice said.

I brought my head up from between my legs, my heart jolting to find Garrett standing right below my face. There was too much chaos inside me to house space for regret. I should have felt like a monster for calling a man to come watch me cry—a man who I had told myself I had stopped loving, a man who was notably getting married in a few weeks. But sometimes, when you can't see the forest through the trees, instead of looking for a way out you roll around in the mud.

"Thanks for coming," I barely managed, as the sobs took over.

Garrett's eyes widened, and he sat down next to me, pulling a strong arm over my shoulder.

"Come here," he said, holding me close to his body.

He was wearing a suit and tie, and I realized that he had been in the middle of his workday when I called him. One voicemail, telling him that Cole Wyan had released my song, and he had dropped everything for me. His magnetic blue eyes tilted to the side, narrowed on my pain.

His jaw tightened and a vein pulsed at the side of his neck.

"Cole can do this—just release your song? Legally?"

"Yeah."

I stared down at my phone, seeing a text from Asher come across my screen. There, in the harsh light of day, was a link to my Spotify song, "Let's Lie."

Proud of you, and also . . . sort of confused. Call me when you have time to chat.

My stomach dropped, guilt and shame swirling like a tornado inside. Guilt that I was sitting here with another man. Pain that I was keeping this from Asher. Shame that this had happened to me. Claws felt like they were inside my throat, and shaking, I turned my phone upside down on my lap, with my hand pressed on the nausea growing in my stomach.

"Maggie, you're going to figure this out," Garrett said, leaning forward to meet my eyes.

"How? The song. The recording. It's just—it's out there for the world to hear. And it could destroy all that comes next."

"Have you listened to it yet?"

I shook my head. My insides were burning with an unknown terror. Terror that I knew wouldn't leave my body until I pressed play. I couldn't escape my own past, even if I tried.

"Do you want me to listen to it with you?" he asked.

I nodded wordlessly but didn't move my fingers.

He took out his phone from his pocket, and I put my hand on his wrist, stopping him. I needed to figure out a way to take back this song, and it didn't start with another person playing it for me. If I could press play on my own hard work, in spite of the monster who stood behind it, then it would be the first step in walking out of the woods. That much I knew.

I brought the heat of my phone up to my face with a sharp inhale, seeing my song right there in front of me, plain as day, on Spotify. And then, my finger shaking, I pressed play, and "Let's Lie" swelled in the air for the first time in five years, and for the very first time in front of the man I wrote it for.

Brush stroke, blank slate
Our time is due
Right there, right now, burning red and deep blue

I couldn't look at Garrett, not at all. Instead, I had my head down on my phone, clenching my entire body.

Paint me anew, inside this room
Don't wipe our slates clean
I quite like this hue
Let's lie, me and you, like new lovers do

I exhaled a relief, my eyes brimming with tears as the tambourine sounded. There was no gunshot. Tears swelled in my throat with the reality that Cole had kept my song the way I wanted it. The monster recognized that my creative version was worthy, and it was complicated and hellish to feel thankful in this moment for the very man who was trying to steal my moment.

Silk shirt, sweat-soaked
Dancing with you
Right there, right now, our bodies unglued

Paint me anew, inside this room
Don't wipe our slates clean
I quite like this hue
Let's lie, me and you, like new lovers do

Your lips, my throat
Don't think it through
Right there, right now holding me like a muse

Paint me anew, inside this room
Don't wipe our slates clean
I quite like this hue
Let's lie, me and you, like new lovers do

Is loving you more worth the fight
Don't answer tonight
You're a big-picture guy scared of a varnished lifetime
Are we worth the fight
Don't answer tonight
Are we worth the fight
Tell me a lie painted white
Just for tonight
Just for tonight

I swallowed hard, daring my eyes to find Garrett, a quick glance to see if he knew who this song was about. His eyes widened around the lyrics as he stared straight ahead. His lips slightly parted, and my heart beat faster. *He knew.*

Paint me anew, inside my room
Don't wipe our slates clean
Our bodies in bloom
Let's lie to ourselves like new lovers do

The airy reverb faded into silence. Garrett sat frozen, staring at the bottom of the spiral staircase, refusing to move. He looked up, slowly letting his eyes narrow onto mine.

"It's beautiful, Maggie. Is that song . . . ?" He trailed off.

The possibility of the answer was so stifling, that he couldn't even finish asking the question. He stared at me, waiting as I studied his piercing eyes, his shifting jaw.

"You know it's about you," I said.

His gaze softened as he studied me for a long, quiet moment. The air seemed to pound and thicken with the rapid beating of our chests, neither of our bodies moving.

"You were wrong," he said, his blue eyes looking into mine. "You didn't love me more."

Air left my lungs. It took me a moment to find words.

"How do you know that?" I cracked.

I watched the way the setting sun fell on Garrett's face—how his eyes scanned mine. After a moment, his large hand reached over, linking our fingers together. His skin on my skin, even just fingers, felt like life and death wrapped in one. Garrett leaned toward me, almost nose to nose, setting his other hand on my cheek.

"Because I loved you more than anything," he said.

49

THIRTY-FOUR

I DIDN'T WANT TO RELIVE the last four years—not for anything. But I needed to. I had been in intensive therapy for over two years, and I owed it to myself to be honest with the guy I was still in love with—the guy who I had pushed away at the very time he was ready to go all in.

The day after I broke down to Summer in Sheep Meadow, she gave me the greatest gift anyone has ever given me, the number to a recommended therapist. Little by little, the only person I started letting down after that was my mom, when I quit my job and picked my guitar back up.

It had been over a year since I had started mending my soul, singing in clubs and venues without having heart palpitations, writing music again, having sex and being able to enjoy it. But the lingering pang of Garrett, of that moment nearly five years ago, it loomed so large—even now. Looming large was also the fact that he was still seeing Cecily, but the regret of not saying what I needed to say felt bigger than respecting what they had. I know that made me selfish. But in therapy I worked to understand that unleashing a very selfish truth might also be life-affirming. Life-affirming was too big a win not to play my hand.

I sat in the little café in Greenwich Village, making blue-inked doodles in my open songwriter notebook around words that had just flowed out of me like lava. I felt a tap on my shoulder.

There he was.

Dressed in a suit with a long wool coat tugged over his broad shoulders. His blond hair damp and wavy from the drizzling rain outside. I hugged Garrett, and he felt stiffer than usual, but slowly he hugged me back, inhaling deeply.

We let each other go, and as we sat down, his eyes looked everywhere but at mine. His usual warm, bright behavior was somewhat on edge. Nervous, even.

"Thanks for coming," I said, closing my notebook and leaning into the table so I could get a better look at him.

"Of course. I've actually—I've been meaning to call you. I wanted to . . . to chat. It's been a while," he said with a tiny smile, eyes now on me.

It had been a while. Four months, exactly. One of our longest stretches, but I surmised that Garrett didn't know what to do with me anymore. I had chaotically disappeared from his life after he got back from San Francisco, then I popped up at birthday parties—his, mine, Summer's, Valeria's. And then, the last two years, I had tried to text more and call, but Garrett returned the distance I had shown him. Rightly so. This friendship was broken because of circumstance. I couldn't blame myself, only what I had been through.

"Can I go first?" I asked, twisting a napkin in my hands.

"Sure."

"I want to talk to you about my thirtieth birthday."

Garrett seemed to go white, and I watched him swallow hard, his hand pinching around his tie. Clearly, this was the last thing Garrett had been expecting me to bring up. And clearly, it still stung.

After a pause, he nodded. "Okay."

"First, I want to say I'm sorry. I'm sorry for what I said to you right before I turned you away. And I'm sorry for how I acted when you tried to kiss me. That must have been so confusing for you," I said, voice level.

I took a deep breath in, closed my eyes briefly, and then opened them on Garrett. His expression softened, taking in how hard this was for me.

"Two weeks prior, Cole Wyan—you remember I started working with him?"

Garrett nodded, eyes searching mine.

"Well, two weeks before my thirtieth birthday, we were recording a song, and it was supposed to be my first single, and—he put his hands—"

I stopped talking, emotions bubbling in my throat. My heart was racing with the heaviness I was unpacking. The rest came out fast. "He touched me where I asked him not to. He tried to rape me. I punched the shit out of him. He threatened my career."

Garrett looked like I had struck him with a shovel.

"He *what*?" Garrett growled.

His vein was pulsing on his neck, his fists clenched.

"He . . . yeah," was all I could say.

"I wish—God I wish you had told me about him."

I looked at his white-knuckled fists, then his reddening face.

"I feel like I'd be visiting you in prison if I'd told you then," I said.

He looked directly into my eyes. "You would be."

Tears clouded my vision, and I looked up to the ceiling, trying to keep my emotions somewhat neutral while I got the rest out. I brought my face back to his. There was a dark storm where blue eyes had been.

"When you touched me, in the bar that night—I—it triggered that moment in the studio for me. I was mortified after that. I didn't *want* to be around you—I didn't know *how* to be around you. And I just want you to know that I—" My voice cracked upon his softened face, eyes blue and inches from mine. "I was in love with you. Deeply. I said what I said that night because I did wish for us to end up together. And I lost myself for a little while, but I've gotten the help I need, and I . . ."

He was frozen. Unmoving. I had to finish. I had to say it all. I was so tired of housing so much regret.

"That time, at the club, on the dance floor, sleeping with you that night—it was one of the most—it was one of the best nights of my life. I felt something there that I don't think many people get to feel. And I hate that we went from that . . . to this."

He blinked me back. I shifted in my seat and looked down at my hands.

"I know you're happy, and I want that for you," I said, my voice smaller. "I just—I can't keep living like this. Pretending that what happened to me didn't happen, and that it didn't take something from us, too. And I wasn't sure it was fair for just me to know that."

I let my eyes find his again. Pain spread across his face as his eyes left mine.

"This is"—he swallowed hard, his focus on his hands—"this is a lot."

His eyes came back toward me. "Are you okay?" he asked. He asked it in such a way that if my answer was no, it might kill him.

"Honestly?" I smiled, staring into his bright blue eyes—ones that now held all of my truths—maybe horrible and horrible ones. "I'm getting there."

He smiled quickly and looked back down at the table. My eyes narrowed again on the way he tugged at his throat—as if he had something he needed to get off *his* chest.

"Thank you for telling me," he said quietly.

We talked idly about his job, his upcoming family vacation to Tuscany, which I knew he was going to with Cecily, but he didn't mention her by name. Neither did I. I hoped she would pass like the rest of them, and that he'd show up at my door. My birthday was coming up in six weeks. Maybe he remembered. Of course he remembered. I'd just brought it up.

We stood to leave, and he stepped forward and hugged me. He held on a little tighter than usual, longer than he'd held me in four whole years.

"I'm sorry," he said quietly, into my ear. "I'm so sorry that you had to go through that alone." He stepped back from me, and with a painful one-sided grin, he squeezed my hand. "I would have liked to have been there for you."

I believed him, and I didn't know where to put that kind of regret.

"See you soon, okay?" Garrett asked.

I nodded, and he walked out of the café.

Through the window, rain slapped down, and I watched Garrett approach the crosswalk, his umbrella curiously closed and limp by his side, rain drenching his body. The light changed to green, but he didn't move. Garrett stood still, paralyzed. He put his hand on the back of his head and looked up at the darkening sky, blinking back something. I caught it—just a glimpse—right as he turned. His face was in agony. Complete agony. And then, he disappeared into the crowd.

50

THIRTY-FIVE

GARRETT AND I WERE AN inch apart on my stairs, eyes locked on to each other, his one hand in mine, his other cupping my cheek. I sat frozen, staring at him for a long while, the way you'd commit someone to memory before the casket closed. My face burned with tears as I tore my eyes away from his. I lowered my watery gaze down to the table, where Garrett's fingers were still wrapped around mine. I slowly unclenched my grip, freeing myself from his hold. He dropped his hand from my cheek.

He knew.

Silence floated between us for a long while until our eyes met again.

"You love him, don't you?" Garrett asked, his voice cracking with the realization.

I nodded effusively, tears down my cheeks.

"Yes."

It was Garrett's hand settling on my cheek, just minutes ago, that made me ache for Asher. I longed to call Asher and apologize for the very thing I was doing—sitting on the steps with another man while I should be sitting next to him. In that moment, I saw a supercut of all the things I'd miss about Asher if I had leaned into Garrett's touch. I saw the beautiful life we'd build, where we'd both cheer each other on, where we'd be there to comfort each other during our dreams and our nightmares, where we'd be the most authentic versions of ourselves no matter what life hurled our way. It took sitting next to a man that I had spent twelve years loving, on one of the worst days of my life, for me to understand that Garrett Scholl wasn't my person. It wasn't just that he was engaged. I knew, the way you just know, that if I wanted Garrett in this moment—that if I asked him not to walk down the aisle, he would have called off his wedding. The way he had just looked at me, trembling hand on my face, eyes full of regret, it told me our entire *what-if* story. And I knew that choosing Garrett would have broken my heart every day. Because I wasn't on these steps sitting next to my soulmate. I was sitting next to The One That Got Away. And I had to let him go.

A gorgeous purple sunset cut through the once-gray cityscape, beaming in through the window in the hallway, and I let my eyes settle on Garrett. He stared down at his hands. The lines on his face were lit with a deep purple hue, making him look almost too beautiful to say goodbye to. It was a fitting ending—the first time I had set eyes on Garrett, he was bathed in a violet stage light. I might as well let him walk into another life under this one.

The last twelve years swept through me like a tidal wave. I pointed my knees toward his, taking Garrett's callused hand in mine, studying his fingers. I hoped he would hold someone like this one day—reading her hand like a map—as if letting her go would be like navigating life without a North Star. I inhaled fresh air, knowing I'd be just fine: I was already found.

"You know this is it for us, right? I can't see you anymore," I said, swallowing a throat of tears. He stared into my eyes, unmoving. "I will *always* remember how much I loved you, and think about you more times than I'll probably want to admit to myself, but I can't love you like this anymore."

He shifted his jaw, pain all over his face. After a moment, he nodded softly.

"Does he make you happy?" he asked, the thought bringing his face together in pain.

"God, he does." I exhaled, feeling it deep in my chest.

Garrett squeezed my hand.

"You deserve that. You deserve it all," he whispered.

He looked me dead in the eyes, and I blinked back at him through tears.

"Maggie, you know . . . I think those Monday nights, that first year we met, those were the best nights of my entire life."

I felt the tears fall down my quivering chin.

"They were pretty damn great," I said. "Goddamnit, now I'm doomed to cry to Fall Out Boy tonight." I laughed through tears.

"Well, if I have to cry to Fiona Apple, that's only fair."

I nudged his shoulder. "I thought you don't cry."

"Pretty sure I'm going to cry tonight," he said, without any shame.

I smiled at him, sadly, but proudly.

"I hope she makes you happy. Like, *really* happy."

Garrett paused for a moment, looking down at his hands in mine.

"I don't think she does. And I know that's not her fault," he said softly.

I gripped his hands tighter, bringing his eyes to mine.

"Garrett, you only get one life. You deserve to have Monday nights like that forever with someone you love. Tuesday through Sunday, too."

"I know," he said, so quietly that I had to read his mouth to understand the words.

He bumped his shoulder to mine, trying to lighten the moment. He always was the guy who made the corners of my mouth dance—who made my body come alive like sunshine on a stormy day. Why should our death be any different? I grinned and edged my shoulder back to his. Garrett threw his arm around me and tugged me close to his side, his embrace springing tears from my eyes.

"You're my favorite person, Maggie May. You know that?"

Here's the thing. I knew I was his favorite person. I knew there was a good chance I always would be. And I knew he'd be one of mine. It was lovely and devastating. It was the right kind of closure.

I reached my arms over and I hugged him tight. I felt his arms go around my waist, pulling me closer, our aching hearts banging against each other.

"I love you," I whispered into his ear, with my tears falling onto the curve of his neck.

Garrett held me even tighter. So tight that I could feel him choke back his emotions.

"I love you, too, Maggie May."

I loved Garrett Scholl; I had since the day I first heard his voice. But you can only be fully in love with one person. It was time for me to be in love with the right one.

51

THIRTY-FIVE

ASHER GREETED ME AT HIS door with crossed arms and a furrowed brow. I swallowed hard and moved my body past him, sucking in tears, trying to get words out before emotions beat me to it. I paced in the kitchen, searching for the very words. He watched me, waiting. And then the words tumbled out of me, quickly.

"So, Cole Wyan—he discovered me a handful of years ago, and then, after we had just recorded one song, he made a move on me. I rebuffed him, he didn't like the word *no*, and he tried to touch me again, and he touched me—and I broke his nose, and he threatened my career, and—"

Asher's face silenced me. It was darker than I'd ever seen it. Outside of the stage and screen, Asher had never embodied anger like this. His eyes narrowed and darted around the room, as if maybe he could pick up something inside his immaculate living room and hurl it into the window, just to expel the fury boiling underneath his cotton shirt.

"I know I should have told you when we saw Cole last week, but honestly, when I saw him, it—it brought me back to a really horrible place—a place I thought I wouldn't have to visit again."

I felt tears around my throat, and the anger slipped from Asher's face, replaced with his default: pure empathy. His eyes softened as he stepped forward, setting his palms on my shaking arms, but I backed away from him with my hands in the air. Hot tears continued to stream down.

"This morning . . . this morning when I found out that Cole had released my song out of nowhere, I ran somewhere else, I ran to another man. A guy who's had this hold on my past . . ."

Asher put his hands on my wrists. His brow was furrowed, like he was trying to keep up.

"Mags, take a deep breath—"

"No. You need to hear this—"

"I don't."

He stood in front of me, and I froze, seeing that there was real hurt behind his eyes.

"I don't want to hear how you ran to someone else, unless this is your way of trying to tell me that you don't want to be with me—in which case, please spare me the details."

He said it forcefully, looking directly into my eyes, and it took my breath away. It was a long moment before I was able to speak again—to navigate past the tears so I could tell him how badly I never wanted to hurt him again.

"Asher . . . nothing happened. I promise."

His entire body exhaled, and he put his hand on his throat, tugging at the chain around his neck.

"Well shit, maybe you could have led with that."

"I'm sorry. I—I ran somewhere else, but I want to be here. And stay here. I want to be with you."

"Are you sure? Because you and I—somehow, we just picked up where we left off, and I didn't venture to ask if you were ready for that. Maybe I was naïve to think you were in this the way I was, and that's not your fault."

I shook my head effusively.

"You weren't naïve. I ran to the wrong person, but I needed to—I needed to close a door. You know me, I suck at lying to you, and I'm not lying when I say I'm all in on this. On *us*."

He took a step forward, slowly.

"If you need to get something off your chest the next time your world is turning upside down, and you can't do it here, with *me*, I want you to tell me. This needs to end if I'm not the arms you want to run into—if I'm not your person."

"You're my person," I said, with tears running down my cheeks.

He hesitated, staring at all sides of my wet face.

"Well . . . can your person hold you already?"

I nodded through a sea of tears, and Asher took me into his arms, wrapping them tightly around me.

I wasn't sure I deserved him in this moment. I felt immense guilt for letting Garrett hold me earlier, and I would try like hell to make it up to Asher.

After a long while, I dried my tears and we ordered some food, both of us exhaling our shitty night over Chinese takeout on the shag carpet as *When Harry Met Sally* played softly in the background. He paused the movie and turned his attention toward me.

"Look, I know I can't make your past go away, but really: How can I help?"

Asher held up his phone. "Do you want to try and call Bex? Do you want *me* to? He called me pretty confused this morning."

"He did?"

"I think he felt like you were toying with options from two different producers—but clearly that's not the case. I know he would direct his anger toward the real monster if he knew the full story."

I finished swallowing a crispy vegetable roll and paused to draw in air, exhaling deeply.

"Don't call him. I don't want Bex to know about any of this. Not yet."

I grabbed my phone off the coffee table. I could feel my spine rebuilding itself, I could feel the heartbreak of a man taking hold of my career turn into white-hot fury. Sometimes, clinging to anger isn't the poisonous venom people make it out to be.

"Who are you calling?" Asher asked.

"Raini."

"Raini?"

I nodded, and as I went to dial her number, I froze. I slowly looked up at Asher, my face softening as I locked eyes with him.

"Thank you," I said.

"What for?"

"For—for showing mercy when you didn't need to. For being here for me. I . . . I really love you," I said, my lips staying open in the awe of it all.

And I did. I loved him fully.

His eyes didn't leave mine. "I don't think I ever stopped loving you," he said, super casually.

"Well that's cool," I said through a teary smile.

A soft grin found his chiseled face. I exhaled again, grateful to be able to give all of my heart to the person who could give me all of his—to the person who I could share a lifetime of hopes and dreams with.

52

SEVENTEEN

My NAKED LIMBS WERE FOLDED between Asher's as we lay on the dock over the sleepy lake, with just a large terry cloth towel covering our bodies. My finger traced the tiny white scar on his chin, slowly, as if I were memorizing his lifeless body before the cops took him away. I let my fingers go to the tattoo on his biceps, raw and wrapped in a clear bandage. There was wild romance in the air. There was death in the air, too. Goodbyes can be complicated.

It was our final night at camp, the night before we were about to go home and then head to separate coasts for colleges.

"Remember that promise we made?" I whispered, burying my face in the curve of his neck, breathing in salt, musk, and sunblock.

"Of course."

He held me tighter, arms around my back, my breasts on his damp torso.

"Promise me," I said.

"Mags, I don't want to live in a world where I would have lost you," he said.

"Just promise me. If we're thirty-five . . ." I trailed off, choking back the reality that I was begging him to save me from a lonely future. Wanting security from another person was pitiful. I was pitiful.

"Hey"—Asher took my chin in his fingers and lifted my face up to his—"I promise. Heck, I'll show up at your door with a ring."

"You better," I said.

I couldn't tell if he was joking, but I sure as hell wasn't.

"But you better not lose me, you hear?" Asher said.

His eyes opened wider, waiting for my answer. I tried to hold every line on his body—as much as my hands and arms would allow. His chin was quivering, already unhinged with the thought of losing me. His eyes filled with threatening tears as he waited for me to speak. It was magnanimous.

Fuck pity. I pitied everyone else.

"I won't. I promise."

"We'll make this work. Right?" he asked, but it wasn't even a question.

"We've made this work for three years. We'll make it work for forever."

He exhaled into a gentle smile, and I kissed him, tears streaming down my cheeks, salt on my lips, and he kissed me back harder, holding me tight as our bodies moved with and against each other in the moonlight.

53

THIRTY-FIVE

SUMMER PHONED ME TO LET me know Garrett had called off the engagement. There was a part of me that believed it was easier knowing he was with someone else, but honestly, I was too in love to let it ruin me. I was, and I mean this wholly, proud of Garrett for choosing himself. I wanted desperately to say it to his face, but I also knew that loving him came with boundaries, ones I had set so that I could be my happiest self.

And I was.

Two weeks later, with the movie's production underway, I sat across from Shelly in her chaotic, colorful office in West Midtown. Summer sat next to me, grinning like a shark. Shelly finished reading the piles of paper in front of her and set them down as she whistled into the air.

"Who knows about this?" Shelly asked.

"The other three names on those pages"—I pointed to Summer—"my unpaid PR rep, my boyfriend, and Raini Perish."

Shelly smiled.

"Well, let's *not* keep it that way. Unpaid PR rep, I assume you have a contact at *New York* mag?"

Summer squinted her eyes, so offended by the question that she refused to dignify it with a response.

Shelly narrowed her eyes back at me. "Before this breaks, your first phone call is to Fin Bex," she said.

"He has my number," I said with a sly smile.

"Christ, I'm going to be dealing with your ego forever, aren't I?" Shelly rolled her eyes at me, and then directed her attention at Summer. "Okay, PR hotshot, let's get *New York* mag on the line."

Stone-faced, Summer saluted Shelly, and then she dialed her contact at *New York* magazine.

I didn't want to hurt Cole Wyan quietly. I wanted to do it loudly, publicly—I wanted to take a baseball bat to his reputation. Shitty men can try to tear our souls apart, but where there is one victim of a man abusing his power, there is almost always more. And when us women find each other, when we lock arms, we have enough collective strength to rise up with fists. And we did.

Over the last couple weeks, I had spent hours on the phone with Raini's cousin, who had been abused and groomed by Cole Wyan. Raini's cousin knew of another woman. And that woman knew of another. We had four victims, including myself—four well-documented cases of Cole Wyan using his power in the worst way possible. It was a slam-dunk case for his mainstream cancellation.

Weeks later, *New York* magazine published a tell-all article: four well-researched accounts of women whose careers were stifled by Cole Wyan. One of them was me.

I was on set the morning the story broke, watching Raini sing the first song I had written for the movie. She, quite simply, took our breath away. It was right then that I looked around, seeing not a dry eye on set—it was right then that I realized I was a part of something real and extraordinary. Something that wouldn't slip through my fingers.

I walked out the stage doors, the sun setting on the backlot as I answered my phone.

"Hello."

"Hi. I have Fin Bex and Shelly Pier for you."

I waited, my heart pounding. I hadn't talked to Fin since Cole had released my song, and I didn't know what was coming on the other end of the line. Fin's bouncy voice clicked through my phone's receiver.

"So . . . turns out that guy's a real piece of shit."

I cleared my throat, almost smiling. "Yeah."

"Shelly and I, we were just talking and thinking: You know what would be a real *fuck-you* to Cole Wyan?"

My eyes widened.

"What's that?" I asked.

"Recording so many songs that 'Let's Lie' doesn't even show up on your top songs on Spotify," Shelly finished.

I exhaled, tears stinging my eyes, relief flooding through every inch of my bones.

"I'd like that, very much," was all I could say.

"I think, however—and Shelly, correct me if I'm wrong—I think you should take a record deal and let me produce the record. Fuck the EP."

"What happened to me getting left for dead if I take a record deal?" I asked, questioning Fin's previous mindset.

"That remains true for so many," Shelly said. "But I just had the head of Sony call me, asking, 'Who the fuck is this Maggie Vine girl?' and let's just say, she didn't need to read the *New York* mag article to know that Cole Wyan is trash. But she sure as hell wanted to help the woman who publicly took him down."

"I would have called you earlier, but I went over to Sony to play her a couple of your demos from the film—I couldn't risk sending them because of confidentiality. She loved you, and she's all in—all in on you," Fin said.

A wide grin split open my face as a blood-orange sunset roared in the sky above me.

"I mean . . . fuck yeah," I said.

"Great. So the next call you get—if it's a 212 number, take it. Her name's Cara."

And just like that, my music career took flight.

—

54

THIRTY-FIVE

I WAS SOARING. ASHER AND I had been going strong for seven months, I was midway into recording my first studio album, the movie had wrapped, and the Oscar buzz had already started—buzz that included Best Original Song. There was only one more box to check, but I wanted to understand my options fully before I approached it with the man I wanted by my side.

I had found a new OB, a woman who specialized in fertility and who didn't mansplain my ovaries to me. Out of an abundance of caution, and because I could afford it, I had her redo all the tests. I wanted someone I trusted telling me about my body.

My OB sat me down across from her, inside a beautiful, cream-on-cream office on the Upper East Side.

"Okay, let's get one thing straight: you're not a lost cause—not at all. If your goal is to get pregnant, I would start with IUI, and I would start as soon as possible. You can absolutely try to do it the old-fashioned way, but I don't want you to waste too much time trying, because with your egg count and your PCOS, the odds aren't great on that end. If you're serious, time is really important here."

She went over the payment plans, and I exhaled. The numbers were still egregious, but they were now affordable to me. I had options. I just hadn't discussed any of them with my live-in boyfriend.

"I'll be back with my partner, and we can go over this with him."

"That sounds like a plan," she said.

My OB stood and smiled at me, her eyes filled with hope for my future. I smiled back, because I knew that she would help me reach my goal—somehow.

I walked back home, listening to a handful of home-recorded demos that I would send Bex later, as I took in the quiet West Village brownstones around me. Asher had moved to New York permanently after filming, purchasing a three-story brownstone on Perry Street so that I could live out all my Carrie Bradshaw dreams—minus sex with other men.

I ducked my head as I passed a stray paparazzo, the guy who always loitered one street back. Holding two coffees, I ran upstairs, finding Asher standing in the living room across from a roaring fire.

The fire lit up the dark gray leather wallpaper and deep green accents where Asher paced in front of a bookshelf lined with the works of Shakespeare and my record collection. I froze—taking him in, watching how he floated back and forth with a furrowed brow, all his attention glued to the script in front of him, his mouth muttering lines for his next upcoming feature. He turned, feeling eyes on him.

"You little lurker," he said, grinning.

"What can I say? I get off on watching you work."

I kissed him hard and handed him his coffee.

"How'd the writing session go this morning?" he asked.

"Great. Halfway there."

He glanced down at his watch, a new Explorer Rolex.

"Shit—we're going to be late for lunch."

He grabbed his leather jacket from the chair and threw it on, and I tugged the lapel of his jacket toward me, so that I could pull his lips onto mine.

"Summer asked to push lunch back thirty minutes—Olivia ran long on a shoot," I said, kissing his lips.

Summer had recently started dating an established makeup artist who really was right for her. Olivia was kind and soft in the places Summer could be loud and bold, and Summer was exuberant in the places Olivia was quiet. It was a perfect yin and yang. And neither woman wanted children. Olivia and Summer hadn't left each other's orbit since I introduced them on Asher's set.

We filed into the airy white marbled kitchen and I took Asher's hand, bringing him toward me.

"Can I talk to you about something?" I asked, my tone even.

Asher studied me, with his puzzled eyes narrowing on my neutral expression.

"What's going on?"

"I went to my gyno today, and we discussed my options."

"Your options for . . . ?"

"For children."

Asher's face went white. My eyes widened, surprised by his reaction.

"You want children . . . *now*?" he asked, his voice so quiet that I had to lean in to hear it.

My eyes scanned the dreadful stillness of his body. I steadied my now-shaking hand on our kitchen island, trying to keep my spine upright. "Asher, I want children, and I don't have a lot of time to do it naturally. I need to start trying *now-ish*. I'm not exactly blessed with the eggs of a twentysomething. Time isn't on my side in this area."

He was frozen, and it took him a moment to speak.

"You should text Summer and tell her we're rescheduling," he said, his voice low.

A sinking feeling enveloped my body as his ashen face didn't seem to melt away. I texted Summer quickly, my heart racing in my throat.

Rain check on lunch. Fill you in later.

Hand on his chest, eyes widened, Asher walked over to the couch in the sunroom, which I called the Soul Room. Everything in here was light and cheerful—soft blushes, yellows, and creams amid leafy plants in the corner. I dragged my footsteps into the room, and the heaviness mounted inside of me as I sat down next to him on the yellow velvet couch. He looked at me, waiting for me to fill in the blanks.

"Asher, I'm almost thirty-six. I want a baby one day. And in order to have the best chance of doing that, one day needs to be very soon. And I love you, and we've looked at rings together, so I know that you see a future with me . . ."

"You want a baby with me." It wasn't so much a question as it was Asher trying to wrap his mind around it.

"That would be ideal, considering we're, you know, crazy in love and want to start a life together. I was looking into doing this by myself before you reentered my life—that's how badly I don't want this moment to pass me by. But yes: I'd love to do this with you. I don't want another baby daddy."

"It's not funny, Maggie."

He stared at me, his head shaking as my face reddened with heat. I had forgotten that Asher Reyes didn't have a sense of humor when he felt backed into a corner.

"Sorry."

"I don't know how I feel about being a parent." He put his hand on his neck and swallowed hard. "Honestly, I don't think I'll have an answer anytime soon, or even in the next year or two."

I could feel my insides tightening, bracing for a fall as my heart seemed to get heavier and heavier.

"My brother—his death and his life were . . ." Tears constricted Asher's throat, and I watched the sadness fill his eyes. "There was so much fear for so long with him, and then there was unimaginable pain. I'm *terrified* of having children, Mags," he cracked, the tears now falling. "I'm terrified of it. I don't know if my heart's capable of trying and losing someone—I don't want to love someone like that without having control over if they're going to be okay. I can't go through what my parents went through."

Asher trailed off in silent tears—his strong jaw quivering at the thought. He shook his head and looked at his hands, as if ashamed, but knowing this was his truth.

"I'm sorry—I'm sorry I don't have the answer that you need right now—" He stopped talking, his voice cracking under pain.

"Don't be sorry," I whispered through tears. I took his hand in mine, pulling his eyes back to me. I sucked in swirling pain and heartache. "I think—I know a child would be lucky to have you. But I can't make you want one right now, just because I'm ready. I—I understand." My voice quivered, tears enveloping the words.

"I'm not saying never, Maggie," he said, squeezing my hand. "I just can't be someone's father right now. I can't conceptualize it. I mean, I just started talking about my brother. I think having a kid right now would wreck me."

I had convinced Asher to open up about his brother, and in turn, he shocked the shit out of me. What was supposed to be a super-sexy *Men's Health* cover shoot and interview became an issue about Asher's struggle with depression, where he shared for the first time the truth about his brother's death. It turned the magazine upside down, in the best way possible. The editors crafted the issue around mental health. I was so proud of him, and all I could think about when reading that article was how attentive and caring of a father he'd be one day—partly because of all the loss he carried for too long. What I didn't know was that Asher didn't want to be a father *because* of all the loss he carried. And I couldn't make him feel like his decision was wrong. I couldn't, because he believed it was right for him.

"One day, maybe I'll be ready to have kids—"

I shook my head.

"No. Please don't—don't make promises for tomorrow that you might not keep. I watched Summer's marriage fall apart because she wanted so badly to promise someone something that wasn't right for her."

He cupped my face with his hands, wiping my tears away even as they kept falling.

"You were supposed to be it for me," he said, his voice breaking.

I watched Asher's chest constrict with the loss, and he kept his warm eyes on mine, tears streaming down his face. All at once, I couldn't stop sobbing. He wrapped his arms around me tightly, our bodies clenched in sadness.

After a short while, I pulled back and ran my hand over his strong jaw, kissing his cheek, his lips, holding his face in my hands.

"I love you so fucking much," I whispered, the truth of the statement splintering me in half. "You've—you've changed my life—not just once, but twice. You're the first person who looked at me and really cared—and you made me really care. You taught me the purpose of loving someone, and seeing the world through your eyes is a goddamn privilege." I caught my breath, heaving tears. Asher choked back a sob, keeping both my hands in his as he watched me continue. "You've given me the chance to have a family. And I wish it was with you, but I understand. I really do understand," I said, the words coming out small, because the feelings were so huge that they could have swallowed us both.

I understood more than he knew. Up until a few years ago, I didn't think children were for me. It wasn't until I unpacked my father wound with my therapist that I started to realize that I desperately wanted a child. I hoped, for Asher's sake, that he would dive into the deep wound left by his brother, even if it meant deciding that children still weren't for him. I knew I couldn't wait around for that answer, nor would I ever want to resent him for taking his time to get there. He deserved more than that. And so did I.

Asher pulled me toward him and kissed me, hands in my hair, tears and longing everywhere. Asher Reyes kissed me like it was the end. It felt like falling off a shooting star—gorgeous and devastating.

We held each other until the sun rose. It was the hardest goodbye of my life, by far.

I couldn't help but think, as I held Asher that night, tears in both our eyes, massive, full love swelling from both our bodies, that maybe I had misunderstood my mom. Maybe this was what happened to her. Maybe she got so much love in that short time from my father that it was enough. Maybe their breakup didn't leave a void inside her. Maybe their love filled her up, so much that there wasn't actually a hole. There was boundless untamed love that they explored—that much I pieced together from their stories—especially from the way my dad talked about my mom. I would call my mom and ask her—I owed her that much. Actually, I owed her a lot more than that.

The love of your life doesn't have to last forever. I would live the rest of my life knowing that loving and being loved by Asher Reyes—twice in this lifetime—was more than enough.

55

SEVENTEEN

I STARED AT THE PHONE, frustration bubbling, pacing back and forth in my tiny dorm room. It was 8:07 at night. Asher had said he'd call at eight. He was never late. He was late.

Already two months into my freshman year, life wasn't going as I expected, so while Asher being late to call me wasn't a crime, it was coming on the heels of my crippling loneliness. I hadn't made a lot of friends at NYU, and everyone in my music classes had the kind of talent I had thought made me rare and sparkly. Not helping was my roommate, Summer Groves, a horrible excuse for a person. Cold and mean, she acted like I had done something unfathomable to her the second I greeted her with a wide smile on our first day on campus. I was thankful that she was at some random rally tonight, not here to flick her eyes at me as I melted down over my boyfriend's lack of calling.

Long distance, the time change, and Asher's and my differing class schedules and commitments seemed impossible to navigate. I found myself saying no to going out and making friends, just so I could spend my dinners talking to him on the phone. This wasn't how I'd pictured college. Asher had a rigorous schedule at USC, the theater program left little time for fun—let alone spending hours on the phone with his girlfriend. And my schedule at NYU, with my major in music production, didn't exactly leave idle time, either.

I knew we were drifting apart. I knew it, yet I didn't want it to be true.

I jumped, my flip phone buzzing in my hands. I flicked it open.

"Hey," I said, a little coldly.

"I'm sorry." Asher sighed on the other end of the line.

"It's okay."

I sat on the edge of my twin-sized bed, swinging my legs back and forth.

"This is hard, Mags. This is harder than I thought." His voice was thick, as if he was wrestling with something.

I could feel a wave of pain throbbing under my lashes, bubbling, waiting.

"Do you—do you not want to do this anymore?" I asked, my voice small.

"It's not that. I don't *not* want to do this—I just—I can't only see you twice a year and talk to you when the timing—when we feel rushed, and it sucks for both of us. That's—that's not a relationship. That's not fair to either of us. I don't know what to do," he said.

I swallowed the tears, my hands trembling.

"Yes, you do, you just don't want to do it. So I'll—I'll do it for you," I cracked.

I pictured him pacing outside his dorm at USC, the gorgeous cream fountains and green palm trees in view, his olive skin bathing in the sun, his face filled with sadness. I wanted to hold him, I needed him to hold me, and I knew, the way you just know, that we wouldn't be holding each other anytime soon, or maybe ever again. And with that brutal thought, my chest caved in, and a special kind of loneliness filled all the spaces he had ever touched. My hands, my arms, my knees, my neck, my heart, my soul—I was consumed by a heavy, dark cloud.

On the other end of the line, so was he.

"Mags," he said quietly, his voice breaking, his tears audible even through mine. "I don't want to do this," he cried.

I tugged myself into the fetal position, holding the phone to my cheek as I buckled, the cries guttural. I'd felt rejection and sadness when my father broke his promises—but his lack of fathering never felt like something that I was losing, like a loss that was permanent. His just felt like a temporary disappointment. This pain was splintering.

Losing Asher Reyes was losing a part of me I would never get back. This was heartache creating a hole inside me that no one else could fill.

No one else but him.

56

THIRTY-NINE

I WENT THROUGH FOUR ROUNDS of IUI to get her. Two years ago, I was sitting in my gynecologist's office going over the overwhelming process of IVF when she stepped out of her office to grab my new lab results from a nurse. She smiled wide.

"Well, this is my second-favorite part of the job. Change in plans. You're pregnant, Maggie."

The other favorite part of her job was delivering a healthy baby, and she did just that nine months later. Willa Vine wrapped her tiny hand around my finger, and for the first time in thirty-seven years, it felt like there was no ache inside me. It felt like this was exactly how my life was supposed to be. I felt full.

> I showed up to every moment a moment too late
> Cold soaked limbs searching for a wave to ride
> Time turned her back on me till you arrived
> My body on a white-hot shore
> So that's what all this fighting was for
> The beat of your heart outside my chest
> Your wide eyes blink back mine
> Time was on my side this whole damn time

Now, two years later, I was cleaning chocolate off Willa's round cheeks outside a bakery in SoHo when I felt a tap on my shoulder. After the movie came out, after "Up North" won an Oscar for Best Original Song, after my first album went platinum, I was used to these taps. I made a point to greet every fan with a big smile—because who the fuck did I think I was to even consider doing the opposite?

I turned around, and I couldn't breathe.

There he was.

Asher Reyes stood in front of me, his thick dark hair swooped to the side, his jawline strong, his amber eyes soft and on mine. A wide smile hit his lips as he took me in.

The fullness left my chest. I remembered, instantly, how much I ached for him. He peered down at Willa in her stroller.

"Well, who do we have here?" he asked, his voice lighting up my daughter's big green eyes.

Willa stuck her chocolate tongue out at him. Asher laughed, and he sweetly stuck his tongue back at her, before turning to me and shaking his head, in total awe.

"Hi, Mags," he whispered, his voice soft.

He reached forward and with his thumb, he wiped falling tears from my eyes. I didn't even know I was crying.

I buried my face into the curve of his neck, and he held me without a question, for a full minute. I felt his chest beat against mine, and by the time I pulled back, there were tears in his eyes, too.

We walked through the city for hours. It was, once again, like no time had passed. Asher strolled beside me as I pushed the stroller through the park until Willa faded into her nap. We hadn't seen each other since the Oscars three years ago. I was pregnant then, and when he saw me and my belly on the red carpet, he looked away quickly, tears forming in his eyes. I could tell that night was impossible for him, even as he won Best Director—the entire night in that ballroom, his eyes kept finding mine. That night was impossible for me, too. I cried in my hotel room, clutching my Oscar in one hand, with my other hand on my growing belly—feeling both like I had it all and I had lost everything.

"That was . . . that night broke my heart all over again," he said, looking at me as we passed over the bridge, autumn leaves crunching below our feet.

"Me, too," I whispered.

"I wanted to reach out and touch you. Hold you. And there you were, growing this very beautiful . . . There you were carrying the reason that I wasn't touching you."

He paused, smiling down at Willa. I peeled my eyes off him, afraid that if I studied the way Asher was looking at my daughter, I might crumple right in the middle of Central Park.

We kept walking as the sun plummeted around us, our shoulders brushing against each other, our steps getting heavier and heavier, our walk slowing, neither of us wanting it to end, until we were back to where we started, outside the coffee shop with Willa sound asleep in the stroller—drool running down her tiny dimpled chin.

Asher turned to look at me as I searched my purse for my apartment key.

"You know, running into you, here, it wasn't by accident," he said.

I looked up. "What do you mean?"

He grinned at me.

"A week ago, I was meeting with a director over there"—he pointed to a brick office building across the street—"and then I saw you walk out of the coffee shop pushing a stroller. I stood there, just . . ." He tapped his heart, implying that it had lived outside his body. "By the time I remembered how to move my legs, you had disappeared through the crowd. Vanished. Like a magic trick."

I pointed to the limestone apartment building above us, adjacent to the coffee shop.

"I live here."

"I know. I asked my PR rep to find out where you lived. And then, I showed up around the same time every day, skulking about the coffee shop, just hoping you'd show up."

I shook my head at him, in awe.

"You could have just called . . ." I said with a little smile, my heart soaring.

Asher reached down and took my fingers in his, taking a step forward. He put his hand on my cheek, my eyes closing and my body melting into his touch.

"It was my turn to show up," he whispered.

I slowly opened my lashes, staring into his kind brown eyes as they scanned my entire face.

"Asher, we want different things," I said, my voice trembling as I looked down at Willa's sleeping smile.

I felt Asher's hand on my chin, lifting my face back up to his. He took another step forward, now only inches from me.

"I want you. I want you, and everything that comes with wanting you," he said, with eyes unwavering on me.

I swallowed hard with my face in his hand, my heart already belonging to him.

"Here's the deal," I said, tears streaming down my cheeks. "Don't you dare kiss me—not unless you plan on kissing me forever."

Asher's hand left my face with his eyes locked on mine. A smile softened his strong jaw, and he tugged at the lapel of my jacket, pulling me into a deep kiss that lit fireworks all around us. After a long while, Asher stepped back and set his hand on my wet cheek, the other moving a stray curl from my eyes. He looked at me like he wanted to take me home and build a life together. I closed my hand around his and squeezed hard, letting him know that I wanted to do the same.

And so, we did.

DIFFERENT SKIES

Sun-kissed shore on the other side of the sea
Bet those copper eyes miss me
Are you holding someone else the same
Will we do this again one day

Do you remember the taste of salt air on my spine
Tears in your eyes when I sang "Strawberry Wine"
Where were you standing when you unbecame mine
I'd float across the ocean just to share that same sky

City streets on the other side of the sea
All these bodies, nobody knows me
Grow up, but please don't change
I need us to do this again one day

Do you remember the taste of salt air on my spine
Tears in your eyes when I sang "Strawberry Wine"
Where were you standing when you unbecame mine
I'd float across the ocean just to share that same sky

Those summers were supposed to be the start
The "what-if" splits me apart
I'll grow old with you somehow some way
Or I'll miss you till my dying day

I fell into stars
Now I'm covered in scars
I fell into you
Now I'm dark blue
We had it all
Was it worth the fall

Do you remember the taste of salt air on my spine
Tears in your eyes when I sang "Strawberry Wine"
Where were you standing when you unbecame mine
I'd float across the ocean just to share that same sky

ACROSS THE ROOM

Blue eyes like the tide
Winning hand in your pocket
You're too afraid to let it show
Aren't you tired of "we'll never know"

Your gaze scans across the room, finds mine
I've been here the whole time
Sunburnt souls on the shoreline
We climb past the sky
Drown in limelight
Take the house, let's just try

My eyes wild for you
With words caged behind my face
I leave the stage with 'em unsaid
Aren't I tired of trying again and again

Your gaze scans across the room, finds mine
I've been here the whole time
Sunburnt souls on the shoreline
We climb past the sky
Drown in limelight
Take the house, let's just try

We could fit like the fairy tale
But you're growing out of Us before we can try Us on
Don't walk someone else's line
Take me back to the "Once Upon a" time

Before this magic wand hits you like a hired gun
'Cause I can see us dancing through the years
When someone else's dream outruns its run
Come to me undone

Sick of this daydream
Tired of opening my eyes
Show me yours
I'll show you mine

LET'S LIE

Brush stroke, blank slate
Our time is due
Right there, right now, burning red and deep blue

Paint me anew, inside this room
Don't wipe our slates clean
I quite like this hue
Let's lie, me and you, like new lovers do

Silk shirt, sweat-soaked
Dancing with you
Right there, right now, our bodies unglued

Paint me anew, inside this room
Don't wipe our slates clean
I quite like this hue
Let's lie, me and you, like new lovers do

Your lips, my throat
Don't think it through
Right there, right now holding me like a muse

Paint me anew, inside this room
Don't wipe our slates clean

I quite like this hue
Let's lie, me and you, like new lovers do

Is loving you more worth the fight
Don't answer tonight
You're a big-picture guy scared of a varnished lifetime
Are we worth the fight
Don't answer tonight
Are we worth the fight
Tell me a lie painted white
Just for tonight
Just for tonight

Paint me anew, inside my room
Don't wipe our slates clean
Our bodies in bloom
Let's lie to ourselves like new lovers do

UP NORTH

I shake myself awake inside a jet-black space
Hug my shoulders just to pretend you're here
Memories shoot through me
A silver lining in a barren atmosphere

Come bring me light
You can steal my night
If you're not a fighter, then take flight

I close my eyes, play us back real slow
Time when you held me like you were afraid to let go
So come keep me warm up north
I know, it's a reverie
Blink back the stars with me
We'd never sleep

I make footprints that refuse to fade
Proof of life on a cold dark day
I hum that song you used to sing me to sleep
My mind's trying to warm the places your skin used to be

Come bring your crown
I'll wear a gown
If you can turn my ship around, do it now

I close my eyes, play us back real slow
Time when you held me like you were afraid to let go
So come keep me warm up north
I know, it's a reverie
Blink back the stars with me
We'd never sleep

Holding on to you is like wishing upon a star I can't see
But hope's always the last friend to leave
So come keep me warm up north
Just you and me
Fold your arm around my shoulder
We could be the real thing

JOYRIDE

Thundering skies
Wet tracks with no guide
I curve my neck to look out your side
Your eyes on me while you drive
You read my mind saying, "beautiful night"
That's right

It's a joyride
It feels like home
Flying down this open road
I remove the safety belt wrapped around my seat

If we go crashing
Let the blow break me

I thought it was always "wait and see"
"See you if I get there," hypothetically
Now you and I are side by side
Windblown grins, no destination in sight

White-hot sunrise
Sweat-soaked dress untied
Two bodies tangled up on your side
The car in park while I drive
I pin your wrists back saying, "close your eyes"
That's right

It's a joyride
It feels like home
Flying down this open road
I remove the safety belt wrapped around my seat
If we go crashing
Let the blow break me

I thought it was always "wait and see"
"See you if I get there," hypothetically
Now you and I are side by side
Windblown grins, no destination in sight
The way the streetlights dance in your blue eyes
The way your knuckles grip around the wheel tonight
We've got scars we can't leave behind
That's alright

It's a joyride
It feels like home
Flying down this open road
I remove the safety belt wrapped around my seat
If we go crashing
Let the blow break me

BONNIE AND CLYDE

I grew up looking down
Held my hands against my ears, silencing siren sounds
I flew out the screaming back door every time
Hugged my shoulders until I found your street
Said I was just walking by
You knew to hold me till I cried

We threw hope to the fire, now I'm floating past Mars
I should know better, I don't see no harm
Letting the ashes of our maybes keep me warm
Floating through Saturn remembering you tangled in my bed
A time before we said words better left unsaid
I float through Jupiter, I still want the moon
I should know better
Darling, it'll always be you

I left the sirens behind
Ran pass your street without stopping for our goodbye
Didn't slow down until my skin was bathed in bright hues
Sandy shores at my feet, feeling golden and blue
I didn't miss running
I missed having someone to run to

We threw hope to the fire, now I'm floating past Mars
I should know better, I don't see no harm
Letting the ashes of our maybes keep me warm
Floating through Saturn remembering you tangled in my bed
A time before we said words better left unsaid
I float through Jupiter, I still want the moon
I should know better
Darling, it'll always be you

Two kids counting stars at night
Your partner in crime, Bonnie and Clyde

Two kids who lassoed the moon
I sure liked loving you

We threw hope to the fire, now I'm floating past Mars
I should know better, I don't see no harm
Letting the ashes of our maybes keep me warm
Floating through Saturn remembering you tangled in my bed
A time before we said words better left unsaid
I float through Jupiter, I still want the moon
I should know better
Darling, it'll always be you

ACKNOWLEDGMENTS

THIS BOOK WAS NOT BORN overnight. Getting here involved tears, an Excel spreadsheet of three time lines, two different endings, tens of thousands of words thrown away and rewritten, epic playlists, and nights that bled into mornings. This novel is so much better for all of the work put into it. And I couldn't have done it alone.

To my children, Max and Zoey. Your excitement for life is what makes mine worth living. One day, I'll write a book that you can read. For now, this right here is just about the only page that is safe.

To my parents. Thank you for allowing me, at a young age, to discover what sets my soul on fire. And thank you for never telling me that my dreams couldn't come true.

There were great writing days, and there were writing days when I googled, "How to write a book." Barry, you made all the days better. Thank you for your unwavering love and support, and for letting me listen to Taylor Swift whenever I want (which is *always*).

To my incredible book agents, Cait Hoyt and Alex Rice. Thank you for championing this story and for truly believing in me as an author. You are both rock stars and dream agents.

To my brilliant editor, Alexandra Sehulster. Thank you for sticking by me when I asked if I could throw away forty pages of an entirely different novel and start this book from scratch. We sure put Maggie Vine through it, didn't we? Thank you for pushing me to go further with her journey. I'm beyond grateful for your patience and your wonderful mind.

To everyone at St. Martin's Griffin and Macmillan who have worked tirelessly to help bring *Maybe Once, Maybe Twice* to life, from the thoughtful social media gurus to the copyediting heroes (who discovered some of my adorable misuses of words). Thank you especially to Alyssa Gammello, Cassidy Graham, Gabriel Guma, Kerri Resnick, Marissa Sangiacomo, NaNá V. Stoelzle, and Susannah Noel.

To the rest of my dream team—Ashley Silver, Austin Denesuk, Berni Barta, Darian Lanzetta, and Olivia Blaustein—thank you for believing in me and always fighting for me to succeed.

To my team at TMG for keeping me out of jail: Daniel Farr, Tracy Porter, and Mallory Zahrt.

To *MOMT*'s earliest readers, the dear friends who I trusted with this story at its various stages: Allie Greenberg, Azita Ghanizada, Jonny Umansky, Julia Duffy, Randi Blick, and Sarah Prinze. Your encouragement meant the world to me during the writing process.

To Freddy Wexler for planting the seeds of this idea into my brain. You are such a talent.

Years ago, my friend sat me down and told me it was "tragic" that I had stopped writing. This truth woke something inside of me, and I haven't stopped writing since. We need the right kind of cheerleaders in our life—those who will push us to be the most authentic version of ourselves. I'm lucky enough to be surrounded by the most wonderful friends and family. You all know who you are, and you know what you mean to me. And to Eugene Kim—from the bottom of my heart, thank you for calling me tragic that one time.

To the woman still reaching for her dreams despite all the obstacles in her way, this book is for you.

ABOUT THE AUTHOR

ALISON ROSE GREENBERG is a screenwriter and the author of *Bad Luck Bridesmaid*. She lives in Atlanta but is quick to say she was born in New York City. While attending the University of Southern California, Alison took her first screenwriting class and fell head over heels. A journey from writing led to marketing jobs before coming full circle back to her first love. Alison speaks fluent rom-com, lives for nineties WB dramas, cries to Taylor Swift, and is a proud single mom to her two incredible kids, two cats, and one poorly trained dog.

Instagram: alison.greenberg

Twitter: @alisongreenberg